Advance Praise for *Keeping Counsel*

KEEPING COUNSEL is the perfect legal mystery. Weaving characters rich with life, in a story packed with action, Forster navigates the reader through a lawyer's worst nightmare. I found it impossible to put down, even when I was supposed to be watching the "Trial of the Century."

—Laurie L. Levenson,
CBS Television Network

KEEPING COUNSEL reinvents the legal thriller, with a walloping premise and a surprising love story. An attorney finds herself bound by the legal code to put her own life on the line for a dangerous client. Read this one with a friend, during the day, with all the lights on—and do not answer the doorbell on any account.

—Polly Whitney, author of *Until Death*
and *Until the End of Time*

R.A. Forster has X-ray vision. You'll feel as if you know these characters from the inside out. KEEPING COUNSEL is creepy and compelling. It's the best read I've had in a long time.

—Herb Nero,
American International Network

MAKE SURE YOUR DOORS AND
WINDOWS ARE LOCKED!
SPINE-TINGLING SUSPENSE FROM PINNACLE

SILENT WITNESS (677, $4.50)
by Mary Germano

Katherine Hansen had been with The Information Warehouse too long to stand by and watch it be destroyed by sabotage. At first there were breaches in security, as well as computer malfunctions and unexplained power failures. But soon Katherine started receiving sinister phone calls, and she realized someone was stalking her, willing her to make one fatal mistake. And all Katherine could do was wait. . . .

BLOOD SECRETS (695, $4.50)
by Dale Ludwig

When orphaned Kirsten Walker turned thirty, she inherited her mother's secret diary — learning the shattering truth about her past. A deranged serial killer has been locked away for years but will soon be free. He knows all of Kirsten's secrets and will follow her to a house on the storm-tossed cape. Now she is trapped alone with a madman who wants something only Kirsten can give him!

CIRCLE OF FEAR (721, $4.50)
by Jim Norman

Psychiatrist Sarah Johnson has a new patient, Diana Smith. And something is very wrong with Diana . . . something Sarah has never seen before. For in the haunted recesses of Diana's tormented psyche a horrible secret is buried. As compassion turns into obsession, Sarah is drawn into Diana's chilling nightmare world. And now Sarah must fight with every weapon she possesses to save them both from the deadly danger that is closing in fast!

SUMMER OF FEAR (741, $4.50)
by Carolyn Haines

Connor Tremaine moves back east to take a dream job as a riding instructor. Soon she has fallen in love with and marries Clay Sumner, a local politician. Beginning with shocking stories about his first wife's death and culminating with a near-fatal attack on Connor, she realizes that someone most definitely does not want her in Clay's life. And now, Connor has two things to fear: a deranged killer, and the fact that her husband's winning charm may mask a most murderous nature . . .

Available wherever paperbacks are sold, or order direct from the Publisher. Send cover price plus 50¢ per copy for mailing and handling to Penguin USA, P.O. Box 999, c/o Dept. 17109, Bergenfield, NJ 07621. Residents of New York and Tennessee must include sales tax. DO NOT SEND CASH.

KEEPING COUNSEL

R.A. FORSTER

ZEBRA BOOKS
KENSINGTON PUBLISHING CORP.

To my brothers
Mike, Mark, Bruce, Jeff, and Gareth
whose wit and wisdom are a constant source
of amazement and amusement

Special thanks to: Jenny Jensen as always, Sarah Gallick
for her extraordinary patience, Theresa Burkhardt for her
knowledge and good humor, and Cheryl Henderson, who
never batted an eyelash.

It is the duty of an attorney to do all of the following: To maintain inviolate the confidence, and at every peril to himself or herself, to preserve the secrets of his or her client.

—Business & Professional Code

Prologue

He hung his head out the window like a dog on a Sunday drive. The whipping wind roared in his ears and slicked back his long hair, baring a wide high forehead. His eyes narrowed, squinting against the force of hot air hitting 75 miles an hour.

Sinister, that's how he looked. Like he could take anyone down.

Women could fall at his feet and he wouldn't give two cents even if they were naked.

That's the kind of man he was.

But if they were naked, he'd give 'em a grin for sure.

"Hah!" he laughed once, but it was more of a shout, just to make sure he was still alive and kickin'.

He was feeling neither here nor there. He had a woman. She didn't make him happy. Thinking about her, he stepped on the gas and the ribbon of road blurred, turning molten under his wheels. The asphalt was hot as hell; still steaming, though the day had been done for hours.

Hot! Hot! Good when you're with a woman, bad when you're in the desert.

Lord, that was funny. True things were the biggest kick of all.

But damn if this wasn't the most lonesome strip of land in all New Mexico and him a lonesome cowboy ridin' it on the back of some hunkin' old steed. Cowboys were the good guys. Had a code to live by, guns to carry. And cows and horses, they just needed a stick in the ribs, a kick in the rear to get 'em going. No need to talk. No questions. No answers.

Do you feel happy? Sad? What are you feeling now? Good. Good. You'll be going home soon. Do you feel anxious? You're so quiet. Do you feel? Good. Good

He was hot like a stove top. Hot like a pot about to boil and damn if he wasn't sitting right on the burner, all these thoughts in his head making his lid start to dance. He'd blow the top of his head right off and out would tumble all those good jokes, and lines that would make women weep. Hot damn. Make 'em weep.

He shook his head hard and wrapped one hand tighter around the steering wheel while he pushed farther out the window, head and shoulders now. The old car swerved but he got it back on track, straight on that dotted line.

He loved those dotted lines. Man perforating the world. A place to rip it in half. Tear here. Send the part with him on it back for a refund.

He shook his head like the dog he was pretending to be. His lips went slack and he heard them flapping, even over the noise of the wind. What an ugly sound and he wasn't an ugly guy. So he turned into the wind and it blew his head empty. When he turned it back, the hot air ran straight at him and made his eyes tear.

Life was wonderful again. Television a blessing. Doctors cured themselves of cancer with a thought. Smart and fancy women could be had with a smile and a wink.

Damn, life was good. It had taken a while but

he was cookin'. He was the most scrumptious thing on the menu.

"Whoeee!" he hollered, and the wind lashed that sound around and threw it right back at him as he hung his head out the window. He pulled it back inside just a snail's trail before the semi whizzed by.

He thought about that close call and making love and a cigarette all at the same time. The close call was past so he tossed aside the image of his head rolling around on the asphalt. His lady was a pain in the ass, so thinking about her was idiotic. The cigarette, though, he could do something about that.

Two fingers burrowed into his shirt pocket. He was already tasting that first good drag and swore he could feel that swirly smoke deep in his lungs. But the pack was empty and crinkled under his fingers. His smile was gone. He didn't feel like hollerin' anymore.

Two hands slapped atop the steering wheel and he drove with his eyes straight forward on the lonely road. He just wanted one lousy cigarette.

But anger wasn't right. He plastered a grin on his face. The new him. New and improved. He accelerated down the four-lane, singing at the top of his lungs in a voice that he was almost sure didn't belong to him. It was too smooth.

Smooth like the turn of the wheel, the slide of the stop he made four miles down. He was still singing when he palmed the keys and unwound his long legs, and stood like a rock 'n' roll god in a pool of fluorescent light at the Circle K convenience store.

He took a minute to admire himself in the side mirror. He didn't like the way his dirty ice eyes looked, so he admired the night sky. Nothing like these black New Mexico nights. Stars as plentiful as rice at a weddin'. He tucked in his shirt so he looked really good. Handsome. _Damn, life was fine._ Whistling softly, he moved on.

Pushing open the glass door, he stepped inside, surprised at how vibrant everything seemed now that he was straight. Michelle Pfeiffer looked like she could just walk right off the cover of _People_ and give him a little hug. The slurpy machine's neon blue and pink letters quivered as if overjoyed to be colored pink and blue.

He ambled over to the register. Little Fourth of July flags were taped all over the place: flags next to the Smokey Joe Hot Salami Sticks, flags wavin' over the stale donuts under the Plexiglas counter box, flags pokin' out of the almost-hidden condom place on the shelf behind the counter.

Hot damn! Independence Day. He almost forgot. Good day for him. He did what he liked, when he liked. No one around to tell him anything. Only his cowboy conscience, only his roamin' man code to keep him in line.

The smokes were neatly stacked on a metal thing above the counter. He looked for the Camels. Left, third row down. Filters one row lower than that. It was the same at every Circle K. What a mind! He could remember everything.

He wandered toward the counter, lay his hands atop it, and peered over, half expecting a pimply-faced clerk to pop up like a stupid kid's toy. Nobody. Just worn linoleum, a wad of gum stuck to it turning black. Great. He could take a pack. Just reach up and be on his way.

But he knew right from wrong. He wanted to follow the rules and felt bad when he didn't. It took a while sometimes for that feeling to happen, but it always did.

Then he saw her.

She was fixing coffee at the big urn right next to the two-for-ninety-nine-cent burgers in those shiny gold and silver wrappers behind the glass, under the red lights that never kept the damn things hot. Whooeee, he loved those burgers.

The woman was another matter. He could tell what kind of woman she was right off: fat and fussy. She was wearing a stupid little Uncle Sam hat that didn't fit. The store manager probably made her wear it, but he still hated it. She should have some pride.

He hated her. She didn't even care he'd come in. She was supposed to care. *Hop to it. A little service here.*

With that thought, the heat caught up with him. Just exploded his head like a potato too long in the fire. This time it wasn't funny. This time he felt sick. The lights were too bright. Too much pain inside his head. Hand out, he found the door and pushed it hard, his other hand held tight to his temple.

The heat smacked him good when he walked out of the white light and frigid air of the store and back into the desert night. He pressed his temple harder as he walked to the car and got in.

He checked himself in the rearview mirror. His hair was a mess. He'd feel better if he looked better. Get the comb. He leaned over to the glove compartment thinking his head would split wide open, and laced his hands around the first thing he found. It was cool and it was metal and he held it to his head.

No comb. He needed a comb. Maybe that damn

clerk would notice the second time he walked into her store and sell him some smokes and a comb. Then he'd feel better.

He looked through the window of that Circle K again. She was still making coffee. Ignoring him.

He needed a cigarette bad. He needed a comb and now he needed some aspirin. He hurt so bad he could cry and she was just standing there making coffee.

Inside again he turned right, and walked up to the woman who was putting the big lid on top of the huge steel urn that would brew coffee for whoever it was that might come to a godforsaken place like this in the middle of the night. He walked right up to her and she felt him coming because she turned around. Her eyes were hazel and real clear and he saw himself in those eyes, reflected back the way people saw him.

Hot damn, he was a good-lookin' cowboy.

And when he smiled at himself, she smiled right back. She didn't have a clue. They never did.

One

Tara Linley was the last of a long line: a family that had started with the Indians and bred with the Spanish until the Anglos put in their two cents over the course of a hundred years.

Her cheekbones and blue-black hair were a legacy of the ancient pueblo dwellers. Her tawny skin was a credit to her great-great-grandfather, Juan Montero. The blue eyes were Irish, but had never gazed upon the Emerald Isle. Old family photos showed a succession of handsome women to whom credit could be given for her height and slim-hipped, lush-chested figure.

From her mother, an artist, came Tara's spare sense of style and her love of home and hearth. From her father came Tara's confidence, but not his fondness for power and prestige. Her mother had died before Tara could talk. Her father had raised her until his death. The law was her sister, politics her brother, and both were poor excuses for family, but Tara hardly noticed.

Now her father was dead, and at times like this, she felt his absence so keenly it hurt. He would have been sad to see her alone. For all his success, the most important thing in his life had been his daughter. She missed his friendship and his counsel, especially now when Albuquerque was changing and she was standing still.

On the North Rio Grande, horrid East Coast clapboard mansions were being constructed by immigrant yuppies, springing up faster than Tara could blink. The interlopers planted trees and bushes imported from parts of the country where water was less valued and more readily available. They complained of the heat in the summer and the cold in the winter, leading one to wonder why they chose to live there in the first place. Thankfully for Tara, all was not lost.

The glorious Sandias, mountains that had stood watch over this land since the beginning of time, remained stalwart. Pink and surreal in the sunset; formidable in the light of day. Real New Mexicans preferred to live properly on the land, respecting it as they blended into their surroundings. Here, in Tara's Albuquerque, adobe houses with their flat roofs and long porches, low walls and weathered gates were the norm; brush, sage, and cottonwoods the natural landscaping. Wreaths of chiles still hung on front doors. And five days into the new year, Christmas luminaria still lined roofs and walls, lighting the way of Mary and Joseph and Jesus.

Tara's home was like these. It had been in the Linley family for generations, on land they had claimed when a neighbor was the person a hundred miles to the south. The souls of all those who had gone before still dwelt in the walls, looked out of the deep-set windows, held tight to the heavy beams that crossed her ceiling, and warmed themselves by the cavernous fireplaces. Each ancestor had added something more to the original structure: a barn, a small nursery (now her office,) a corral, the lean-to by the river, a guest house. Her home was Tara's reward for a young life at the mercy of politics, spent in cities so alien they might have been half a world away. She loved this house and the tradition and the stability of her life.

She hated change, but her life was changing. Carlos, the man who had tended the Linley land for as long as she could remember, was needed elsewhere to deal with family business. He had stood on this porch, hat in hand, explaining how it was.

Tara watched him drive away. She pulled the blanket she had thrown over her shoulders tighter even though she couldn't see the truck any longer. It had been an awkward conversation, since Carlos was a man of few words, but already she missed him.

She poked her hand out from beneath the blanket and looked at the note he'd given her. Neatly printed were the phone number of the place he'd be in Arizona, and the name of the boy who would come to take care of her horse for the duration: Joseph. She hoped he would be as good as Carlos said. She knew he wouldn't be.

"Tara, hon? Where do you want the gold ornaments?"

Tara closed the door and sloughed off the blanket. She'd half forgotten she wasn't alone. Folding the blanket as she went, Tara entered the living room just as Charlotte finished packing the gold ornaments from the tree into the wrong box. Charlotte looked up and smiled with prettily bowed, very pink lips.

"Is this the right box?"

"Sure." Tara tossed the blanket onto the couch and took over the dismantling of the Christmas tree. "You shouldn't do that. I don't want you to get messed up before—wherever it is you're going."

"The high school. Woodrow's giving a speech.

Reception afterward so he can listen to everyone's complaints." Charlotte waved a cigarette, unapologetic for her displeasure at the upcoming event. "You don't mind if I smoke, do you?"

"Woodrow thinks you quit," Tara said. Charlotte arched one well-defined eyebrow. "All right. Your secret's safe with me." With her hands full of strung chiles, Tara nodded toward the fireplace. "There's a lighter over there."

"Don't think I need one." Charlotte snapped open her purse. "Oops, wrong." She was across the room in three long steps. Tall and slender, she was nonetheless substantial. She was a doer, and a perfect political wife for Woodrow. Charlotte could sit with her ankles daintily crossed for hours, or run roughshod over a room full of volunteers until they dropped from licking too many envelopes.

They'd known each other since high school, and Charlotte Weber still intrigued Tara Linley with her single-mindedness and generosity. Thankfully, she always managed to get what she wanted, too.

The cigarette was lit, the first drag taken, and Charlotte was happy.

"Oh that tastes good." She leaned back against the huge fireplace. "You know, I still can't figure out how you managed when you were a kid. Keeping up with the schedule of a man in public life is difficult even for an adult. Knowing what to say, when to say it, what to do—" Another drag and a thoughtful expulsion of a spirit of smoke. "But you followed your father around through three federal appointments and an elected office. That was a big career for a man on his own with a little girl." The next puff was more perfunctory. "The gang and I didn't sympathize very much. We went out cruising while you hung out at the high school watching him give speeches."

"I liked being with him. I didn't need any sympathy." Tara pulled a box toward her with her toe and laid the dried chiles in a nest of tissue paper. The mis-boxed gold ornaments went in after.

"Yes, you did. You're just too proud to admit it," Charlotte said.

"Okay, a little would have been nice." Tara grinned. "Happy to know you were right?"

"No. I like guilt," Charlotte sniffed.

"You've never felt guilty in your life." Tara laughed.

"You're right. But it's only because I've never really done anything to feel guilty about." Charlotte put her hand to her neck, tired of rehashing history and uninterested in delving into her psyche. "Do you think these pearls are too much?"

Tara looked over her shoulder and shook her head. "No, they're fine. You look like you could take over the governor's mansion tomorrow. Hand me those scissors, will you?"

Charlotte looked around, tossed what was left of her cigarette into the fireplace, and grabbed the scissors off the mantle. Though she handed them to Tara, her eyes were locked on the cards neatly displayed on the rough-hewn wooden mantle.

"You got one too, I see," Charlotte said evenly. "What?"

"Ben's announcement." This time her voice was flat. Tara's snipping stopped but she remained stooped over the box. Finally, pulling a piece of tape across the seam, she sealed it tight.

"I think everyone did," she said. "I saw Charlie in court the other day and he mentioned getting one. No big deal."

"It might not be a big deal to Charlie," Charlotte said, conversationally nudging the opening into Tara's private life wider. "But he's kept in touch with Ben. You haven't."

Tara nodded and lifted the box, neatly stacking it on the one she had managed to pack before Charlotte arrived thirty minutes early. It gave her an excuse for not looking Charlotte in the eye. She could kick herself for even bothering to display that card.

"He sent flowers when Dad died last year. He was in Los Angeles, I think. Didn't even mention coming back. Not that there's any reason he should. It's been over twenty years." Tara straightened and put her hands on the small of her back. She smiled at Charlotte. There was less sparkle and more strain in her expression. "Look, I've just about had it for tonight. You can toss those Christmas cards in the fire. At least the mantle will be cleared. I'll finish packing up the tree tomorrow."

"You don't want to save Ben's card, just in case?" Charlotte ignored her given task and fingered the red card resplendent with gold cherubs, one with its hand on the other's breast. Ben always did have a subtle, but healthy, libido. Fleetingly Charlotte wondered if it was still intact. If someone like him could even manage to—

Tara interrupted her thought. "No. Thank you very much. And if I hear another word about it, I won't go to your fund raiser tomorrow night."

Charlotte quietly put the card back. "In that case, I'm out of here." Charlotte gathered her things, the subject of Ben Crawford closed. She glanced in the mirror above the hearth, gave her St. John suit a tug, and grinned. "I'm really sorry I couldn't stay longer. I hate leaving you alone tonight of all nights."

"Not the first birthday I've been alone. Besides,

Caroline took me out to lunch and the court reporters sent flowers to the office. Two judges even remembered. The bouquet you brought was icing on the cake, and I'm thrilled you thought of me, considering how much you have to do tonight."

"It was nothing," Charlotte said, lifting her chin a tad. Tara leaned in for an air kiss and walked her friend to the door.

"Tell Woodrow hello for me and wish him luck."

"Certainly will," Charlotte murmured, her spouse voice fully in force, her face closing, changing into the public one that no one could read but every voter loved. When she looked up, her smile was in place and wouldn't droop until the last reporter had left the high school. Tara had long since ceased to be amazed. She'd watched those in public life morph since she was ten. It was an art she'd never perfected.

" 'Night then." Tara opened the door and shivered. It was a cold, clear January night. The last place she wanted to be was in the high school auditorium listening to Woodrow Weber wax poetic on various and sundry political agendas.

"We could meet you for a late dinner and celebrate," Charlotte offered.

Tara shook her head, too quickly. "No, thanks. I'll see you tomorrow. Where is it again? What shall I wear?"

"La Posada Hotel. Right after work. Everyone will be in suit and tie. Do me a favor. Wear a dress instead of pants. I'm going to put you in front of the cameras with Woodrow and your legs are fabulous," Charlotte said. Suddenly her arms were around Tara. "Wish us luck tonight."

"Of course." Tara patted Charlotte lightly, then held her away. "I always do, you know that."

"He just wants it so much, Tara," Charlotte said quietly.

"I know."

What else could she say? Woodrow was a politician. There was always hurt for the women who loved that sort. Hurt and joy. Rejection and acceptance. It was all the luck of the draw, the whim of the people. Thank goodness her fortunes were dependent only on her actions.

Charlotte's public face had slipped. She took a moment to put it in place.

"All you can do is your best, Charlotte," Tara reminded her. Charlotte fingered her purse as if the thought made her nervous.

"I know. I guess I just keep thinking there's more somehow."

"There isn't. Just keep smiling. That's what the voters want."

"Guess you should know. See you tomorrow. Happy birthday."

With that, Charlotte was gone in a cloud of lavender perfume. Tara closed the door with a chuckle, picked up the mail that the cleaning lady had laid neatly on the hall table, and wandered back to the living room.

Bills, an invitation to speak at a women's conference in Taos, a letter from Franklin, the last in her short list of lovers, and the dearest. She opened that envelope swearing she smelled his aftershave as she pulled out the card. Franklin was getting married. Good for him. He would make some woman a marvelous husband. At one time she thought she might have walked down the aisle with him. But Franklin wanted to live in the bustle of New York, and Tara clung to her Albuquerque roots, unlike many of her friends and family. Those she had liked, and some she had loved, had left. But now Ben was back and that wasn't something Tara had counted on in this lifetime. Thankfully, Albuquerque had grown. They wouldn't be running into one another anytime soon.

Impulsively, Tara stepped up to the mantle and gathered the Christmas cards into a haphazard stack. They were in the fire, curling at the edges, before she could think twice. The red card with the gold cherubs was the first to go. Watching awhile longer, Tara finally turned away. Knowing Ben was close again made her feel lonelier than ever. She didn't want to question the choices she'd made, not on this particular birthday, anyway.

Feeling antsy, Tara went to her bedroom, and peeled off her sweater and her too-short-for-court skirt. She pulled on her jeans, tossed on a flannel shirt, tied back her hair, and grabbed her denim jacket. A night ride was in order. Shinin' would love it as much as she.

Tara tugged her boots on, groaning with the effort, and heard a knock on the front door at the same time. Her heels sounding an echo on the tiled floor, Tara flipped on the lights in the living room and reached for the doorknob. Charlotte must have forgotten something. She pulled on the huge knob. Impossible to fling, the massive door opened slowly but it wasn't Charlotte who waited on the other side.

"Surprise!"

"Oh, my God," Tara breathed, sagging against the door, her forehead resting on the thick wood. She lifted her head.

"You didn't think I'd forget, did you, Tara?" The woman on the doorstep burst into Tara Linley's house, handing over a bouquet of roses that had half hidden her, pressing on Tara a magnum of champagne. "God, if you only knew what it took to get here! You have no idea, I swear. Happy, happy, happy, you old broad, you!"

Tara laughed as Donna Ecold filled every available bit of space with her gifts, her chatter, her laughter, and her presence.

"I don't care what it took to get here. I'm just glad you made it." Tara kissed her friend's cheek, holding her shoulder as if she were afraid she might flit away.

"Of course you are, my love," Donna trilled. "I knew you'd be bummed. Everyone is bummed when they hit forty. So here I am, to get you through your birthday crisis."

Donna chattered, but not without noticing that Tara wasn't listening any longer. The tall woman's face had fallen to a look of bewilderment. Donna looked over her shoulder and giggled. She flung her arm around Tara's waist, pulled her close, and gave her a little squeeze.

"Okay, so it's a little more than me, myself, and I. Tara Linley, this is Bill Hamilton. Bill, this is my very, very best friend in all the world. The smartest woman you'll ever meet. The best attorney on the face of the earth, Tara Linley."

Donna's little head swiveled from one person to the other. Her grin could have lit up Albuquerque from one December to the next, but its radiance was lost on Tara. Her eyes were locked with Bill Hamilton's and she had the strangest feeling that she should shut the door before he stepped over her threshold.

Two

"There I was giving this lecture in the Taos library on the structure of children's books and Bill walks in. I mean, the entire room is filled with old ladies hoping to make their fortune spinning their little tales into best-selling books, when suddenly I see a hand raised for a question, and there he is. I ask Gorgeous if he has a question and he says 'sure.' So he says 'Would you have a drink with me when you're finished, ma'am?' The place went nuts." Donna reached over and patted the hand that lay so quietly on Tara's dining room table. It seemed Bill Hamilton was used to being touched. He turned his electric smile on Donna, and Tara was mesmerized.

"Come on, Donna. Tell it straight. Those ladies just thought it was a bit odd for a cowboy to be hangin' around a library." He turned that grin Tara's way and his gray eyes sparkled like a pool of quicksilver. Tara smiled back. Oh, but he had the magic. Ben and betrayal, Charlotte and failure, her father and the loneliness she felt without him—everything was forgotten the moment Bill Hamilton walked in and turned that smile her way.

"Are you saying I'm not in my right mind?" Donna pouted, leaning into him. Tara watched. How lovely that he put his arm around her, tipped her chin with just a crooked finger before saying, "You've probably been out of your mind since you were a kid and that's all the more luck for me."

Gently, he set her upright and laced his hands in front of him. Good strong hands. Dark hair ran up his wrists, and disappeared into the turned-up cuffs of his denim shirt. Tara forced herself to look him in the eye so she didn't go on speculating about the map of that curling hair. It was no hardship. He looked like a movie star without the ruse of a public face. What you saw was what you got with Mr. Hamilton, it seemed.

"I'm just amazed you stopped to listen to a lecture on children's books," Tara said, as Donna snaked her hands around his arm and held on tight. Tara could see the years slip away from her friend's face. How lucky. How amazing. How almost unbelievable after all these years for Donna to find happiness with a man like this.

"I like kids. Takes a special person to talk to them the way they need to be talked to," Bill said.

"You have children?" Tara asked. She stacked dinner dishes. The haphazard feast had been made better because of the company. Immediately Bill half stood as if to help. Tara waved him down. Donna attached herself once more as Tara turned, not realizing her question had been ignored.

"Don't you dare move. You're my guests. I thought I'd be spending this depressing evening all by myself. Here you both are to rescue me from the forty blues."

"If you're what forty looks like, women should be beatin' down the door to get there." Bill's hand covered Donna's, but his eyes were all for Tara. He held her gaze, then turned it on Donna. "You're both poster girls for makin' time stand still. Damn if I wouldn't swear you'd been drinkin' from the fountain of youth. Oh, I almost forgot." Bill was up and heading toward the front door.

Donna sighed, giving Tara a wink. "He is just a dream, isn't he?"

"Almost too good to be true," Tara giggled. The giddiness of these two lovebirds was rubbing off on her like wet paint on a bench. She hoped she'd get rid of it soon. She had to work the next day.

"Don't tell me he's got a brother in his pocket," Tara whispered to Donna.

"If he did, I'd make him show me first," Donna giggled. They pulled apart. He was back, all legs and slim hips moving toward the table. He stopped at Tara's elbow and leaned down close.

"Happy Birthday. Didn't want to come empty-handed. My daddy said never, ever go to anyone's spread without somethin' to offer."

Bill Hamilton held out a heart-shaped, black and gold box. Where on earth he'd found Valentine's candy when people were still nursing New Year's hangovers Tara couldn't imagine.

"Thanks. That's so sweet." And she meant it. Sweeter than all the lovely gifts she'd been given over the years from admirers with more than Bill Hamilton would ever have. Putting down the dishes, Tara took the candy. "I was wondering what we were going to do about dessert." She laughed and pulled open the top only to stop short. Her head cocked. She looked at the man with fog-swirl eyes and held out the nearly empty box. "Two pieces?"

"But they're the best two pieces. Marzipan," he said with a wink and a chuckle. "Donna told me they were your favorite. I tossed the rest. Wouldn't want you to have anything that wasn't right up to snuff. Not a lady like you." Those eyes were still trained on her as she put the top back on.

"Well, thanks," Tara said, flustered and flattered and just slightly put off. "That is definitely the most unusual gift I've ever received. I love it."

"I guarantee you aren't going to be forgetting this night any too soon," Bill said quietly, moving toward Donna, running his hands across the back of her neck until his fingers were coupled around her throat. "Nothin' good should last too long. You lose appreciation for it. Ain't that so, Donna?" Tipping her head back until her neck stretched long and taut, Bill leaned down and kissed her lips, slowly.

"Everything but us," she purred back and that delighted Bill Hamilton.

"We're better than good. We're perfect."

Donna raised her lips to be kissed again, then shot Tara a how-'bout-them-apples look.

"Can you believe this?"

Tara shook her head and chuckled.

"It's tough, I must admit." With that, she took the dishes and headed for the kitchen. A moment alone was definitely in order. For her or them, Tara wasn't quite sure.

Tara glanced at the clock. Fifteen minutes. The dishes were almost done. Every once in a while she could hear Donna laugh. Her little girl voice was getting tinnier with age. Tara closed her eyes, hoping against hope that Donna wasn't pulling her moppet act. What was charming in a sixteen-year-old might drive a man like Bill Hamilton home to the range if Donna didn't watch it.

Rinsing the last of the silver, Tara leaned over

and peeked through the open door. Bill and
Donna still sat at the table; Bill looking like the
handsome young whip he was, Donna looking
more than her age. Donna the natural teller of
tiny tales, and the tall-tale cowboy. Two yarn spin-
ners happily weaving their own May-December legend. As she retrieved the champagne flutes, Tara
thought it seemed a perfect match.

"Well, what do you think?"

Tara looked over her shoulder. Donna was standing in the doorway in her short, light flowered
dress. A poor choice for an Albuquerque winter.
In a nod to the nip in the air, she'd layered it
over a turtleneck. Her thin legs were encased in
black opaque stockings, her shoes were thick-soled
boots that added two inches to her height and
nothing to her panache.

"He's fabulous." She pulled down the glasses
and turned around.

Donna grinned. "You're not mad I brought him
with me?"

"No, of course not." Tara laughed.

Ready for a chat, Donna settled at the kitchen
table and toyed with the salt shaker. "I'm not fooling myself, you know. He is special and I am so
happy. He's funny. He's surprising. He's darn good
in bed." Her enthusiasm melted into a sigh and
she rested her chin on her upturned palm. "You
know, I'm glad you like Bill. It's always been important that you like my men, but it's really important you like him."

"Donna, as long as you're happy, I'm happy. If
Bill's doing it for you, then that's great." Tara's
eyes flicked over Donna's head toward the doorway
as she joined her at the table. "What have you
done with him anyway?"

"Nothing." A Cheshire cat grin followed. "He thought we needed some time alone to girl talk so he's making a fire. I love a man who thinks about stuff like that."

"Better all the time," Tara agreed quietly, letting her observation dwindle to nothing.

"It's not awful for you, is it? I mean the way it was for me when I turned forty?" Donna gave Tara a little poke in the arm, misreading her silence. She got a wry grin for her efforts.

"Nothing could be that awful." Tara rearranged the three flutes. They now sat in a line instead of a triangle and she seemed satisfied with the symmetry. "I'm actually just glad we're not sixteen anymore. Remember? Washington was awful, wasn't it? We were such babies."

"Yeah," Donna caught the mood and drifted with the memories.

Washington, D.C. Two girls whose fathers had been big fish in that exclusive small pond. Tara, adored by her widowed father, had hated Washington because it wasn't New Mexico. Donna's barely-there mother was consumed by Washington. Committees and charities, luncheons and dinners, dressing for balls, recovering from balls, having a ball with everyone but her husband, all took precedence over her daughter.

Donna still searched for a place and people to call her own. Unfortunately, she put her faith in an odd assortment of people who used her, sometimes abused her, and left her without a thought when the happy-go-lucky, trilling-voiced little girl became a woman afraid of growing old and being alone. So Tara had given Donna a place to be herself, where no one judged her. In return, Donna had an uncanny knack for knowing when Tara's privacy bordered on reclusiveness. They saved each other from their own little quirks. Tara pushed the champagne bottle across the table, not wanting to talk old business.

"Long time ago," she sighed, "Let's enjoy the moment."

"Damn straight." Donna took the bottle, hitched up her skirt, and planted the magnum between her bird legs, as tiny a body as Tara was statuesque. She couldn't saddle a horse, but she had a fast thumb with a champagne cork.

"How long have you been seeing him?" Tara asked.

"A month and three days," Donna said. Her bottom lip disappeared between her teeth. She worked on the cork so she didn't have to look at Tara.

"Four weeks," Tara mused. "Bet you haven't written a thing. Bet you haven't talked to your agent."

"You know me too well." The cork squeaked, but it was her voice that was tight.

"Where does he live?" Silence. Donna almost had the cork out. Tara drew circles on the table. "Is he staying at your place?"

"I'm waiting," Donna said.

"For what?" Tara lifted her hand, innocent in her ignorance.

"I'm waiting for the lecture on looking before I leap. Let's get it over with. Tell me I'm moving too fast. Point out how much I have to lose now in a palimony suit. Talk to me like a child. Tell me I don't know where his hands have been," Donna sniffed.

Startled, Tara spoke carefully. Her curiosity wasn't judgmental. All wasn't well in paradise if Donna was so defensive.

"I thought you wanted to talk about him."

"Don't be ridiculous," Donna said angrily. She worked the cork furiously, revving herself up again, charging the battery that allowed her to whirlybird over reality. With a huge pop, the cork exploded out of the bottle. Tara ducked as it ricocheted around the kitchen, narrowly missing her prized kachina that sat in a little niche high above the huge oven where her ancestors once baked their flat loaves of bread.

"Nice shot," Tara laughed, swooping in with a glass to catch the overflow before it drenched Donna's lap. "Friends?"

"Okay." Donna feigned petulance and filled Tara's glass. "Good?"

Tara took a sip and nodded. Donna's taste was impeccable as always. Tara put the glass down and laced her fingers around the stem, studying the simple design. Belgian crystal. Beautiful and serviceable like everything in the Linley family home, from the ladle that Margaret Linley had used to fill the glasses at the saloon she and her husband Jesse ran in the eighteen hundreds, to the Navajo rugs that hung on the thick adobe walls. This was history. This was permanence. This was a sense of belonging that couldn't be bought. Yet now she looked around and it seemed that much of what she loved had lost depth of meaning. She could recite the history, but not feel it. She could admire the workmanship, but not be moved by it. Tara sighed, half listening as Donna's good humor returned.

"So, tell me what's been happening with you? Slain any dragons lately? Stood up for the poor? Won a case for the rich?" Donna filled the other two glasses, pushing one away, ready to fulfill her role as confidante to a woman who liked to think she didn't need one.

Tara made a motion as if trying to erase the question. "None of the above. Work and more work. I don't know where the time goes. Haven't got anything to match the prize in the other room," Tara said.

"Come on, there has to be something—someone? Talk to me," Donna prodded.

Tara chuckled and exaggerated her melancholy. "You're beginning to sound like me. I don't know." She crossed her arms on the table, leaned over and whispered. "It's the weirdest thing, Donna. I go to court, argue a case, present a motion, do my paperwork, go to dinner, see people for drinks, then go home and have this been-there-done-that feeling that's driving me crazy."

Donna sat back and crossed her legs, her boot-shod foot pumping up and down, stoking the burners of her mind, Tara's problem the kindling.

"Honey, every woman goes through this. But it's harder for someone like you. Someone who's all alone."

"Oh please." Tara guffawed, thoroughly entertained.

"I'm not kidding. This whole autonomous thing—men and women living on their own, no real commitment—it's against all the laws of nature. I've got a book I want you to read. It's called *Living Alone: The Danger Zone.*"

"Donna, really." Tara rolled her eyes and leaned back in her chair. "Of all the nonsense. You're telling me I need to be married? Why? I've got a dozen male friends and a few that have been much more than just friends." Tara tsked.

"And all these friends?" Donna demanded, not to be put off. "Where are they tonight, on your fortieth birthday? I don't see any big surprise party.

I didn't burst in on you getting ready for that date-to-die-for. That table out there wasn't set up for a cozy dinner for two, was it?"

Tara raised a shoulder as if to say her solitude, like Donna's need for companionship, was by choice. Donna didn't buy it and made a sound that left no doubt.

"I don't need parties. I have flowers and good friends offering best wishes."

"It's not the same, and it's about time you faced up to it." Donna poked her finger. Tara batted her hand away and laughed. Donna was being ridiculous and Tara loved her for it. She only wished she knew when to quit.

"Tara, a committed relationship can change the way you look at everything. You need someone to wake up to every morning. You've never had a man to hold your hand, and worry with you about one thing or another day in and day out."

"I have nothing to worry about . . ."

"You haven't washed someone's underwear and not minded."

"What a thrill."

"You haven't . . ."

Tara clucked. "I haven't cooked breakfast naked, run after small children, or enjoyed the delights of picking up his shirts at the laundry."

"Stop it," Donna said quietly. There was something in the air now that gave Tara pause, and she became attentive. "I hate it when you laugh at me. You think I don't know what I'm talking about, but I do."

"I'm not laughing at you, Donna," Tara insisted. Donna shook back her hair and ignored her.

"Look, I know you love me, Tara, but I also know there's a part of me you don't respect. I've been married three times. I've had my share of lovers. At least I've tried to live a full life. But you haven't." Donna had found her footing. Her dark eyes were on Tara's blue ones and they weren't about to let go.

"Donna, I don't think less of you for the way you live."

"If I was a man, you wouldn't give me the time of day. I've watched you, Tara. You pick your lovers over until you find the cream of the crop. You quote the guy's curriculum vitae, for goodness' sake, instead of telling me what a good tush he has."

Donna had been fingering the stem of her flute and now pulled the glass toward her.

"I loved each of my husbands," Donna said. "I adored belonging. The sound of Mrs. before my name was like music to my ears. My heart just filled up when I opened the closet and saw my clothes hanging next to someone else's. Sometimes I would spend hours looking at the ring on my finger." Donna's hand went to her nearly flat chest. "That ring meant I was so special that someone wanted me forever. Even if we didn't make it to forever, it was still wonderful to think we tried."

Donna put that same hand to her head and ran her fingers through her blond hair as if that helped her think. Her eyes wandered from Tara's.

"Men and women aren't meant to live the way you do." She sighed and looked back at her friend. "If people didn't make commitments, the human race would have died out a long time ago."

"If the human race had to depend on me, we'd be in trouble." Tara laughed, unsure how to continue this personal, so deeply private, conversation.

It was usually Donna who dug into her soul and bared it. Tara wasn't crazy about hers being mined.

"You might feel differently if you met the man of your dreams," Donna suggested.

"I don't dream about men," Tara joked.

Donna was tenacious.

"You did once." Tara's brow furrowed as she silently pleaded a defective memory. Annoyed, Donna went on, "Georgetown. Seventeen and you had your first drink. Probably the last time you were ever out of your mind. You told me about him then."

"Those were the fantasies of a little girl," Tara said testily. Ben Crawford. She didn't want to talk about him tonight. Not with Charlotte, and certainly not with Donna, who had never met him.

"You were a young woman."

"I was a little girl, and that was a long time ago." Tara stood up and collected the glasses, ending the conversation. She looked down on her friend and spoke softly, more gently than was her first instinct. "Marriage and a man aren't what I need, Donna. So don't try to make a girl's daydream into a woman's reality. It just ain't going to happen because you want it to. I do love you for wanting to make things right. Just don't go too far."

With a look she terminated the conversation, but Donna touched her arm, speaking in a voice that chilled Tara.

"One day soon people will stop calling you beautiful. Instead you'll be handsome. Someday you won't be asked to give the keynote speech at a fancy conference; you'll be talking at rubber-chicken luncheons about 'my career as a lawyer.' Even if your name is Linley." Tara moved. Donna tugged at Tara's shirt to make her listen. "There are fashions and you won't be part of them. Your father's gone. He was a legend here and some of his aura clings to you. But it won't last forever."

Donna dropped her hand and leaned away from her friend. Her eyes fluttered down. She'd made her pronouncements sadly, as if even she, the teller of enchanted tales, couldn't find a happy ending for this one.

"You've walked through life cutting a straight path, guarding your privacy and your home. You didn't look at what you left behind or shoved aside to keep all this safe. You've always been headed forward to a destination only you could see. You have no great ambition because everything came so easily. You substituted tradition and comfort for great passion. You've never been tested, Tara. That's why you're sad. Half your life is gone and you haven't taken the time to give someone all of yourself." She sighed and looked straight at Tara. "You're the last of the Linleys and it's a pity to see such a fine family end with you. Think about it. Lie awake some night and let yourself be afraid of something, for something. Find some passion in your life, even if it's to mourn what you haven't passed on to another generation."

Tara listened, enraptured by this odd soliloquy, delivered with such precision and deliberation. She wanted to rebut this fantastic nonsense, yet she found herself mute and embarrassed, wondering if Donna wasn't one hundred percent correct.

"Fire's a blazin', ladies."

Slowly Tara turned to the doorway, trying to clear her head. Bill Hamilton leaned casually against the doorjamb, one jean-clad leg crossed over the other. Slender, on the right side of rangy, he seemed to belong there in her desert house. Perhaps this was what Donna was talking about. A man to dream of. A man whose looks could steal your breath, whose smile could warm you fifty feet off. Tara was almost smiling when Donna shot out of her chair. Their moment was over and now the evening belonged to three, not two.

"Honey, that's marvelous!" Donna's hands fluttered over him as she joined her man of the moment. She looked at Tara a minute longer but spoke to Bill. "Girl talk's over. You've been so patient. I think we're ready for that champagne, aren't we, Tara?"

"Absolutely," she said and walked behind them into the living room, where she sat in the high-backed chair while Bill and Donna cuddled on the couch.

Three

"Towels are in the front room cupboard. I've put a coffeepot in the bathroom so you don't have to come to the main house for a cup. There's shampoo and there's a hair dryer. Extra blankets in the chest. It gets cold out here."

Tara stood back and surveyed the guest house. It was a cozy little cottage that backed onto the Rio Grande. In the spring and summer there wasn't a more magical place on the face of the earth. The little adobe structure was shaded by the graceful arms of cottonwoods in bloom, sage sprang up around the courtyard, and the river tumbled by at a lazy pace. Unfortunately, in the winter there wasn't a chillier place. Still, it was preferable to having Bill and Donna in the guest room next to hers. They could frolic to their hearts' content out here in the frosty bungalow and she'd get a good night's sleep.

"This is great." Donna tested the bed with a little jump and a giggle.

"Real nice, Tara. Thanks. Couldn't have asked for a better welcome considerin' we just moseyed in here without so much as a phone call." Bill stowed his gear in the closet and looked around, obviously pleased.

"Considering nothing. It's been a wonderful evening. And I still reserve the right to a challenge match on Yahtzee. I've never been beaten that badly in my life."

"You got it." Bill cocked his finger and shot her his promise.

Tara lingered, touching the quilt rack by the door. "Back door's open at the main house. Donna knows where everything is, so help yourself." Tara was headed out when she turned around. "Listen, I've got to go to a fund raiser tomorrow night for Woodrow Weber's gubernatorial campaign. Shouldn't last too long. Would you two like to come? We could have dinner in town after."

"Sounds wonderful!" Donna grinned and clapped her hands. A party. Her favorite thing.

"Aw, I don't think so." Bill talked over her.

Tara waited for an answer. A look passed between the two. Donna smiled apologetically and explained.

"Bill's not one for crowds of fancy folk, as he puts it. How about we settle for dinner?"

"Sounds good. I'll leave directions on the kitchen table. It's cocktails after work so plan on meeting me in front of the hotel around seven-thirty. Or eight." She looked from one to the other for confirmation.

"You're on." Bill grinned, sat on the bed, and draped an arm over Donna's shoulder. He buried his face in her hair, keeping his smiling eyes on Tara. That was her signal. Three was a crowd.

Tara smiled a goodnight and stepped outside, shutting the door behind her. She hooked her thumbs in her belt and peered at the night sky. It was clear and lovely and she wasn't quite ready for bed. Walking to the paddock, she planted her boot on the lower rung of the fence and hoisted herself up, putting her crossed arms on the top board.

"Shinin'. Pretty boy," she called softly, though there was no need. The horse sensed her presence. He pranced toward her, bringing the animal warmth and companionship Tara loved. A strong creature, this horse of hers, bigger than life, yet gentle. If he were a man, Tara would have no trouble falling head over heels in love. She made affectionate noises as he laid his muzzle over her shoulder and nuzzled in.

"That's right, old boy. That's right. You love me. I'm not going to be an old shriveled-up prune, am I?"

Tara put her face against his warm, silky jaw. He snorted gently and tossed his huge head back. Tara chuckled and raised one hand to pet him, balancing herself on the wood as she had since she was a girl. In those days she'd petted a dozen different horses, cared for by half as many ranch hands. In those days the land had stretched for miles, instead of acres, on either side of her home.

The horse threw his head and danced away from her, teasing, wanting to play. Tara wasn't in the mood. A lot had happened that night and her mind was full: Ben Crawford's return to Albuquerque, Donna's observation of Tara's loneliness, a man like Bill Hamilton sitting in her home as if he'd visited for years. Tara shushed Shinin', then held out her arms. He walked back into them and she ran her hands down his shoulder, noting how well his winter coat had come in. He'd be warm tonight. She gave him one more pat.

Jumping down from the fence, Tara brushed her hands on her jeans and surveyed her domain. The champagne and the cold, Donna and Bill behind closed doors, and the age of the evening convinced Tara it was time for bed. If she was destined to be a crusty old broad, a courthouse fixture, then so be it. If it ever really bothered her, she'd deal with it. She'd give herself a deadline, make a list, do some research, see a shrink, learn a new joke, but she sure as heck wouldn't read any of Donna's self-help books.

Head down, she chuckled at herself and Donna and the world at large while she watched her feet kick over the hard-packed ground. She needed new boots. The dry winter showed no signs of changing. There was a gopher hole that needed to be filled in. Tara looked up. The cottonwoods, so lush and green in the spring, surrounded her like skeletal remains planted upright instead of laid in the grave to rest. She shivered. The night had suddenly gone beyond cold. She tipped her head back and looked at the black sky, trying to feel for any hint of snow. There was none. Eyes earth-level, one last over-the-shoulder look at Shinin', she gazed past the trees to her house, so softly lit on this winter night, and knew that something had changed.

Tara was tired, but not so weary that the difference in the space around her went unnoticed. Alert, hardly panicked, she narrowed her eyes, scanning the corral and the entrance to the barn. Every hair prickled, every muscle tensed for confrontation. An animal? No. Shinin' would have been skittish. Whatever was out there was ahead of her, not behind. Irritated, she took her hands from her pockets and walked two paces, stopped, and breathed easy.

"You don't need to hide," Tara called.

She counted the time in heartbeats, waiting for

the silence to end. Finally Bill Hamilton broke free from the black shadow of the huge cottonwood that stood between the paddock and the main house. He paralleled her, his fingers digging deep into his back pockets. Even in the dark Tara could see the flash of his teeth, the glint of those opaque eyes of his. She imagined he shook back that long, straight dark hair of his but it was hard to tell, blending in with the night the way it did.

He wore no jacket. It was as if he had come out of the guest house quickly, looking for something, instead of being prepared for a late night stroll. There was no cigarette held up to explain his presence, no embarrassed laugh to pretend that he'd snuck out to explore her property, curious about his lover's friend.

"I wasn't hidin'." He offered no alibi.

"Oh?"

"I was lookin' for you."

"Really?"

He moved idly toward her, his feet kicking at the dirt with each step, his eyes never wavering.

"No sense beatin' around the bush."

He was closer now and she could feel him. She felt the heat of him, the vibrations of an unusually intense man who knew his power though, perhaps, not how to use it. Tara was intrigued, and no longer guarded. Champagne, conversation, and charisma were a deadly combination. He was close now, almost shoulder to shoulder, and her reaction was getting stronger.

"Is there something you need?" Tara took charge, but Bill didn't seem to notice.

"Nope. Not really." He gave the ground beside her one last scuff, walked over to the fence, and hopped up on the first rung the way Tara had done. He missed his footing, grabbed for the upper rail, and pulled himself up. Cautiously he turned around and hung on so that he was looking at her, listing toward her.

"Nice horse." He half turned again and held out one hand to Shinin'. The horse danced back delicately, hoof-over-hoof. Shinin' snorted and threw back his head. Surprised, Tara moved forward to calm him. But Bill Hamilton had turned away from the animal, almost lost his footing again, and then righted himself. He laughed and there was an excessiveness to it that bothered Tara, but Bill Hamilton gave her a glow-in-the-dark grin. Tara stood her ground, seeing he needed no help.

"You're not a cowboy at all, are you?" Tara said.

He shook his head, let go of the railing with one hand, and put a finger to his lips, "Shhh. Don't tell Donna. She decided I was a cowboy, 'cause I dress like one. Probably sound like one, too. I'm not educated like the two of you."

"Doesn't make you bad," Tara assured him.

"Doesn't make me a cowboy either," he chuckled. Feeling more comfortable on his perch, he locked his elbows and hung away from the fence. "My daddy was a cowboy though. He worked on ranches in Montana, Northern California. He's a good guy, my dad. My mom too. She was a waitress for a long time. Both of 'em worked real hard."

"Are they still working?" Comfortable now in the dark with him, Tara moved around and closer.

"Nope. They were pretty old when they had me. Retired now. But my dad's still a cowboy. Taught me to love the life. Music especially. I do so love that music. Everyone's so darn sad and strong in those songs. Don't you think? Especially the women. On their own, men leavin', men cheatin', and they just go on. Keep all that hurt inside. Damn, those are sad songs." He jumped down from the fence and examined the palm of his hand as if he'd picked up a splinter. Just when she thought to help him, his eyes flicked her way, his grin almost hidden by the angle of his head. "Strong women. Like you, I guess, huh?"

"And Donna," Tara reminded him.

"Naw. Donna's the soft one. You're the strong one. That's what she tells me, but I could see it myself. You may live quiet, but I wasn't fooled. Not like Donna, who lives big but needs things at home that belong to her. That little lady thinks the world of you, you know."

Bill Hamilton began to walk, tracing a path toward the river. Tara joined him. They turned and headed toward the house, only to stop near the cottonwood where she'd found him. Sweet talk rolled off his tongue like sap down a wounded maple.

"We've been friends a long time, Donna and I."

"I know. She's told me every story about fifty times. Wish I was buddies with someone the way you two are."

"Looks like you've found one now." Tara cocked her head toward the guest house. He followed her gaze and she swore his eyes softened almost to tears.

"She really saved me. That's one special lady." He collected himself and reached down for a pebble. He looked at it closely and then gave it a snap. It danced over the ground and they picked up the pace again.

"You had something you needed to be saved from?" Tara asked.

Too personal. She could see it in his eyes. Before

Tara could make light of it, he went on to something else. "Donna says you're a good lawyer. One of the best."

"I don't know how she'd know, but I appreciate the accolades." She smiled, pleased with the compliment. He could charm the rattles off a snake, or even turn Tara's head, without a problem.

"Only speakin' the truth the way I know it." Another kick and a pebble went flying. Ten yards and not a word was said.

"What kind of law do you do?"

"General practice. Civil, some criminal," Tara answered. "This isn't exactly a big city. It's difficult to specialize. I've got some corporate clients who make me comfortable. With those fees I can afford to help people who need a voice in the system. You know, just like Joan of Arc or Susan B. Anthony. I'm right up there." Tara chuckled and walked slowly. In the morning she would thank Donna for bringing Bill Hamilton, for talking to her, for making her see that it was time to enjoy for the sheer sake of enjoyment. She would put an ad in the paper. *Wanted: One good-looking cowboy to make me feel like a very special woman.* They'd double-date.

"That's good. I like that. You really help the folks who come to you, even when they aren't rich?"

"I try. Sometimes I can't help. Most often I can."

"I bet you manage better than you know." He twirled in front of her. Tara stopped. He looked toward the guest house. "You'd talk to anyone who needed help, wouldn't you?"

"Sure. Can't hurt to talk. If I couldn't handle the problem, I'd refer it to someone who could," Tara said, realizing the tone of the conversation had changed. "Do you know someone who needs to talk to a lawyer?"

"I do. Yes ma'am." They faced each other square, Tara almost as tall as he. Between them was something, a field of anticipation so palpable that Tara swore she could reach out and touch it. But this thing had nothing to do with charm; this was no feminine short circuit. She looked at him curiously now, seeing beneath the brightly lit eyes, something she hadn't noticed at first. A seriousness, an intelligence and intensity that made him all that more compelling. "I need to talk to a lawyer, Tara, and I was hopin' you might consider being the one to help."

"Nothing serious, I hope?" She put out professional feelers, but nothing came back. No dread, no fear, no nothing. She breathed easy.

"Got me, but I know I need a lawyer. I'd like to hire you." His hand was on her shoulder, and Tara was almost sure that when he removed it, the imprint would remain.

"Of course. I wouldn't have you go anywhere else. I'll help if I can." She moved out of touching range. He took no offense and fell in step with her again. They were headed back toward the house now, river sounds serenading them. It was time to sleep. "I've got a hearing in the morning. I'll be in the office about ten. Ask Donna. She'll tell you how to get there."

"Sounds good. I'll be there. We'll do it." He did some finger popping and put one hand over the fist he made with the other.

"I'll see you then." He turned toward the guest house then pivoted back, "Oh, I know you're pretty high priced. I just want you to know I'm good for it. Don't you worry. I got money, Tara."

"Didn't cross my mind. Good night, Bill. I'll be honored to help you out." Tara gave him a nod. They parted only for Tara's professional curiosity to get the best of her.

"Bill?"

"Yep?"

"I'll need some idea of what it is we're going to be discussing."

Tara's words bolted into the air, froze, and rang in her ears. The silence stretched into a thin, cold line and finally, through the dark, he spoke.

"Summer," he said. Tara beetled her brow and shook her head though he probably couldn't see. "There was a big to-do out at a Circle K on the highway."

"Yes?" Tara waited for an explanation.

"I'd like to talk about that," he called back, and Tara could see he was grinning. He was still grinning when he shut the guest house door behind him.

"I wondered when you'd be back," Donna said.

Alert, Bill stood quietly in the dark. Without moving, he surveyed the scene, his demeanor snake-like, slow-moving as he positioned himself for a strike. There she was. In this dark room she almost vanished in the big bed. She was talkin' like she deserved to have an attitude.

"I thought you'd be in there awhile," he said, taking a step toward her, turning his head, indicating the bathroom door.

"Cold porcelain holds no allure on a night like this. It's freezing in there. Freezing outside, too." She smiled, a little sourly. "Were you stargazing?"

Bill chuckled, low and deep and a little mean.

"Ah-ah-ah." He waggled a finger, keeping time

with it as he walked her way. "You're jealous. You think I'm chasin' tail, don't you?"

"Don't be ridiculous," she snapped, but her voice was a whisper, almost as lost in the dark as she was in her need to keep him.

"Naw, naw, naw." Bill was prancing now, having fun. His right hand pulled at one side of his shirt, his left the other. He bared himself while he danced, just that little bit of skin, a little teasing song. He was a lean machine, a man on the move. He was the Marlboro man. Oh, if she only knew.

"You can't fool me, you little bit of nothin'. You can't. You can't."

The man's fingers were on his fly. Down went the zipper. An inch. He was close enough now and Donna could see his tongue snake out and roll around his lips. Not for the first time she understood there were some things she didn't like about him. Some small and base things that bothered her to no end. Down that zipper went another inch, then two, the metallic grate background music for his striptease. His tongue disappeared and he was right by the bed now looking down on Donna. She saw him in his best light, shadowed and softened. The fine set of his lips, the thick lashing of those sharkskin eyes. She could have died for looking at such a beautiful face, or turned to stone, or lay down at his feet and let him step right on her.

Now she was looking at his bared chest. Somehow he'd managed to unbutton that cowboy shirt of his. Her hand shook. She reached out and touched the precious line of fine hair that ran down from his navel, disappearing into the denim that hung on his slim hips. The tip of her nail touched that space, the flat of her hand was itching for the feel of flesh, when her wrist was wrenched back, her arm angled sharply away so that her body followed suit. Donna grunted, surprised by the sudden attack. Not really afraid. Not really an attack because now he lay her hand back where she had wanted it in the first place.

He just wanted to be the person to put it there. He spoke to her sweet.

"You're not thinkin' I'm after Tara out there, are you?"

"I saw you," Donna said, her voice shaking, tentative in her reproach, unsure of him when he should be the one worried about being ditched. She had the money. She had the house. She had the prestige. But he had the power and he used it now, pouring it over her like honey, licking it off with every word he spoke.

"Aw, baby, baby. Shh, you sweet thing," he purred, his fingers still tight on her wrist. "You just saw me and Ms. Linley doin' some business. Remember what I told you? I got some old business and she'll clear it up for me." Bill pushed her hand closer to his crotch, but not close enough for her to find out if he thought her interesting in the least.

"What kind of help? I could do it for you," Donna breathed, her fingers jerking as he held her tight.

"Nothin' but my business, man's business." Bill pushed farther and Donna moved closer, the covers falling off her naked body. Bill's eyes flicked over her. She had no idea whether she pleased him or appalled him. He was such a hard man to read. She had to hear words, she had to know.

"That's all?" She shook him off, no longer willing to be directed, and put her hands on his hips. Quickly, Donna pushed away the denim and the cotton beneath until there was nothing left to push away and she found what she wanted.

"Do you care?" Bill asked, gently, softly, like a man talking to a child, a lover talking to a beloved.

She didn't hear all those things in his voice, nor did she answer his question, which was just as well. Just as Goddamn well as far as he was concerned.

"Hey, I'm not going to stand up here and spout all that stuff about honesty and integrity. You've seen my track record. You know me. My wife's family has lived in New Mexico since before it was a state. I don't like rhetoric. I'm just going to tell you straight. I want to be your governor because I want to make sure New Mexico doesn't become California. I don't want our schools at the bottom of the educational barrel and I don't want us living on top of each other. We shouldn't wonder if our neighbor will lend a helping hand or cut ours off when we reach out. I'm ready to be your governor. I'm ready to follow through on my promises now!"

Woodrow held up his hands as if the crowd in the high school auditorium had raised their voices in a collective roar of approval, instead of putting their hands together in a polite acknowledgment that he had finished speaking. Harriet Klinger got up from her seat, shook Woodrow's hand, and gave him back to Charlotte, who looked at him adoringly as he took his seat beside her.

"Well?" he whispered through clenched teeth.

"You did fine. So well." Charlotte's assurance came through a brilliant, unmoving smile.

Their attention was fixed on Harriet.

"Thank you, District Attorney Weber. We appreciate you coming here tonight to talk to us about your views." Harriet was addressing the crowd.

Woodrow grasped Charlotte's hand while he nodded to their hostess, who had looked back at them briefly.

"Are there any questions for the district attorney?" Harriet waited an excruciating ninety seconds before announcing, "Fine. There are cookies and coffee in the back of the room. You'll have a chance to mingle with Mr. Weber and his lovely wife in a more relaxed atmosphere."

Class was dismissed and Woodrow mingled with Charlotte in tow. He munched on cookies and drank red punch and made polite conversation. Charlotte passed him twice, giving him a minimal roll of the eyes. One of those signals. Things were a little better, but on the whole the evening hadn't gone well. They'd been off by a beat all night for some reason and the crowd sensed it. But then this audience was older and few cared about education when their children had been out on their own for twenty years. They might worry about overdevelopment, but that was a toss-up. They probably worried about crime, but the cops did a decent job. Woodrow needed a sexy position on something and he needed it soon, though the campaign was young. In the meantime he'd smile and munch and shake hands.

Then he saw something he didn't like at all. Out of the corner of his eye he caught sight of a younger face, a woman's face and a familiar one at that. He couldn't remember her name, only that he had felt uncomfortable in her presence. But another voice called to him. His smile was back and he leaned into the greeting, giving the caller his full attention. Still, the little niggle of worry stayed with him for a good long while.

"Hi, sorry I'm late."

The woman had the kind of style that doomed her to anonymity. Her hair was dirty blond and hung to her shoulders. She never cut it, though it never seemed to grow any longer. Despite her comely features, without makeup she was undefinable. Her clothing was clean and old enough to show some wear, her shoes were low, her skirt too long. In short, she was ordinary. She had chosen her outfit deliberately. She hadn't wanted to come to this place, but the man had insisted he had no time to make other arrangements. Besides, Weber wouldn't remember her. It had been too long; she had been too minor a player. Perhaps the man was right, but she'd caught Woodrow's eye and now wasn't sure. She wanted this over with as quickly as possible.

The man she came to see was easy to identify. He didn't look bored or enraptured and those seemed to be the only two expressions on the faces of those who came to hear Woodrow. She made a beeline for the expressionless guy.

"You're from the governor's office . . ."

"I'm the man you came to see." He talked fast and low and for some reason she imagined he never spoke any other way. "Do you have it?"

"Yes, I do," she said, slowing things down a bit, not quite sure this was what she wanted to do even if she had to do it. She looked over her shoulder and saw Charlotte Weber, beautiful and put together as if she didn't have a care in the world. That made her mad—and uneasy. Some people

had quite a bit to care about. Some people had
worries. Maybe the politicians should think about
that. She looked back at the man. "Could we at
least step outside?"

"Sure. Yeah. I've heard enough. The guy gives
a good speech, but he's gotta learn to tailor it to
his audience. He was all over the place."

"Everyone's a critic," she murmured and led the
way out the door and into the parking lot. People
were already leaving, headlights coming on, weaving
about, illuminating them now and again. The
woman skirted past a red Volvo, hugged the auditorium wall, and slipped around back between the
cafeteria.

"Happy now?" The man was holding something
out to her. She looked surprised, even though she'd
asked for it. "I brought it, so let's get on with it."

"It's only a memo. Maybe it doesn't mean anything." A twinge of conscience.

"Look, you read it to my boss's secretary. She
took it down and read it to him. If they think it's
worth something, then it's worth something. I don't
make those kind of judgments. Now, I've got fifteen
hundred dollars. You want it, take it. Give me what
I came for."

She hesitated a second longer, then opened her
purse and took out a crumpled piece of paper.
She handed it to him. He flipped on a penlight
and she could see he had bad skin for a man his
age. Funny, she didn't think guys got acne past
sixteen. His eyes flicked up.

"You couldn't put it in an envelope?"

"I wasn't thinking." She fingered the one he
had given her. It felt light for fifteen hundred dollars. She half smiled. She'd never had a bill in her
wallet bigger than a twenty. Government work

didn't pay much. After the last cut it didn't pay anything at all. "Sorry. Is it what you want?"

He looked it over, clicked off the light, and pocketed it and the letter. He was neater about it than she.

"Yes, this is what I expected. Thanks. See you later."

"That's it?"

"What? You want to get a receipt?" the man asked.

"No, but I just thought there should be something—some assurance . . ." Her voice trailed off.

"That's rich. You're screwing Weber's career, and you want assurances that you won't get caught. Lady, you're not cut out for this kind of thing. If I were you, I'd take the money and run."

"I'm going to. But you should know, I wouldn't have done this if I wasn't desperate. I just found it in the personal stuff I took when I got laid off. I was kind of mad when I called about this. Now, I'm not so sure I should do this. I mean people could get hurt, couldn't they?"

"Boy, lady, you are a rocket scientist, aren't you?" he muttered as he walked away. The woman was forgotten and so was her concern.

Behind him she was left to think about her life. She was a really good secretary. It wouldn't be long before somebody recognized that. Heck, if Woodrow Weber could convince people he was gubernatorial material, she certainly could convince someone to give her a job. Now, with the money in hand, she could wait it out until the right job came along. Another minute and the woman walked to her car, her step lighter than it had been in weeks.

The man she'd been talking to watched until she was gone. He went across the parking lot and got into a nondescript sedan. Inside another man waited. That man turned on the reading light and they both looked at the memo. Albuquerque. District Attorney's Office. Recommendation to indict Strober Industries for fraud and endangering the public through shoddy building practices. All this in specific relation to the construction of the new county building. The memo was long. It was thorough. It was specific. Across the face was a note, written in Woodrow Weber's hand they presumed, denying prosecution. Both men smiled. The one who had met with the colorless woman in the parking lot pulled another sheet of paper out of his breast pocket and glanced at it.

"I think the governor is going to be able to use this when he really starts campaigning. Strober wasn't even thoroughly investigated. Seems Weber nixed it pretty quick. Six months later his war chest gets a nice fat check from Strober Industries. Then Strober begins work on three major developments doing business as three different companies. Weber's dead meat if the governor keeps the heat on."

"He will," the other man replied. "He's a pro."

The first put the key in the ignition and chuckled. "Don't you just love politics?"

Ben Crawford rubbed his eyes. It had been a long day. Five interviews. Five reports to make and the last bit of unpacking to do. He had assumed it would take Social Security at least a month to get him on line with work, but he'd barely had time to get the kitchen in order before he was up and running—so to speak. Government. Slow as molasses or quicker than a jack rabbit. After this last move he would have preferred a little more molasses.

With a groan he threw his head back, rotated his neck, and attempted to knead the muscles at the top of his shoulders. A wife would have been nice right about then. Someone bustling about, whipping him up a little something to eat after a long day, massaging his neck. Ben snorted, knowing he'd never survive a wife like that. But women were on his mind and it wasn't because he was hungry or tired.

Charlotte Weber had called. Charlotte, who always had an ulterior motive for every lovely thing she did. She'd invited him to cocktails. *Had he been out yet?* Only a few people. *Had he reacquainted himself with any of his old friends?* A little business, a little pleasure. *Woodrow was running for governor, did he know?* Fund raiser? *Well, yes. Actually.* But more a chance to renew acquaintances. Old acquaintances. People she was sure he remembered. *Tara Linley, for instance?*

Charlotte had said the magic words. She had stopped him cold with that one and he wondered if he should be grateful. Now he was thinking about the woman he'd been trying not to think of since he'd hit town. It had been a long time, after all. Water under the bridge. Fond memories. Loving memories. He'd leave it at that. Unless, of course, he happened to run into her. Unless, of course, he happened to involve himself in something like—well—politics.

Ben laughed outright and switched off the desk light. The reports could wait. He was hungry. He was tired. He would decide about tomorrow night, tomorrow night. Then he wondered who he was kidding.

Four

A lawyer shall not knowingly use a confidence or secret of his client to the disadvantage of his client or for the advantage of himself or a third party, unless the client consents after full disclosure.
—Canon 4, ABA Model Rules of Professional Conduct

"Ms. Linley. Would you care to respond?"

Judge Mason put a finger alongside his rather fleshy jaw and pushed up so that his right eye was almost buried in a fold of flesh. He raised the brow on his left. He wasn't quite bored, but he was getting there.

"Yes, Your Honor." Tara stood up and away from the counsel table. Ignoring her paperwork, she spoke from a heart that was filled with joy. Her esteemed opponent was sweating bullets. "I have not changed my mind, Your Honor. I respectfully put before this court a motion for summary judgment in this matter. The facts are clear and in evidence. This is not a case of fraudulent behavior or malicious intent on the part of my client. Rather, it was a case of men experiencing an unfortunate and universal downturn of the market, which both acknowledge was risky. They also concurred that the possible return on investment warranted such a risk.

I have fully documented statements to these facts. I have deposed the plaintiff and offered to this court the exhibits which should convince Your Honor that a summary judgment is not only wise, but the only course of action."

She sat down. Enough said. Judge Mason let that finger slide down his cheek, allowing his face to resume its normal, hangdog, expression. She decided he wasn't bored, only tired. Divorced a year ago, either the dear judge was worrying about alimony payments all night or he was trying to keep up with a new honey. Tara would put her money on the former.

"All right, Ms. Linley. As usual, your work is impeccable. I've read over the myriad of exhibits you have given this court and would thank you to remember, sometime in the future, that our time is limited."

Masking a smile, Tara half stood. "Yes, Your Honor."

"Unfortunately," he continued, "while I see there might be ground for a summary judgment as you request, I'm going to deny your motion. There are gray areas that might warrant further consideration. You have shown no interest in settling this case . . ."

"As well we shouldn't, Your Honor, since my client has done nothing wrong." This time Tara didn't stand. A wise decision. He spoke over her.

"The plaintiff seems to be champing at the bit, as they say." His honor gave the attorney on the other side of the room an ominous look. "I think we have no choice but to go to trial and see what a jury has to say about this. I will, however, point out to Mr. Blackwell that he may be well advised to have a heart-to-heart with his client before that time. Were I the plaintiff's lawyer, I would be considering the long, hard road that I would have to walk to prove this case in his client's favor. Motion for summary judgment denied. We will see you here again for jury selection in four weeks' time."

The end. Other lawyers were already moving about, ready to take their places in front of the bench. Tara gathered her things. She checked her watch. Ten 'til. Good timing. She pushed through the swinging gate of the bar, nodded to Faith Cornlow, who was waiting to pass the other way. Tara headed down the aisle toward the door and freedom. Gary Blackwell followed behind, briefcase under his arm, day planner already out as he called.

"Tara, hey, wait up." He was hot on her trail now, almost beside her. She grinned and kept going until she was through the door and in the hallway where spectators weren't interested in their conversation. Now she had time for Gary. Not much, but enough. Strangely, he seemed disappointed her motion had been denied.

"I gotta tell you. This date just isn't good for me. You gotta cut me some slack on this. Jury selection in a month . . ."

"Can't do anything about it, Gary. It sounds good from where I stand and my client wants his name cleared so he can get on with business. Have your client drop the proceedings, and you won't have any trouble with the hearing date. You know you don't have a leg to stand on anyway." She was revved up now, loving the pull and push of this business. It was like trying to control a horse once you've given it its head. "Your client's trying to tell the court that my client was in on some conspiracy to defraud him. That's ridiculous. He doesn't even have a partner. Who was he conspiring with? His dog? Besides, we've got the records."

Two attorneys they both knew passed them by with a nod and a greeting. Tara and Gary smiled back and Tara moved in closer.

"We've got your client's approval on all transactions and memos indicating the risk involved in some of those transfers and purchases. The entire market went into the toilet the same time your guy was trying to second-guess the global economy. You can't blame my man for that. His advice was as solid as it could be in the face of your client's avarice. Now you're trying to recoup his losses at the expense of my client's good name and limited resources. That's the way I see it. That's the way I'll argue it." Tara gave him a pat on his shoulder and moved on. "I have to run. Have an appointment at ten-thirty."

"That's not true." Gary hurried after her again, dodging an old lady resplendent in Navajo dress. He took a minute to admire it. Nothing like the real thing. Then he sprinted after Tara.

"My client didn't understand what he was signing when your man gave him the transaction approval. My client is seventy-five years old. He's infirm, Tara."

Tara turned on her heel, grinning from ear to ear. "Then he needed you before the fact, not after. And if he's so out of it, how come he had the presence of mind to even question what my client was doing? If he's that bad, he should be in a home where he can wheel and deal over a game of Monopoly." Tara hitched her briefcase and laughed. "Come on, this is such a waste of time. I haven't been sitting on my hands. If we go to trial, I fully intend to call the last three financial advisors your client has retained. To a person they will testify to his erratic behavior. The man wants to be Howard

Hughes, but he's a small-time investor with dreams of grandeur and paranoid delusions.

"My man's five years out of business school with an unblemished record. All his other clients are satisfied. He's got a sweet little wife and twins on the way. Put your client's track record of professional abuse up against that saintly picture and take your chances. You want to go to trial? Fine. It'll be fun. But if I were you, I'd drop the whole thing." Tara gave him a thumbs-up and walked away with a "call me" thrown over her shoulder for good measure. Time was a-wastin' and she had a new client headed her way. Wishing last night she'd gotten a little more information, Tara now hoped Caroline had managed to work her magic and throw together some quick and dirty research on any summer problems at Circle Ks. She walked back to the office, pushing through the door at five after, a little flushed, anxious to get on with her day. Amazing what a good night's sleep and some company could do for an attitude. She felt wonderful.

"Hi! I'm home," Tara called as she burst into the reception room, her coat already unbuttoned. Immediately her fingers went to her lips. Caroline was busy. Her hands were on the word processor and the phone was propped between shoulder and ear. She was muttering a mantra of "uh-huhs," so Tara tiptoed past, dropped her briefcase, hung up her coat, and sat at her desk.

George Amos, the esteemed chief of police, had called. Not her favorite fellow in the world, but useful. She picked up the pink message slip. He wanted information on the deposition of one of his officers in the Johnnie Rae Riskin matter. She almost set it aside, but thought twice. She settled into the high-backed chair and dialed George. There might be information to be had for her, too.

"George Amos. Tara Linley returning his call." Their connection wasn't meant to be. "Yes. Okay. No, just tell him I returned his call. I'll catch him later."

"Knock, knock." Caroline bustled in, all decked out in a signature floral dress, before Tara could pick up the receiver again. "Here you go, hot off the presses."

"You're a doll. Sorry to have called you so early about this, but I wanted to be up on things before Hamilton gets here." Tara held out her hand and Caroline gave her a sheaf of papers.

"How's Donna?" she asked. "Haven't heard from her in a month of Sundays." Caroline settled herself in the client chair.

"Fine. When you see her new boyfriend, you'll understand why the phone hasn't been ringing off the hook." Tara flipped through the papers. "Did you open a file on him?"

"Much as I could. A name doesn't really constitute a file. When he gets here, I'll fill in the rest."

"Fine." Tara abandoned the papers and pushed them aside. "Fill me in on all this stuff. I'm still in overdrive after this morning. Blackwell doesn't have anything and Mason knows it. We'll probably settle, but I was so ready for a fight."

"Today might be your lucky day if you're feeling feisty," Caroline said. "I don't know what Mr. Hamilton's coming to talk to you about, but it should be interesting." She leaned over, almost rounder than she was tall, and pulled the faxes and Xeroxes her way, putting them in order like a gambler organizing his hand. When she was done, she had two piles: one large, the other considerably smaller. She talked about the smaller one first. "Okay. We've got a couple of Circle K incidents last summer. One in early June. Had a trucker raped and beaten nearly to death." Caroline shook her head sadly. "Sometimes I wonder if women's lib did us a favor. Women shouldn't be driving those rigs."

They sat in silence a moment, Tara thinking how lucky she was to have a choice in life, Caroline thankful she'd found Tara and this job when she did.

"Anyway. There were four robberies in Circle K parking lots and two assaults on clerks. All in the early morning hours. Kids were doing the robberies. Some in the city, some not. A drunk trucker was arrested for one of the assaults. Never found the perp on the other one. And that brings us to July fourth. You've got to remember that one."

"Refresh my memory." Tara reached into her desk drawer for a compact and lipstick. She flipped it open, gave her lips a swipe, and put it away. Caroline was running through the list.

"July fourth. Cops have the file open, no leads, no evidence or witnesses as of the last writing, which was"—she referred to the Xeroxes—"October third. I haven't been able to find out if anything has changed since then, but it's still early."

"Not to worry. I've got a call into George Amos. I'll ask him. Let's keep going."

"This was a really sad one. It gives me the creeps to even think about it. The lady was alone working the graveyard shift. She'd been doing it for a long time, really knew the ins and outs. Anyway, it seems she was surprised while she was making coffee. There was no struggle. She was shot, I don't know exactly where or how because they kept the details out of the paper. But I suggest you take a look at the July fifth and July eighth articles. That's going to give you a good overview in case this is the thing he wants to talk about." She shivered and pushed herself out of the chair. "I hope this isn't the one he's got on his mind. It was just awful. I wouldn't want to be involved in it even in the smallest way. Just the thought of being alone in one of those stores all by myself late at night is enough to give me cardiac arrest. Not knowing who's going to walk in, nobody to help if the wrong person does. I know there isn't a good time to die, but so early in the morning?" Caroline wrapped her arms around herself. It wouldn't have surprised Tara to see the younger woman cross herself. "I don't even know anyone who's up at three in the morning, much less thinking about killing someone in a convenience store just for fun—or whatever makes someone do something like that." Caroline tried to read over Tara's shoulder. Tara gave her the eye. She straightened up.

"You're giving me the creeps," Tara said before pulling out the articles Caroline indicated. "How do you do this? I can't believe you got this much information in a few hours."

Caroline beamed, her disquietude forgotten. It was lovely to be needed.

"My cousin works over at the *Trib*. His girlfriend is the receptionist in research. Her aunt knows how to work the new computer system and here you go, everything you ever wanted to know about the latest in criminal activity. It is what you wanted, right?"

"I'm sure this is it. Thanks, Caroline. As usual, I couldn't have done it without you." Tara shooed her away, anxious to begin. "Close the door on the way out, please."

"You got it." Caroline headed out, but paused

and gave a wink just before she slipped through the door. "You look great, by the way."

Behind the closed doors Tara read accounts of the robberies and the rape. The reports were informative and seemed accurate. She set them aside, fundamental facts committed to memory. The assaults were interesting, but nothing to write home about. There was only the murder left to review.

Suddenly tired, Tara sat back and twisted her chair toward the bank of windows behind her. Outside it was cold but not frigid, a blustery kind of day that she usually loved. Nine stories below was a sweep of concrete that was Tara's stage. But today the plaza was a lonely place. People didn't pepper the weatherworn benches, or chat as they made their way in or out of the building, or stand together nursing takeout coffee. The few who straggled in and out of the building were uninteresting for their lack of purpose, small and insignificant from this height. Nothing but dark specks blowing around the landscape.

Dark little . . . specks.

Tara froze before sitting up straighter to peer more intensely at something—or someone—who caught her eye below. There. She tagged it. Movement. Behind the concrete pillar. Third on the left. Beside the fountain was someone who didn't move. Watching her. Her window was one out of hundreds in the high-rise yet Tara knew with certainty there were eyes on her. Unwavering, intent, vicious eyes. Her heart thumped hard and there was a pulse farther down in the pit of her stomach that quickened. It was an ill-defined feeling, half pleasurable and half frightening, and it filled her to bursting.

Tara sat forward in her chair, so close to the expanse of glass she felt the tug of vertigo. Yet she couldn't move away, nor take her eyes off that dark spot below. Her mind was atwirl with the possibilities of what this speck might become. Man? Woman? Fantasy creature come to haunt her from some forgotten nightmare? Then it was gone, turning behind the pillar in a blink, leaving her breathless and intrigued and thoroughly amused by her own nonsense.

Someone was simply waiting, or having a smoke. She looked again and the thought that someone had waited or watched for her was still there. How horrible to think about it. Faceless, unknown to her, but not she to him. Tara shut her eyes, feeling so vulnerable and small, laid bare like a lady of the night being picked for a ten spot by the meanest man in town.

"Knock, knock."

Startled, Tara jumped and swiveled back to the door, her cheeks burning red with embarrassment.

"I scared you. I'm sorry. I should have known. Reading that stuff will make you a basket case. Here, I just brought some tea. Sorry." Caroline backed out of the room, apologizing quietly until the door was closed. Tara turned back. It was only a cold, blustery day outside. The kind she loved and now there was no one at all in the plaza, not a speck or a man or a creature from a long-forgotten nightmare.

Tara turned away from the window, but found it necessary to breathe deeply before she began to read about the killing at the Circle K.

Six articles. The first had run on the front page of the *Journal,* wrapping over to page three, describing a sadly senseless murder of a woman who had a lot to live for. Marge Hogan had been a two-year Circle-superior employee when she was killed in the aisle near the coffee urn. Inventory checked out. Not even a stick of gum had been taken. Mrs. Hogan had no criminal history. Post mortem, her praises were sung by one and all. This wasn't a hit. It wasn't revenge. There wasn't even a jealous boyfriend waiting in the wings toward whom the long finger of the law could be pointed. The lady with a half-dozen bullet holes in her had been happily married since she was sixteen and was the mother of four children.

A tragic death, softened, she supposed, by the fact that the woman had been loved and lived well. Tara read on, grateful she didn't deal with this kind of thing every day. Johnnie Rae's drunken spree had ended in a manslaughter charge, but that didn't come close to matching this unjustifiable act of violence.

Marge Hogan hadn't crossed anyone, bore no grudges, and was scheduled to sing her first solo in the church choir the following Sunday. And at the time of her death, the lady was pregnant. Pregnant! A jury would draw and quarter whoever had killed her. In a place like Albuquerque, where life from bug to bush was considered a treasured thing, a pregnant woman was as close to sacred as you could get.

Tara flipped through the next few sheets. As expected, coverage of the Circle K killing diminished with the lack of information until, finally, Marge Hogan, her grieving family, and her unborn child were relegated to the back page and two paragraphs, a journalistic mumble that indicated police would continue to work on the case. By October, she had disappeared from the public eye. Everyone had given up on Marge.

Tara shoved the papers aside, remembering the

crime now, remembering the detached outrage she had felt. Tara even remembered thinking how interesting it would be to work on such a case, a crime curious for its lack of rhyme or reason. How small of her to have had so little respect for the horror that woman must have felt, the grief the crime had caused. What if it had been someone she loved? What if it had been her? Tara shoved away from the desk with a mental mea culpa and a fleeting thought that she could easily let her imagination run away with her if she read stuff like this on a daily basis. That was when Caroline interrupted again.

This time she simply put her knuckles discreetly to Tara's office door. It swung open, but instead of bustling in, Caroline called from outside the door, making her announcement like a crier to the queen.

"Mr. Hamilton."

Five

Tara didn't stand though it was her usual habit. Perhaps it was the account she'd just read, the odd angle of her chair, or the surprise of seeing Bill Hamilton again that kept her in her seat. He was a sight to behold. She smiled and he settled himself in the client chair as easily as he had relaxed in her home. Good old boy. Rhinestone cowboy. He did have a way about him.

"Hope it's okay, Tara," he said, "I'm a little early. Hung out for a while but I'll tell you, it's damn cold."

"Too cold to stand around outside." She moved her chair closer to the desk.

"Gotta get me a better jacket." He held open his denim one. It was old, well worn, and unlined, a jacket no self-respecting gigolo would wear.

"So where did you leave our friend? Still getting her beauty sleep?" Tara made small talk as she usually did to settle a new client's nerves.

"Damn straight." Bill laughed, shifting again, crossing those very long legs. "Donna's just like a kid. If she has a big night she sleeps 'til noon. Never seen a woman who wasn't up and about at the crack o' dawn. Guess that's the difference between city women and country women, huh? You're up early, though. Saw you out there with that horse of yours."

"You should have come out." Tara lost her smile, at the same rate his eyes lost some of their humor. He looked hard and she wondered if he was more than simply a sleepless man. Yet what more could he be? There wasn't much to watch in the early hours on a place like Tara's. Nothing but the countryside—or her. "The coffee's free, you know. You should have joined me."

Bill shook his head and Tara saw a prism behind his eyes, the third dimension of his optical biology. It was as mesmerizing as the bedroom voice he now used.

"Naw. You looked too good just standin' there. Must be nice to be that way. Content. Know your place."

"It has its advantages." Tara inclined her head, more to break the spell than to acknowledge the correctness of his observation.

"Yeah. I just bet it does." These words were clipped and impatient in tone though he tried to hide it. Fear was there too. The story of his trouble wouldn't be long in coming.

He smiled again, but it wasn't the electric grin of the night before. His hands went to his thighs, massaging the lean muscle. Then one arm was over the back of the chair again.

"So, now that you're my lawyer, I guess we better get to it, right?" Bill moved and pushed his hair back. Both hands seemed unable to find a place to light. "I'm gonna have to tell you, Tara, I'm grateful as can be that you took me on. I'm a little nervous about this. Never talked to a lawyer before. Lot of doctors, but that's different. This feels weird." His whole body rippled in a nervous little wave as if he was excited beyond containment.

"There's nothing to be afraid of. A lawyer is like

a doctor or a priest. What you tell me, as your lawyer, is confidential." Tara said the words the way she'd said them a hundred times. And a hundred times, she wished for some like experience so that she could understand her client's apprehension. The only thing to be gained in the confines of this office was help and, she hoped, a resolution to the problem at hand.

"A preacher'll die before he tells what you told him. Is that true for lawyers, too?" Bill chuckled.

Tara couldn't help but smile, "You won't find many martyrs in our ranks. We'll go into the lion's den, but we'll talk it to death before we let it eat us. However, we do take our oath of confidentiality very seriously."

"I'll just bet you do." Bill made it sound like a prurient act. Then he perked up. "It's amazing." He raised his hand and twirled it in the air, ready to flick his lasso and capture her. His nervousness vanished. The cowboy was back. "Don't know, Tara. I don't think I could do it. I'd spill the beans for sure. 'Specially if it was somethin' bad. Or really evil."

"You wouldn't if it was what you believed in. Priests and lawyers, doctors, too, are each two different people. One part of them is just like everyone else. They laugh and get hurt and have all the emotions everyone else does. The other part though, is separate, above the pull of emotions. If that weren't true, a lawyer couldn't defend someone he knew to be guilty, a doctor couldn't operate for fear of inflicting pain, a priest couldn't give absolution because his human side would cry out for retribution of the sin."

Tara swung gently in her chair, lost in thought. It had been a long while since she'd considered any of this. Bill was quiet, hanging on her every word. She indulged them both.

"In law school they tell a story I'll never forget. A man told his lawyer that he had murdered two people. He told him where the bodies were. The lawyer went to that place and found the bodies. He took pictures and, in the process of taking pictures, moved one of the bodies. He went home, put the film away, and didn't do anything. He didn't go to the police. He didn't call the newspapers. He didn't call the victims' families. His client was never arrested. The question is, what did the attorney do wrong?"

"That one's easy," Bill said, delighted with the story. "That lawyer's supposed to tell the police where the bodies are without saying who did it."

"No. He was under no obligation to anyone except his client. He was bound to keep the client's confidence regarding the murder *and* the location of the bodies," Tara answered. "The only thing the attorney did wrong was interfere with the scene of the crime by moving one of the victims. That attorney went about his daily life, conducted business, and the professional part of him lived with the knowledge of those bodies and that crime. That's just the way it is."

"Damn, that's something. That's cool. Kind of a biker code thing." Bill hung his head and let it swing. Tara could almost hear the hogs gunning their engines in his brain and her own turned over in amazement that Donna had found this unlikely paramour.

"So," Tara said, voice low, professional, and leading. "Let's see what confidences I'll be keeping for you. What is it you need help with?"

"Thought you'd figured it out. Donna said you were smart as a whip."

"Being smart doesn't mean I can read minds," Tara said, suddenly and briefly annoyed.

Bill nodded toward her desk. Such sharp eyes. Tara put her hand atop the stack of information Caroline had given her. She glanced at it, then back at Bill.

"I have a very efficient secretary, but I'm afraid it was a hot summer and Circle Ks on the highway seem to be where things happen. There were quite a few incidents." Tara pulled a legal pad close and touched the tape recorder to her right. "Do you mind if I tape our conversation? I'll have it transcribed for your file and then the tape will be erased. My files are also confidential."

Bill was quick as a lizard, leaning over the desk, his hand strong and warm on hers. Tara's eyes snapped toward him and her lips opened. She remained mute, too surprised to protest. Shaking his head, Bill let his hand slip away while his grin came back in exact proportions.

"We should just talk a bit, you and me. I'd feel a heap better that way," he said softly. Cautiously, Tara nodded once.

"All right. I'll take notes. I'll need some notes as much for your protection as my edification. There might not even be a legal problem. If there is, I'll need something to refer to."

"Yeah. Okay. I guess that makes sense. But I don't think you'll need 'em. You'll remember. I know that sure as I know my own name."

Tara saw those eyes of his flash metallic. Her gut wrenched with a horrible sensation that came upon her quickly with intensity and depth. Unnerved, she waited, trying not to think ahead, refusing to read anything into Bill Hamilton's words or actions. She nodded at him, poised her pen. He was on.

"Well, listen here." He scooted around in his chair, found a position he liked, cocked his elbows on the arms, and held his own hands. "Let's get to this. What I'm looking to do here is get somethin' off my chest."

Bill dipped his head again as if his thought process was clearest in this position. He'd parted his hair in the middle today and it fell in soft wings over his broad forehead. He looked like a prince in a fable, but he wore jeans, not tights. Tara had a funny feeling she wasn't in for a fairytale ending to the story he was about to tell.

His head came up, showing a hardened face, closed to her scrutiny. Steel-colored eyes looked right at her and Tara knew, in that instant, that this was not the same man who had eaten her food and laughed at her jokes. This was not the same man who Donna Ecold adored. This was not a man Tara could have imagined being this close to her in her wildest dreams.

"I was in the Circle K where that woman was killed," he began.

Tara jotted a short note. It was the date. It meant nothing. Relief was on the horizon. He was a witness, frightened, holding his emotions at bay. She gave him a slight nod of encouragement. He ran with it like a racehorse out of the gate.

"I killed that woman, Tara," Bill whispered.

Stunned, Tara sat perfectly still. *Those aren't your lines. That's not what you're supposed to say. You were there, right? You saw who did it, right? You're afraid, right? That's what you're supposed to say.*

Bill Hamilton sighed, slid back down in the

chair, and lounged with his long legs in front of
him, the tips of his boots touching the bottom of
Tara's desk. He let them slip just enough so the
tips of his toes brushed those of her pumps. A
tremor ran up the right side of Tara's body. Another inch and they'd be playing footsies. His chin
lay in one upturned palm. He seemed to be looking past her into a sky that matched his eyes.

"I feel so bad, yes, ma'am." He jerked his head
off its support and snapped the fingers of that
hand before it fell back into his lap and he was
hers once more. "I can tell you, it's been bad living with this in my head." He seemed to segue,
his voice taking on a faraway quality as he painted
pictures for Tara. "I think of Donna and she's so
sweet and so good. And you. Look at you. A real
lady like my mom. I would have wanted to kill the
son-of-a-bitch who did anything to you good
women. Then I took the life of someone else's
good woman." Bill nodded to the articles Tara had
put aside. "I saw all them stories. I know about
her. Church-goin' woman. Lots of little kids. I felt
so bad, thought my heart would break. Spent days
not doing anything but sittin'. You know? Do you
know? I swear I thought it was a dream and I'd
wake up. Sometimes I couldn't remember it, the
actual doin' of it, then I'd remember everything."
He raised his head an inch, his eyes narrowed, and
he gave Tara a look of despair. "Every little thing."

Tortured, he played to his audience. What could
he say? he seemed to ask. How could she know
what it felt like to take a life? How could he ask
her to help him when he was a fraud? He'd slept
with her best friend, sat in her home, was close
enough to take her life last night had he chosen.

Anesthetized, his audience listened. What did he

expect her to say? Nothing, since he shifted again.
Deciding the chair wasn't big enough to hold him,
he got up to pace the length of her desk.

"Understand now, Tara, it wasn't like I planned
it. Not premeditated or nothin'. No way in hell
was it that." He guffawed, suddenly oafish and
crude instead of charmingly countrified. "It's
somethin' that just happened to me. I stop being
for a minute sometimes. Hard to understand, but
that's the only way I can describe it."

He was under full steam when Tara found her
voice. Though the pen in her hand shook, her
voice didn't.

"If this is a joke, Bill, it isn't funny. If it isn't, then
I want you to sit still and talk to me. No more stories,
no more editorializing. I want . . ." Tara took a
deep breath. Her professional life was passing before her eyes and she scanned it, looking for anything that would give her a clue as to how to handle
Bill Hamilton and his confession. The stereopticon
of her life was incredibly precise, but she found no
help in the frames. This was to be a new experience,
one with a myriad of opportunities for failure. Even
winning would bring no joy. "Bill, I'm turning on
the tape recorder."

"I wouldn't do that," he warned, hands splayed
on her desk. She thought no longer than a second.

"Then you're not here for help."

They looked at one another for a long moment.
Blue eyes on gray, will against will.

"That a scared woman talkin' or the other half
of you, Tara? The one that's gonna help me without being concerned about what I did?" he asked
lazily.

"It's not a scared woman, Bill, I'll tell you that

right now. And I am concerned about what you did—as a lawyer."

Those eyes were still on her but she didn't waver. Finally Bill smiled, small and convincing as if he truly was licked.

"Okay. Okay. We're on."

"Fine." Tara's hands disappeared beneath the desk. She clutched her right in her left, trying desperately to tame her shakes. She began to talk, falling into the persona that so fascinated Bill Hamilton, finding some comfort in her detachment. "There could be a lot of reasons why you're here, not the least of which could be that you're telling me the truth. If it is anything but the truth, I want you to think very carefully before you say another word. Fifteen minutes of fame isn't worth the fire and brimstone that will rain down on your head if you confess to this crime." Tara raised the pen. Her hand no longer shook. She pointed it at Bill Hamilton, confident behind her professional guise. "Now, if you're telling me the truth, tell it without all the nonsense. Start again or leave."

Bill's lip curled. If he'd had a toothpick, he would have tackled it with his tongue and twirled it to show his prowess. Instead, he waited an interminable minute before his lips relaxed into an almost quizzical expression. Tara hoped he would walk out.

He sat down.

He leaned forward.

He said, "I killed the woman in the Circle K on Route 47."

Behind his eyes was the truth and Tara couldn't read it.

"Have you done this before?" she asked quietly.

"Nope." Bill straightened up, relaxed now. Relieved perhaps. "Never hurt anyone before."

"Where's the weapon, Bill?"

"Don't know, Tara, and that's the Lord's own truth."

"Cut the crap."

Bill chuckled. "Can't." She accepted that. It was probably the truth. "Gun's gone. I don't remember where. Don't remember a lot in my life. When I was a kid, my mom sent me to a doctor. I walked into that office for sixteen and a half years. I know I was sick, but I was sick of takin' them pills too. I was sick of bein' sick so I just up and stopped the whole thing." He scowled, he would have spit, but he had some decency. "I saw a doctor on TV who cured himself of cancer and I was better'n that guy. I could do that. I didn't even have cancer. I fired that bastard doctor's butt. He never got excited about anything, never listened. I showed him good. Cured myself—for a while." He gave her a little click of the tongue and a sad wink as if to say the fun didn't last long. "Then there I was, at that Circle K wanting some smokes. Next thing that woman was dead. And"—he opened his hands, widening his eyes—"there you go."

He was done. Confessed and cleansed. Tara hadn't taken a note. She hadn't moved a muscle. The tape still turned. He smiled. *I chopped down the cherry tree and there's nothing to be done.*

"Does Donna know you're here?" Tara asked, her voice flat but audible.

"Yep."

"Does she know about this?"

He shook his head. "Nope."

"Have you had any thoughts of hurting her?"

Tara looked at him hard, hoping her eyes seemed as unforgiving and cold as his had.

"I swear I'd never hurt Donna. Not for the world." He seemed genuinely disturbed and made a small gesture as if to say, "Tara, come on. It's me, Bill." Yes, it was Bill, but not the Bill Hamilton of last night. That man couldn't have done what this one was confessing to.

Tara looked away briefly, finally understanding specifically what drew Donna to this man. Sincerity. It was difficult to find these days and Bill Hamilton breathed his adoration most convincingly. What, she wondered, had he had sincerely felt when he pulled the trigger and killed a lovely, married, church-singing, pregnant lady? She put a hand to a chest that felt brittle and tight, as if she could reach through and pluck out her heart to see if it was still beating.

"All right," she said, exhaling the words with a thoughtful breath. She double-checked herself, running imaginary hands over her brain to make sure everything was where it should be. Rational. Intelligent. Her tone was right, her body language regulated. "I think we better formalize our business. After I outline the terms, it will be up to you to choose whether or not you want to continue our professional relationship. Should you decide not to, I am still bound by my oath of confidentiality. No one, not even Donna, need know of this conversation. You will be free to seek other counsel without fear of recrimination."

"I won't be changin' my mind, Tara. No siree. I need your help. I need you, Tara, and I need you bad. I been waitin' a good long while to find a woman just like you."

She looked at him sharply and he looked back

mildly, perhaps even playfully. His lips were turned up at the corners. She felt not triumph from him, but mischievousness, as if the fun part was yet to come.

"All right, Bill. I must advise you, I have never handled anything quite like this. If you're charged, it would most likely be for first-degree murder. I can refer you to someone in Santa Fe who specializes in high-profile cases such as this if you so desire."

"No thank you, ma'am," he said.

Tara caught his rhythm and didn't miss a beat.

"My fee is two hundred and fifty dollars an hour. You'll be charged for any out-of-pocket costs for trial exhibits or investigative services as necessary. I will require a retainer of five thousand dollars." She paused. He didn't flinch. Neither did she and the last memory of the playful talk of the night before vanished. "I'll require that now."

"Yes, ma'am." The checkbook was out of his pocket. He laid it on the desk like a gunslinger. *I'll see you and raise you one.*

"Do I have your permission to call your bank to verify your balance?"

The request diminished Tara because it was made spitefully and that realization unnerved her. This was not simply business. She wanted to bring him down a peg or two, she wanted him to falter, to question, to do something other than look at her with a cocksure grin or furrow his brow as if frustrated, concerned, or any number of expressions that seemed to change with the light. Bill Hamilton was not just a client arriving by referral. He was Donna's lover, firmly implanted in Tara's own backyard. This weed that she was trying to uproot threatened her, and that dispassionate person she had spoken of only moments ago was no-

where to be found. The emotional Tara hung on
for dear life.

"Absolutely. Sure thing. Business is business,"
Bill said.

Tara gave him a pen and buzzed Caroline. The
check was handed over. The door closed. They
were alone again.

"I'd like you to move out of the guest house
and not see Donna while we take care of this."

"I don't think so. I think you can take me at
my word that Donna'll be cared for. We gotta trust
one another, Tara," he reminded her.

"How old are you, Bill?"

Down to business.

"Twenty-nine." He clicked his tongue and stuck
the tips of his fingers in the coin pocket of his
jeans.

"You have family. Where are they?"

"Arizona." He rattled off a phone number. Tara
jotted it down. He was getting antsy again. This
man didn't like to sit for long.

"Now, I gotta be truthful with you on that one.
I haven't seen them for a while. We had a falling-
out, and I am not real sure if I can swear to that
number. I just want that on the table between us,
okay?"

"That's a start." She jotted a note without looking up. "Where do you live?"

"With Donna."

"Before that?" Tara shot back, happy to have
found that part of her that couldn't be touched,
that dealt only in strategy and laws and loopholes.
She would have wept with relief if she'd been able
to.

"All over the place. I get rooms. Sometimes I
stay with other people. Depends on what comes

up. But I think I'll be stayin' on with Donna now, if you know what I mean."

"Does your father know about this? About this woman you claim to have killed? Have you told any friends? How about your mother?" Tara watched him carefully from under her lashes, looking for any sign that he was disoriented by the illogical course of her questions.

"No." He hesitated. His eyes lowered quickly, his fingers winding around themselves now. Interesting how the mention of his mother bothered him. "I don't think my mama would be very proud of that, do you? She'd be shamed for sure. She can't do nothin' for me, so I don't want her to know."

And what, Tara wondered, did he think would happen when he was on trial for this? Tara would want the woman front row center in a courtroom. The point, though, was moot. If Bill Hamilton was charged with this crime, he'd be lynched before his mother could cry. The intercom buzzed. Tara picked up the receiver instead of putting the call on speaker. It was Caroline. Bill Hamilton was good for the retainer.

"Do you work?" Tara asked, replacing the receiver.

"I've worked just about anywhere they'd hire me. Doin' anything. I'm not lazy, that's for sure. I like my money too much. Do what I gotta do to get it." Again the grin.

"Did you rob the Circle K?"

Bill shook his head, "Didn't need any money. Just a pack of smokes. Late night. Lonely road. Just a pack of smokes was all."

"Are you employed now?" Tara continued, unimpressed with his glibness. As far as she was concerned, he was a liar. Whether it turned out that he had actually pulled the trigger or made up a story, he was a liar. He had lied with the first smile and the last compliment and he could still be doing it.

Bill Hamilton gave his answer and the answers to every question after that. He worked when he had to, got money where he could, and it seemed plentiful. Women liked to care for him.

"And I always give them back just what they need. Exactly what they need," he whispered, and they were off again, holding his life up for scrutiny. Not a care in the world, a lady to love him, money in the bank, a gun in hand. What more could a young man ask? Just that one little blemish on his record.

No criminal history, he insisted, and she knew she would have it checked before he made it down the elevator. Married? Naw, not a cowboy like him. Lived with a gal. Yup, a gal.

"Hard to believe, Tara, but that woman decided she just didn't like me anymore. And I'll tell you one thing, yes siree, I gave that woman all I had to give." He raised a finger as if lecturing her. "She put me out like a dog, Tara." Bill grinned. He laughed. This was obviously a private joke.

And they were off for another run, talking about Bill's philosophy of life. *Just gotta take what comes, then pay the piper.* Bill's hatred of his psychiatrist and disdain for his own illness and terrible weakness. Donna's precious clothes. A dead woman. Until Tara touched the middle of her forehead, a fortuneteller still connected to the other world.

"What do you want from me, Bill?" she asked evenly.

"Help," he answered, astonished she should have to ask.

"What kind of help? Are the police on to you?"

"Naw." He shook his head and his hair caught the light. There was a golden tone in it.

"Do you want me to go with you to turn yourself in?" she suggested.

"God damn, no." He laughed and slapped his leg lightly. "I couldn't go to jail. I'd never make it in there. I'll tell you, Tara, I swear I'd never make it. I know that what I did was wrong, but I wasn't in my right mind. Hell, I just had a blackout and *boom*. Don't even know what I did with the gun. Don't know how I walked out of there." He pursed his lips and blew out the bad air, took in some good.

Both hands were in his hair and he pulled the pretty waves up into wings. He pulled so hard his eyes changed shape. "I need help to just straighten out. A place where I could find a doctor who understood me." He thumped his chest once, and smiled sweetly, "Maybe straighten me out. I want a bunch of 'em to take a whack at me, just to be sure this time I'm gettin' what I need, you see? Not just one guy pullin' a fast one. Not just one bastard who thinks he knows everything. He'd be the kind to hold all this over my head. Like I failed him, personally. There's only so much of that a man can take, you know?" He lowered his hands and leaned heavily on the desk. All the smiles were gone. "So just do that. Whatever I need to do so I can get me into a hospital and I won't go to jail. Just get me some help."

Mr. Happy-Go-Lucky had vanished. This man was tired, and if she had to guess, he was afraid like everyone else who came to her. Tara knew where she stood now. She was ready to act. As his advocate, not his friend, she would work miracles for him. Tenting her fingers, Tara tapped them against her lips.

"I need proof that you're telling the truth, Bill. Convince me. Give me permission to check your information with the proper authorities. The police released no details of this murder. If they have matching information, that will help me to make some decisions."

"What decisions do you have to make?" Bill asked. "You're my attorney, ain't you? Just sign me in someplace. Get me to a hospital. Let me lie low. I don't want to black out again. I don't want to hurt anyone again."

Donna's face flashed in Tara's mind. She'd like nothing better than to lock him in a loony bin and throw away the key. Her throat tightened and she said nothing. But Bill tired of the silence, so he filled it.

"You better do this, Tara, or it won't be good for you." His voice was gentle. Tara was lulled by it. "You couldn't live with yourself, never really knowing what had happened to me. I mean if you decided not to be my lawyer, you still couldn't tell anyone the stuff I told you. You'd have to sit here by your lonesome, and just think and think about it. Then Donna and I would go away, and you'd think some more. I'd bet my saddle you'd rather be in the thick of it all, instead of on the outside wondering what's what. I think you like being what you are. Two people, one who has the power. Am I right? Did I hit the jackpot?"

The silence that ensued was strangely thin, one that wasn't stuffed with his apprehension and regret the way Tara would have expected. Instead it was like a fog further clouding her now darkened sky. Tara looked at this man who had appeared at her door to celebrate a birthday and had, instead, aged her light-years.

"You're right about one thing, Bill. I have the power. But it's not limited. It's my conscience and my ethics, not my power, that will make me work for you. But I will only work for you if you're straight with me. You could be a nut who simply likes to confess to other people's exotic crimes. You may be covering for someone. I won't know until I confirm what you've told me with details. Now, give me the information, give me your permission to use it then leave me alone to do my work because you need me more than you know."

"You're a good one, Tara." Bill laughed, his head back, dark hair grazing the collar of his shirt. "I need you, yes I do. You help me and keep me laughing. I feel so much better when I'm laughing."

"We'll see." Tara picked up her pen. Bill winked, a knowing little gesture that sealed their bargain. Then he told her a thing or two about that night at the Circle K. When he was done, Tara spoke again.

"My obligation is to help you receive the medical treatment you need and desire. I'll represent you as a mentally disturbed person until the truth of that is determined by the law. I will do my best not to jeopardize your well-being in any manner that might result in your incarceration without the opportunity for medical evaluation."

"Fine and dandy, Tara. Just fine."

"You can go now, Bill. I'll think about this. I'll see what I can do," Tara said wearily.

Bill stood up, tugged on his jacket, and put out his hand. Mechanically, Tara took it while he chatted. "Now I'll sleep just fine. A real load off my mind, Tara. Hey, mind if I use your phone? Gotta call Donna, see if she's ready for me to come on home."

Tara waved him to the reception room, unable to bear him as close as the phone. He picked up the receiver on Caroline's desk and punched out the number to the guest house from memory, turning his back on her when he began to speak. Caroline buzzed on the other line.

"Yes?"

"George Amos, returning your call."

"Tell him I'll call him back," she said, her eyes still on Bill.

"You got it."

The connection was broken. Bill Hamilton hung up, too. He looked over his shoulder, gave Tara a little salute, and killer grin. He walked out of her office firmly established in her life.

Six

When the other line rang, it startled her. Then it annoyed her. Still listening to the phone in her guest house ring, Tara hesitated, then punched the blinking button on line one, hoping against hope it was Donna calling from somewhere.

"Tara Linley."

"Where are you?"

It took a minute for Tara to adjust to what she was hearing. This wasn't Donna's little-girl voice crying for help, or wailing over a broken heart. The voice on the other end of the line was a contralto, not a soprano, and the woman talked about Woodrow Weber, not Bill Hamilton. Tara switched gears.

"Tara? Come on. Woodrow's expecting you."

"Charlotte, I'm waiting"—she stumbled over the lie—"I'm trying to get hold of someone. I can't talk right now. I can't make it tonight."

"But Tara, it's almost seven. I thought you were coming around six." Charlotte's voice changed, softening to honey. "I'm sorry. I know you're busy. It's just that we'd planned on you being here. This is such an important evening. We've got everyone who is anyone here, and you've been asked for more than once."

"Charlotte, I'm sorry. I'm so sorry." Tara stood

up and turned toward the window. The phone cord wrapped around her middle. She pulled it away and let it snap back, anxious as she looked out into night. Last she remembered it had been four-thirty in the afternoon. She'd drafted a letter and attended a deposition that ended before it began when the plaintiff's witness didn't show up. She'd begun writing a speech that ended up in the trash can, then initiated a list of possible solutions to the problem of Bill Hamilton. Then she started to worry—not about legal ramifications, not about the professional disposition of this predicament—but about Donna.

So Tara started to call. She must have redialed a hundred times and now Charlotte wanted to know where she was. Why wasn't she making small talk with bankers and politicians at Woodrow's fund raiser? Charlotte asked. *Well, honey, because a guy who just confessed to killing a woman in cold blood is hanging with my friend.* Instead she said, "I don't know where the time went. I don't think I can come."

She begged off, standing firm against Charlotte's noises of hurt and dismay that normally would have reeled her in. Then Tara realized seeing Charlotte was just what she needed to do. Donna and Bill were going to pick her up after the fund raiser. They were out and Tara wasn't where she was supposed to be. She had to be where Donna expected her to be.

"I'll be right over," Tara said quickly, anxious to get off the phone now. "I'm sorry. I truly am. It was a bad day, I'll be right there."

"Okay. If you're sure," Charlotte said, but now there was a note of concern. If Tara was on edge, she might not be a sterling guest. "But only if you're up to it. There'll be lots more times."

"Of course. Of course. The sooner we're off the phone, the sooner I'll be there."

"We're right in the lobby. Can't miss us. They still have the tree up. It looks so wonderful. Lots of people are passing, talking about what's going on—"

"Charlotte," Tara sighed, "hang up. I can't come until you hang up."

"Right. Hurry now."

Tara indulged in necessary primping. Her sun-kissed complexion had taken on a sallow cast, her hair looked as if she'd just rolled out of bed. She managed some lipstick, a comb, and a splash of cold water to wake herself up. It would take ten minutes to walk to the hotel; she'd spend forty schmoozing. Time would pass more quickly. She couldn't panic. Nothing was wrong in the guest house. Donna and Bill had gone out. Nothing had happened last night, nothing would happen tonight. Bill needed Tara and he needed her happy. As long as that was true, Donna was safe.

In front of her, past the towering Christmas tree hung with ribbons and bows and dried chiles; past the tiled fountain topped with a spray of impossibly exotic flowers; under the garlanded archway and the towering beamed ceiling; milling about the rough-hewn wooden tables and chairs and the gleaming bar were the shakers and movers who had come to wish Woodrow Weber well and add a little something to his gubernatorial war chest. It was a good crowd. Thirty or forty people at least. Charlotte had sounded desperate for Tara's presence, but she'd obviously been missed more by Charlotte than anyone else. She unbuttoned her winter-white melton coat, put on a smile, and found her hostess.

"You made it. Oh, thank you. I was getting so worried. I just don't think things are going very well. Everyone's being awfully tight-fisted tonight. Maybe you can loosen a few wallets. Look, there's Mrs. Houghton. She adores you. A word and she'll get that old fogy husband of hers to write a check." Charlotte had Tara by the elbow and had steered her to the bar. "What do you want to sip on?"

"Water," Tara said, shaking her head to indicate she wasn't going to be picky tonight. The man behind the bar shot some into a glass, tossed in a sliver of lime, and handed it to her. "Thanks."

"So, you want to tackle the Houghtons first?"

"Charlotte, I'm sorry. I don't really feel like tackling anyone. Couldn't I just kind of mingle? You're early anyway on the fund raising. It's not even two weeks since New Year's. Even rich people feel the pinch right after Christmas."

"I can't believe you, of all people, are saying that. You know how much it costs to run a campaign. Besides, our esteemed governor already has two million backing him. That wife of his pours her own money into his campaign like it was water. I wish I had something I could give Woodrow. Something really substantial."

"You give him more than you know," Tara answered, as if by rote. "Where is he, anyway? I wanted to have a word with him."

"Not about business, I hope. We're leaving all that district attorney stuff until tomorrow. Promise it won't be about business, and I'll find him."

"Okay. No business," Tara answered reluctantly, hoping Charlotte would disappear long enough for her to find out what Woodrow knew about the Circle K matter.

"Go mingle. I'll find him and be back."

Charlotte was gone, touching an elbow here, whispering in an ear there, doing her candidate's wife thing so beautifully Tara was impressed. Charlotte was gobbled up. Tara was on her own. She wandered, her eyes roving toward the door over and over again. She half expected to see Donna burst through it wild-eyed as she screamed for help, Bill Hamilton after her with a gun in his hand. Tara shook her head to clear it. An assistant U.S. attorney she'd been casually acquainted with tried to catch her eye across the room. She turned the other way, toward the phones. One more call. Just in case they had simply been outside watching the river, taking a walk, doing something normal and safe. Just in case Donna hadn't heard the phone.

Tara turned sideways, murmured her apologies, held her drink above her head, and managed to slip into the alcove without being stopped for a conversation. Leaning against the wood, she put her sparkling water on the right side of the phone, her purse on the left, then leaned her head back and closed her eyes. Her head was splitting. Funny she hadn't noticed it before. A wave of laughter erupted from the party. Tara smiled. It was nice where she was. A good place to wait.

"Need a quarter?"

She opened up her eyes. The first thing she saw was a corroded quarter. The second thing she saw was a most attractive hand. Then she saw an arm. But it wasn't held out to her, it was held up. Tara looked down and hoped she was hallucinating.

There was Ben Crawford. She'd thought about meeting him like this—by surprise—often enough.

She'd even thought about what she might say. She would be warm. They would exchange pleasantries, maybe become misty-eyed if the pleasantries lasted long enough. They would part. An awkward meeting made bearable because the suspense was over; a volatile situation finally diffused. But this wasn't any day and Tara wasn't ready for this particular surprise. Her stomach fluttered. Her mouth went dry. Her lips parted and no sophisticated, inspired words eased her through these first awkward moments. Her hands were orphaned. She found no place where they felt graceful or casual or even comfortable. Tara's eyes darted here and there, finally resting on Ben and locking onto eyes that had grown older, but no less kind. Under that gaze, Tara's faltered. Her eyes skittered away and she found herself looking at the wheelchair in which he sat. Immediately, she looked back at his face, a safer focus.

"I'd almost given up on you. If I'd known you were hiding, I would have started seeking sooner. Woodrow never did know how to throw a party."

"Ben, I . . ." What was there to say?

How've you been the last twenty-four years? Like your chair. Do you mind I didn't call? Any chance you're ever going to walk again? Did you miss me when I stopped coming by? Did you lie awake knowing why? Wondering why the letters stopped coming? I did.

But Ben was gracious, and Ben was good, and Tara felt her heart a little blackened because in his greeting there were no accusations, only pleasure that he'd found her here.

"Okay. Be that way," he said sweetly. "Don't talk. Bend down here and give me a hug."

She did, grateful for his mercy when he could have exacted a pound of flesh. Tara rested her hands on the hard black arms of the wheelchair, and closing her eyes, she lay her lips against his cheek, realizing it was no longer fear in the pit of her stomach, but that age-old draw of him that swelled inside her. He smelled so good. A man's scent where once there had only been the changing essence of a boy. He was strong too. The arm that wrapped around the back of her was iron-like, unbreakable, secure. But her eyes opened as she knew they must. She saw his legs, shriveled and useless, as she backed off.

"How are you?" Tara said automatically. She lay her hand on her purse, knowing she looked like a colt ready to bolt.

"I'm fine. You look miserable, though. Need to make that call, or can I interest you in a quiet corner and a sympathetic ear? You look like you could use both."

Tara chuckled self-consciously, "I don't think there's a quiet corner to be had out there. In fact, I'm surprised to find you here. I didn't know you were interested in politics."

"I'm not. Charlotte told me you were going to be here."

"Did she send you to find me?"

Ben looked over his shoulder. Charlotte was watching. He gave her a little wave. He smiled, then looked at Tara. "Yes."

Now she really did laugh. "Honest as always. I always thought that was an odd trait in high school. You and I were probably the only ones who had perfected the art of telling the truth."

"Except to each other?" Ben asked. Tara's expression clouded.

"I don't think I'm up for this discussion tonight, Ben. It's great to see you, but—"

He held out his hand. She was going to leave and

he didn't want that. "I'm sorry. You're right. That was clumsy. There's just so much to catch up on."

"And you want to start where we left off? Not exactly the most pleasant time in our lives." Tara slapped her purse under her arm. "I thought maybe we could start with the basics. What do you do? Married? Kids?"

"Psychologist. No. I don't think so," Ben said quickly, adding softly, "I'm sorry."

Tara took a deep breath. She held it. She looked to the ceiling. They were in a small space. It would be tight for two people standing. It was impossible with Ben's chair. She had to get out of there and he seemed to know that. He twirled his chair. No more than a flick of those hands—lovely, masculine hands—on the chrome wheels. If she didn't know better, she would have sworn he'd turned on his heels.

"Wait," she said, hurrying after him though it was only a few steps.

"It's okay. I wasn't leaving," Ben said seriously. "It's the only way I know to back off. You can't possibly think I'm going to make this easy for you." It took thirty seconds for his eyes to soften and crinkle and for Tara to understand that he was teasing. Not much had really changed about Ben—not much and yet everything.

"No, I wouldn't expect you would. I guess I'd kind of gotten it into my head that this town was big enough for both of us."

"It is," Ben agreed, "no matter how we decide to live in it. Sorry I came back?"

Ben began to move forward. Tara fell in step beside him.

"I don't think that's for me to say," Tara answered.

"Maybe not, but it's something I need to hear."
Ben's fingers moved lightly over the wheels. "You
forgot your drink. What were you having?"

They had made it to the fringe of the crowd.
Those who noticed Ben's chair made way. The
women did double takes. He was a handsome man.
Strong-jawed, tan, hair just long enough, mustache
just bushy enough, and eyes so beautifully blue and
knowing. Tara then saw the disappointment in the
women's eyes as they noticed the wheelchair and
turned away. Ben was oblivious.

"Sparkling water. I don't really need a refill."

"I think you do. In fact, you probably need
something stronger right about now." He cocked
an eyebrow. She shook her head, hugged her
purse closer, and looked around. She smiled at
people across the room. She checked her watch.
She thought of Donna and the day threatened to
overwhelm her. She watched as Ben ordered the
drinks and kept an eye on her. An old world of
memories fell in on her. His timing was lousy.
About as horrible as hers had been twenty years
ago. Only difference was, she was still standing.

"Come on." He was back. Two drinks in one
hand, the other maneuvering his chair. "Let's start
again. I'll ask you how your day was. You complain.
Everyone will leave and then we'll really have a
good chat." He was moving ahead of her, looking
over his shoulder, smiling gloriously when Woodrow caught up with them.

"Tara, I'm so glad you made it!" Woodrow's arm
was around her, his lips on her cheek. He whispered, "Thanks. I really appreciate it."

Tara gave him a pat, "My pleasure. I'll make you
pay me back one of these days."

"You got it," he promised.

"Sooner than you think," she whispered and stood away, still cradled in the crook of his arm.

"I see you found Ben. It's great he's back in town. How about a picture?" Woodrow tipped his head. A photographer appeared. Ben moved out of the way. "My man, where are you off to? Come back here."

"Nope. I'm the new kid in town again, but I don't need the publicity. You go on." Ben grinned, happy to be out of lens range.

"Jane, come on over here for a picture with Tara and me," Woodrow called, taking Ben at his word.

Tara gave him a wry look then smiled broadly. She could feel his eyes on her, even as she tried to stand tall and look good for the camera. Woodrow didn't notice how tight she was, how uncomfortable despite her grin and chit-chat. But Ben knew something wasn't right. She played the game, he watched from the sidelines—amused and confused because it had been a long time and he couldn't put his finger on what was wrong. The trio smiled, the flash popped, and it was done.

"Ben, you don't mind if I borrow Tara for a minute, do you? There's someone over here who knew her father well." Woodrow had Tara by the hand, but they didn't go far. "Well, here he is. Tara, do you remember Jim Beckley? He was in Washington when your father was attorney general. He was a Reagan appointee too. Now he heads up his own organization for senior citizens. The main idea is to create a network of transportation opportunities so that our older folks can get around safely day and night. Safety is a big part of my campaign."

Tara put her hand out. She'd heard Woodrow's speech on crime a thousand times and would bet that poor Mr. Beckley had heard it once more than she.

"Of course I remember. Jim, it's lovely to see you again. I know that Woodrow is very committed to our senior citizens. I'm delighted to see you here tonight." She made it through the speech without screaming. Small talk wasn't right. Not now when Donna was out there with that man.

"You've grown a bit since I last saw you, young lady," the old man chuckled, delighted to be remembered. Tara swiveled and held out a hand.

"Have you met Ben Crawford? He just recently came home to Albuquerque from—from parts unknown."

Ben offered a hand. The older man took it between both of his. "You're a man I'd like to talk to. The handicapped have a lot in common with us old folk. Or is that what they call you these days?"

"Physically challenged," came the reply, but it wasn't Ben who had spoken.

The small group turned to look at the well-groomed middle-aged woman who had offered the politically correct answer in an even more politically correct manner. Woodrow obviously didn't know her, but that didn't keep him from recovering nicely. There was more handshaking. Woodrow gave it a you-mean-a-lot-to-me emphasis.

"Nice to see you. Nice of you to come," he said.

The woman gave him a watery smile and severed their connection. Obviously, she wasn't as thrilled as Woodrow was.

"I'm a freelance journalist, Mr. Weber. I wanted to ask you some questions. I think I could sell the story I'm writing to one of the national news magazines if it checks out, but I need some corroboration."

Woodrow's mouth turned down thoughtfully to keep his grin from flying off his face. National coverage. The night was a success.

"Happy to carve out some time for the press. Why don't we go find someplace that's quiet?" Woodrow reached to steer her away, then stopped. He snapped his fingers as if he'd just had a marvelous idea, and said, "You know, we could set a time tomorrow for an interview if you like. Lunch, perhaps. Hard to get the full story on certain things if you're rushed for time. I could make sure we weren't interrupted, Miss . . . ?"

She ignored him. "No, that's all right. I'm kind of booked up and this really won't take long." She pulled a recorder from her pocket, pushed a button, and held it out to Woodrow without apology. "Is it true that you refused to prosecute Strober Industries when investigators in the district attorney's office found that they had used inferior materials in a county building, making those buildings dangerous to the public? Did your investigators also find that full payment was authorized for the originally spec'd materials after their conclusions had been reached, knowing these materials were useless?"

Woodrow had taken more than a minute to process what was being said. Tara watched his smile tighten, falter, then fail. He tried to move out of the circle of people. Jim Beckley was enthralled. Ben's face had tightened as he realized what was going on. Tara tried to run interference.

"Woodrow, I'm afraid I've really got to find Charlotte. I do hope you'll forgive us," she said to the woman as she stepped between them.

"Of course, Tara. Let me take you to her." Woodrow took the hand Tara offered. She was now solidly between him and the reporter, but the woman was a pro and was hanging in. He called over Tara's shoulder, smiling but nervous. "Call my office and I'll be happy to discuss this with you. I'll provide information that you'll find very interesting." Woodrow was sweating, saying too much, too loudly.

Ben wheeled himself into the fray, further distancing the woman. "Woodrow, I'm afraid I've got to run, but I did want to have a word—"

"Mr. Weber," the woman called, attracting too much attention by design. "Did Strober, in return, funnel over thirty thousand dollars into your campaign coffers from various subsidiaries? Mr. Weber, this isn't a hard question. Are they still giving you money at the expense of public safety?"

Stunned, Woodrow stood beside Tara. His hand on the small of her back trembled, but his political sensibilities were intact. He moved slightly, facing the stringer, smiling just in case a rogue camera was about.

"I think you have some misinformation. I'd like to talk about that situation rather than give you quick answers that could be misconstrued. Now, if you'll give me your card, I'll call you personally and set up the appointment. I can see by the look on your face that you want to make this more than it is. Give me my say, that's all I ask. I'm not going to fight with you. So either accept our hospitality and enjoy yourself tonight, or let's set up something between the two of us. After that, print what you like."

The woman eyed Woodrow, assessed the situation—Ben, Tara, and a continually curious Mr. Beckley—then made her decision.

"I'll call you," she said.

They watched her back as she beelined for the front door. Woodrow mumbled his thanks to them all as he fished for his handkerchief, wiped his brow, and went the opposite way. Ben had wheeled backward as Mr. Beckley moved in on the group, wondering what that was all about. And Tara, who almost turned her eyes away when the reporter pushed through the door, was thrilled a minute later that she hadn't. Donna Ecold burst through, a tiny little thing blown in with the wind. Her eyes were wide. Her hair disheveled, her lips parted. To call for Tara? To ask for help?

Tara slid away, the world falling out of focus. She barely heard Ben call her name. She wasn't aware that Charlotte had joined Woodrow. Tara only knew she had to get to Donna. Slowly at first, then faster she went, until her heels seemed to crash onto the tiles in her haste. She was stopped by a knot of people. Tara feigned left, then right before getting around them. That's when Donna saw her.

They were so close Tara could almost reach out and touch her. She was almost close enough to talk, but before Tara could ask if she was all right, before Tara could ask where Bill Hamilton was, she saw his reflection in the door. His image was liquid and one-dimensional in the glass. Bill Hamilton, time traveler caught between dimensions. Then he saw her too, and the mother-of-pearl-colored Bill Hamilton smiled slowly, contentedly, and gave her a wink just as Tara gathered Donna into her arms.

"Tara, please, not in public." Donna laughed and pried herself away.

"I'm sorry. I'm sorry," Tara breathed, her eyes flicking toward the door. He was gone, reflected now only in her mind. "I'm sorry. I'm just so happy to see you. You looked so worried when you came in. Then Woodrow. There was this incident. Hey, nothing. Sorry. I'm not making any sense. Long day." Tara ran her hands down Donna's arms. She felt good. So little, but intact.

"Must have been a killer," Donna said.

"You have no idea," Tara answered, drawing her into the lobby.

"Hey, what are you doing?"

"I thought we'd go in." Tara stumbled, realizing how ridiculous that sounded. She couldn't drag Donna away from the man outside without an explanation and she couldn't give an explanation. What Tara knew about Bill Hamilton couldn't be shared even with the woman who climbed into bed with him every night. "Nothing. I don't know what I was thinking." Her smile was shaky but she managed it.

"Good," Donna put her arm through Tara's. "Now, where's your coat?"

"Left it over there." She tossed her head back and followed the gesture. Coat in hand, she was retracing her steps when she saw Ben watching her from across the room. He made no attempt to intercept her. Tara almost wished he had. Realizing it was best, she lifted her lips sadly in something that could have been a smile but passed more as an acknowledgment that situations had never been on their side. She left La Posada without another word to anyone and joined Donna, who was already cuddled up with Bill Hamilton in the car.

"Tara, you hardly ate anything. We should have gone somewhere else. Greek was never your favorite."

Donna was draped over the back of the seat, her arms crossed, her chin atop them.

"It was fine. I'm just tired."

"Long day, huh, Tara?" Bill yawned and used his free hand to touch Donna's hair. She cooed and got closer to him. "When you gonna get a real job, babe? Somethin' that makes a difference in the world."

Donna giggled and turned her head into his caress. "I do make a difference. Every little kid who reads one of my books believes that there's a happy ending just waiting for them out there."

"I haven't read your books and I believe that too." Bill Hamilton was purring, his hand on the back of her neck now. Tara looked away. In the dark of the car the scene was too intimate—too frightening—but Bill wanted her attention. "What do you believe, Tara? You believe in happy endings?"

She put her hand to the side of her head and rubbed her temple. She thought she did. She'd been living a happy ending all her life.

"I believe in the right ending. The one that's best for everyone."

"Does that always mean the bad guy gets it in the end?" His eyes were in the rearview mirror. Tara could only wonder if they were also on her.

"I don't know, Bill. I don't know," she said, her voice a worn-out whisper.

"I don't think so. Bad guys can have reasons for being bad. What do they call that? Extenuating circumstances. That's it. Damn, I love those lawyer words. What do you think, Tara?"

"Oh, let her rest," Donna murmured, turned around now, her head on Bill's shoulder. "We've been playing all day and she's been working. Don't tease her."

"You're right, Donna. I won't tease. I'll just drive. Man, I love to drive."

Donna mumbled her thanks. Tara let her head fall back on the seat and closed her eyes. They would be home soon and she could think. But the car was moving strangely. Faster now than Tara knew the speed limit allowed. Bill took a left. Tara opened her eyes. She rotated her head to see the landscape changing. They weren't headed home, but out of town. She sat up. Even Donna noticed the change in route.

"Bill, where're you going?" Donna sat up straighter, shaking off sleep. Her shoulders didn't clear the seat. She looked like a child sitting next to him. "Honey, come on. Tara's tired, Bill."

But Bill wasn't with them any longer. He was somewhere else, seeing something else on the road, and he was speeding toward it. Both hands on the wheel, he suddenly snapped his arm and flipped a switch. The window rolled down, smooth and silent, letting in the roar of the highway wind.

"Bill?" Donna had scooted away only far enough to turn toward him and lay her hand on his shoulder. "Bill, where are we going?"

In the backseat Tara clutched the armrest, her eyes bright, her heart slowing as she saw where they were: nowhere. Nothing but desert, a house or two, a mile out, blurring as they sped by. Suddenly Bill threw himself toward the door and his head went out the window.

"Whooeeee! I am the Marlboro Man! Hot damn!"

He hollered and the cold, cold air blew his hair back and the wind whipped through the car until Tara was sure she would freeze to death or die of fright in the face of Bill Hamilton's insanity. It had to be insanity.

"Bill. Come on. Stop," Donna hollered over the cacophony. "Come on. It's cold."

The car swerved off the road and Bill slammed on the brakes. Donna was thrown forward but he caught her before she hit the dashboard. Tara's breath was knocked out of her, the tight belt holding her midriff in place while the rest of her jack-knifed.

"Ow, baby, that was fun. Wasn't that just a dandy ride? Just a hell of a ride." He pulled Donna to him and held her tight, then he grinned at Tara. A little boy done wrong, a little boy with a secret. His voice lowered. They might as well have been alone together. "I just wanted me some smokes. Just a pack of smokes."

With that he sat Donna upright, opened the car door, and got out. Tara watched him saunter across the hard dry ground. She watched him reach in his back pocket and pull out a comb, run it through his hair just as he hit a pool of light. She watched him open the door and she watched him disappear inside the Circle K.

"Isn't he crazy? I swear, that man is crazy," Donna muttered and Tara thought she heard a note of pride.

"Yeah, I think he is," Tara answered and in her voice was a note of surety.

Seven

"I cannot—repeat—cannot believe this. What is it? Is the entire world conspiring against me? Explain this debacle, Joanie. No, don't try to explain. Let me just go over the facts, and see if there's a glimmer of hope that somehow this can be explained to me."

Woodrow Weber measured his paces to the window of his office, looked toward downtown Albuquerque, noting the gleaming high-rises and the fine architectural figure the Hyatt Hotel, tallest structure in the city, cut across the sky. Then he looked down and considered the unpaved, dirt parking lot that surrounded his own, square, ugly, brick building. He pivoted, clasped his hands behind his back and paced back again, passing his secretary on step five. He held up his hand, the pointer finger heavenward.

"One. The rapist that's terrorizing the university is caught in the act. With great fanfare we—I—make the decision to indict. With greater fanfare, we go to trial. I assign our finest team with the full confidence in their ability, believing every assurance they give me. Then, with the greatest fanfare of all, the district attorney's office bites the big one and there's a mistrial because of our incompetence. We have to start from scratch.

"Two." Up popped another finger. "We finally find out who's been fixing the high school basketball games. George Amos makes an arrest. The kid's been in high school for six years, making more money taking bribes and flunking his classes while he plays basketball than he ever could pumping gas. Now half the city is in an uproar because we've arrested a child. A child, they call him! The other half of this city is mad because we're not already in court sending the bastard up for daring to tinker with the outcome of a sporting match."

"But Mr. Weber, we're going to pretrial hearings," the young woman began, knowing she shouldn't be put in the position of defending anything in this office. She wasn't an attorney.

Woodrow held up his hand, did a precision turn, and headed back. He stood over her, the scent of Aqua Velva wafting down upon her. He spoke gently, carefully, and condescendingly.

"Joanie, don't try to make it better. What does the public know about pretrial hearings? What, I ask you?" The poor girl shrugged, having no clue what the proper response was. Not that it mattered. The entire conversation seemed to be rhetorical. "I'll tell you what they know. Nothing! Nothing! The voting public thinks I try every case myself. I swear, the way the editorials have been running lately I might as well. It couldn't get any worse. And now this!"

Woodrow stopped, held out his hands, palms up, inviting her to look at the pamphlet on the desk. Joanie turned her head but her eyes were closed. She'd already seen it.

"Five hundred thousand mailers." He whispered and stepped forward. "Five hundred thousand direct mail pieces that are supposed to convince the good people of the entire state of New Mexico that I would make a wonderful governor. Now." He took in a ragged breath and let his eyes flutter shut for a moment. "It is my understanding that a good mailer, one that should convince people to vote for the right candidate, the one who would be the best governor, should at least spell the candidate's name properly. Don't you think, Joanie? Don't you think that someone . . ." He bent from the waist and looked at her close up, his middle-aged gnome face taking on unusual and unattractive proportions. ". . . someone who was responsible for proofreading such material, might have noticed that the name 'Woodrow Weber' is not spelled Woobrow Weder!"

Joanie slid her eyes his way. His face was purple. It wasn't a pretty sight.

"I suppose the last person who saw it should have caught that mistake," she squeaked, as defiant as she dared be. He was, after all, the person who had signed off on the proof. With everything else that was going on around the office, he shouldn't expect her to be responsible for his campaign literature. It wasn't in her job description and she would have told him except, as usual, they were interrupted. Gratefully, Joanie stood up and grinned at Tara Linley.

"Hi," Tara called from the outer office and walked right into Woodrow's. One look at him and she wondered which of them was worse off. "Sorry. I interrupted. I'll wait outside."

"No, no," Woodrow said and waved her in. He looked better already. The purplish color was draining from his face. "Might as well interrupt now before I kill someone or jump out the window. Look at this, Tara. Just look. Woobrow Weder.

Five hundred thousand of these were drop-shipped this morning."

Joanie slipped past Tara, gave her a pat on the arm, and disappeared. Tara closed the door to Woodrow's office and went to the sideboard. They could both use a cup of coffee. Cream in his. Hers was black.

"Here," she said, handing it to him while he keened over his misprinted mailers. She patted his back and stood for a silent minute.

"Tara, I don't know if I'm cut out for this. Running for district attorney was one thing, but a governor's slot, I don't know." He shook his head, pushed up his tortoiseshell-rimmed glasses, and stuffed his hands in the pockets of his winter-white pants. His bucks were white too. A blue-striped shirt, old school tie. She'd bet her bottom dollar there was a blue blazer hanging around somewhere. Such a dapper guy. She loved Woodrow because he had style and he was smart and still there was something awfully vulnerable about him. It was a unique combination in an educated man.

"It's a huge leap, Woodrow. Maybe there was a stepping stone you should have taken before you went for the big one," she commiserated.

He breathed in through his nose and out through his mouth. A word came with it. "Maybe."

He sounded so despondent, Tara felt terrible for even suggesting it.

"Hey, Woodrow, I wasn't thinking. The old gov himself is going to make mistakes, too. Besides, Charlotte called early this morning and said that you'd taken in more last night than you'd expected." Tara hoped this would brighten his mood a bit. She needed to have his complete attention.

"You really think this isn't a disaster?" He

picked up the offending material and looked at it.
Tara slipped it out of his fingers.

"I know it isn't. Really. But it's not going to help
if you keep it on your desk and look at it all day
long." She took it away and put it under a stack
of papers on the credenza. "Drink your coffee. It'll
make you feel better."

"I guess you're right. Oh, before I forget . . ."
Woodrow had coffee in hand. He headed for his
chair, turned, and backstepped into it. "Are you
going to that tea Charlotte's giving for the Women
Voters Coalition?"

"I don't know," Tara said wearily. "What if I just
send a check? Couldn't I just do that?"

"Come on, Tara. You know that's not it. I don't
want your money," Woodrow insisted. "I mean
money's really appreciated, but it's you I want. You
show up and the fact that a Linley's hanging
around will really give me a boost. And boy, do I
need a boost. Especially after last night and that
thing with Strober Industries. Could you believe
that? I've had Sandy trying to figure out who that
woman was and who she worked for. I don't know
what she's got but it was damn scary, I'll tell you."

"Any truth to it?" Tara asked, seating herself.

"I don't think so. I mean that investigation was
so long ago. I swear, I really think the decisions
made were a matter of expediency. I hadn't even
decided to run yet. I'm going to review the file,
of course, but as I recall, the civil division was over-
extended when that came across my desk. Inspec-
tors had approved changes. The company paid
some kind of fine. It was arbitrated." He rubbed
his eyes with his free hand. "Boy, I'm tired. I don't
know how Charlotte keeps up with all this. She's
always fresh as a toothpaste ad and on to the next

thing." He let his glasses fall back on his nose and pushed them into place. "Speaking of which, that tea isn't for a few months. And no, you don't have to go. I just appreciate all the support you do give me. I won't push it." He chuckled affectionately. "Won't make the same promise for Charlotte, though, so if you can't come, I suggest you lie low."

"I'll try. I will."

" 'Preciate it." He drank his coffee. She stared at hers. He studied her over the rim of his cup. When Tara didn't speak, Woodrow took it upon himself. "I guess you didn't come in to scream at me for a miserable evening last night."

"When have you known me to scream?"

"Never. You're more formidable when you don't, actually. Always throws me when we're in court together, and you pull that righteous persona out of your hat. Hard, smart, sure of yourself. Meticulous."

"That's how I am in court, huh?" Tara smiled and put her coffee aside.

"In court. Not now." He cocked his head. "Something's on your mind. Charlotte get under your skin by setting you and Ben up last night?"

Tara bit her bottom lip. She looked away from him. He owed her for last night and a few other things so he remained patient. It was one of his best traits—and his worst. He'd patiently followed Tara around in high school, driving her crazy, until finally realizing Charlotte was the woman of his dreams. Funny how things worked out. Charlotte and Woodrow a steady item, she and Ben strangers. But even Woodrow's patience had a limit.

"Earth to Tara." She looked at him.

"I'm in a bind, Woodrow. I'm not happy about

it. In fact, it's really thrown me for a loop. The good news is, I think I have a solution to my problem if you'll help." Tara laced her hands together.

"Off the record?" Woodrow asked.

"Pretty much. I'm not going to give you much. I don't want to compromise you, or myself, in any way."

Woodrow nodded, sagely. Enough said. He was a good attorney, a dedicated attorney. She'd been up all night working this out and he would understand what she needed. There was no other way for Tara to discharge her duty as a sworn officer of the court, be faithful to her client, and keep Donna safe.

"Woodrow, I've taken on a new client. This person came to me for help. I believe he's mentally unstable, but lucid. He is very intelligent and knows exactly what he wants. This client has given me specific instructions as to the disposition of his problem."

"Tara, you sound like you're giving an opening statement. It's me. Spill it," Woodrow said quietly, concerned now.

"Woodrow, I am bound by my oath as an attorney to do what is in the best interest of my client."

"Tara . . ." Woodrow warned.

"He says he killed that woman, the clerk, at the Circle K last Independence Day. The murder on 47."

"Whoa," Woodrow breathed, his coffee cup tipping as his hand went slack. Luckily he had enough presence of mind to right it before a drop of the dark stuff spilled on his creamy slacks. Quickly he put it on the desk and pulled his chair closer. "Are you sure?"

Tara laughed lifelessly. "I'm not sure about anything. I talked to him at length before I took him on as a client. I met him in a social situation. He came recommended. I didn't pick him up off the street, he wasn't waiting in my office, he didn't put a gun to my head. He seemed like a nice, normal kind of guy initially. The last thing I expected to hear was something like this. But there are other things, feelings of apprehension, odd behavior of his that comes and goes. I'm not a psychiatrist, but I've seen enough to think that I'm not dealing with a sociopath. I know he has been under the care of a doctor for much of his life. He hasn't come asking for punishment. He wants my help to get him off the streets."

"We should call George on this immediately. You know that, don't you?" Woodrow said, yet he made no move to pick up the phone. He had nothing. Not a name, not a clue as to whom Tara was talking about.

"Woodrow, please. I didn't come here for such a simplistic resolution, you know that. I'm not here to turn him in. The man believes, and I believe, that he is mentally disturbed. He's asked me to get him help. If he truly is the Circle K killer, he needs it and I'll want to get it for him fast. I don't want him on the streets, and quite truthfully, I don't want him near me."

"Hmm." Woodrow harrumphed in a most thoughtful manner. He looked at her from under his lashes, a look she'd seen him use on many a cowering witness when he was demanding the truth. "If he's threatening people, Tara, you're fully privileged to breach the confidentiality. I will make sure that your client is separated from you quickly and kept incarcerated until there's a resolution to this problem."

"He isn't threatening anyone, Woodrow. That's the point. He's concerned that he might have another episode. The idea of that doesn't constitute a threat. But if he's concerned, so am I. And you are too, if I had to guess. So all three of us want the same thing."

"I suppose that's true. We may not want it in the same way." Woodrow twisted in the chair and crossed his legs, ankle over knee. He had a rather handsome profile. He didn't quite look so gnome-like from that angle. He had been smart and was photographed that way for some of his campaign literature. He looked back at her too soon. "Why not tell me what you want first? Since this is new to me, I need time to mull it over. Better if I have your take to think about at the same time."

"Okay. Fair enough." Tara watched him carefully, trying to discern if there was anything going on in Woodrow's head. There were no vibes. Either she was more unnerved than she thought, or Woodrow was simply taking it all in and the wheels weren't turning yet. She began to talk. "There is a way we can do this so that everyone wins and justice will still be served. Since I'm not sure if this guy is just spinning a tale, I asked him for some specific information. I'd like you to go to George Amos. Get the status on this thing and the lowdown on those details. I've already confirmed the file is still open. I have my client's permission to give you this information only."

Woodrow nodded. Tara was walking a fine line and she was doing it beautifully. Woodrow searched for a pen and paper as he talked. "You don't think he might be covering for someone else? Using you to do exactly this so that he can find out what the status of this thing is?"

"The thought crossed my mind," Tara admitted. "A lot of things have crossed my mind. Believe me, if he's a confessor or playing some kind of game, I'll be thrilled to cut him loose." Then she'd tell Donna about her beloved's strange sense of humor. This bit of information she kept to herself. "But my next step has to be predicated on what you're going to do. Will you see George?"

"Why not ask him yourself, Tara? It would be more expedient." He faced Tara. She looked tired. Beautiful, but tired. Ben had been the luckiest guy in high school to have her. Too bad they all had to grow up.

"I don't think it would be wise." Tara shook her head. "Caroline found out George knew the woman. George isn't exactly the most judicious law man in the best of situations. I don't want to make this personal, and I don't want to give his imagination something to work on. You can approach this like a routine inquiry. Tell him you want to make sure your calendar is clear if there's anything new. Make it casual, Woodrow. Just take a look at the file and check out these details. Please."

"And once that's done?" He was playing with a pen now, his coffee getting cold, his eyes downcast. He was thinking. Tara could almost see the wheels.

"When we're sure this man is who he says and has done what he professes, then I'd like the District Attorney's Office to petition the court for hospitalization for my client. If your office makes the petition, my client is hospitalized with impunity. Anything said to the doctors can't be used against him in a court of law. He's safe from self-incrimination. I have done my duty and remanded him to the care of professionals who can monitor his behavior and, hopefully, help him."

"And this office has made that possible," Woodrow objected, his brows pulled together tight. "I think it would be more judicious to get him behind bars. We're not talking about jaywalking here."

"Woodrow, if he did this, then he's got real problems. He needs to be given all protection under the law. And," she said quietly, "you run a risk if you arrest and attempt to indict. If the grand jury won't return a true bill, the public will be outraged. This isn't fixing a high school basketball game, Woodrow. If you try and fail, the voters will just see you chasing your tail again. I'd hate to see that. I'd hate for you to jeopardize your position, or the governor's seat."

Woodrow's gaze never left hers. They didn't war with their eyes, their body language never changed, but in their heads both knew what had transpired. Tara had thought this through and was willing to play hardball.

"I suppose it could happen," he said finally. Smoothly he pulled his coffee toward him, lifted it, and drank. Tara knew it had to be cold, but he didn't react if it was. He was being decisive. Theatrics were dear to an attorney, as much for buying time as masking a disadvantage. Finally, he said, "All right. I'll take the first step. Let's go for it. Give me what you got."

Tara closed her eyes, a little prayer of thanks flitting through her mind as she reached into her briefcase. From it she withdrew a sheet of yellow-lined paper, neatly folded. She didn't hand it to Woodrow. Instead, she unfolded it, held it in front of her so that he couldn't see her notes, and looked up before she began to read.

"Let's do this as quietly as possible."

* * *

"Exactly correct. Down to the pinky finger. Look here. See where it's wrapped around the metal thing that's sticking out from the shelf like she's kind of holding on to it? Whew, this guy is good. I can't remember the last time I peed, and he's got a dead body from six months ago locked in his head down to how her fingers looked. Jeez, that's weird."

Harry Johnson made the comment. His partner Clay Williams took up the task.

"The other stuff checks out, too. The cardboard hat she was wearing, the positions of bullet entry, the one that just chipped her skull right here."

Woodrow listened without a second glance at Harry and Clay. No doubt they had many endearing qualities that set them apart from the rest of the human race and each other. Yet when they worked, the similarities were uncanny. They finished each other's sentences and came to the same conclusion within seconds. They dressed alike: short-sleeve shirts, brown Sansabelt pants, lace-up shoes, black and brown ties that hung halfway down their bellies. They were guests Woodrow had been unhappy to see at this particular party.

"Good pictures," Woodrow said, eyeing the corkboard on which the coroner's photos were laid out helter-skelter. Woodrow wasn't skittish. He'd seen a dozen murder scenes, but he didn't take delight in lingering over them. Clay, or Harry, was showing them like they were last year's vacation stills. Woodrow glanced at it again, sorry to find himself thinking what a wonderful exhibit they would make in front of a jury. Damn effective.

"Thanks. I've always said this department was particularly talented that way." George Amos threw his feet on top of his desk and laced his hands behind

his head. He was a handsome man. Woodrow could
just imagine a campaign poster with him on it. He'd
give anything to have half the man's looks in this
day and age of television campaigns. Not that
George could have done what Woodrow had. Not
in a million years. He cared too much about kicking
butt.

"Yeah," Harry piped up, "look how great this
one is. That hole right near her thorax is clear as
day. Good thing somebody found her pretty quick
after it happened. She was still warm. Time of
death is real accurate."

"Who found her?" Woodrow settled himself on
the credenza opposite the chief of police and
hitched one leg up and under him, then let it
drop again. He hadn't been able to get comfortable since Tara left his office. He almost disliked
her for sticking another thorn in his side.

"Hey, Woodrow." He looked up. George wanted
an audience since Woodrow had asked for the
show. "You want to hear this or what?"

"Yeah. Sorry."

"The guy who found her just stopped for cigarettes and a candy bar. Can you imagine seeing that
when all you wanted was a Snickers?" He shook his
handsome head but forgot to wipe the smile off his
face. "Called us right away, then split."

"Maybe your guy is the one who found her.
Might be," Harry speculated, hitching up his
Sansabelt pants, looking sincerely at Woodrow. Clay
seemed to have lost interest in the conversation
and was still checking out the photos of the body.
He tired of it soon enough, gave George the high
sign, and received a silent acknowledgment that he
wasn't needed any longer. Clay tugged at Harry's
sleeve. Harry was still waiting for an answer.

"Yeah, that could be," Woodrow said, anxious to be away from this place and these people who seemed to enjoy their work more if it was just the wrong side of distasteful.

"I don't buy it for a minute," George said and his tone had an edge to it. The big guys could be honest now that the underlings were gone. "Why phone it in that night and then turn yourself in six months later? No percentage in that. The guy was totally freaked on the 911 tape. He drove a rig, couldn't afford to get involved. Apologized all over himself when he was coherent." George tossed a wad of paper onto the desk. Woodrow hadn't noticed him toying with it. "Naw. My bet is he was an upstanding citizen, doing what was right and scared to boot. That's not the guy you've got, is it, Woodrow?"

"I've told you, I haven't got anything but some information, and now you have that too," Woodrow complained, tired of George trying to draw him into a speculative discussion about this case. Woodrow's brow knit as he looked askance at the chief of police. "You talk about this like it's a game. Doesn't it bother you at all?"

"What? That woman dying like that? Damn, Woodrow. I hate it."

"Doesn't sound like it."

"I'm a professional," George said softly. His eyes slid toward Woodrow, his gaze an accusation. "I don't wear my heart on my sleeve. You start doing that, and you're in big trouble. You start doing that, and you won't think straight. I think straight all the time, and I've got patience. That's why I knew I'd be hearing this someday. I hoped I'd be the one to track that sucker down, but if he wants to stroll right in here, that's fine with me too. I knew that woman, Woodrow." He heaved himself up, grabbed another piece of paper, and settled down again. Instead of crumpling it, he began to fold it. Over and over and over itself until Woodrow was sure he couldn't fold it one more time. He tossed it back on the desk. "I knew her since we were kids together, and I want that boy hangin' from the nearest tree. Now we've got him, I want to do this right. No screwups."

"George, there are a dozen possibilities here that you simply can't discount. He could be the trucker, he could be someone who likes to confess, he could be covering for someone, he could be insane. I'd have to think he's insane to do that," Woodrow mused, bothered with this whole conversation. He had wanted in and out in minutes. This little chat was going on an hour and George Amos was making vigilante noises. George, sensing the other man's caution, backed off, even managed a little grin.

"You're right. Can't rule anything out, Woodrow. But this poor lady died bad. It was cold. I mean when you think about the mop . . ." George put a hand to his mouth and let the sentence dangle. Woodrow didn't rise to the bait. Two could play at this game.

"I didn't come to talk about the mop, George."

"We should talk about it. We got a great set of prints off the thing and they're just itching to be matched up to somebody." George's feet were off the desk, his hands atop it now. "We've either got a fine upstanding citizen who's never been fingerprinted in his life, who suddenly went berserk and kills this lady, or we've got a sociopath who kills all the time, has never been caught, and therefore has no fingerprints on file. Or a little bit of both with a morbid sense of humor thrown in to boot. Now I'd want someone like that off the streets. I'd think you would too, Woodrow."

Woodrow held up his hand. "I want to do what's right, sure, but I'm not going to go off half-cocked on this. It isn't personal. This is about what's legally possible."

"Bull. It's personal. If you don't think that, then you should get into another line of work."

"And if you believe that, then you shouldn't be in law enforcement," Woodrow drawled. "You're the most dangerous kind of lawman."

"No." George stood, facing off with the man across the room. "You're dangerous because you calculate every move without the right kind of motivation behind it. Everything in this world is personal, Woodrow. Now I'm not going to do anything stupid where this guy is concerned. But when I get him, within the parameters of the law, you better believe I'm going to feel personal about it. I'm going to do everything in my power to make him pay for what he did. If you don't feel personal once you get him in the courtroom, then he's going to walk and all my hard work is down the drain."

Woodrow slid from his perch and buttoned his double-breasted blue blazer. Over that he threw a dark trench and grabbed an umbrella. His business was finished, but George wouldn't let go.

"So," George said quietly, "where you got this fellow hidden, Woodrow?"

Woodrow shook his head and gave George a wry smile. George never did give him enough credit. "I don't have him. An attorney came to me and asked me to check it out, confirm that the information she'd been given was correct. I promised to look at the file, not tell half the police force. So next time I ask you a favor, George, let's keep it between you and me. Just to keep relations good between the cops and the DA."

George ignored the wrist slap. He loved the cops-and-robbers thing.

"Who, Woodrow?" George prodded. "Marcia Mabley?" Woodrow buttoned his coat. "Sue Farmer. That's who, right?" Woodrow rolled his eyes. Even he wouldn't have thought of Sue Farmer. "Tara Linley," George guessed. Woodrow looked him right in the eye.

"Cut it out, George. It's a stupid game and I have better things to do." Woodrow's poker face cracked enough for the other man to know he'd guessed right.

"Tara Linley's going to defend this creep? Miss Upstanding Citizen herself?"

George read people well, but sometimes he misinterpreted the message because of the medium. Woodrow's chin nuzzled near his tie as he arranged his coat collar. Woodrow ignored him.

"It doesn't matter who's got him. I'm not going to do anything with him. I'd never get it through the grand jury much less a pretrial hearing and you know it better than anyone. There's no case."

"Give me a warm body, Woodrow, I'll get everything you need. Let me pick him up and talk real nice to him. I promise, Woodrow, I'll give you something you can use."

Woodrow turned a jaded eye George's way.

"George, I don't even know if he's in the state, much less the city. All I have are the few details I gave you. I understand that this is an emotional thing with you, but it's not with anyone else. I want to make that perfectly clear." Woodrow hoisted his briefcase. The eyes behind his glasses were hard. "His attorney's got an agenda for him that works for me, too. There are laws and we will work within them. Whether we like it or not, those suspected of a crime have rights too. If I agree with this attorney's proposal, we may eventually get the guy up on charges. If I don't follow that game plan, we might get him into court and watch our case fly out the window because we haven't done the proper psychological screening." Woodrow sighed. "Now, don't fly at me like that again, George. There's a difference between personal and passionate. I'm passionate about my job, but I also know the limitations of the law. I work within it like most attorneys. I've had enough trouble lately. I'm not going to take on something I can't win. If the guy wanted to confess, he would have done it. He didn't. You making an arrest just means a headline. It doesn't make a case."

"Who gives a shit what *he* wants, Woodrow?" Woodrow stepped back, fearing for a moment George was going to rush him. Instead the bigger man slid onto the desk, half sitting, and looked hard at Woodrow Weber before he smiled. "I'm not questioning your commitment to the law, Woodrow. But you've got other things to think about too. A big trial would do more for you right now than winning all of the piddly little ones you've been working on. Half the women in this city—probably the state— would be rooting for you to be governor if you did finger this guy. You're running on a tough-on-crime ticket like everyone else. Here's your chance to milk this."

"There's nothing to milk. We're not going to discuss it further," Woodrow wailed. "I haven't got a case, and I want you to be very clear: you haven't got a suspect."

"I'll get you one, Woodrow. I promise you."

"Then make sure you do it right. Bring me a name, solid evidence, an eyewitness, and I'll prosecute. Without that, I'm going to do what is legal, ethical, moral, and expedient." Woodrow raised a hand in warning. George shut his mouth. "And I am concerned personally about this, but not in the way you think. Tara Linley is responsible for a great deal of political goodwill, and she's an old friend. I'd be committing political suicide if I screwed up on all fronts. End of story. I've got to go. Four reverends, their wives, and two monsignors are coming for dinner tonight."

George shrugged, not quite finished. "Fine, Woodrow. It isn't my campaign. But maybe Tara knows something we don't, and that's why she's pushing to commit her man."

"Like what?" Woodrow's hand was on the knob but he had a minute more for George.

"Maybe we're close to finding something, and we don't know it yet. Maybe there is a witness. Maybe her man did another job and we're going to be able to tie him to this one. Anything's possible." George talked faster, outlining his scenario. "She holds out the carrot, says 'Woodrow, do your constituents a favor and get this guy into a hospital and off the streets.' You agree, then all hell breaks loose. The perp can't be prosecuted because you've got him in the hospital, certified." Woodrow glared at George. The chief backed off. "Okay. She's a friend. Probably wouldn't do something like that. But she's a lawyer, too, and the law swings a lot of different ways. She knows how to use it as well as you do. Just my opinion."

"I appreciate your input." The door was half open when he looked back. "I'd love to hang this guy if he's really the one. I'm not unfeeling, but I have to be prudent where everyone is concerned. Everyone, George. Even Tara's client."

"Sure, Woodrow." George was dismissing him, already settled in his chair and looking at paperwork. "Just keep me apprised and let me know if you need anything on this." George looked up as if surprised to see Woodrow still there. "Have a good dinner. Maybe those reverends will say a prayer for all those people you're concerned about and one extra for your campaign."

"Maybe they will," Woodrow said and he was gone.

"You're going to need it, you wimp," George muttered to the closed door.

Eight

Tara waved as she got out of the car and tried to remember the name of the boy who was crossing her land. He was coming from the stable headed toward the cottonwood tree, walking that insolent amble young men affect at a certain time in their lives. He seemed without purpose until he turned toward the pump.

"Tara," she chided herself, "how condescending."

Closing the car door she walked out to meet him, her breath turning into a cloud as she called, "Hello." They met halfway across the yard.

"I put the horse down for the night 'cause I didn't know if you were going to be late." He looked surly, and anxious to get out of her way as soon as possible.

"Thanks. I appreciate it. I'll check him later," she said.

"I did it right." He glared at her from under thick, dark brows that almost came together over the ridge of his nose. Tara tried not to smile. She'd seen tough and she'd seen odd. Tough and odd were embodied in Bill Hamilton. This boy didn't come close to being either.

"I'm sure you did, Joseph." Finally, the name

had come to her. He twisted his shoulders in what Tara assumed was an expression of embarrassment.

"Yeah. I did," he mumbled. "So do you need anything else?"

"No. Just wanted to say hello," Tara said, her eyes darting toward the guest house. "Carlos is a good teacher. I'm sure everything is fine. Was there anything around here today that bothered you? Anything that I need to attend to?" Eyes to the guest house again. "I mean, I have guests. I thought that they might have gotten in the way."

Leading the witness.

"Nope." Joseph shook all the way down to his shoulders and stuffed his free hand into the pocket of his worn down jacket. He waited a minute longer, assumed he was dismissed, and turned away, forgetting the water he had come for. Tara called after him.

"Payday is every Friday. I'll leave it on the front porch in an envelope."

He raised a hand above his head and Tara knew he was smiling. She passed Donna's car, hitched her briefcase, and shuddered. Memories of their wild nocturnal ride were still fresh in her mind. So where were they now? Inside? The light from the bedroom shined golden and low. Lovemaking light. Tara shuddered at the image.

Were they waiting, perhaps watching from a window in the small house? Bill whispering things to Donna. Telling her his stories while they watched Tara walk toward the main house? Donna believing them. Donna wanting him so bad she'd believe—or do—anything for him.

Tara frowned. There was something she hadn't considered. Donna not as victim but partner. Certainly not in murder. Donna could never con-

science such horror. But she could be drawn in
and partnered to Bill's madness. She'd have to find
a way to talk to Donna about Bill, naturally skirting
the issue of his homicidal résumé.

Preferably, Donna would have already tired of
him and he'd be gone. That would be lovely.

Tara pushed open the gate. The hinge was almost off. She walked slowly over the pavers.

Perhaps Bill was gone, Donna left behind and
something of value missing. Tara could notify the
cops. She would suggest they look a little closer at
the thief. She would suggest they ask him about
places he'd been. Perhaps ask him about the
Fourth of July. She'd be a bug in their ear. Her
record would be clean—a suggestion was hardly a
broken confidence. Someone else could figure out
exactly what they had in him and Donna would be
safe. Fat chance. Daydreams.

Mail was in the basket. She flipped through it
as she pushed the front door open with her hip
then stopped cold. The house smelled. Garlic and
oregano and onions. The scent wafted on a wave
of heat from the kitchen and washed over the
front room, tainting everything in its path. Tara
followed the smell, briefcase and mail still in hand,
coat still buttoned up to the chin. She hung back
before quietly stepping into the kitchen doorway.

Bill Hamilton, apron-clad and wielding a wooden
spoon, grinned at her, greeting her as jovially as a
bridegroom awaiting his bride.

"Well, there you are. Damnation, I'd almost
given up on you, girl!"

Tara didn't smile. This man didn't belong in her
life, much less in her home taking liberties with
her kitchen. Things had changed.

Tara stood quietly, her expression unreadable.

Bill Hamilton seemed to thrive on reaction and the last thing she wanted him to do was flourish. Cautiously she moved into the kitchen, circled, and stood opposite him, the table between them. She unbuttoned her coat slowly and stashed her briefcase on the closest chair. The mail went onto the table.

"Where's Donna?" she asked carefully.

Bill gave the pot a little stir, dipped his head, and slid his eyes toward her. He leaned over from the waist, his eyes darker in this light, but still bright. The steam from the pot he tended curled around his head forming a hellish halo, his smile curled as lazily as the mist.

"In the closet with a knife through her heart," he whispered, then laughed, letting it wither into a chuckle. Upright a moment later, he ignored Tara's pallor and the pain that was raw, swift, and deep in her blue eyes. "Hope you like spaghetti. Thought I'd do you a little favor and cook tonight. Long hard day for the lady lawyer." He laughed hard once, then twice, then gave her a wink. "You should be thankin' me. Donna told me you were feeling out of sorts. Give me a hearty handshake, Tara, 'cause I'm changin' your life."

His good humor tortured her. Tara fought for her voice, found it, and lay her hands on the back of the kitchen chair for support.

"Where's Donna?"

Bill's eyes snapped her way. He was peeved, unhappy that she didn't find his little game fun. He stirred the contents of the pot precisely. Still pleasant, he was no longer good-humored. "In the guest house. You know her. Gotta dress just right even if it's just family at the table."

Tara shivered, so relieved she felt ill. But he was

watching her and she wouldn't give him the pleasure of seeing her so.

"You're not family, Bill."

"Oh, I know that," he said and held up a handful of noodles. "What do you think? The whole pound?" Without waiting for her answer, he cracked the pasta in half and dumped it in the water that boiled on the back burner. "Don't worry. I haven't been steppin' where I don't belong. Really. Just an expression. That's all. Words are funny things. Donna likes to talk about words. They mean a lot to her. They mean a lot to doctors, lawyers, merchants, chiefs. Damn, I'd like to be a chief. You're a chief, Donna said, and I can see it now. Little town, big lady. Real classy the way you handle it."

"What about you, Bill? Are words important to you?" Cautiously, Tara slipped out of her coat. Her jacket seemed tight. She'd give anything to change her clothes but not when Bill Hamilton was in the house. Not when they were alone. She wouldn't take her eyes off him for a minute "Do you want to change any of those words you used today? You want to tell me a different story?"

"Nope," he answered. "Hand me the oil, will you?"

Tara looked, spotted the olive oil, and walked around the table to retrieve it. She went close, handed it to him, and looked him in the eyes. He needed to understand she wasn't afraid of him. She wished she wasn't.

"Okay. If that's the way you want it. Soon it's going to be too late, though. If this is a joke, I want to know now."

"Why?"

Those eyes were moving her way again as if they had a life of their own. Tara moved two, three feet back, out of the circle of his influence. Bill Hamilton shimmered with a bizarre ascendancy. Under his sway, other people would do unpleasant things without question because those things felt good, felt mean and nasty and free. This was what Donna found irresistible. Words, important though they may have been to her, were nothing compared to a hard, willing body, the gift of youth and abandon Bill Hamilton offered.

"I need to know if you want to change your mind. It will make a difference in the way I help you. You may not want me to be your lawyer if you can't accept what I decide," she lied.

"Not that easy, Tara. You want me to say I want someone else to talk for me. That won't solve the problem." He spoke quietly, intent on his culinary task. "If I told you something different, you still couldn't tell anyone else. Even if I fired you, you'd have to sit with two different things in your head, trying to figure out which one is right. Even if you said you couldn't be my lawyer, I'd still be with Donna and you'd still know about what I did."

Disgusted, Tara turned away but Bill reached for her. Taking her arm, he held her firmly in his grip. Her breath slipped into her throat, scraping between her teeth. Instinctively her hand covered his, her fingers digging into his. She fought no further because he was so close and she could see the sheen of his cleanshaven skin, smell a scent that made him unique and beautiful. He moved closer to her, his lips parting as if he might kiss her. Instead, he spoke gently, those beautiful lips of his moving just outside her peripheral vision. Tara closed her eyes. She trembled.

"I told you the truth. Don't be mad at me. We've gotta work together. Together." He gave her a little underscoring shake. "You're my hope. So hang in, babe, okay? I am one sick sucker. I'm so good sometimes, then sometimes I feel"—he sighed—"nothing."

Mechanically Tara opened her eyes, terrified to the very core of her being. She leaned away and looked at his hand. Finally she found the courage to look up at him. He was evil or he was sick, but one thing she knew with certainty—he was smart. He let her go. Spoon in hand, he changed again, chameleon-like, quick and captivating. Conversational once more.

"So, did you find out anything? Did you go and ask whether or not the stuff I told you was right?"

"Yes," she almost stammered. "I told someone what you'd told me and he promised to check it out."

"That's all, right? You didn't tell him my name. You can't do that, right?" He tried to smile but she saw the worry behind those eyes of his. Tara shook her head. He was satisfied. "Incredible. Against human nature if you ask me, but whatever. Did you figure something out? I don't want to go to jail, Tara. Donna would understand a hospital but not—"

"Thank goodness! You're finally home!"

Startled, Tara half jumped out of her skin and twirled toward the doorway. Donna stood with her arms out, half hanging on the jamb like they were monkey bars on the playground. She looked perfect. Jeans, a big sweater that hid impossibly tiny hips, its cowl neck hanging just right. The shades of purple offset her platinum hair. She wore lavender cowboy boots, so pristine it was impossible to imagine they'd ever been worn outside much less in the presence of a horse.

"Hi." Tara's voice was so small she had a hard time finding it. Tara touched her brow, the sign of an exhausted woman, not one unnerved. But Donna wasn't paying attention to Tara. She pranced into the kitchen, wound her arms around Bill's waist, gave his back a kiss, and grinned at Tara.

"I'm starving, but Bill insisted we wait for you. He said everyone deserves a good hot meal after a hard day's work." She breathed deeply, her eyes closed. "Smells heavenly."

"I usually just have a salad." Tara turned away but Donna caught her arm.

"Don't be a spoilsport," Donna said, a plea in her voice, fear that he might go play somewhere else if they weren't nice. "He's worked so hard. Even put out some munchies. Make an exception, just this once."

"Tara is one of those women, Donna, who makes exceptions for friends. Bends over backward, right, Tara?"

Bill didn't wait for an answer. He put his hands on both women's waists and herded them out. "Fire's a-goin' in the living room, little snacks, everything you need to relax 'til dinner. Now get, both of you. I'll call when chow's on. Go."

Tara didn't need to be told twice.

"Oh, look at this. Cheese, crackers. Not exactly inspired, but sweet. I swear, I didn't even know he could cook. Come on, have some."

Donna settled herself on the couch and put a piece of cheese on a cracker while Tara thought about Bill Hamilton rummaging around her cabinets, touching things that belonged to her and her family. He had violated her subtly, in so many ways—her mind, her home, her friend. This was detestable, sick or not.

"I don't want a cracker." Tara took off her jacket, avoiding Donna's curious gaze. "I'm just not hungry, Donna. It's been a long day, and I'm not crazy about coming home to find someone using my things."

Slowly Donna put the cracker back on the plate. The wine was forgotten, the good mood broken. "If you don't want us here, you should have just said so."

"Don't be ridiculous. Of course I want you here."

"But not Bill, is that it? You're mad about last night. You're mad about his little prank with the car," Donna said quietly. To her credit she didn't pout.

"Oh, Donna, no," Tara said. Spent, she slipped onto the sofa beside Donna, her shoulders curled in as if she were exhausted. "It was stupid. What he did was dangerous, but I'm not mad about that."

"Then what? You weren't yourself last night. It was like you went out the door in the morning and came back someone else that night." Donna drummed her fingers on the table and glanced at her friend. "That was Ben last night, wasn't it? At Woodrow's cocktail party."

"Yes."

"Had you ever seen him in that wheelchair?"

"No. He was still in the hospital when Dad and I had to leave for Washington," Tara said quietly.

"Guess you just went from one needy soul to the next." Tara looked up, confused. Donna smiled. "Me. I meant me. That's when we met. I just didn't know about Ben. I didn't know for the longest time that you were having some troubles of your own. You really keep things in tight, Tara. Maybe all those feelings you kept in about Ben when you were a teenager are coming back now. Is that what's making you act so strange?"

Tara laughed, a short despairing sound. "No, I don't feel badly about seeing Ben. His accident was years ago. We're adults now. It actually feels . . ." Tara paused, having no words to describe what she felt about her encounter with Ben. Those feelings were too wrapped up with this nightmare.

"He's handsome. Still looks good. Looks great as a matter of fact," Donna said brightly, but her good cheer was forced as she tried to find her way in the labyrinth of Tara's new mood.

"This isn't about Ben." Tara patted Donna's knee. She got closer, throwing her arm over the back of the sofa, an idea taking root. "Look, I think I was just fooling myself. I am upset about turning forty. I need a vacation and I want you to come with me. Please."

Donna was content. This she could understand. "Of course I'll go with you. Don't be ridiculous. Where do you want to go?"

"I want to go far away. Europe maybe. Right after I clear up something with Woodrow." Bill's name burned itself into her tongue, but she didn't say it. "I have a case that will be great if it works out. If it doesn't, then I'm out of here. I'm going to run away, and I want you to run away with me. How about it?"

"Tara, I swear you're losing your mind."

"No, I'm not," she insisted. "You're my best friend in the world. Pay me back for your fortieth. You can do this for me, can't you?"

"Of course. I haven't been for ages, and Bill would love to see Europe," Donna soothed.

"No!" Tara half came off the couch. She stood up, covering her panic as she poured a glass of wine, calming herself with the mechanics of it. She couldn't look at Donna and spoke with her back turned. "No, I want us to go. Just girls. He'll be here when you get back. Please, a few weeks. That's all." When the silence stretched, Tara looked over her shoulder. Donna was considering her, her expression troubled. "Wine?" Tara asked.

"No, thank you." Donna put one elbow on her knee before resting her chin on her upturned fist. "Tara, is there something between you and Bill? Something you're not telling me?"

"Oh, Lord," Tara muttered, defeated.

"It's okay if there is. I understand. Believe me. He's young, you're vulnerable. He's charming, you're overworked. He hit me that way too. Women react that way to someone like him."

"Please, Donna. It's nothing like that," Tara groaned and took her seat again. "I just want to go away with my best friend and relax. That's it."

"It's more. If it's not Ben, and it's not Bill, then it's something even you don't understand." Donna rested her leg on the couch, the other dangling over the side. "I still think you're lonely. I can help you work through it, really I can. Or at least let me give you the name of my therapist."

"Donna, I don't need a therapist. I need a hammock under a beach umbrella. I just turned forty, I miss my father, and work just isn't . . ." Tara chose the next word carefully: ". . . challenging."

"Honey, I can't take off right now anyway. I've got book commitments. Besides, if you and I are going to travel, I want to do it in style. Why rush it? Let me finish up my work and we'll plan a whopper of a trip." Donna reached for the cheese and crackers again. She gave one to Tara and took one for herself. "I'm still going to give you the name of my therapist, and I hope your incredible pride won't get in the way of calling her. Talking to someone who doesn't know you from Adam can be so freeing. No judgments. Just help." Donna took a bite of the cracker and spoke through the crumbs. "Kind of like your job. You help people who come to you without questioning why they do what they do. You know, Bill was in therapy since he was a kid. He's benefited so much from it."

"How'd you find out Bill had been in therapy?" Tara asked cautiously.

Donna smiled beautifully, transported to some private moment she held dear. Tara shivered at the thought of Bill Hamilton and his confessions. "He told me. Soon as we met. That's unusual for a man to admit something like that."

"Sounds like his problems were bad if he was in therapy as a child."

"I can't say. We shared our history in confidence, Tara," said Donna, sober as a judge.

Tara responded quickly, working the opening. "I would just worry that his problems might create trouble in your relationship. I'd hate to see you hurt again."

"That's so sweet," Donna whispered. She looked like she might cry, and then she looked pleased. "You're feeling bad and you're worried about me. It's nothing like that. He has headaches—episodes—where he doesn't remember much. Poor thing." Donna leaned closer, "Between you and me, I don't think his mom and dad were as wonderful as he makes them out. But he's strong, and he's optimistic. He doesn't even see his therapist anymore. Just as well. It sounded like the man was taking him for a ride in the last few years anyway."

"How so?"

"You know, keeping Bill on for the monthly check. I was surprised to hear it because when Bill mentioned the man's name I thought maybe we had the same doctor. I was so silly." She laughed at herself. "I took that as a sign that we were meant to be together. But my Dr. Carol wasn't his Dr. Carrol because mine was a woman and she liked to be called by her first name and his doctor had the last name spelled with two *r*'s."

"So much for fate." Tara forced herself to keep her lips tight together so she wouldn't sing an alleluia. She would have thrown her arms around Donna and crushed her in a bearhug, but then she'd have to explain herself. "The mistake's understandable. Albuquerque's not that big a place. I can see how you'd jump to that conclusion."

"Oh, that was even sillier. His doctor Carrol isn't even in Albuquerque. He's in Santa Fe." Donna opted for a handful of crackers this time, no cheese, and sat cross-legged on the couch, happy the conversation was lighter. She picked through the crackers looking for those that were perfectly golden. "I'd be a basket case if I had to drive all the way to Santa Fe to see my shrink. Wouldn't you?"

Tara laughed, "I don't know. I think I might drive that far if I thought that was the doctor who could help me."

"Reverend Halliday, it was so good of you to come. I hope we'll see you again.

Charlotte shook the reverend's one hand in her two and smiled sweetly. He was a huge man with more than his share of extra padding. She'd spent most of the evening wondering if her delicate dining room chairs would hold up until dessert. Now she was sending him on his way, with a little prayer of thanks. The chair had survived. "I enjoyed myself thoroughly, Mrs. Weber."

"Charlotte, please," she responded generously.

"Charlotte. Well, I always thought Woodrow would make a fine governor, but after meeting you I think he's the perfect candidate. It would be wonderful to have a woman in the mansion who enjoyed doing the things women should. The current governor's wife seems to think that she should have her hand in matters of government. Absurd."

"Well, I enjoy keeping house, boring as that is. And I'm so glad you enjoyed the dinner. The only problem I'd have as the governor's wife is dealing with all those people who'd want me out of the kitchen."

Reverend Halliday laughed, gathered his own wife, and lumbered down the walk, leaving behind a pleased Charlotte. She felt triumphant, even though evenings such as this belonged to Woodrow. She set the stage, he stood center. Charlotte was very proud of him and would be his partner to the end.

"Good night!"

Woodrow was beside her now, calling out to the retreating figures. They didn't turn. They hadn't heard him. That was fine. Woodrow put his hand on her shoulders as she closed the door. He kissed the top of her head.

"Come on, I'll help with the dishes."

"You don't have to, honey," Charlotte said, secretly pleased when Woodrow trailed her to the dining room and began stacking. "You had such

a miserable day I'm surprised you made it through
the dinner. I can't believe Tara asking you to put
that man in the hospital just like that."

"Charlotte, she has a point. I just can't imagine
winning that one, and I've taken such a trouncing
on the rapist case and now this basketball betting
scam with the high school."

Woodrow raised his voice. He was talking to the
air. Charlotte was already in the kitchen with the
water running. He carried in six dishes, three
wineglasses, and a handful of silver. He deposited
them in the sink, sank into a chair, and rubbed
his eyes under his glasses. Charlotte was his best
friend, his confidante. Luckily he hadn't married
someone with problems as big as his own.

"I'm no expert, Woodrow, but it seems to me
that George has a point. Any press is good as long
as your name is in front of the public. The governor is getting so much coverage with this crack
baby thing. Then he adopted that little baby.
Sometimes I wonder if he didn't do that just for
press value."

"Charlotte." Woodrow verbally waggled a finger
at her overstatement.

"Well, Woodrow, you never know. I do think if
there's anything to Tara's client's case, you ought to
go for it. I've listened to you talk about the law.
From what you say, a jury would be sympathetic to
the victim in this case. They wouldn't need a lot of
evidence, would they? I mean sympathy counts for
a lot. Look at those two brothers who murdered
their parents in California." Charlotte stacked a few
plates in the dishwasher, stole a look at her husband,
saw the hurt in his face, and quickly amended her
lecture. "But of course you're the expert, honey.

Whatever you think best. I'm sure you know what's right for everyone."

Woodrow stood up. He was too tired to talk anymore.

"It's not a matter of making a decision, Charlotte. Sympathy wouldn't hold up on appeal even if I managed to convict on one piece of evidence and sympathy. And Tara hasn't told me who this man is."

"Oh, you could figure it out," Charlotte said brightly, holding her soapy hands over the sink. "You are the smartest man I know, Woodrow Weber. I'm so proud of you. You'll get what you need. A confession or something."

"Or something," Woodrow said quietly. "I think I'm going to bed. Do you mind?"

"Of course not. You go on. I won't be a minute."

Her hands were back in the water. She was happier doing the dishes alone anyway. The chore freed her mind and she let it roam. Plans for the Women Voters Coalition tea were refined. She mentally composed a short two-fold mailer with pictures and she thought about all the things Woodrow had told her about Tara. Another pitfall was the last thing Woodrow needed.

Charlotte sighed and rinsed the last of the glasses. She flipped off the kitchen light and headed upstairs, taking off her jewelry as she went. She turned off the stairwell light on the landing, and began to unbutton her blouse. She'd slip into the pink negligee Woodrow liked so much. But when she got to the bedroom, Woodrow was asleep, his glasses askew on his nose, an unread brief lying on his chest.

Gently Charlotte took the brief, put it on the

bedside table, and kissed her husband's forehead. Woodrow mumbled, his sleep disturbed, and turned on his side. Charlotte covered him, then changed into the flannel pajamas she kept for nights just like this.

Finally, crawling in beside her husband, Charlotte put her hand on his shoulder and patted, wishing for all the world that she could make all the bad things go away so Woodrow could do what he was meant to do.

Nine

Tara took the Turquoise Trail, a winding trek that degenerated from four lanes of blacktop to two just outside Albuquerque as it headed straight into Santa Fe. It would have been faster to take Interstate 25, but Tara needed time alone. Away from Albuquerque she might be able to decide if she was crazy.

During the last two days Bill Hamilton had been a perfect house guest. He had fixed a fence rail. Tara had heard him laughing, making suggestions for Donna's latest book. And always, when they happened to cross paths alone together, he asked if she had heard anything. Oh please, he would say politely, had she heard? And Tara lived this odd nightmare and she hadn't heard anything. That really scared her. That terrorized her in the bright light of day instead of the dark of night. She needed a break and she needed to do something constructive.

Her eyes drifted to the mesa as she drove. She was dazzled by the red blanket of earth and the seamless canopy of robin's-egg blue sky, the breathy clouds, the hidden sun, and a flutter of snow. The scene empowered her and she hated the thought of it. Empowerment! A crazy concept concocted by the media to make women think they weren't living up to some stunning potential. But Tara believed one either had power or didn't. At least she'd believed that until Bill Hamilton had come into her life.

He had taken away her power of objectivity because Donna was involved. He had destroyed the power of her position; it was now at odds with her emotions as a friend. Now Tara wondered if he'd made a dent in her power of persuasion. What should have been a simple series of inquiries was now suspect because of Woodrow's silence. He hadn't returned her calls and that left her uncertain and nervous. Bill Hamilton should have been in a state mental facility within days, yet he still lounged in her home, grinned at her, and slept with Donna Ecold.

Swinging the Jeep onto the shoulder of the road, Tara left the car and stretched. She breathed in, raised her face, closed her eyes. She prayed silently, standing, that some surety would come to her soon. If she'd thought it would help, Tara Linley would have knelt on the earth and clasped her hands, begging to be captain of her own destiny again.

Tara opened her eyes. No burning bush appeared at her feet; the earth didn't open up to spew forth its spirits. She was alone with this unfamiliar turmoil. Tara got back in the car and went forward, not back.

She made Santa Fe by noon. An easy drive into a town she appreciated, but never really enjoyed. There were too many people, too close together, spending too much money on things they didn't need. Tara honked at a woman in an immense fox coat who had left the door of her yellow Mercedes wide open while she ran into a shop to drop something off or grab something up. Maneuvering the

Jeep around the open door, she hoped the car behind her would take that door off its hinges. To keep frustration at bay, Fate gave her a freebie. A parking space big enough for the Jeep opened up on Canyon Road. Tara tucked the car into the space, hopped out, and started looking for the office of Dr. Stanford Carrol, psychiatrist.

She found it in a pink stucco building above a lovely store, its windows full of antiques and unusual collectibles from third-world countries. A tin box caught Tara's eye. She passed by easily. Donna was on her mind. She climbed a narrow flight of stairs, once painted brick red and now charmingly chipped and worn. Bill moved into her mind with Donna. Tara stumbled. The mere thought of him unnerved her. These were the steps he'd climbed even as a boy. She wondered if his mind was as disturbed then as hers was now. Did he frighten himself? Did he feel *nothing* as he walked to his appointment? She stopped to admire the beautiful little courtyard and calm herself. Tara reveled in the quiet as she slicked back her long hair and twisted it into a rope.

To her left was a door painted hunter green. The door to her right was cornflower blue. Straight ahead was one stained the natural color of the wood. Stanford Carrol's name was printed neatly in black on that one. An interesting psychological statement, this. No color, wood laid bare. She walked through it into Dr. Carrol's office.

There were no bells or whistles, not even a receptionist in a short skirt and Indian-pawned silver waiting to offer her assistance in a subdued, but lyrical, voice. Instead, Tara found herself in a small, whitewashed room. The walls were bare, the furniture exquisite: a small table, two overstuffed

armchairs, and a love seat. There were side tables
at either end of the love seat, a giant ashtray on
one of them. Nice touch. Nonjudgmental, this Dr.
Carrol, or simply aware that when the mind is
cracked, a nasty habit can be calming. Very cute.
Very chic. Very Santa Fe. Very quiet and it was this
last that unnerved Tara most.

She waited, reassessing her surroundings. No
one came in after her, but no one came out from
behind the office door, either. Tara paced in the
small room, then knocked on the door. Nothing.
Her heart lurched, her stomach churned, and she
hated herself for it. Fantasy had never been her
thing, and now she was indulging in it on a regular
basis. In her mind's eye she saw the door flung
open. Bill Hamilton here, surprising her, a mania-
cal head doctor hot on his heels, both of them
reaching for her . . .

Tara tsked, a noise of loathing at her own ridiculous imagination. She reached for the knob,
and just as she touched it, before she actually had
a grip, the door flew open and Tara screamed. So
did the young woman on the other side of the
door.

"Oh no! Look what I did!" she exclaimed, whipping a huge cloth from the back pocket of her
very short shorts. She fell to her knees, putting
aside the giant watering can she had in the other
hand. She scrubbed furiously. "Hey, you scared the
bejeebbies out of me. I can't believe this. Stan will
be furious. He's really funny about his carpets. Not
like you can hurt wool with water. What about the
sheep, for goodness' sake? They stand out in the
rain and everything." She wiped a little more then
glanced up. "Oh, hey, I apologize. You look awful.

I scared the living daylights out of you, too, huh? Come on, sit down."

Tara had laid herself back against the wall, the breath knocked out of her. In her mind's eye it had been Bill there, Bill screaming back at her. Perhaps it was the idea that her imagination could be so fertile that paralyzed Tara more than anything else.

"No. No, really." Tara backed away from the girl. "I'm fine, honest. You just surprised me. I knocked and no one came, so I assumed I was alone."

"I was way in the back. Can't hear a thing in Stan's office 'cause it's soundproof. That's so no one hears what's going on inside." Her fingers posed for emphasis and Tara was reminded of a Balinese dancer. For some reason it seemed odd that she wasn't chewing bubble gum. "Stan can't hear outside his office. There's a light on his desk that tells him when people come in. Want to see it?"

Tara's smile was shaky, but she managed it. This girl was so cute she couldn't help but like her.

"No, thank you. Is he back there though? I do have an appointment."

"Oh, you're the one." The moppet-coiffed girl backed off and retrieved her watering can. "He told me you might come while I was here. I'm the Green Girl." Proudly she held up her watering can and patted a plant spritzer at her waist. "I take care of the plants in offices around here. I have a key and everything. They all trust me, you know, so that's why Stan gave me a message to give to you. He said you could either wait or meet him at the Loretto Chapel. You know where that is?"

"I have an idea."

"Good, 'cause I'm busy. I have a ficus that's

weeping all this sticky stuff and it's really yucky."
She stuck out her tongue and screwed up her nose
and looked cuter than Meg Ryan.

"I wouldn't want to take you away from that."

"Oh thanks. I'm so glad. I wouldn't mind walking you over there, but this is kind of important,"
the girl said. " 'Course it's not as important as
what Stan's doing." She moved and Tara smelled
spring. "The reason he's not here is because Mrs.
Rey had a breakthrough. I didn't mean to hear
that, but I did. I can't even imagine what it is. I
mean do you think Dr. Stan is like helping her
have a religious experience or something since
they're at the chapel?"

"I don't know," Tara answered quite seriously
despite her amusement.

"I don't either. Well, that's the message. You
okay now?" She held out a hand and touched
Tara's shoulder, giving her a little push as if to see
if she was stable.

"No problem. I'm fine. You don't know how
long Mrs. Rey's religious experience is going to
take, do you?"

The Green Girl shook her head. "Haven't a
clue."

"I think I'll go on over to the chapel and find
him. What's he look like?"

"Oh, cute. Tall. You know. Thin." Those fingers
went askew again.

"Right." Tara gave her a thumbs-up accepting
the description as the best she was going to get.

"Good luck. Hope you find him. And don't
worry, you'll be fine. He works wonders for people.
I was so depressed when I started seeing him and
now, well." She held out both hands to show her-

self off in all her glory, and a glorious picture she was indeed. "Need I say more?"

"Not another word," Tara panned. She was halfway to the front door, the Green Girl an equal distance down the hall heading toward the ficus, when Tara called, "Do you mind if I ask you something?"

" 'Course not," she called back.

"It's snowing outside. Aren't you cold in those shorts?"

"Oh, no," she answered, "these socks are really heavy."

Tara nodded and left the office.

The plaza was quiet in midafternoon. A handful of people were milling about, ducking in and out of the shops. Late lunchers were lingering behind the windows of bistros and burger bars. Tara walked across the now brown grass slowly, rehashing what she was going to say once she found Stanford Carrol. But the plaza wasn't big enough and she reached no decision by the time she stepped into the hush of God's house.

In the chapel, under a cross and under the high windows, a cluster of women knelt and prayed the rosary. One woman's voice called the prayers, while the beads slipped silently through their collectively devout fingers. A family—two parents and two kids—were viewing the stations of the cross, and in the corner, just outside an ancillary chapel, was the man she'd come to see.

He was one of those guys every woman under twenty fell in love with in the sixties. He was tall. He was lanky. His glasses were round and rimless and his hair was long, straight, and parted in the middle. His face was drawn, sensitive-looking, and properly pale.

Tara walked down the aisle toward him. He had no interest in her approach, so lost in thought was he. One hand lay in his lap, the other was draped over the side of the pew. His fingers looked like marble, detailed like Jesus lying in the Pieta's lap. They were exquisitely long and she imagined them plucking a guitar as he sat on some college campus warbling relevant songs that changed lives and broke hearts.

She was abreast of him now and saw that he wore his clothes well. A turtleneck. *What else?* Black. *Why not?* A pair of jeans. *Of course.* And boots. *Well worn, naturally.* He probably had a special occasion workshirt and a tie in a closet somewhere. There on the pew beside him was the requisite tweed jacket. She'd bet her bottom dollar there were leather patches on the elbows. His briefcase would be one that was fashioned by an Indian friend. The doctor would probably swear the leather was softened by the craftsman's teeth. Tara smiled when she stopped. He did not when he looked at her. That didn't surprise her, the man had obviously been thinking deeply. She was taken aback by his voice, though.

"Tara Linley?" That voice was as deep as the Grand Canyon. The guy had obviously been in the wrong line when heaven was handing out vocal cords. She wondered if the Lord enjoyed the sound of it here in His house.

"Yes. I hope you don't mind my coming here." She put out her hand. He half stood and took it.

"You made good time." He drew her into the pew and moved back to allow her room. "And no,

I don't mind your finding me here. I don't say things I don't mean. I gather you spoke to Paula."

"The Green Girl?" Tara grinned. Stanford Carrol looked at her pleasantly. She had his number. The man didn't like to laugh. Probably never cried. He was there as a receptacle for other people's emotions and what a fine one he was. "Yes. She said that one of your patients was having a breakthrough."

The old receptacle actually tipped his lips at that one. "The patient in question has a breakthrough once a month. It's like a progress report. If she has a breakthrough, she can tell her husband she has to continue with therapy."

"You don't mind that?"

"I'm not crazy about it. But I think she needs the attention, and there's merit in that. I'm sure you know people who sue other people just so they can feel as if they're accomplishing something."

"Can't deny it." Tara popped the snaps on her denim jacket. It was hotter in the church than she'd first thought. "Where is she?"

"The miraculous staircase." He tilted his head to the right.

Tara had seen it once, the staircase that St. Joseph supposedly built for the nuns. Whoever did build it had to be a saint. They'd left without getting paid. The church now charged tourists to see it. Tara wondered why, since St. Joseph hadn't stuck them with a bill.

Stanford Carrol was still talking, his deep voice soothing in the twilight of the place. "We come here every time she has a breakthrough. I wish all my patients were so kind as to give me a reflective moment on their hour. So," he said precisely, "I have reflected and here you are. My patient will be in there for at least ten more minutes. You're on."

Tara eyed him. He was so grounded, so up front. She tried to imagine Bill Hamilton sitting with this calmly ordered man who didn't adorn himself, his workplace or, most likely, his life. Bill would have been put off by such austerity, frustrated by his inability to crack Stanford Carrol's demeanor. She could just see him prancing, spinning his tales, growing into the fake cowboy he'd become right in front of Stanford Carrol's eyes. And what had this man done to stop it? What did he know about the process and the end result that could help her now? That's what she had come to find out.

"I'm here about Bill Hamilton. As I told you on the phone, I'm his attorney, and I have some questions for you."

"Do you have a release from Bill?"

"No, I don't." She held his gaze.

"Then I could have saved you a long drive. We could have discussed all that I'm free to discuss over the phone. You realize that, of course."

"I do," Tara admitted. "But I needed to see you. I thought that might tell me something about Bill, too. And truthfully, I was hoping I might be able to convince you otherwise. You're not Bill's favorite person. I didn't want him to know I was coming to see you. This visit is to help me make appropriate decisions regarding Bill's legal standing. I want to assure you, though, I'm not talking a specific point of law at the moment."

"I'm not sure I really understand." He adjusted his glasses from the side, took them off, and held them up to the altar light. Satisfied with what he saw, he put them back on and gave her all his attention.

"Bill hasn't been charged with a crime. I've been retained to assist him in navigating around a problem so that he will not be incarcerated." Tara pushed up the sleeves of her sweater and crossed her legs, ready to work.

"Isn't that what lawyers are supposed to do?" The question wasn't easy. Dr. Carrol went on when she didn't answer. "I find it hard to believe Bill would be involved in anything small. He was a grandiose person."

"He is unusual, and the specifics of his problem aren't really important at the moment. I'm looking for general information. I believe you treated him for a number of years?"

"He was an adolescent when I first started seeing him."

"How young?"

"Twelve, I think. Maybe thirteen. He didn't tell you?"

Tara pressed on, quietly. The family followed the stations of the cross toward their pew. "Is yours a pediatric practice?"

"No. General. I tend to see more men than women. That's simply a personal preference. I like women too much to want to be disillusioned in my personal life by what I hear in my professional one." Stanford looked at Tara, and waited for her next question.

"Interesting." She pushed back her hair, trying to find words that would get her what she wanted. Unfortunately, Tara didn't really know what that was. She started to fish. "Can we talk about Bill's family?"

"In general." He agreed and shifted, recrossing his long legs. "I saw his mother the first time Bill came in. She seemed reasonable, rational. A nice-looking woman. Other than that, I'm not at liberty to discuss his family. Money? Would that be of interest?" Tara nodded. "I can tell you that I was always paid. I got the feeling that it bothered Bill when there wasn't money—not just for me but other things. I never raised my rates for Bill. As we grew older together, I realized I didn't like to see him agitated."

"Did it frighten you when he was like that?" Tara whispered now. The family was right behind them, staring at Christ fallen under his cross. A priest had come onto the altar. The place was beginning to feel crowded. She wished they could go back to his office.

"It didn't make me happy. Bill was not an unusual guy on some levels. On others . . ." Stanford stopped, then picked up his jacket. He held it in his hands, twisting it while he considered what to say next. "But then, to follow that line of thought would be discussing the specifics of that patient, wouldn't it?"

"Not really. This could be a general conversation about, say, Bill Hamilton's tendency to truthfulness. Does Bill tell tales? Does he hallucinate? I suppose we could discuss how reliable those tales are. Neither of us have to talk about what he's told us," Tara contended, though that was exactly what she wanted to do. Strangely, she had the feeling Dr. Carrol wouldn't be averse to a little soul baring either. Tara moved on the hard, shiny wood of the pew, pushing him as far as he would go. But Dr. Carrol was staunch. Tara tried again. "Maybe we could talk about his tendency to violence. Could Bill Hamilton be violent? That's the real question. That's the one I need answered."

The doctor held up a hand. He turned his head away, thought a moment, then looked back at Tara.

"This is walking a real fine line. I could ask you if you're concerned for your safety, or if Bill has made any threats. You might even lie and tell me you fear for your life, but I have a feeling fudging isn't your style." His expression clouded; his body language was that of an irritable man. "Okay. Let's talk clinically." He tossed the jacket aside. Obviously it gave him no inspiration, or comfort, to hold it. He gazed at the altar, not Tara. "Where there are violent tendencies, there are no hard-and-fast rules. For some people, violence is manifested quickly and sporadically. This is almost a physical necessity like breathing. Others are violent at will for psychological reasons. The violence makes them feel better about themselves, satisfies a desire for power, that kind of thing. Generally drugs such as Prozac and lithium can be used for control. That might be of interest to you. You could extrapolate from there. Other than that, may I suggest you call when you have a signed release from Bill."

"Okay. How about this." Tara knew she'd been given a gift, but it wasn't what she wanted. She wanted to return it for something bigger. "Can these people work? People with violent tendencies?"

The doctor's eyes flickered with something— amusement or irritation, she wasn't sure. "Many of my patients are well enough to hold jobs. Some are actually classified as disabled. Then Social Security picks up the tab."

"Was that the case with a certain patient?"

The doctor was tiring. It had been irritation behind his eyes. "I never really concerned myself with where the money came from."

"Can I see his emergency information?" Tara asked.

"No," he answered smoothly and started to rise in the same way. He was standing when Tara put her hand on his arm. They must have made quite a picture, the tall man, the woman pleading with him, her hair falling down her back. Very biblical.

"Doctor, there's a lot at stake here. I'm scared and I don't know if I should be. I'm afraid for other people, too, but he hasn't really done anything."

"And all I have is your word that you represent Bill Hamilton," he reminded her. The family had moved on. A small woman in a plaid dress had come through the chapel doors and tagged Stanford. Tara didn't have much time.

"Do you want to call him?" Tara bluffed, hoping he wouldn't take her up on it. She had no idea how Bill would react if he knew she was there.

"I want a written release, Ms. Linley, or a written request from another doctor for a transfer of medical records. I'll accept either one. Let's put it this way—when you're discussing crazy people it doesn't hurt to be very, very careful."

"Okay. Okay." The woman in plaid was bearing down now. Tara was out of time.

"Look," came the rumble of a voice. Tara's head snapped up. He was giving in—sort of. "I have no doubt you're who you say you are, but I don't want to be on the wrong end of Bill Hamilton. I don't want to know about him or why he needs a lawyer. When he terminated me, I washed my hands of him gladly."

Tara was mute, afraid to scare him off by asking another question. Stanford looked over his shoulder, made a motion, and the woman in plaid held back. She sank to her knees in front of a statue painted blue and white. Tara had him for a moment longer.

"I'll tell you this. Puberty often creates a crisis for certain types of patients. Where medication may have worked before, it may not after that particular change in life. You think you're making progress, then *boom,* you're back to square one or even lower. Stuff happens. I guess sometimes I think more of my skills than I should. The one saving grace is that *certain* people"—he put the emphasis on the right word and Tara listened up—"certain people are truly distressed when their actions cause injury. I would worry if that ever stopped. Hopefully, if we were to talk about a mutual acquaintance, someone is monitoring that emotional meter. The fact that honest anguish follows or precedes violence is important here. Certain people need medication and I hope someone makes sure that they get it."

Dr. Carrol started to sidestep out of the pew. While Mrs. Rey knelt in front of the statue with her hands folded, her eyes were on her doctor.

Tara followed him. "Could you order medication for me if I needed it?" He stopped and spoke quietly, remorsefully.

"Lovely thought, but no. I can't do anything without that person's consent, and that will never happen. It seems in this case, an infomercial has more credibility than I."

"Is there anything I can do?" Tara asked. Stanford Carrol looked heavenward, then back at her.

"Pray?" Tara's disappointment was so evident that he clucked an expression of commiseration. "Sorry. Best I can do is suggest you get him to see someone. If he trusts you, and I'm assuming he does, then he'll follow your advice."

"I have no idea whether or not he trusts me, Doctor." Tara looked at the floor, wishing she had found answers here instead of another door closed in her face. "He may hate me. He may admire me. I'm not sure who he is, or what he is. Sometimes I think he's jerking my chain, sometimes I think he's as scared as I am. I've never had a client like him. I wish there was something I could do."

"Just take care of business best you can," Stan said. "That's about it. In all the years I saw him, I'm not sure I accomplished anything. It can be disconcerting."

"It can be downright scary."

"It can be dangerous," he said seriously, then added, "though I wouldn't really know about that."

Tara could almost see the small print of that statement: *This doctor has made a statement that can be construed neither as the truth nor as a judgment on his former patient Bill Hamilton.*

"One last question," Tara said, her eyes darting to the impatient Mrs. Rey. "If you had a hypothetical patient whose violent tendencies were controlled with Prozac and lithium, and that hypothetical patient quit taking these medications after an extended period of time, how long would it take for the patient to revert and the violence to take hold again?"

"Difficult to say. Everyone is different."

"Three months?"

"Three months would be reasonable."

"Would reasonable apply here, Dr. Carrol?"

"I doubt it, Ms. Linley."

They parted. He went off to deal with the mystical Mrs. Rey; she left to find the only earthly person who could work a miracle: Woodrow Weber.

Ten

"Hello! Hello!" Out of breath, Tara fell on the phone. The receiver slipped, she juggled it, and it dropped to the floor with a thud. It was back in her hands in a flash. "Sorry. Hello? Who is this?"

"Tara, you okay?"

"Woodrow! Woodrow, this is great." Relief actually did come in waves and she was drowning in them. Tara tossed her purse on the nearest chair, checked the yard, saw that no one was about, flopped onto the window seat, and put her feet up. She felt exhausted from her drive when she walked through the door, but Woodrow's voice had rejuvenated her. "I've been so worried. You haven't returned any of my calls. I expected to hear from you yesterday at the latest. I was about to come find you."

"This isn't the only thing I have to do, you know." Woodrow was testy. Tara took two deep breaths, calmed her beating heart, and gave herself a mental whack on the head.

"I'm sorry. I really am. I just assumed you wouldn't have any trouble getting George to show you the file. I never wanted to put you out. I know how busy you are."

Come on, come on. You have no idea what kind of person this is. Help me, Woodrow.

"Hey, I didn't mean to snap either. I'm sorry.

One thing led to another, Tara, and I had to do some checking on things. I had to think." Woodrow sounded tired. "Did you see the paper this morning?"

"Yes. This whole thing with Strober is getting out of hand." Tara closed her eyes and let her head rest against the wall. Home felt good. Gossiping with Woodrow felt good. Her life was almost normal for a moment and she gave in to the pleasure.

"That's so, but I checked the file. It was arbitrated to the people's satisfaction. I didn't see a damn thing about that in the write-up. Or anything about the fines they paid. Or the fact that permits were pulled until everything was fixed. Oh," he went on, sounding as close to outright anger as she'd ever heard him, "I loved the quote from Chris."

"I don't remember," Tara said, having done nothing more that morning than skimmed the headlines.

"The governor is appalled that I would even consider running for his prestigious seat when I can't be trusted with the public safety. It's bad, Tara. Charlotte knows it. I know it. The voters take this kind of thing and latch on to it." Tara remained silent, waiting for him to play out so she could get to business. "I've had to do some major disaster control over here, so I just can't sit up and take notice when you demand things and ask favors. You understand that, don't you?"

Tara rolled her eyes and checked out the crack in the ceiling, biting back the six or seven retorts that came to mind, half wondering if there wasn't something else going on here. She was fairly sure she had a killer on her hands. She knew, after her visit with Stan Carrol, that Bill was certifiable. But

Woodrow had never met Bill Hamilton. Confined by her confidence, Tara had no way of convincing Woodrow how urgent this matter was. Luckily, she didn't have to try.

"Listen." He sighed. "I've talked to George. I need to talk to you. Could you meet me at Lindy's around five?"

"Maybe it would be better if we settled the details over the phone. That way I can do whatever I need to do and deliver him to you in the morning with all the paperwork. You sound awfully tired to be doing this tonight," Tara said.

"Lindy's at six, then. Would that be in your schedule?"

"Sure, Woodrow. No problem," Tara muttered, properly chastised by this unusually terse Woodrow. She put out her feelers with a tease. "If you beat me there, order me a milk shake, huh?"

"Sure, Tara." But there wasn't a chuckle to be spared.

"On second thought, don't bother. See you then. And Woodrow, thanks. I really appreciate all you're doing."

The line went dead without so much as a good-bye, but his voice still rang in her ears. He had sounded embarrassed, even a little guilty. Holding the receiver close for a minute, she finally hung up, hoping Woodrow wasn't burning both his bridges during this campaign. He'd find himself out of a job if he couldn't control either end of his life.

She checked her watch. It was only four. She needed to clear her head and be ready for whatever Woodrow had for her. A ride would get rid of the cobwebs.

* * *

"Hello you," she called quietly, forcing herself to keep her eyes on the paddock instead of the guest house. She didn't want to see Bill, though she'd kill to see Donna. It was an awful feeling and one that would be nonexistent in a few hours. Until then, she would suppress her urge to do an about-face, find Donna, and tell her that she was in lust with a nut.

Tara slipped the paddock latch open, and eased herself into the corral. Shinin' was on her in seconds. A nuzzle, a pat on his long, strong neck, and they walked together as far as his stall. Like a dog seeing its leash, Shinin' bolted in delight. Tara smiled and let her eyes flick over the stable yard. Joseph had everything in order.

Whistling, she checked her English saddle and decided it would do. Her hands ran over the well-worn leather of the girth, held it, and pulled it off the wall. Half turned, already feeling the cinch of the thing on Shinin', she grabbed the bridle. A second later she heard a frightful noise and it was coming from her own throat.

Woodrow walked slowly out the back door into the garden. It was bare this time of year. The shrubs looked sad without the spring flowers to cuddle up to. Charlotte was on her knees, digging in earnest as she planted bulbs in precisely dug holes. He pulled up a garden chair and sat beside her. She sat back on her heels.

"I hope I'm not planting these too early."

"I'm sure they'll be fine."

"Yes, I am, too. Did you call her?"

"Yes." Woodrow ran a finger around the intricately designed wrought-iron chair and wondered why on earth they'd ever bought them. They were darn uncomfortable.

"And?"

"And she's meeting me at Lindy's at six. I don't know about this whole thing, Charlotte. It gives me a very bad feeling. I sure don't want Tara to be hurt."

"Woodrow, I don't want anyone to be hurt. I know you've been having second thoughts about this, but you have to do what's best. Believe me, this is best."

"I suppose you're right. Charlotte?"

Her eyes hadn't left him since he sat down but she smiled as if he'd just caught her attention.

"I'd like to cancel the next couple of engagements. I really think I should be at the office a little more. You know, get things under control. What do you think?"

"Well"—she lifted a shoulder—"it's up to you. You know what's best."

"Yes. Yes, I suppose. That's it then. I'll cancel the next engagements."

He started to get up but Charlotte put her hand on his knee, "Unless you'd like me to step in for you. I could make those speeches. It might look just right if we did that. It would make a good impression, a candidate so dedicated to the people that he was risking a campaign." Woodrow took it all in. When he remained silent, Charlotte smiled gently. "You don't have to decide now. Just think about it."

"I will. It's a good idea. I think I'll go shower and lie down a bit before I have to meet Tara."

"Woodrow," Charlotte called to his back. She smiled wider when he turned around. "Don't worry about Tara. She'll be fine. I know it."

"I don't want to do anything that might hurt her," Woodrow said and Charlotte nodded. Charlotte hated the thought of someone she cared for hurting too.

Tara was on her knees howling in pain.

Horrified, she looked down to see blood gushing from her right arm. Her skin was ripped in the same jagged pattern as her shirt. From wrist to elbow she seemed perforated by jagged holes. Beside her lay the pitchfork. The damnable tines, sharp as a sword, had caught her full force on the tender skin that protected against damage to more than vital veins. Jesus, how did it get there? Poised above that bridle where it never should have been. She yanked. It fell. Jesus, Lord above, there was blood everywhere. And she hurt. She hurt so badly.

Small sounds came from someplace deep in her lungs, bubbling out of her lips. A mewling of horror that popped, faded, and was lost in the echo of that first scream. Now mute, Tara watched her life's blood pumping from the horrendous rent in her arm. Oddly aware that she was in shock, mindful that the pain was now nonexistent, she clutched her right arm with her left hand. But the wound was too long. The blood poured through her fingers, flowed under her nails, stained the ground around her, and mixed its scent with the dirt and dung. She was sweating in the cold, but the sweat became icy and the noises in the corral surrealistic.

Feeling faint, Tara forced herself to let go of her arm long enough to push herself up. Terrified her arm would fall off if she didn't clasp it again, Tara

held it tight against her stomach, half stumbling,
half running out of the corral.

Shinin' was on her instantly, nuzzling and pushing, alarmed by the scent of blood. Feebly she
tried to push him away, but he stood fifteen hands.
Whole she was hardly a match if he decided to be
against her, wounded she was his victim. Somehow
Tara managed to get herself out of the corral.
Nausea rising, she stumbled toward the pump that
seemed to fade in and out of her line of vision.

"Please. Please, God," she mumbled, sure He
wouldn't hear such a frail cry but she felt better
for it. She heard herself sobbing into the frosty
day, the sound trailing around trees and bushes
hoping to find someone to hear and help.

Suddenly strong arms were around her. A voice
whispered comfort. Tara was caught up against a
strong chest, and in her relief, she half held up
her arm, half cried, half smiled as she looked up,
not into the face of a savior, but that of a gray-eyed
devil. Bill Hamilton held her and there was no
choice but to put her faith in him.

"I'm hurt," she whimpered. "I'm hurt."

"Damn if you aren't, little lady." He held her
tighter, pressing her arm against his chest, working
the pump with his other arm until the cold water
ran hard and fast as it came out of the spout.
"You've had yourself an accident. Damnation. Bad
one. Bad. Bad. Bad."

He whispered and whispered and turned her
around so she was cupped into him like a lover,
held affectionately from behind. With care he
moved her arm, so gently she didn't know why she
resisted. The cold water flowed over the wounds
and Tara's knees buckled with relief. She was
saved. Closing her eyes she fell back into him, half

conscious but fighting for the whole of her senses all the same. Something wasn't right. Something just wasn't right.

She forced her eyes to open. The water was still pumping. But so was her blood. Bill's hand around her arm was pressing from the side so the blood flowed more freely than ever. She struggled feebly, knowing now he wasn't trying to help her at all. Insane. He was insane. Holding her arm lower than her heart so the blood poured out of her and into the drain. No one would ever know what he had done. She would be dead. He would live.

Swooning, her sudden weight caught Bill Hamilton off guard and down he went with her until they were both kneeling in the bloody, muddy earth. With one last breath, Tara rallied, refusing to let him kill her. Refusing to be another woman lost to his moment of nothingness. Her life was worth more than that.

"No," Tara whispered, weak though she was. "No," she said again and struggled as best she could, blinded by the hideous exhaustion that was overtaking her. With her free hand she pushed him hard as she could. Off balance still, he fell and the stream of water stopped as suddenly as it began. Tara managed to find her feet. Woozy, she took a step. Then another. But he was fast, up and grabbing for her. He twirled her into him and held her tight against his chest. Too tight. She couldn't fight him and she knew it. She couldn't run and she knew it. And her blood was binding them together, her wounded arm caught between her and the man who tormented her. Through bleary eyes she saw him smile, grin really. He opened his mouth.

"Donna!" he yelled and grinned once more so

that Tara would know he was saving her. He turned his head, his beautiful expression of endearment changing to one of panic. Tara closed her eyes and lay against him. There was nothing more she could do except listen to the vibrations in his chest of his liar's call for help. "Donna! Come quick!"

"Bill! Tara!"

Tara was in other arms. Thin arms were holding her. Tiny hands caressing her. A golden head and angelic face hovered above hers. They slipped on the pulpy earth until she was lying half on her hip and half in Donna's lap.

"Help me, Bill. Help me now. I think she's in shock. Come on, quick."

Bill picked her up and they got to the guest house with Donna trailing behind making hysterical noises. That was the last thing Tara remembered until she opened her eyes to find Donna cleaning her wounds, heedless of her dress, touching her as if she was the most precious thing on the face of the earth.

"No stitches," was the only thing Tara could think to say.

"You need stitches. I've cut butterflies, but I don't know if they'll hold." Donna didn't look up but Tara could see that her face was tearstreaked even as she worked the gauze around her arm. "Tara, this was so ugly. I've never seen so much blood gush out of one person. I thought"—she hiccupped a sob—"you were dying. I thought I wouldn't have you anymore. What would I do without you? Thank goodness Bill was there. What would have happened if Bill hadn't been there?"

"He hurt me," Tara managed to say but her

mouth was dry and dirt-encrusted. She tried again but Donna lay her hand on Tara's forehead.

"I know, honey. He had to press so hard." Donna cooed her soothing, gentle words. Tara shook her head back and forth, half out of her mind with fear and pain and anger.

"Holding so tight," Tara croaked.

"I know, sweetie, I know." Donna pushed her back once more and secured the bandage. "He had to, honey. To stop the blood. You have to understand."

"No," Tara said, near tears. "Before, Donna. Before."

"I found it."

There he was. Bill Hamilton, savior, standing with long legs apart as if he owned the place. In his hand was the pitchfork, on his body a blood-drenched shirt. Donna flew to him, Tara forgotten. He was Neptune ready to spear his little fishy with his muddy, bloody trident. A little appetizer before indulging in the already helpless main meal.

"This did it?" Donna whispered. Bill ignored her.

"How's she doin'?" She followed him meekly until they both stood over the couch looking down at Tara. But Tara only had eyes for him. He bent his knees; he balanced on the balls of his feet. He smiled at her so gently Tara thought she might cry. Had she imagined Bill Hamilton malicious and savage when he was only saintly? Had she dreamed of her blood running river-like down the drain? She closed her eyes, but he touched her shoulder. "You rest, little lady. You should be tired," Bill cooed, his lips so close Tara could feel the warmth of his breath on her. "You made a hell of a mess out of me, didn't you?" Tara was mute. He leaned into her and maybe his lips brushed her hair. Perhaps he only leaned too far as he stood up and handed Donna the pitchfork, knowing Tara watched him from under lowered lashes, feeling safer with her eyes on him.

One. Two. Three buttons. Bill Hamilton's chest was bared on six. He slipped off his shirt and even Tara could see the stain of her blood down the front of his naked torso. It had matted the dark curling hair that covered his chest and ran a fine line down his stomach to the buckle of his belt. He ran his hand over that hair, his lips parting so slightly Tara hoped she imagined it.

"You should shower, honey. Go on. I can take care of her." Donna was tugging on his arm, taking him away from Tara, reclaiming him for her own. There was no reluctance in him. He turned and kissed her atop her head, touching her own bloodied clothes.

"You need one too," he said and kissed her again, on the lips, a triumphant statement of his hold on Donna that he made her forget about the wounded Tara.

"Later," Donna breathed the moment he let her up for air.

Tara turned her head, too tired to watch him go or see Donna look adoringly after him. Too tired to figure out what was going on here.

"Tara?" Donna touched the wounded woman. "Honey, do you think you'll be all right 'til Bill and I clean up or do you want to go to the hospital now?"

Panicked, Tara struggled to sit up. She held out her good hand. "No. I don't need a hospital. Please just get me home, to my house."

"I'll do no such thing," Donna gasped. "You've got to have a doctor stitch that."

"I will. I promise. Not now. Please. I have an appointment. I have to go." Tara knew how irrational she sounded, but for her, Woodrow was the key to life and death. Her arm was only a painful inconvenience.

"Don't be ridiculous," Donna protested, but Tara already had her feet planted on the floor, her head and arm exploding with a fiery pain she tried to hide without success. With a screech Donna was on her. "Tara, go to the hospital, please. You'll die if you don't. I couldn't be here without you. You're the most important thing in the world to me. Please, Tara. I'm not good at this. Please go—for me."

Donna cried big, real tears. They fell out of her eyes in glops, taking her mascara with them. Tara saw the fright her friend felt. But what could she do? There was no choice as long as that man, that puzzle, remained in her life.

"This can't wait, Donna. It can't," Tara half sobbed, half insisted, pushing Donna up as she forced herself to stand. Donna held on, her grip loosening, afraid to hurt Tara if she held too tight.

"Tara. Tara."

"I have an hour and a half. Just do this for me. Help me get to the house. Put me in a hot bath. I promise, if I'm not feeling a hundred percent better, I'll cancel. Let me try. Please."

"All right, sweetie. All right," Donna fussed, sniffling, afraid Tara was out of her mind. Gingerly, Donna wrapped her arms around her friend and helped her cross the yard. They stopped more often than Donna liked, Tara crumpled once too often. But they forged ahead.

In the house Tara sat on a small vanity chair

watching her bath water run, wondering when she would see it run red, tinged with her own blood somehow spit up from the ground. She couldn't take her eyes off it even as Donna ever so gently stripped off Tara's clothes. Deftly she wadded them into a ball and took them away. When she came back, Tara was already halfway in the tub. Without another word, Donna eased her in. When she was settled, Donna disappeared again, only to return with a huge glass of orange juice. This she put on a small table beside the claw-foot tub.

"You shouldn't go, Tara," Donna whispered, sadly aware that she didn't hold as much sway over Tara as Tara did over her. With a sigh, she closed the door and left Tara alone in the steaming tub.

A second later Tara heard the back door close. She willed her eyes to stay shut, wanting to see nothing but darkness. But the darkness was full of pictures. Blood and mud, gray eyes, a smile, lips that whispered. Donna standing in the arms of a killer or a madman or both. Still Tara Linley kept her counsel and that made her a part of the darkness too.

"Hi."

Tara slid gingerly into the booth knowing she looked like death warmed over. Woodrow had the courtesy not to say anything, or he had a bee in his bonnet that was buzzing like mad and didn't notice how horrid she looked. From his expression Tara assumed it was the latter because he'd forgotten himself too.

Usually a picture-perfect gubernatorial candidate, Woodrow looked like a man on the edge of his luck. He wore a sweater, not a jacket, and Tara noticed a hole in the sleeve. His eyes were red-rimmed. He was a tired man. A defeated one? Just looking at him made Tara feel her own debilitation more acutely. Donna was right. She should have postponed this meeting. But another day with Bill Hamilton was unthinkable. Exhausted, sick, or even dying, she had to finish this.

"I saw the file," he said without ceremony or eye contact. *Along with every photo, statement, and opinion given by everyone involved.* "There's a good chance your guy is the right one. A very good chance, Tara. All we need to confirm is his finger-prints. There was a clean set lifted at the scene and that would be conclusive if we could do a comparison."

"Who's 'we,' Woodrow?"

Woodrow started to lie, then changed course. His mind was made up so no amount of affront could sway him. "George," he said, his eyes leveled at her collarbone.

"You told George?" Tara's voice was so plaintive Woodrow looked her in the eye and his brow twisted in commiseration.

"I did. I told George because I wanted to hear more about the investigation. It's my duty as—"

"Woodrow, please don't try to make it better," Tara moaned.

"And don't try to railroad me," he said, lowering his voice. "We may be friends, Tara, and colleagues, but I have to make my own decision. I didn't accept your proposition on face value. And now that I've seen the photos of that woman, I don't think I could live with myself if I just signed your man over to a hospital and left it at that. Tara, a woman died."

"Oh, Woodrow," Tara sighed. Her arm

throbbed, her head pounded with this unexpected turn of events. "Don't you think that's all I've thought about? I know a woman died. Women die all the time and their killers aren't caught. Sometimes they're killed by the men they love and sometimes by men they don't know, and I don't want another one to be victimized by my client. But he is my client and his welfare has to be uppermost in my mind. I know that sounds hollow, I know it sounds cold, but that's the way it is. The ethics of our legal obligations are in question now. Not just mine as a defense attorney, but yours as a prosecutor. You're not bound to prosecute every case presented to you. You're bound to do what's right for your constituency. I think you've proven you can do that if we take the Strober incident."

"That wasn't murder, Tara," Woodrow snapped.

"It could have been if that building failed," she reminded him quietly. Her voice trailed off until there was hardly a sound made on the last all-important word. When she spoke again, there was a sadness in her voice that pained her to listen to it. "Woodrow, please tell me this isn't what I think it might be."

"Tara, listen to me. I'm in a bad spot. I'm sorry, I really am. At any other time I would stand by you. But I talked it over with George and he agrees. This is big. It needs public closure."

"And it sure as hell wouldn't hurt your campaign if you could deliver the Circle K killer, right?"

"No, it wouldn't. I'm not going to lie to you and I'm not going to tell you this decision has been easy. You have no idea what I've been going through trying to come to it."

"And I don't care," Tara said curtly. "I didn't think you were this low, Woodrow. In fact, I'd al-

ways been proud to death of you. I thought you
had guts. Now I can see you're just like every other
sleazy politician around."

"Your father was one."

"No, he wasn't. Not like you. He never traded
a life for a vote, or justice for a long shot. My
father was a statesman. You're a politician and
that's all you'll ever be. You're using that woman's
death to try and cover up the fact that you want
my client for your own purposes. You don't want
to see her put to rest."

"And you do?"

"Yes. No." Tara shook her head. "I want to do
what's right. Woodrow, listen." Her hand snaked
out to touch his, but he moved it away. "Listen to
me. I spoke with his doctor. The man is afraid for
him and of him. He didn't tell me much, but it
was enough for me to give my client a fifty-fifty
chance of being totally insane. You can't try an
insane man. Where will that get you if you try?"

"He's the one, Tara. I know it and you can't
hide behind the sanity question."

"You haven't seen him."

"You haven't seen what he did." Woodrow's
voice was shrill, the picture of the murder scene
fresh in his mind. "I confirmed everything. The
paper hat, the bullet wounds. Granted, I could be
off base. He could be the trucker that found the
body and called it in. I don't know. If we could
test your client's prints against the set we have,
then we'd know for sure because the driver told
us he didn't touch anything except the pay phone
outside. So either you've got the perp, or you've
got the guy who turned it all in."

Woodrow sighed and ran a hand across his eyes.
As if he'd willed it, a waiter appeared and flour-

ished menus. Tara shook her head. Woodrow did too. The waiter left, none too pleased. Woodrow leaned over the sparkly red laminate table, folded his hands, and looked at her. "I'm not going to petition for anything on behalf of a man I haven't met. What you've given me isn't enough.

"So many things could be going on here. I would be derelict in my duty as district attorney if I didn't take a look at this from all angles. Let him come in and talk to me, Tara. Or George, if you want. Just talk. You know we can't force him to be fingerprinted. Just convince him to come in and tell us what he told you. Let me evaluate him myself, and I'll have George open the file to you. We'll put our heads together."

Tara shook her head in disbelief. Bill Hamilton had messed up the rug of her life and Woodrow Weber had just pulled it right out from underneath her.

"Woodrow, I thought you were my friend," Tara said quietly.

"And you're mine," he challenged. "See, it cuts both ways."

"And so it's a standoff?"

"I guess so," he sighed. "I don't know that there's any other solution. I can't budge on this, Tara."

"Neither can I. I am *legally* bound to my client and intend to honor his request. Even if he wasn't my client anymore, I couldn't hand him over to you." She leaned over the table, lowering her voice. "Have you forgotten what it means to be a lawyer just because you want to be the lawmaker?"

Tara hung her head, not in defeat but to buy time to think. When she raised it again, she was breathing easier, all her energy directed at a solution to this new problem.

"He's been under a psychiatrist's care, medicated since he was an adolescent. He's complex, he's unstable, he isn't a clear person for want of a better term. This man will not blithely walk in and let you question him. I promised to be his advocate when I accepted him as a client. Don't do this, Woodrow. Don't put me in a bind like this."

"I don't want to, Tara, but you're not the only one with principles," Woodrow said, finding it difficult to sound convincing. "I'll make it easy. Just give me his name. I'll run him. I'll do all the work. You don't have to tell me anything except that. You've done your job by asking me to petition. Now I'll do mine."

Tara cocked her arm and propped the elbow on the side of the booth, hoping the change in position would alleviate the throb. Her thumbnail disappeared between her teeth. She looked past Woodrow as she thought. He looked at her wrist. Slowly he reached out as if to touch the bandages. Tara started, then pulled her arm down and put it under the table.

"Did he do that?" Woodrow breathed.

"No," Tara said, unsure if that was the truth, but she exploited the change of subject. "He helped me when this happened. Now I want you to help me. I want him out of my life, Woodrow. I want him off my property. But I want it done the right way."

"He's on your property!" Woodrow paled. "What in the hell have you gotten yourself into? Is this personal? Does this man mean something to you?"

"Yes," she answered, seeing a crack of light behind the door he was closing on her. "It is personal. But not in the way you think. It's a friend of mine, Woodrow. A woman I care deeply about."

"Then you have no choice," he said gravely. "Give him to me."

"Only if you agree to hospitalization," Tara answered, frustrated and tired. He was missing the point and it wasn't even a fine one. "If the doctors find he's sane, they'll release him, and he's all yours, but I'll have fulfilled my obligation. You've maybe waited a few months while he's being evaluated. That's nothing."

"I don't have a few months," Woodrow shot back.

"You do. Stop it. Stop worrying about your campaign," Tara insisted. "You know the rules as well as I do. I can't give you anything that can be used against him: not his name, not a set of prints, not a piece of physical evidence, nothing. I am bound by my oath of confidentiality and I will not breach it." She almost lay across the table, looking very young and almost defeated. "Woodrow, what's it going to take to convince you that he's not arrestable, much less indictable, at this point?"

"I only have your word that he's unbalanced, Tara. I haven't seen a psychological workup, I haven't met the gentleman in question. Bring me something that says he's certifiable, and I'll consider petitioning. I wouldn't have a case anyway if he's legally insane. If you can't do that, then convince this guy to talk to us. He made the first step in contacting you and giving you permission to partially disclose. Obviously he wants some kind of resolution. Do it, Tara. Either one, but do it quick."

Tara hung her head. Woodrow was right. Bill Hamilton had cried out for something. But what? Was this the whimper of a flawed man? Or a cry that was a prelude to a laugh because the joke was on her? Stanford Carrol was closemouthed and Woodrow was taking the goal and going home.

"Okay, Woodrow." Lifting her head, so tired she could cry, Tara Linley acquiesced. "I'll get you what you want. But I want your word that he will be committed per the State so that anything he says to the physicians cannot be used against him in a court of law. Your word, Woodrow."

She'd given as much as she could. If Bill Hamilton was going to stand trial, he would do it with a clean slate. No medical file open to the prosecution should he be judged sane. If that could be arranged, Tara would have done her job.

"I'll see, Tara. I'll do my best," was all he said.

Wearily she slid out of the booth and, without a backward glance, left Lindy's and Woodrow Weber, but not her worries, behind. She drove in a trance, never once tagging the unmarked car that followed her all the way to the driveway of her home.

For the first time in her life Tara locked the doors of her car and, once she was inside, the doors of her home. Ten minutes later she was in bed, a painkiller working its magic on her throbbing arm and her aching head and her heavy heart. Failure was not a familiar or comforting bedfellow.

Almost asleep, it was a struggle to answer the phone when it rang. But answer it she did, only to hear nothing on the other end. Sleep coming fast, she almost hung up when she heard a sound like wind through the cottonwoods. But it wasn't wind, it was someone sighing. A beautiful, almost deep voice pulling in a breath and exhaling it, and in the rhythm it made, Tara was sure she could hear a word. Over and over again she heard the word.

"Bang."

"Bang."

"Bang."

Eleven

"Are we billing this time?" Caroline stood in front of Tara's desk, notepad in hand, waiting for instructions.

"Darn right we're billing this," Tara muttered. The night had been too short, her sleep too disturbed by ridiculous dreams, to make her anything but out of sorts. Bill Hamilton was disturbing every minute of her life; he might as well pay for it. "And if Mr. Hamilton doesn't get his check back posthaste, then we drop him."

Bravado. It was a ridiculous indulgence. She wanted Bill Hamilton to disappear, but on her terms. Putting her fingers to her eyes, Tara wondered if the likes of him could ever be exorcised. No matter what the outcome of all of this, he would color her life, and Donna's, forever; he would shadow their friendship until the end of time and Donna might never even know it.

"Maybe you should cancel your appointments today." Tara lowered her fingers and a worried Caroline came into view. Tara smiled.

"I'm fine. Really. I just didn't sleep well last night."

"Can't imagine why," Caroline drawled. "Did you have anyone look at that arm yet?"

Tara laughed. "Not yet, but I will. Donna went

through my address book this morning and made an appointment for me. Pushy, pushy."

"Good for her. I should have thought of that." Caroline raised an eyebrow. "Are you going to keep it?"

Tara looked at the bandage peeking out from under her buttoned cuff. "The appointment or the arm?"

"Very funny." Caroline pulled a face and held up her notebook. "Are we done with this?"

"Not unless you have something." Tara handed over a pile of correspondence to be typed.

"Messages and mail," Caroline said. "Gary Blackwell still can't get his client to settle. You're going to start picking a jury as scheduled. Johnnie Rae's mother called. She wants to know why it's taking so long to get a trial date."

"Have her take that up with the court clerk," Tara responded quickly, immediately sorry she'd spoken so flippantly. "No, don't tell her anything of the sort. I'll call her. Poor woman is beside herself. Johnnie Rae's her only child. It's got to be hard for her."

"She is a sweet lady. She also started making noises about her bills." Caroline bit her lip, hesitant to bring it up.

"Take care of that, too. We'll put her on a payment schedule. I'll let you know what we work out so you can adjust the records."

"Last one. Ben Crawford called. Wanted you to call him back at your convenience. Nice voice." Caroline handed over the pink message slips. Tara took them, glanced at the top one, and let the name imprint itself on her brain. It was a name she actually etched into her notebooks in high school. It still looked good. Strong letters. The sight of it written still gave her a sense of security.

"Thanks. I'll take care of all of them this morning." She set all the pink slips aside, tapping them thoughtfully. "Nothing from any of the psychiatrists I've talked to?"

Caroline shook her head, hating to be the bearer of bad news.

Tara sighed. "I did think that last one might bite."

"Janet Gardner?" Caroline remembered them all. A steady stream of psychiatrists had been called and summoned and cajoled, but not one wanted the job Tara had to give them. Caroline could only imagine what Tara was telling them. It must be awful. No one she knew ever turned down work.

"Yes, that was the one. Gardner," Tara mused. "Unfortunately her practice was new and she didn't want to get involved in anything that could result in bad press."

"You told her that?" Caroline was astounded.

"I had to. It would take about three seconds for her to put two and two together. Woman murdered, pregnant woman no less, and our guy looking for hospitalization. Women's groups, Right-to-Lifers, they'd all have a field day with it. Dr. Gardner said she wasn't a crusader." Tara pushed aside the message slips and Caroline put the mail in front of her. "Funny thing is, I don't think I am either."

"Don't be silly," Caroline scoffed, already halfway to the door. "You work for a zillion causes."

"Not the kind that are going to ruin me."

"Anything I can do to help?"

"Find me a psychologist who's willing to medicate our new client and consult with him even if our client doesn't want to be medicated or consulted with," Tara said with a half-beaten smile.

"I'll work on it over lunch."

"Thanks," Tara said with a laugh. She waved her off only to call her back. "Actually, would you mind bringing in our hit list? I may give one or two a call again, and see if I can't be more persuasive this time."

"Now?" Caroline asked.

"When you've got a minute."

The door closed and Tara was alone. She riffled through the mail, pushed it aside, put her feet up, and lay back her head. Eyes closed, she thought of what she needed. A psychologist who didn't mind bending the rules a bit, a shoulder to cry on, a voice she trusted, to help her through all this. She couldn't blame a self-respecting psychologist for not wanting to take this one. After all, would she try to convince someone they needed a lawyer? The shoulder to cry on would have been Donna's if this was any other problem than the one at hand. A voice she trusted? Tara fingered the message from Ben, then pushed it aside.

She thought of her father and tried to remember exactly how he looked, how his voice sounded. Desperately she tried to recall his sober demeanor, the way he spoke with such surety, his talent for considering a problem from all angles. But he'd been dead a year and the sound of his voice wasn't as clear as it once was. Harold Linley couldn't help his daughter. No one could help except Woodrow. She would try him one more time.

Unwinding, feet on the floor, Tara had the receiver to her ear when Caroline buzzed. She punched the lighted button, but before she could speak, the door flew open and in popped a friendlier face than the one Tara had been thinking of.

"Hi, sweetie!" Donna's head popped in, but she held the door tight against her neck as if, by exposing only one-eighth of her body, she would bother Tara less.

"Well, hi. Come on in." Tara stood up and waved her in, a grin on her face that wavered but came to full bloom when she saw that Donna was alone.

"Hi yourself. I'm glad to see you so chipper. In the middle of something horrendously important?"

"No, come on." Tara went around her desk to meet Donna halfway, fighting to contain the wash of relief that came over her at times like this. Tara gave her a hug, realizing how easy it would be to whisper in that ear about a secret she was keeping. What would it hurt? Who would know? A well-placed word. A broken pledge, a professional deceit. What was there to lose?

Everything.

Tara's serenity of conscience. Her license to practice law. Bill Hamilton's right to representation and the right to be considered innocent—or at least impaired—until proven otherwise. Donna Ecold's life. Tara's own, perhaps.

But Bill had done nothing unequivocally threatening. So the philosophical triumphed over the physical once again. The law recognized only the extreme threat of harm, or the reality of it, as a basis for breaking faith with a client. Justice could indeed be blind—so she smiled a bit more broadly at her friend and pretended Bill didn't exist.

"Come in. This is wonderful!"

"You're sure you're not busy?" Donna asked.

"No, I told you. Nothing that can't wait for a while."

"Good," Donna reached behind the door, took Tara's coat off the hanger, and held it up. "Then we can have coffee after your doctor's appointment."

"You were so brave! Oh, I just hate stuff like that. I would have passed out for sure. Thank goodness I never had children. I'd hold the pain over their stupid little heads forever." Donna snapped her napkin and rearranged the sugar and creamer. "This place is adorable."

Tara laughed, still shaky. "I hope I can get a good stiff drink."

"I think it's tea only," Donna whispered. "Want to take off?"

"No. I was joking." She touched her arm gingerly. She hadn't expected the stitches. In fact, she had assumed it was too late to do any more damage. How wrong she'd been.

Donna raised her hand and hailed a waitress, tired of their medical talk. The girl who came to the table was a cute little thing dressed like Miss Muffet. Donna gave her the once-over and ordered. "Two Earl Greys and a plate of whatever you have that passes for tea cakes." She waved the speechless girl away with a quick call, "And two waters, please," before turning to Tara. "She looks like she belongs in one of my books."

"You're so uppity. Poor thing looked terrified," Tara clucked. She reached over and touched Donna's hands. "Thanks for making me go to the doctor. I admit, I was going to conveniently forget about that appointment."

"So tell me another." Donna lay her napkin on

her lap. "You needed to go. Someone's got to look out for you, and I love you best," she said softly.

"Thank you, Mama." Tara laughed. "I did need to stop for a minute and just enjoy myself. I'll admit that. So what do you say? Let's keep the momentum going. We'll have our tea, then swing down the street and go shopping. We'll wind up with a late dinner at Rio Bravo. That would be so good . . ."

"I don't . . ."

"Okay. What do you feel like? Something fancier? I know, Le Marmiton. That would be lovely. Just like old times."

"Tara, sweetie," Donna said. "I'd love to poke my head in a few shops and maybe do dinner tomorrow, but I promised Bill I'd make him one of my famous burgers tonight. That is if you don't mind me messing up your kitchen again," she added quickly. "I thought we could all eat around seven, and then maybe we could play Yahtzee again. Like your birthday. I'd really like that, Tara. I'd like it more than I can tell you."

"Sure. Yes, why not," she said. Tara's chest tightened. Flash points of resentment banged about in her brain. "Sounds like a heck of a lot of fun."

"Boy, that was convincing." Donna rolled her eyes. "We can hardly wait for you to get home if you're going to be such a fireball."

"Donna, give me a break. It's been a tough day. I've been to work, had needles poked into me, and I've still got things waiting for me at the office that I didn't finish."

"Hey. Hey." Donna called a time-out. "A minute ago you were ready to go on a shopping spree and stay in town late for dinner."

"And a minute ago," Tara reminded her tersely,

"I thought I might have some quality time with my friend. Isn't that the reason you came here in the first place? I thought you wanted to celebrate my birthday, not flaunt a new piece of a—"

Miss Muffet returned with their tea and a plate of lemon squares. The two women sat back, ignoring both, glaring at one another. Tara managed a thank-you before the girl flounced off.

"You're jealous," Donna teased, honing the impertinent edge to her voice, a mean intonation like little girls use on playgrounds.

"That's absurd," Tara said, disgusted. "Unfortunately, it's exactly the kind of interpretation I would expect from you. Donna, it's time to grow up. Stop hanging out with juveniles and see if you can hold your own with real men. Maybe then there'd be some merit to that kind of charge."

"I was just joking, Tara." Donna crossed her arms on the table. "But it is interesting what flies when you throw it up, isn't it?"

"I think you're reading a heck of a lot into a situation, and I think you're giving yourself credit you don't deserve."

"Well, now we get to it. I'm stupid, you're not. Big lawyer, Tara; dopey children's book writer, Donna. Is that it? Well, I may not have enough brains in my head to attract the Pope, but you've lost everything that could possibly attract a real man like Bill." Donna spit those last words at Tara. People were looking and she didn't care.

"I'm not going to sit here and listen to this nonsense," Tara said, crumpling her napkin and tossing it on the table. "I have better things to do."

"That's it. Run away. Just like you always do. Run away from Ben when he needed you, run away from love, run away from me now that I'm happy.

You know why you're going to run? It's because I'm strong now. I never was before, but Bill gives me strength and you don't like it. It means that you aren't the center of the universe anymore."

Tara was up, tossing bills on the table, her lips tight, eyes downcast, anger bubbling just below the surface.

"You don't know what you're talking about."

"Yes I do. It's been coming for years. You're hiding, Tara. You try to make it seem that you're just thinking things through but you're hiding. You hid behind your father when he was alive. I always thought you were selfless, helping him where you could when you could. But you were really comfortable, back there behind him. It meant people wouldn't approach you. You were defined without ever uttering a word. That was so safe, wasn't it, Tara?"

Tara turned on her heel, aware that every eye in the small teahouse was on them. She walked to the door, identifying sounds of disarray behind her: overturned china, Donna wiping up tea, finally ignoring it, and hurrying after her.

"And what about Ben?" Tara pushed through the door, Donna followed, a Mutt to Tara's taller Jeff, annoying as she hopped around, dogging Tara's steps. "How convenient for him to have an accident that kept him in hospitals and rehabs. How convenient so Tara didn't have to deal with the ugly, seamy side of life."

"And what about your job? What about that?" Donna crowed. "It's bloodless. There's no life in it, no compassion, no—"

"There's honor in it, damn you." Tara had turned so quickly Donna had to jump back. Tara towered above her, righteous indignation etched on every feature of her face. Anger colored her neck but left her cheeks pale. When she spoke again, her voice had lowered, the tension was heightened. "There's honor in the way I live and in what I do. You, on the other hand, haven't a clue. You run around, jumping into situations, and cry when they turn against you. Let me tell you, Donna . . ." Tara moved closer, leaning into her friend. "You're in a hell of a situation now. Jealous is the last thing I am. Concerned. Frightened. Those adjectives might work. But you, little lady, are thinking with something that isn't even close to your brain and you don't have a clue what you've got your claws into."

Tara turned and punched the button that would give her permission to cross the street. She punched it so hard it sent a shot of pain straight up her injured arm. Donna grabbed her and there was another kick. She turned angry eyes on Donna. The other woman backed off, a fleeting expression of sorrow and guilt on her face. Tara exploited it. "And if you want to talk about changes, look at you. You used to be so happy-go-lucky. Now you're so anxious you need constant reassurance that Bill is the jewel you keep swearing he is. Are you having second thoughts, Donna? Or maybe you realized he's just a little off, but you're too proud to admit it. Maybe you don't know how to untangle yourself and you're hoping I'll give you a good reason. Maybe you're trying to goad me into saving you."

"Nice theory. So tell me what I've got myself into, and let me make a real adult decision about Bill. Let me actually think about our relationship instead of just lying on my back and spreading 'em. Isn't that what you think, Tara?" Donna moved closer again. "Or maybe that's the part you're jealous of."

"That's disgusting and beneath you," Tara snapped. "I'm Bill's attorney. Did you know that?"

"Of course." Donna raised her chin proudly, but kept her lashes lowered. To hide the truth? To save face? Tara would never know. "He told me you were doing business."

"Did he tell you what kind?"

"No. Tell me. Go on. Shock me. Make me shiver. Tell me what's got your holier-than-though panties in such a knot, Tara."

"I can't," she screamed.

Donna was breathing hard. Her cheeks were red with the cold and now Tara thought Donna looked a little silly in her head-to-toe chile pepper ensemble. She pulled away, looking at her with the dispassionate eye of an attorney. How many women were there like this, dependent upon men who didn't deserve to follow them down the street, much less lead them? With a tremulous, defeated breath, Tara spoke.

"I can't tell you, Donna. I won't tell you. Go ask Bill. Go crawl into bed with him and ask why he needs my help."

"I will," Donna whispered. "And while I'm doing that, why don't you just lie all alone in yours and figure out why it probably won't matter to me at all."

Across the street, the little illuminated man flashed on. It was time to walk. Tara did.

"Hi." Charlotte was sitting on the porch, cigarette in hand, flicking ashes over the railing into the rosebushes below.

"Hi," Tara called, coming up the walk.

Charlotte took a last drag, expertly flipped the butt into the flower bed below, and stood at the top of the stairs waiting for Tara to reach her. When she did, Charlotte gave her a kiss and put her arm around Tara's waist to walk her into the house.

"I'm so glad you could come. I meant to get back to you about taking you to dinner for your birthday, but things got out of hand." They stepped into the house. Tara loved Charlotte's calming taste, all muted colors, peach and beige, green and blue. Small patterns on chairs, dark wood, a feeling of permanence. She closed the door behind them. "I just couldn't get Woodrow's schedule and mine together, so I decided not to try to do anything fancy and just make it the two of us."

"I'm glad you didn't." Tara dropped her purse by the door. "Believe me, your timing was perfect. I was desperate to put my feet up and be waited on. I don't think I could have faced another restaurant."

"Sounds like you've had a rough day. I'm glad I called then," Charlotte said, walking on ahead and calling over her shoulder. "Come on into the kitchen with me. Since it's just us girls, I figured you wouldn't mind casual."

"As if anything you ever do is casual." Tara laughed, pushing herself to good humor. Unfortunately, the memory of her icy parting with Donna blocked the effort. Tara slipped out of her jacket and tossed it onto the couch as she passed.

"I've made a new dish. You're going to love it. Bacon, sun-dried tomatoes, and that's just the pasta. The sauce is even better." Charlotte was bending over to peer into the oven when Tara joined her. "Homemade bread too."

"Beats burgers," Tara muttered.

"What?" Charlotte checked a pot atop the stove and an incredible scent filled the air. Tara smiled properly now.

"Nothing. Private joke." She was feeling better, here where life was stable with a predictable friend.

"Oh. Hope it's a good one. We haven't been doing much laughing around here. This whole thing with Strober Industries is causing Woodrow such grief I've never seen him so disheartened, Tara. Sit." She motioned to a ladderback chair. Tara didn't need to be asked twice. Charlotte had the wineglasses filled and was sitting opposite her ready for a good chat.

"I saw the interview with him this morning on television. He looked good, he sounded good. What he did was perfectly ethical. The problem was taken care of and that should be that."

"It would be if this wasn't election time. You know they found out how it happened, don't you? How the governor got hold of this information?"

Tara raised a brow. "Really? I didn't know there was an investigation."

"All very quiet, naturally. Sort of a personal inquiry," Charlotte told her. "Woodrow had Sandy looking into a few things. What else is a campaign manager for after all? Want some munchies?" Tara shook her head. "Anyway, it was a woman who was laid off ages ago. She passed the memo along to person unknown for a fee. Now she's terrified Woodrow will prosecute for theft even though that's not what it was at all. She just found it in her personal things."

"He's not going to, is he?"

"Of course not," Charlotte sniffed, her arms crossed as she rested against the counter. "Can you imagine? Woodrow prosecuting a woman who's been out of work for almost a year, for giving the authorities something that could be construed as proof that Woodrow is the real culprit. He might as well stand on the Senate steps and wait for the old knife in the back."

"Well," Tara sighed, "I'd say that Woodrow is about due for a change of fortune. He's really been weathering one storm after another."

"I'll say. I could have shot that stringer who showed up at the party at La Posada. Everything was planned so perfectly, then there she was. I should have seen her coming." Charlotte poured the wine and gave a glass to Tara.

"The way I should have seen Ben coming?" Tara asked. Charlotte colored, smiling a sweet and innocent smile.

"Mad?"

"Nope," Tara admitted.

"Heard from him?"

"He called," she said.

"And?"

"And I've been busy. I'll call him. I promise. I actually would like to apologize for running out on him that night. Your pot's going to boil over." Tara raised a hand and Charlotte jumped to rescue the pasta.

"I saw that. You were out of there like a bat out of hell. What was going on?" Tara ignored the question; Charlotte ignored the silence. "So you're feeling better?" Charlotte drained the pasta, added a squirt of olive oil, and smiled at Tara.

"What?" Charlotte nodded and Tara raised her arm. "Oh, much, thanks. I can't imagine how that happened. My mind was on other things."

"Things can happen that way. I know I worry

about Woodrow when he has a lot on his mind."
She sipped at her wine, stirred something in another pot, opened the oven, and checked the bread. "I think of him having a car accident, or having a heart attack or something. But sometimes I just worry about him failing because that would just kill Woodrow."

"Everyone fails sometimes, Charlotte," Tara said. "You can't protect a grown man from that. Besides, Woodrow can hold his own. Grief is something he can dish out."

Tara twirled her wineglass and looked out the picture window onto the Webers' impeccable backyard. Charlotte's husband, that selfless public servant, wasn't all he appeared to be, but it wasn't her place to point that out.

"I hear you're giving some back," Charlotte answered, taking her attention from the stove, giving it to Tara. "Grief, I mean." The two women looked at one another for a minute that stretched to two. Charlotte smiled and held out her hand. "Pass me that colander, will you, Tara?" It was in her hands and a second pot of pasta drained by the time Tara recovered her wits.

"Charlotte?" Tara was cautious and Charlotte was chatty.

"Get the salad out of the refrigerator, will you?" Tara stayed where she was. Charlotte got the salad herself. They both knew what was coming and Charlotte had the chutzpah to force the issue. "Tara, come on, we'll talk about it over dinner. Sit down again, have some wine. It's no big deal."

Charlotte made up a plate for Tara and was holding one for herself. Tara looked at neither. Her appetite had died. Charlotte fluttered her lashes and finally put her plate on the table.

"Okay. I'm sorry I said anything, but I couldn't help it. Woodrow's worried about this thing between you and him, and I'm worried about him and you. There, I said it. Now, please eat. I worked all day on that."

"Woodrow put you up to this, didn't he?"

Charlotte lay her fork down with great deliberation. She reached for her throat, but the pearls weren't there and this wasn't a meeting of the sisterhood of homemakers. "Of course not. Woodrow can fight his own battles. I'm telling you as a friend that I'm concerned that this Circle K thing could ruin a friendship that has stood for years."

"It can't possibly, Charlotte. Our profession has nothing to do with how we feel about one another. Those are two different relationships," Tara answered, knowing if Charlotte went much further she would amend that statement.

"Not if what you're doing professionally affects your friend's ambitions. Not if you are deliberately holding back information on a dangerous man, one whose incarceration could result in a safer community as well as help Woodrow get what he wants."

"I'm not a part of Woodrow's campaign, Charlotte"—Tara pushed away from the table—"and I'm not sure you should be quite so well versed on the details of the district attorney's business."

"Now that's ridiculous," Charlotte laughed humorlessly. "I'm Woodrow's wife. You think he doesn't tell me what he does with his day?"

"I would have thought he'd keep information general, but it seems that Woodrow likes to fill you in on the specifics. And you're the second person today who doesn't seem to think there's anything wrong with shading a line here or there between professional ethics and personal curiosity. What's this world coming to?" Tara drawled and pushed the chair into the table as she headed out.

Charlotte put her hand on Tara's wrist, pulled back as if afraid she'd hurt her, then realized it wasn't the one that was bandaged. Tara shook her off. Instead of trying to stop her, Charlotte followed.

"Tara, there are no secrets between a husband and wife. Jobs are things that last for a while and then you go on, but trust and friendship between two people who are married is forever. I just don't understand why you're upset."

Tara laughed, a short harsh sound, and called over her shoulder. "Charlotte, you sound like one of those commercials for marriage counseling videos. This is so weird. First Woodrow makes all this harder than it should be and now he sends you to convince me that I'm the one who's being unreasonable? Or is it dishonorable? This is so rich, Charlotte, I can't tell you how it makes me feel that you and Woodrow have decided to be so supportive. I'm glad you've had a chance to discuss your strategy in detail. It's a damn sight more courtesy than your husband has shown me. He gave me two minutes in a coffee shop before he decided to hang me out to dry."

"Stop it. He did no such thing." They were in the living room now and Charlotte looked odd in the half light, too thin, too pale, too tight. But she softened quickly, so effectively that Tara wondered if she was the rigid one, taking out her anger and frustration over Donna on everyone. "Woodrow is very concerned about the decision he made regarding your client. And I think that you shouldn't be so inflexible. There's a lot at stake here, Tara, and it's not just Woodrow's standing in the polls. There's the safety of the community to consider. You don't seem to think about that at all. You interpret Woodrow's stand as purely political when it seems only right to bring a man like this to trial."

"I'm not going to discuss the individual versus the community at large. What I will point out is that you are acting as if my client is guilty of this crime."

"But he confessed to it. That's what you told Woodrow."

"And, may I remind you, that was a confidence I had been given permission to share with Woodrow. Besides, he hasn't been proven sane enough to stand trial," Tara stated. "Charlotte, after all these years of living with an attorney you should understand a lawyer's obligation to his client. I won't consider Woodrow's career needs, I won't discuss your concerns or criticisms of my actions. I will listen to my conscience. If you and Woodrow bend the rules, then you live with that. Any behavior can be justified. I could even justify murder in a court of law. But I'm not going to do that. I'm going to help my client."

"Very nice, Tara, but hardly the real world."

"In the real world the finger is pointed your way when you don't do what someone wants. I'm selfish, I'm jealous, I'm endangering the public wellbeing. I've heard it all now, Charlotte, and the one thing you forget is that there is no evidence against this man. No one has seen him. No one has examined him. No one can tie him to anything that happened at the Circle K. This is a witch hunt and I am not going to be the next one to speak in tongues." Tara grabbed her jacket and put it on.

"And you're forgetting that he admitted killing that woman—unless you're lying about that."

"To what purpose?" Tara challenged.

Charlotte shrugged. "I wouldn't know. That was a stupid thing to say."

"Thank you for that anyway." She buttoned up, ready to go.

"But think of how you could help your client if you worked with Woodrow instead of against him. The longer you leave this man hanging, the greater the chance he'll hurt someone else."

Tara searched for her purse. "Did Woodrow give you a script? I have to tell you, the more you talk, the more determined I am to honor my client's wishes. I'm glad he came to me. If he'd turned himself in, he would have been lynched by now." Tara took a deep, rattling breath and glared at the other woman.

"Charlotte, I can't stay in this room one more minute. I don't blame you at all for trying to change my mind. But I have been pummeled and knocked around today by people I love and respect and I've had it up to here." She swiped a hand across her forehead. "I'll call you when I cool off. Just do me a favor. Don't put your nose in this one."

"Hi, you two." Tara whirled toward the door as Woodrow pulled it open. "Something smells good."

He stopped as if physically restrained by the angry charge in the room. "I would have been here sooner if I'd known you were coming for dinner, Tara." He smiled hesitantly.

"Don't worry, Woodrow. I'm not staying for dinner," she said.

"Tara, please . . ." Charlotte made an effort to stop her but it wasn't a very heartfelt one.

"Bye, Woodrow. Call me. I think we better talk." Tara passed him fast, pivoted, and came right back. "You know, Woodrow, you're not batting a thousand these days. If anyone should be helping anyone, it should be you. My dad lent his name to your campaigns and so have I. We've given money. I've done everything I can when we are on different sides of the courtroom to conduct myself professionally so that we don't have problems like this. I respected you and I trusted you, Woodrow. But I don't anymore.

"From here on, until this situation is taken care of, we're going to do this the right way. No more unrecorded meetings. No more handshakes. No more social engagements. No more fund raisers. I'll memo you on your promise to petition if I supply a psychological profile. I'm going to get you that profile. Then we'll go back to the way things used to be."

Tara walked out of the Weber house. Charlotte came to Woodrow's side and together they watched Tara until she got into her Jeep and drove off. It was cold but both of them stood in the open doorway awhile longer.

"I'm sorry, Woodrow," Charlotte said. "I thought if I asked her woman-to-woman, she'd come to see things your way."

"I wish you'd talked to me, Charlotte, before you talked to her," Woodrow said. He put his hands on her shoulders and kissed her neck. "I think I've just lost her support for the campaign."

"You can win without her."

"You think so?"

"I know it," Charlotte said and turned toward the kitchen. "Dinner in five," she called over her shoulder, taking out a cigarette to calm her nerves as she went. Woodrow would just have to understand. It was only one—in the house—after all.

Woodrow closed the door and went to wash up. Looking in the mirror he decided Charlotte was right. The Linley name was old and respected, and looked good on fund-raising programs, but times had changed. It wasn't the draw it once was. The only thing Tara Linley really had that he wanted for his campaign was the Circle K killer.

Twelve

She'd walked through the kitchen, exchanging a polite but restrained greeting with Donna. Bill sat at the table. He gave her a "hey-little-lady" and Tara thought she would burst. Clothes changed, she went outside and saddled Shinin'. There had been a moment when she reached for the bridle that had given her pause, but Tara was just angry enough to let it pass. At this point a pitchfork through her heart might be enough to put her out of her misery. She cinched the girth with a vengeance, apologized to Shinin', and swung herself into the saddle a minute later, only to be stopped by a call from the dark.

"Tara?" Bill Hamilton stood in front of the gate to the corral. Shinin' danced, anxious to leave yet wary of the human being in his way.

"Not now, Bill," she said, angry he'd followed her out. She glanced quickly at the house. Donna was in the window, shadowed and still. "You better go back in. You've caused enough trouble for a lifetime."

"Heard you and Donna had words. I'm sorry 'bout that. Damn shame, if you ask me. I never wanted that to happen." He took a step forward, then another. Shinin' was shying but Tara held the reins tight.

"You don't feel bad at all, Bill. Maybe you're in your playful mode, having a little joke at my expense. I think you like this, me and Donna at odds. Exactly what kind of kick do you get from it?"

"None. I swear." He held a hand to his chest. He was close now and she could see him clearly in the night. He wore a denim shirt, open almost to the waist, and an expression closed to her. His eyes glittered but she couldn't see them clearly. That was a blessing.

"Did she ask you about our business?"

"Yep. But I couldn't tell her. I care for that woman too much. I don't want her to wonder, don't want her to ever wake up in the night and think I'm gonna do her wrong, understand?"

"She already thinks so. She thinks you want to get in my pants, Bill. What do you think about that?"

"Nice to know she figures I have good taste." He laughed. "She thinks the same about you, Tara."

"I know. Donna gives herself too much credit."

"That's harsh, Tara. And too bad," Bill was so close he stood just under Shinin's jaw. The horse threw his head. Bill put up a hand, calmly, casually, as if he could will the creature away. "You are a pretty lady. Not delicate like her. A little handful, that's what Donna is. And a bird in the hand . . ." Bill leaned into her, his chin almost on her knee. "You know what they say about the bush?"

"I know, Bill," Tara said quietly.

"Good. So you know I'm sincere about her. Real sincere. Same as about you gettin' me help."

"Can't do it, Bill. Not without your cooperation." Tara looked into the night, talking as if he wasn't even there. "The DA wants a psychological workup. You've got to cooperate on that one, and until you do, we're in a standoff. Simple as that."

"Nothin's that simple, babe. You know what I am. You tell him. We don't play games, you and me. Find me the right doctor and I'll sure think 'bout doin' a couple of tests. Trouble is, I might flunk." He looked sorrowfully at her. "Then I'm out on a limb. I'm on the run. I'm with Donna forever." He was whispering now and Tara felt his face as he lay it against her thigh. He nuzzled there, spreading his arms cross-like over Shinin's flank, reaching all the way to the horse's neck as he pressed against her leg and the gold-colored animal. The contact was so surprising, so electrifying, Tara bolted beneath it. Without thinking, frantic, she dug into Shinin', letting loose of the reins, allowing him to tear through the gate and into the night without concern for the man she left behind.

Tara sped through the darkness, across her land and beyond to the fields that no longer belonged to her. She rode until she saw the lights of home, civilization she had no desire to confront. With a cry she wheeled and headed back again, only to do the same before she reached her house. The cold night was cut by her cries of frustration and those same cries urged Shinin' on until he breathed as hard and deep as she. Beneath her thighs the animal moved with a surety and might that excited her. Tara leaned into him, commanding him with a flick of her wrist, a tug at the rein, a press of her knees into him. And he responded: right, left, right again, and a full head. On his back Tara pressed into the saddle, erasing thoughts and replacing them with a physical pleasure that erupted inside a part of her so private no one had ever touched it. Until tonight. It wasn't just the horse, or the ride in the black night; it wasn't the cold or the feel of her own body responding to the pleasure she felt. It was Bill. He had touched her. He had laid his head on her body and pressed himself into the horse, becoming a part of both of them. God forgive her, she had felt what Donna must feel. She had felt desire so swift and intense as to leave her mindless. What was in him had passed to her and she felt the madness like a gift.

That was what she wanted to rid herself of. Instead she used it, matching it with her own anger and frustration. And when she was done, when the horse stood panting in the middle of the field in the middle of the night, with his exhausted rider lying over his back and stroking his mane, something came into Tara's head. A glimmer of an idea, just a seed of a thought. Perhaps this was what he'd wanted in the first place. Perhaps it wasn't Donna at risk at all. In some way, somehow, Bill Hamilton's next victim was her.

Tara walked Shinin' back across the fields, staying close to the river as she went. The extravagant sensations, the unbridled inference she had imagined alone in the dark, had been tamed. There was no conspiracy here to victimize her. Bill needed Tara too much. Donna was in no danger. A meal ticket seldom was. Her home was still there and standing, glowing golden through windows where a light had been left on. By design or mistake she didn't care. What had been up was down, those who had loved her loved themselves more, and an oath taken when she had passed the bar so many years ago seemed suddenly a tremendous burden. All she wanted now was food, rest, and in the morning she would step closer to the middle of the road on this thing. Surely she and Woodrow could work out something that would be acceptable to Bill.

Slipping from Shinin', she bedded him down with a pat on the neck before peeling off her gloves as she glanced toward the guest house. It was dark, Bill and Donna sleeping tangled in one another's arms, she imagined. She didn't speculate on what they dreamed, but strode on, pushing open the door to the main house, equally hungry and tired. Hunger overrode exhaustion. The kitchen was the next stop.

Flipping on the light, Tara blinked in the brightness, thinking that soup would warm her. As her eyes adjusted, she stopped thinking about food, and looked around to see if anything was out of place. The kitchen was pristine save for an ebony-handled carving knife, its blade embedded in the butcher block. Tara blew on her hands, trying to warm them, as she went to fetch it, only to pause. Atop the impeccably scrubbed butcher block, beneath the blade of the knife, was a note written in Donna's childish scribble. Tara's hand went behind her back, instinct telling her not to touch it, common sense telling her that caution was ridiculous.

Touch it she did. The news was a flash, scrawled in the throes of excitement. Donna was engaged. Bill Hamilton was a bridegroom to be. Around the message she had drawn a curlicued heart and through the heart the knife had been jammed, its handle obscuring the bottom half of the page. Grasping it tight, Tara wiggled it, yanking it out of the wood. With her other hand she picked up the note. In bold, block print, the message had been amended, Bill laughing while he wrote " 'Til death do we part" before he had driven the knife through that papery heart, drawing no blood but making Tara's run cold.

Sick. Furious. Appalled at the grossness of the joke, the intimate inference that they shared a dangerous understanding of the way Bill's mind worked. She didn't want to think about it, much less understand it. Tara wanted rest. She wanted her life back. She wanted her friends back. She wanted to wake up in the morning and know there was a calendar for her to follow. No more insane teasing from Bill Hamilton. No more idiotic accusations of jealousy from Donna. This lunacy would stop now. Tara threw open the back door and stormed across the yard.

"Wake up! Bill, get out here." Tara banged on the door, dancing on the doorstep of the guest house, jumping off the steps to look through the window. But the curtains were drawn and the night was dark and silent. She lay her fist on the wood again, pounding and pounding. There was no one to hear if she screamed at the top of her lungs and she wished there were. Let someone ask questions, let someone call the cops. Let them take this out of her hands. Send her anyone else, but not someone whom Donna loved. Anyone but that. She raised her fist and dropped it again. One. Two. Three times.

Bill was right. He was nuts. He needed help, but if she was going to get it for him, then he had to stay out of her space. She could not, would not, live with him. That was Donna's choice, not hers.

"Bill," she screamed, "I want to talk to you now. Get out here."

The door opened. She shut her mouth and clenched her jaw. One step back and the knife was held at the ready. Tara knew only that it was there and that holding it made her feel safer. But the door stopped opening. Tara stepped forward and gave it a little push, her knees buckling in the face of such frightful uncertainty. He had touched her tonight, laid his hands on her. He had watched her and she was shaken. What was left? What would he do now that she had come for him? With a courage fueled by desperation, Tara pushed a little harder.

"Don't you play these sick little games, you bastard," Tara hissed. "I don't care if we wake the dead, you're going to explain this and all the rest of it. The phone call. I know I didn't dream it. The . . ."

Slowly the door opened all the way. Donna, half asleep, held on to the knob and leaned against the jamb.

"Tara, come on, that hurt." She mumbled, her voice slurred with a sleepiness born of pills. "What time is it? What are you doing?"

"Donna, I need to talk to Bill. Just go back to bed and send Bill out here. I need to see him. Now . . ." Tara's voice broke.

"Don't you ever give up, Tara. Talk in the morning," she muttered and the door began to close again. Tara put her hand out, more gently this time so she could reach around and take hold of Donna and pull her outside onto the stoop. Swiftly she closed the door behind them.

"Tara, don't. It's freezing. I'm not dressed," Donna whined, coming awake now as Tara wanted. She held Donna close, not for warmth but from a need to be secretive. This was better. Much better than confronting Bill.

"Listen to me, Donna. Listen good. Look at this." Tara held up the knife. It looked uglier in the dark, a dull gleam running up the backbone of the long blade. She held Donna tight, shaking her as she ordered, "Wake up and look at this."

"What? It's a knife, Tara. I've got twenty at home." Donna twisted, trying to squirm her way out of Tara's grip.

"Ever had one through your heart?" Tara growled. "Huh? Ever thought about that?"

"Wha . . . ?" Donna was shaking her head now, her eyes blinking like crazy as she fought the effects of her sleeping pill.

"Through your heart," Tara said, punching each word for emphasis. "That sweet little note you left me about your engagement. Well, your intended left his own little message. He drew another heart. He wrote, ' 'Til death do we part,' then stuck this through the heart. Through it, Donna. Don't you understand? Don't you see what he's trying to tell me?" Tara took a deep breath. Her eyes darted to the door. It was still closed, the house still silent, Tara still frightened. Her whisper grew more urgent still. "Don't get any clothes, just come with me to the house. I want you to leave tonight. Bill can stay here, and I'll take care of him. He needs help, Donna, and I don't want you around if it gets ugly."

Donna was staring now, standing quietly in the circle of Tara's arm. She looked drunk. She looked astonished. Finally she looked amused, and then she started to giggle.

"Tara. You are getting weird. Very, very, very weird." Donna put her hand out, touched the knife, then backed off to the door, clearly annoyed. "It was a joke. He thought our news would be like a knife through your heart. We shouldn't have laughed about it, but we did. He stuck the note to the board with a knife. Big deal."

"Donna, you don't understand. Donna . . ." Tara insisted in a frantic whisper, but Donna already had the door open.

"I'm freezing, Tara. Go to bed. Sleep it off or whatever." She waved behind, shooing Tara away from her.

"I'm not drunk," Tara said, throwing herself against the door and holding her hands across the frame. "He hurts people, Donna. He's going to hurt you."

"Oh, please." Donna turned back and rolled her eyes. "That man loves me. He took me to bed tonight and touched me and loved me and I loved him back. Want to look?" She held out her arms. "See any scratches? Bruises? Want to watch next time just to make sure I come out unscathed?"

"I'm not crazy," Tara said flatly.

"Really?" Donna asked. "Could've fooled me."

The door closed. Tara was alone in the cold dark wondering if maybe, just maybe, she had lost her mind.

Quietly, in a fog, Donna slipped back into bed with Bill. She turned on her side, asleep before her head hit the pillow. Beside her, Bill Hamilton lay quietly, his eyes on the ceiling, his mind on the pain that shot through his head. Then, there was nothing.

Thirteen

"Damn right, I'm mad. I'm furious, Woodrow. I've never been so humiliated in my entire life. George Amos called first thing this morning. I thought it had something to do with Johnnie Rae's case. But, no. He wants to ask about the accessory thing. Like he would even have a clue. Accessory, my foot. The man has lost it if he's trying to intimidate me on my turf. And I blame you. You've put me and my client in an untenable position. I'll be lucky if my client doesn't go to the bar with a complaint."

"Tara, I swear, I didn't know he'd do anything like that. He's just trying to do what he thinks is right."

"Don't you dare defend him! If he's that ignorant, read him chapter and verse about the laws against harassment."

Tara walked faster and Woodrow had no choice but to catch up. The snow had finally come, not in fat lovely flakes but in flat wet drops that had a terrible tendency to transform themselves into hail pellets every ten minutes. Tara's head was down as she walked, her fedora pointed into the mess. Woodrow had run out after her call without hat or umbrella and now his fine hair was plastered to his head. He looked ridiculous and Tara was glad. It was a small thing, but she was feeling petty today.

"I wasn't going to defend him. Give me a break, Tara. I thought he'd be discreet. And you're the one that put me in the mess anyway. Did it ever occur to you that if you'd simply asked me for state-ordered commitment without the details we wouldn't be going through this?"

"Oh, right. You'd do that without asking for particulars. Woodrow, I trusted you. I tried to do everything aboveboard and you're the one who screwed the whole thing up."

"I reiterate, Tara, I did as you asked, I satisfied my own curiosity about the case. You know you're not the only one concerned with doing the right thing. I wasn't going to just waltz in to George and peek at a file and come back and report to you. I have responsibilities, too."

Tara took a hard left and hurried across the plaza, past the drained fountain and its signs warning against swimming, past the weatherbeaten benches under the concrete pavilions that shaded downtowners when the sun was high and hot. But it was cold and this plaza was deserted except for a knot of homeless men gathered around a trash can, chatting and moving back and forth on the balls of their feet trying to keep warm. It obviously hadn't occurred to them to risk the wrath of the city and build a fire in that can.

They shared the space with a hot dog vendor who braved the weather to hawk his wares. The dogs smelled great, but Tara would wait to fuel the fire. She pushed through the glass doors of the Bernalillo County Government Center and waited for Woodrow to catch up before she started again.

"I do give you credit, Woodrow. I always have.

It's not easy being a government attorney. But you miss the point. Ambition I understand. I even understand wanting to use this situation. What I can't understand is how free you've been with information. George didn't need to know it was my client. Charlotte certainly shouldn't be involved in any decision making. I can't believe either one of them held a gun to your head and made you tell. All you've done is muddy the waters on something we agreed could be handled fairly and discreetly."

Tara tapped her foot. She didn't look at Woodrow any longer as she continued through the building.

"I confided in you as a friend. I told you that there was someone involved that I cared about. You decided to ignore that very human factor in this equation. If you hadn't, business would have been taken care of and he would have been out of her life and mine and I'd be sleeping a whole lot easier." She turned on him to make her point. "Woodrow, did it ever occur to you that *I* might get hurt? Did you ever wonder what would happen if you did prevail and sent this guy to prison? Did you think about him? Do you know what happens to unstable guys in prison? Do you, Woodrow? They die and it isn't pretty what's done to them before they die. Which of these scenarios is worth an election?"

"Okay, okay. I get your point." Woodrow peeled off his gloves as he followed her to the elevator. They waited. Tara pushed the button, Woodrow opened his wet coat, reached in the back pocket of his slacks, and pulled out a comb. "Look, Tara." The comb was back in his pocket and he spoke quietly to her. "You know, Tara, I live here too. I worry about Charlotte, knowing a guy like that is out there. I worry about all of us. My stand is valid too. You've seen the system. You know that some-times the cracks are huge and someone can fall right through. I don't want him committed only to find him unindictable because he spilled his guts to a doctor who can't be subpoenaed."

Tara looked at the floor, some of the fight going out of her. "I know it's tough, Woodrow. You've got a lot of irons in this fire. I don't think you're being malicious." She sighed again, not as angry, but still wary and wishing she could explain this so he felt what she did. "You haven't seen him. That's all. You haven't talked to him."

"I'd like to."

"Why can't you take my word for it?"

"Because I can't, and I'm sorry about your friend. Really I am. That's the pits. And I know it doesn't count much that I'm concerned too, but I'm not going to let you railroad me, Tara. I'm just asking to talk to him. If we have something to hold him on, I will, but he'll get a competency hearing."

Tara rolled her head back and forth. "Woodrow, you keep thinking it's an easy thing for me to give you this man's name. Even if I did, even if some-how we skirted all the ethical issues, then what? All you'll have is a name. What are you going to arrest him for? He hasn't done anything. Nope, introducing you two is a lousy deal." Tara shook her head and punched the up button one more time. "This whole thing is a lousy deal. Why is it that elevators take forever?"

"Tara, that won't do any good." The bell dinged just as Woodrow admonished her. She gave him a tired and wry smile, then stepped in ahead of him and whipped off her hat. Her hair cascaded past her shoulders, her cheeks were red with cold, her eyes snapped blue like the color of a brittle winter sky, an Albuquerque sky. But today it didn't come together, something vital was missing to make her beautiful. She lay back against the wall.

"Woodrow, I'm sorry for all this." Tara took a deep breath. "Never in my wildest dreams did I imagine I'd have a situation like this on my hands. Last night he did something strange and I thought I'd come to you and see if we couldn't come up with some compromise. But then George called." She looked up to find Woodrow looking back at her. "I realized then that this man, incompetent or not, could not be used by anyone. The only good I can work for is his. Can't you see that, Woodrow? If we wheel and deal and fudge the rules, then we're not representatives of the law anymore. We're simply advocates of our own goals."

"You can let me talk to him, Tara. It isn't unreasonable for me to want that. Even you have to agree. Even you would want to assess a situation personally before doing something that might hurt your career. You would, Tara." Woodrow's eyes softened as if he hated being the one to hold the mirror up for her. Tara rolled her head back along the wall of the elevator.

"But you won't see it, Woodrow. You won't see how crazy he is. He's . . ." She could not describe Bill Hamilton. She looked back at her companion. "You feel the insanity, Woodrow. He's so good. He's so . . . so personal about it."

"What about your friend? What does she see? Maybe I could talk to her."

"No." Tara pushed herself off the wall. This was defeat. "She wouldn't be able to help you. She is involved and love is blind."

Woodrow put his hand on Tara's shoulder. "And you're the only one that sees this clearly, Tara?"

Startled, Tara paused, thinking hard for an instant. "Yes. There's no black and white here, Woodrow. I don't know what he really wants. I have to take him at his word. I have to assume that he knows he needs a doctor's care. The roadblocks he throws up may be his madness. Like a child throwing a tantrum so the parents will prove their love. I don't know what the real story is, but I will protect him until I find out."

They stood silently together, each thinking. Finally, Tara spoke.

"Woodrow?"

"Yes?" he murmured.

"You didn't push the button."

"You could have pushed it," he noted. They stared at the panel a little longer, Tara thinking it wouldn't be bad to hide here a bit longer. She was the one who finally poked it and the one who finally laughed once.

"We're going to be late."

"Yeah, but I didn't mind the breather. Did you?"

"No, I didn't."

The elevator jerked gently. They were on their way. Friends again for a minute. The other side of her, Tara thought. The side that didn't keep secrets and needed a friend. Oh, how she needed someone to count on. They reached their destination and Tara split herself. The attorney Linley walked out and waited for DA Weber, who went ahead to announce their arrival.

"Mr. Weber. It's nice to see you again."

A mild-looking middle-aged man stood as Tara

and Woodrow entered his well-turned-out office. Wood desk, leather chairs, real paintings on the wall. The bar obviously thought more of its employees than did the state. Woodrow said his hellos then passed the man's hand on to Tara.

"Nice of you to see us. This is Tara Linley." Woodrow stepped back, his arm out as if to usher her into the inner circle. She didn't give him a glance as she passed.

"Nice to meet you," Tara said and she meant it.

"Lovely to meet you. I was privileged to hear you speak to the Bar Association last year. Lovely speech. Well delivered. Please, sit down." He smiled gently, and Tara did as he suggested, noting that he had gracefully managed not to refer to the content of her speech, the title of which even she couldn't remember.

Frank Sepada laughed. "I'm delighted you called. I'm afraid I don't see many people as the Bar's ethics liaison. I field phone calls, write letters, answer complaints. To see living, breathing human beings is truly nice. However, I'm aware that your presence here can mean only that your situation is serious. Compromised, if I might make that assumption."

They both nodded.

"Mr. Sepada," Tara said, anxious to be heard first, "I've been retained by a person who confessed to me that he committed a horrible crime."

Tara told the story again. Personal involvement, heinous cold-blooded murder, odd behavior, psychiatric history. When she was done, Frank Sepada turned to Woodrow.

"Mr. Weber?"

"I'd like to at least talk to the man before I take a step regarding state commitment." Woodrow leaned forward in his chair, his posture that of a concerned public servant. "I have already agreed to make a decision based on the evaluation of her client by a qualified psychiatrist. I simply can't take her word for a psychological diagnosis. She is a lawyer, and, with all due respect, this might be a rather unique ploy by her in preparation for a defense. She hasn't given me the evaluation I've requested. I'll have to refuse any action, unless you can provide us with another solution. We have agreed to abide by your decision."

"This is refreshing. Seldom do I have adversaries willing to work even this closely together." He cleared his throat and tapped the side of his cheek. "Ms. Linley, has your client threatened anyone or exhibited such odd behavior as to put himself in danger?"

"No," Tara said, a flush coloring her neck as she remembered the night before, his head on her thigh, crucifying himself to Shinin'. She shook off the tremors that caught hold where the two men would never see. "No, but the potential is there. I'm sure of that. He's unpredictable. Smart. Frightening. But there have been no overt threats."

"You've corroborated his medical history?"

"Yes, with his psychiatrist."

"And what did he tell you?"

"Nothing specific. He confirmed the man's violent tendencies, but he wouldn't do so on record, citing privilege."

"I see. Well, Ms. Linley, I suggest you get more than that. It seems you have only two choices. Immediately seek Mr. Weber's help should your client become violent, and barring that, determine if your client is competent to waive his rights and release you from the attorney-client privilege. If he is, then you must explain the situation to him and offer him the option of working with the DA. If not, then I'm afraid the law can do nothing for, or with, this man." Mr. Sepada fluttered his eyes toward Woodrow, an oddly nervous gesture for a man who was so very calm. "I'm sorry, Mr. Weber, but I can't deliver her client into your hands because you wish it so. You'll have to work for him."

His eyes were back on Tara again.

"Ms. Linley, I would prefer to see you determine your client's competency and convince him he has options rather than wait for a violent outburst of any sort."

"I had hoped for something more, Mr. Sepada."

"Believe me, Ms. Linley, I wish I had a bag of tricks."

Tara nodded her understanding. "We're sorry to have wasted your time."

"Not a waste of time. I wish you the best." Frank Sepada stood up. "I do want to say, though, that I don't envy either of you. Your position, Mr. Weber, yours by virtue of the elected office you hold, has got to be based not only on legal considerations, but also on political ones. I wouldn't venture to guess how the percentages break down on your motivation."

He looked at Tara.

"I might say the same of you, Ms. Linley. You are torn between concern for your client and concern for your friend. These are considerations that I can't take under advisement. What we lawyers promise is to work only for the good of our client within the confines of the law, and to remain silent regarding issues that have been told to us in confidence. It is the same difficulty priests pray about and doctors lose sleep over. The general perception that lawyers do not agonize over questions such as these always amazes me. I'm sorry, but I'm afraid Ms. Linley is, to use a nonlegal term, stuck."

They left Frank Sepada's office in silence. It wasn't until they were outside on the sidewalk once again that Tara found her voice. Standing close to Woodrow, she spoke over his shoulder, near his ear, looking at the building on the other side.

"Woodrow, I'm sorry about last night. I'm sorry about being angry. I'm asking you to please issue the petition for hospitalization. Please." Her voice dropped to a whisper. "The injury on my arm, Woodrow. I think he had something to do with it. I think he was trying to get me to bleed to death, but my friend showed up. Last night I found the carving knife stuck into a note on the butcher block. I think he's watching me. I think . . ."

Woodrow shook his head. "I don't know what I think, Tara. You're pulling every trick in the book to get me to do something I know isn't right." Woodrow clamped his lips shut. There was pain in his expression, there was fear. He warred with his evil twin who, Tara knew, whispered against her. Woodrow needed her man and hated himself for it.

"My position is clear. I see him, I evaluate him, or we do nothing." Woodrow put his hand on her arm and pressed, offering his assurance. "Tara, I'm your friend, and you know it. Anyone else would have manipulated the little you've given me. I could have gone to the press. I could have just posed the questions: What if a local attorney knew who the Circle K killer was? Who do you think is right, Mr. John Q. Public? Tara protecting the rights of a killer, or me wanting to get him behind bars? We're pretty basic out here, Tara. You know what the answers would be. You know the public doesn't care about philosophy when it comes to their safety."

"I didn't think you had this in you, Woodrow," Tara muttered and stepped back. She had begged him and he wanted her on her knees. Now Tara didn't want to be anywhere near Woodrow.

"I'm not threatening. I'm only showing you this can play a hundred different ways. You have my offer. I don't want to see you compromised, but I have a lot at stake too. I'm not throwing it away."

Woodrow gave her arm one last squeeze and walked away. Tara let him go. Anxious, tired, her arm hurting, she got behind the wheel of her car, turned the ignition, and sat quite still. Finally, tired of listening to the motor idle, tired of just about everything, Tara threw the gear, pulled out into traffic, and made a U the first place she could. Home wasn't where she wanted to go. She wanted to be with a real friend.

"Woodrow, if you don't stop pacing, I'm going to hogtie you. Now, either you have something to say, or you don't. If you don't, then I've got work to do."

Woodrow stopped and glared at George Amos. George threw back his hands, giving up.

"Okay. Okay," he chuckled. "I'm sorry I called Tara. I'm sorry I tipped my hand. She already yelled at me. You don't have to."

"I don't see anything funny about this, George." Woodrow stopped his pacing. He was thoughtful. He was concerned. "I just don't know what you thought you'd gain."

"Nothing," George answered. Woodrow's eyes

snapped his way, challenging him. "That's the truth, Woodrow. I didn't expect anything. I just wanted confirmation. I'm entitled. You put it on my plate, I can push it around a little bit."

"That's intimidation."

"Hell, she couldn't be intimidated," George scoffed. "But there's a lot to be told by someone's reaction. And Tara Linley reacted like a cat in a bath. She is skittish and she's got something hot."

"All that from a phone call, huh?" Woodrow drawled. "What a lawman."

"Better doing something than just sitting around waiting to do her bidding like another lawman I know."

"Look . . ." Woodrow put his hands on the back of the nearest chair. "I don't want to be a part of your game. I want to do this right. I'll hold out and that's legal. You're going down a road that might be a little crooked. I just think you should consider that."

"Woodrow, get off the fence. Don't you think this is going to come out sooner or later? It may not be a big to-do that breaks it. Maybe a little whisper here or there. Maybe a secretary will gossip about something she overheard when you finally get this mess straightened out. And when it does come out, people will know Tara Linley did the best for her client. They'll know I did what I could to find out who this guy was so I could keep an eye on him. And you? You'll be the one who sat back and waited. Do you think the voters will respect a man who doesn't take a stand?"

"I've given her options," Woodrow said quietly.

"And if she doesn't take advantage of those options?"

"Then it's her problem."

"That will seem so special to all those women who want to run to the Circle K for milk at midnight for the baby," George drawled. "Woodrow, I don't have time for this. I'm going to put that poor woman's soul to rest if I can. You can either help me or you can stay out of my way. And if I break the law, then you can come after me. But until then, you just go back to your office and sit there and wait until Tara brings him in, or I find out who this guy is and I find a reason to bring him in, or . . ."

"What?" Woodrow asked.

"Or we find Tara Linley dead somewhere. Hadn't thought about that one, had you?"

"Go to hell, George."

"Not before Linley's client," George said. Woodrow was at the door. "Oh, Woodrow, did you see today's paper?"

Woodrow turned back and George tossed it his way. He caught it and took the rubber band off. "You made the front page. Governor's going to form a committee to look into the contracts awarded to Strober Industries. Starting with the board. According to that article, you went to law school with one of the board members."

"The article's wrong."

"That's what I thought," George said, "but it makes good reading. Since there's nothing else interesting to read about. Like a good collar. Or a murderer brought to trial." George swiveled in his chair and tapped at his computer. "See you, Woodrow."

Woodrow didn't move. He held the newspaper in a hand that was suddenly sweaty with an arm that felt weak. George whistled and it irritated the heck out of Woodrow. He opened the door, closed it again, and said:

"George."

"Yep, Woodrow."

"I am worried about Tara. I wouldn't mind knowing what was going on at her place. Keep an eye on her and let me know if you see anyone suspicious around her house. A discreetly watchful eye. Might help."

"I can spare some men for that kind of public service. I hate to see a fine attorney put in a bad position because of our negligence."

"Yeah. Just remember, I'd hate to see any of us in a bad position."

Fourteen

It was perfect. The kind of place Tara imagined Ben would have. A stucco bungalow bigger, she was sure, than it appeared from the outside. On this short, half-moon street, there were only six houses that at one time had been home to families, the porches host to bicycles, the yards the domain of children. Now the porches were bare and each of the freshly painted buildings housed a business. A doctor, a paralegal, and a dentist were on the left. An accountant sort of in the middle, considering there were six houses and no middle. And on the right another dentist and a psychologist.

Tara stood in front of the last house. Neat and white, it sported a tasteful brass plaque on the far right. She'd driven there without thinking. Now she was thinking twice.

Tara looked at the unpretentious building and walked up the steps, ignoring the long ramp running from sidewalk to porch. She rang the bell and stepped back, holding her purse in front of her, looking like a trick-or-treater anxious to see what surprises this place held for her. No one came, so she rang again and stepped farther back and to the right, hoping to peek through the window. It was draped.

"Hi!" Tara twirled. A woman leaned over the

railing that wound around the porch of the dentist's place. She was dressed all in white. Tara would have pegged her for the dentist but noticed her nails. No way she could work on anyone's mouth with those. "You looking for Ben?"

"Yes, I am." Tara walked to the end of the porch on her side so they wouldn't have to yell. "Doesn't he keep regular office hours?"

"Usually, but he's testing today."

"Oh, I better come back then," Tara said quickly. "He probably won't feel up to seeing anyone."

"Are you kidding? He loves company after those things. They get him so pumped up. You might as well go watch. He's just around the corner." She pointed a purple talon north and Tara looked after though there was nothing to see except traffic. "You can't miss it. It's the little place with the blacked-out windows. I don't know the name but it's not even a block up."

"If you think it's all right."

"Believe me, I know it is."

"Okay, I'll see if I can find it," Tara called. "Thanks."

"No problem. If you miss him, want to leave a message?"

Tara shook her head. "No. If I don't find him, I'll come back another time. Thanks again."

Tara went down the stairs and at the sidewalk paused. She looked back over her shoulder and gave the woman a nod, then headed in the direction she'd indicated. A walk would do her good, and if she found Ben, all the better. Thankfully, the need for a sympathetic ear wasn't as urgent as it had been. She turned the corner and began looking at the storefronts, and wondered if seeking

Ben out was wise. The floodgates of their relationship were rusty. They might not open as she anticipated. There might be one rejection more today, but there also might be salvation.

She checked out the shoe repair and next to it an empty storefront. Next to that was a small boulangerie, a twirling sign outside announcing that the bread was fresh today. There it was, next to the boulangerie. A store with blacked-out windows. Nothing announced what business was taking place behind the worn door, but the woman had said Ben was testing. Tara put her hand on the knob, hoping she wouldn't walk in on some therapy session, and pushed. The door opened and it was the sounds of combative men she heard.

Tara stood in an anteroom. There was a narrow doorway on the far right. She headed toward it cautiously, listening to the sounds of battle. Cries and slaps, thumps of bodies hitting the ground, came from the room beyond. Cautiously she looked through the door, registered what she was seeing, then slipped into the larger room and sat on a folding chair, one of six against the wall.

No one noticed her. Not the eight men kneeling against the wall to her right, not the one man standing between them and the mirrored wall to the left, and certainly not the two men warring in the middle of the room with the killing moves of karate. One of these men was Ben.

He was magnificent. Dressed in white cotton pajamas, black slippers on his feet, a brown belt around his waist. He faced off with another man. This one was standing, and Ben seemed disadvantaged in his chair. Yet the man on his feet was more often on his back. Ben pulled on him and he went to the ground. With a horrendous cry Ben mocked a killing blow to his throat. His opponent was up again and this time was brought to his knees with a feigned two-handed strike at the kidneys. The man reacted as if he had actually been hit.

Over and over again the exercise was played out. Sweat glistened on Ben's face, rivulets ran down his chest, and Tara was mesmerized by the beauty of such a deadly art and the man who indulged in it. His arms, corded with muscles, cut through the air, creating sound by the mere force of motion. His fingers curled and stretched into weapons designed to disable and kill, yet he used his knowledge with such precision that he and his partner seemed connected by respect, not by fear. There was a moment when Tara turned her head, terrified that Ben had made a mistake, that his hands had actually made contact with flesh and blood. But after the final cry, she looked to see his opponent standing, the two of them holding their fists downward and bowing from the waist in a sign of respect for each other's skill.

Ben was breathing hard. The man who had watched, the master, didn't smile, but he was obviously pleased. The men kneeling against the wall were impressed, but no more so than Tara, who sat spellbound. With little fanfare, the master walked to Ben, handed him a black belt, backed off, and gave him the same fist-down salute his opponent had. He turned to the men against the wall and went through the same ritual and then Ben was looking at her, wiping away the sweat with a towel, while he wheeled toward her with the other.

"Your timing is impeccable. Nothing like being surprised when you're doing something good."

"It looked better than good." Tara grinned ear to ear. "I don't know much about karate—"

"Kung fu," Ben corrected, snapping the towel and folding it into his lap. He gave her a smile. "Most damage, least movement. Great for someone with limitations."

"Like a wheelchair?"

"Like a simple mind," he countered. "You ought to try it."

"Thanks. I never thought of myself as simple-minded," she said, laughing.

"I meant you ought to try it for the fun of it. You could work out some of the kinks."

"I didn't know they showed." Tara shifted in her chair. "Do you have anything else you need to do here?"

"Nope. If you can wait 'til I shower, you can help me celebrate. I'm officially a black belt. You were here when history was made."

"Far be it from me to snub history," she said softly. "I'd be honored to help you celebrate."

"Great." Ben nodded and touched his hair once more. He nodded again and the grin was the same one he'd given her when she said she'd go to the Sophomore Christmas Dance with him. She smiled back, fighting the urge to mourn the fact that he didn't dance anymore. "Great. I'll be out in fifteen."

"I'll be here."

"I'm sorry. I apologize. I can't believe I forgot my wallet."

"Ben, I could have bought you dinner, you know. We are celebrating your black belt, after all."

"Sorry. Some things haven't changed. I'm still

old-fashioned that way. Won't take me a minute,
come on in."

Ben was wheeling up the ramp under his own
steam as easily as Tara climbed the steps to the
porch. She beat him by a second and followed him
into the bungalow.

"I made the front into my office," he said, chatting as he went down the hall. "Don't really need
a receptionist but I keep the living room for a
waiting area. I still do see some private patients
even though most of my work is with Social Security."

"What do you do for them?" Tara poked her
head into a large and airy room, sparsely fur-
nished.

"I do evaluations to determine whether or not
applicants are mentally competent for employment. Sometimes I evaluate test scores, other times
I actually have to see the applicant. Privately I'll
deal with occupational therapy, helping those who
are newly disabled to cope."

"You'd be good at that," Tara said.

"I hope so. Welfare isn't on my agenda." He
flipped on another light. "This is where I do the
real work if you can't tell." Tara's neck craned
again. Ben had stopped and stayed by her side. "I
love this room. All my toys are in here. See up there
on the ceiling? That's the first ski board I ever used.
It's amazing what they can do with sports equipment
for people like me. My diplomas. Really proud of
those. The wind-up toys are favorites too. The paperwork is secondary. Ignore it."

He wheeled on, continuing with the tour, stopping only when he realized Tara no longer dogged
him. Silently his chair rolled over the hardwood
floors.

"Hey, you coming with me to hunt for that wallet?" He touched her. She turned her head toward the wall. "Oh, Tara. Come on. Sit."

Tara shook her head, but he nudged her into his office and put her on the couch. At that moment, Tara Linley began to cry.

She put her hands over her face and Ben came to her, stopping when there was nowhere else for him to go. Their knees almost made contact, but he had to lean over to touch her shoulder. She wished it could have been an arm he wound around her. "I had no idea you'd be so overwhelmed by my humble abode."

He chuckled, chucked her chin, and didn't seem at all put out when Tara raised her face and turned her head away from him. True to form, knowing her so well despite the years between them, Ben simply did what had to be done. He handed her her purse and sat back.

"Thanks." Tara sniffled, flipped it open, then closed it without bothering to ruffle through. "I don't have a Kleenex." She sniffed again. Ben went to the desk, opened a drawer, and came back with a box. Resisting the urge to swipe her sleeve across her nose, she dug in and pulled some out. "Do you mind?" she asked, miserable at this turn of events.

"I've seen people blow their nose before," he assured her.

"Crying isn't something I do well," she insisted, tissue at the ready.

"You're doing a fine job." He went away before she could decide if he was making fun of her. He was across the room, politely ignoring her while she composed herself. When he came back, he had a cup in each hand, his chair running by itself.

He stopped it with an elbow on a button. Handing her a cup, he waited. Tara balled up her Kleenex in one fist and wrapped her other hand around the mug.

"Thank you." She drank. "Hot chocolate!"

"Everybody can do coffee," Ben said. "Hope you noticed the miniature marshmallows. Only special visitors get those."

"How could I miss them? Nice touch. Pastel colors." Tara laughed a little, still disadvantaged by the sniffles. Taking a deep breath, she fell back against the cushions and crossed her legs, knowing she was wound tighter than a spring.

"I guess this wasn't such a good idea."

"Depends on what the idea was, Tara." Ben said softly. He set aside his mug. "Want to try and tell me?"

Tara shrugged, "Boy, I don't even know anymore. Guess I wanted to be with a friend."

"You don't have any of those?"

"With someone I could trust."

"That's narrowing it."

"With someone I admire." She looked him in the eye. It wouldn't go any further than that.

"I'm glad I made the cut," Ben said.

"Are you being facetious?"

Ben shook his head, his lips tipped and the smile wasn't quite sad, but almost, as if he expected her to know him better. "No, I'm not. I know it's hard for you to be less than strong with someone. Some things don't change in twenty years. I count myself lucky to be the person you came to with your trouble. There's been an empty spot, Tara."

"I missed you, too," she said. She put her mug aside too, knowing there would never be a better time to climb over the wall between them. "Things got crazy when we were kids. I always felt bad about that. I had to go with Dad to Washington . . ."

"I had to learn how to use a wheelchair," he said. No accusation, simply a statement.

Tara's jaw stiffened, their eyes were tight on one another.

"All right. No excuses," she said, surprised to find anger, not regret or sadness, buried deep inside. "I made the choice. I deserted you."

"That's not what I wanted to hear. I led you into that and I'm sorry." Ben looked out the window behind the desk. "You were sixteen, I was seventeen, and that car took away the next ten years for me. Sounds like it took all twenty out of you and you didn't know it 'til now." He looked back at her and smiled for real this time. "We could really get into this, couldn't we? You want to talk about it now or want to do what we'd planned on doing in the first place?"

"Hunting for your wallet?"

"Dinner."

"I don't know," Tara said, suddenly wearied. "Ben, I'm sorry, too." For the years, the accident, the abandonment, the love they had lost and missed.

"We're even," he said, and she knew it was true. No judgments, no recriminations. They could, indeed, pick up where they'd left off. Unfortunately, where they'd left off had been a bit more innocent than the here and now. Tara still had Bill Hamilton to think about, Donna to worry over. "Let's start again. I'm so happy to see you."

"Me, too, Ben. I'm happy to see you so well settled." She took account of her surroundings.

"Finally. It took a while. I'd love for you to think I was this pulled together all these years but I wasn't. I was mad, Tara. I was hurt. I was lonely and I was a horror to be around. Then one day, it kind of happened. New friends, resources, people who show you how to do the same old thing just a little differently. I've hiked in Colorado. I've played basketball in New York. I've sailed in the Atlantic. There's a guy in California who was paralyzed when he was a kid. Incredible person. He's a kung fu master. When I saw him, I knew that's what I wanted. It's a powerful sport. So controlled. You need to make judicious decisions. A centimeter can mean the difference between life and death, literally. It's not about anger and I think that's what I like about it. If you can control your body that precisely, you can control everything else in your life."

"Including your emotions?"

Ben tipped his head, "That doesn't sound like a do-you-still-love me question."

"It isn't," Tara admitted.

"Want to talk about it?"

"Do you mind? It's big stuff, Ben. Not exactly small talk for two old friends."

Tara looked at him and realized how inordinately beautiful he had become. Old friends indeed. She had missed seeing him change but oh, how wonderful the change was. His features were chiseled, hardened in a way that wasn't threatening, only a testament to determination. His eyes were crinkled with wrinkles that fanned out from the corners as if he'd spent the last years trying to see into the future. His lips, from what she could see under the full mustache, were still as they'd always been, the lower one fuller than the

upper but not so full as to be pretty. They were
lips that were wide and, in repose, could be stern.
But when he smiled or laughed, Ben was Ben all
over again. Tara forgot the wheelchair. But the for-
getfulness lasted only moments, and the remem-
brance had less to do with Ben's painful memories
than hers.

"I'm glad you still wear your hair long," he said,
as if reading her mind. "And I'm glad you've come
to me, no matter what the problem."

"I have nowhere else to turn," she said. "I want
you to know that. It doesn't mean I don't value
your opinion. I just don't want you to think that's
the only reason I came."

"It's nice of you to be concerned." Kindly, Ben
didn't make her pay for her sins of omission during the past years. He settled himself in his chair
and waited.

Tara put her hands together as if she were praying. "I've got a client. He's been violent in the
past. I believe he's dangerous now. He's taken up
with a good friend of mine."

She talked, poking into every worrisome cranny
she could think of, until the whole story was told.
When she was done, Ben considered her closely.

"Sounds like a problem."

"I don't know where the lines are drawn anymore. I honestly don't know if this man is mentally
ill or just mean. That's what makes it so frightening. If Woodrow chooses to do nothing about this
and wait until my client tips his hand, this guy
could be with my friend for a very long time."

"I can understand a psychiatrist not wanting to
get involved. Private practice is something you have
to protect like a lover. With Social Security evaluations I don't rely on the consumer base for my

clients. I can evaluate him if you can get me to him."

"A formal interview?"

"If we have to do it some other way, we can. I don't think that's unethical. Just remember, I'm not a psychiatrist. I can't prescribe medication. Woodrow might reject my evaluation if what you say about his agenda is true."

Tara took a deep breath, pushed aside her purse, and slipped out of her coat. She rolled it up, held it tight, and wound her legs underneath her.

"I feel helpless, Ben, and that's the worst of it. When I took that oath to defend anyone accused, I know I never considered all the permutations. A criminal was almost glamorized in my mind back then. In all these years I've been able to practice it impassively. Sort of split myself in two. I was so darn proud of that."

"You should be. You've always been able to do that. Even when we were kids. You were the most disciplined person I knew." Ben touched the top of her hand. "That wasn't bad, mind you. Everyone was amazed when you were handed a problem or a project. Your eyes would glaze over and you wouldn't surface until the objective was accomplished. That's what makes you a good lawyer. That's why this is so difficult. You can't suppress that urge to do right when your emotions are involved."

"Funny, that's what Donna said too. Only she wasn't quite so polite. She said I'd never experienced true passion because I always had my eye on the goal."

"Maybe you've just been waiting for the right

moment to turn off the straight and narrow road. Maybe passion's still ahead."

"Possibly," she said. "I hope it is."

"Guess only time will tell."

"Yes." Embarrassed, Tara unwound her legs and put them on the floor. "I'm beginning to think I'm a hysterical female. The only vibes I'm getting are scary ones, and I'm getting them over little things. Things other people interpret as normal."

"At the risk of being trite, do you think all these little things could be a cry for help and you're the only one he's crying to? Maybe he's feeling like he wants to strike out again and this is his way of telling you"

"He should have called a crisis line."

"Tara." Ben looked heavenward. "This is satisfying to him. I don't need to see him to know that. It's a lot more interesting than simply waiting for you to do your thing. There's drama in his head and he's acting it out. Didn't he tell you he felt nothing? Well, this way he feels all the time. He's making up ways to get your attention."

"Why me and not Donna?"

"He may actually love Donna, and want to spare her pain. A sick mind doesn't negate real emotions. Who knows what you represent to him? Who knows anything until he gives you a chance to see beneath it all?"

Tara caught the fever. Ben was interested. Ben would help.

"You know what really bothers me? This isn't a legal issue at all. If he were accused, I could stand up for him in court. If he wanted to confess, I could be by his side with counsel. But all he's done is tell me this horrible thing and give me permission to dangle a carrot in front of Woodrow and

George. I hate that I took the bait. I hate that I didn't think it through better."

Ben countered, "There was nothing to think through at the time. You had a problem. You had a friend in need. You had a solution and you had no reason to think that it was anything but an expedient and judicious one. Lighten up, Tara."

"Good advice, but wrong. He's in my guest house. He . . ." Tara stood up quickly, the memory of Bill touching her a confession on the tip of her tongue. Ben was the last person she wanted to share that memory with. "He's Donna's lover. Anyone else, and I wouldn't count this as a problem. I would just let it go until circumstances changed and I could actually make a difference. He would be on the other side of the wall that separates my work life from my real one. I'm not quite sure what my next move should be. All I know is I can't release his name to the authorities or talk about his crime to my best friend."

Tara verbally threw up her hands. Ben's brow was knit. He sat quietly, then reached for the phone.

"I think we need to put our heads together on this one. Just a minute."

Tara could only guess what was going through his mind as he punched in a number, held up a finger, and listened to the ring. Tara moved closer, curious as to who he might call to help solve this dilemma. He smiled at her and ordered a pizza, a salad, and a six-pack of soft drinks.

"I can't think on an empty stomach," he said, and held out his hand.

Tara took it. It felt good in hers even though in her memory it wasn't like this. Not hard and dry, the hand of a purposeful man. How well he'd grown despite his accident. How very wonderful. How very attractive. She slipped her hand out of his. He stopped, looked back and up at her.

"Will you see him, Ben? If I can get him here. Will you?"

"Sure."

Tara smiled and closed her eyes. She stood back and let him go through the door, peaceful for the first time in days. Ben was here to help and she appreciated it more than he would ever know. They would be partners. Professional to the last. Why, then, when she followed him, did she feel almost disappointed?

Home. Full of pizza. At peace. What more could a girl ask for other than finding a solution to a miserable problem. Smiling, Tara swung out of the car, slammed the door, and was about to head in when she saw Joseph slogging across the yard.

"Joseph!" she called. "Wait. Please."

Tara hurried to him. Nothing much had changed. The teenager still looked sulky. He stopped, glared at her, and waited for her to come to him.

"Joseph, I'm sorry to keep you, but do you know what happened the other day? My arm?" She held up her arm, still bandaged, and he peered through the dark.

"I put that pitchfork away where it was supposed to be. I put it on its hook, and I didn't have nothing to do with moving it. I swear I didn't."

The surly youth transmuted into a frightened boy before her eyes. Not at all the reaction she had wanted. Fear closed mouths as often as it opened them.

"I didn't say you did, Joseph," Tara assured him. "I was only asking if you knew how it came to be balanced behind the bridle. I just wanted to make sure you hadn't made a mistake, and if you had, I'd show you where the pitchfork is supposed to be kept."

"Well, I didn't. I've never hurt anybody, and I do what I'm told."

"I believe that. Carlos never would have left you in charge if he hadn't thought so too."

That threw him. If there was no attack, there couldn't be a defense. "Well, then. Okay."

"Okay," Tara said, and he dismissed himself. She called after him. "Payday tomorrow. Don't forget."

He waved his hand over his head. She was beginning to think of that as a rather endearing gesture. With a lighter step for having confirmed her fears, Tara stopped by Shinin's stall. Joseph had indeed done his job properly and therefore someone—Bill Hamilton—had to have specifically moved the pitchfork. He had wanted her to be scared, if not hurt. That had to count for something on the nutty scale. She was closer to her goal now. It wouldn't be long with Ben on her side. Not long at all. With a final pat for Shinin', she headed in.

"Just wait, Mr. Hamilton," she whispered to herself. "We're almost home now."

"Tara! Tara!"

Tara stood in the half-open doorway, thinking how like a mother she'd become. Her ears were always pricked for the sound of Donna's voice, the sound of distress. But distressed was hardly what Donna seemed. She whirled up to Tara, her long black wool skirt flapping around her riding boots, the sleeves of her turtleneck sweater pushed up her arms. She looked charming. She looked mad.

"Hi." Tara smiled but Donna was determined to set the tone of their talk.

"Tara." She nodded curtly. "I think we need to talk."

"I'd love to," Tara said. "Come on in. Let me make some tea. I'll tell you about Ben. I saw him and—"

"I don't want to talk about Ben. Not until we've straightened things out about Bill. I've been thinking about this all day and I've got to get it off my chest. I came all this way to celebrate your birthday and you have done nothing but ignore me, attack Bill, and imply that I am stupid for having feelings for him. Tara, I have to tell you. Last night was the last straw and I want an explanation."

"Donna," Tara said flatly, "I gave you an explanation. I'm seeing Bill professionally. He asked for help on issues that I think are serious. I'm not going to get into a cat fight over that man. I'm his attorney, and as such, I can't be your friend on this matter. Either you trust me or you don't. You can honor the years we've known each other or the weeks you've known Bill. Your choice. But I can't pretend that things haven't changed since he retained me. They have. I'd prefer you didn't see him until we settled this matter and that's about all I can say."

"What a high-and-mighty mouthful," Donna taunted. "Any other orders, Sargeant?"

Tara shook her head, and took a step closer to her friend. "Donna, I just want you to understand that I'm in a difficult position. I wish you trusted me enough to act on my instincts. Since you don't, things will have to change."

"Meaning you and I can talk, but Bill can't come to the party."

"Yes."

Donna sucked in her breath through pursed lips. Then she pushed past Tara and went into the house, shutting the door after Tara followed.

"I think we'll leave in the morning, Tara. Bill and I. I think we'll just head on back to my place. But before we go, I have a few things to say. First, we're either friends or we aren't. If we're friends, then you owe me an explanation. You can't hide behind your oaths and potions and pledges. You talk to me straight, or you hug me goodbye until you're ready to pick up and be friends again. But I can't take this anymore. You're just like Jorge."

Tara tried to steer clear of the conversation, fussing with her coat, running a finger over the hall table, trying to place Donna's second husband. "Why on earth would I remind you of Jorge?"

"Because you're gutless." Silence. Deep, show-stopping silence enveloped them. Donna dug in. "You are, Tara. You don't have the guts to tell me to my face, so you're pulling this long-suffering, you'd-never-understand-in-a-million-years act. One of us has got to do something. Since you don't have the guts, I will." Donna sighed and plopped herself down on a kitchen chair. "You know, Jorge did the same thing to me. He wasn't happy if the house was too clean because it meant I didn't have enough time for him. He was unhappy if I spent time with him, and the house went to pot. I was too loud in front of people, or too shy. I couldn't win."

"This isn't really about you, Donna. Not in the way you think."

"Of course it is. It's about the man I adore. Everything that touches him, touches me." She slapped her knees with her hands and pushed herself off the chair. "I learned my lesson with Jorge, Tara. When someone acts that weird, when you can't get a smile from them anymore, when they run away or stick their nose behind a book and send out those cold, colder, coldest vibes, it's time to move on. And you're hitting the freezing point, Tara. So either talk, or it's *hasta la vista* and we pretend this was a lovely visit. Your call."

Tara paced, finding it hard to be stationary while she listened to Donna's accusations. Finally she leaned against the thick wall, then slid herself into the deep windowsill and rested there.

"I have nothing more to say."

"You made him feel so welcome that first night," Donna said, pleading for Tara not to throw her away.

"He's calculating. He makes things up."

"He's anxious to please. He likes to entertain."

"He's taking advantage of you."

"I'm using him!" Donna threw up her hands. "Tara, he's young, he's handsome, what on earth is he doing with me? I'm not paying him. Thank goodness I haven't fallen to those depths yet. He hasn't asked me for a thing. Not money, not clothes, not a car. Nothing. It's not like that at all."

"You're being used and so am I."

Donna took a few steps and waved a hand as she shook her head. Now she had the picture. "There it is again. *You're* being used. You know you diminish my relationship with him by insinuating yourself into it. You've been doing it since the minute we got here. Flirting and blushing. When that didn't work, and he came to you for help, you used that to make yourself more important in his life. Now you're suggesting that he and I separate.

It sounds very strange to me, Tara. It sounds like you're using everything you can to get next to him."

"That man is a fraud," Tara said quietly. "He's not a cowboy and he's hiding a lot of ugly things, Donna."

"So what?" Donna wailed. "Who doesn't have secrets or faults to hide? Are you so perfect that you don't hide? Please. You're the worst. First you hid from Ben behind your father, then you hid from the world behind your profession. Admit it, Bill reminded you that you're a woman and you don't like it. It's as simple as that."

"That's disgusting," Tara rejoined, her eyes narrowing. "That may be the way you see my world, Donna, but it's not my way. I don't slip between the sheets and share my home just because someone pays attention to me. I'd have to know more about him than he's good in bed."

"Jesus," Donna breathed, her dark eyes wide and hurt. "Do you think I'm a whore or something?"

Tara held up her hands and crossed them in the universal sign of time-out. "No. You act on instinct. You need to step back. I know how you need to be needed."

She got up and reached out, but Donna's arms were crossed. She backed off and Tara did too.

"I'm just saying that you're a giver, Donna. You always have been. I've been overly cautious and even miserly with my feelings. I think our ways have made both of us needy and lonely at times. Neither way is right. But this time, I know, in the bottom of my heart, that Bill is dangerous."

"You are sick."

"I am right," she whispered.

Donna passed Tara, their shoulders brushing as she went. Tara stood alone in the silence of her home. She looked at the floor, her chin on her chest. It took three minutes for her to analyze what had happened and conclude it was wrong. Donna was at a disadvantage, without a frame of reference, and that made Tara's responsibility greater.

She'd grovel if she had to. If she couldn't get Donna to send Bill away, then there was a greater percentage in keeping them together and near, just to make sure that Donna remained alive and kicking.

She knocked on the door of the guest house twice. When no one came, she touched the knob, turned it, and walked in. The place was quiet. Bill wasn't about. Tara would have felt him if he'd been within fifty feet. Something rolled off that man, an emanation of energy, that couldn't be identified as evil, nor could it be counted on for good. It was simply there, pulsating, incessant, and overwhelming as he pushed himself through her life.

"Donna?" Tara stood just inside the door and called.

Nothing.

Then she heard a drawer slam in the bedroom. *Come find me. Here's a little noise to guide you. You make the first move.* Tara walked toward the bedroom, following the audio crumbs Donna was tossing out. But Tara froze in the doorway.

Every drawer in the dresser was open and most were empty. Donna's small lips were set in anger, her blond hair flying back and forth as she turned to grab a piece of lingerie, a forgotten ball of

socks, a last sweater. On the bed her suitcase was
almost filled, and it was on the suitcase that Donna
focused, knowing full well that Tara was watching.
Tara slipped into the room and hugged the wall.

"I'm sorry." The apology hung in the air long
enough to be frozen by a glance from Donna.
Without missing a beat she leaned over the bed,
and pushed and shoved the clothes into a different
configuration. Tara's eyes flickered to the floor.
Bill's duffel was ready to go. Tara pushed off the
wall and hung on the bedpost. "Don't, Donna.
This is just plain silly. A man isn't worth our
friendship, is he?"

"Our friendship probably isn't worth anything,
Tara." Donna's voice was as tight as the packing
job. She pushed down the lid and leaned on it to
get the left clasp shut. She did the same to the
right and talked through clenched teeth. "I'm
sorry, too. Truly sorry it's come to this. But you've
been impossible. Wonderful and welcoming one
minute, and the next you're treating Bill like he's
a psycho, and me like I'm an idiot. If Bill is so
damned dangerous, then what's he doing hanging
out here? Huh? No answer, right?"

Donna took a second to glance at Tara, who
didn't bother to answer. There was nothing more
she could say.

"You've got a serious case of attitude, and I
don't care how big a lawyer you are, or how busy
you are, or what an upstanding citizen of Albuquerque you are—it wouldn't have killed you to
be straight with me. That's what friends do. Or
you could have pretended that nothing was wrong.
Because that's also what friends do. You couldn't
do it, and it wasn't 'til tonight that I figured it
out." Tara heard a snap. The suitcase was loaded

and ready to go. Donna turned, one hand on her hip, the other atop the suitcase. She was breathing hard from the exertion of her job and her emotions.

"You're transparent as glass. You're lonely and you're jealous that I always have a man and you don't. I thought you really liked him and were happy for me, but you wanted him. Admit it."

"I will do no such thing!" Tara's voice rose an octave to stop Donna's tirade. She rounded the bed and sat down heavily right under Donna's nose. "Have you ever seen me do anything stupid because of a man? You haven't. Don't deny it," Tara asked. "How can you reduce this to such simplistic drivel?"

"Because that's all it is," Donna snapped.

"Get real. What Bill means to me has nothing to do with middle-aged hormones, sweetheart. If anything, he's the one that's been after me. He came out to the corral that night you guys fixed dinner. Ask him about that. If that wasn't a come-on, I don't know what is."

Tara waited, her upturned face a showcase of triumph. She waited for Donna to collapse next to her, stunned into silence. Tara was sorely disappointed.

"I know exactly what went on. We laughed about it, Tara. He told me how you bolted, terrified of him. All your big talk and you're still terrified of a real man. You ran away from Ben when he was whole. Yeah, I know all about that night. I think it's pitiful."

Speechless, Tara locked eyes with Donna's. Bill Hamilton's spirit stood between them, destructive and gleeful.

"Is there anything else? I have a few things more to pack before we leave."

"You're being stupid, Donna. Very, very stupid. I don't know how he's turned you against me. I'm not afraid of men. I'm afraid of Bill Hamilton."

Without another word Tara started to leave, pausing long enough to scoop up a bright red blouse Donna had dropped.

"Don't forget this. I'd hate for you to come back for anything." Tara lay the red silk blouse across Donna's palm. As she did she caught sight of a twinkle of silver just outside the window, a short flash of something glittery. So many things came into her mind's eye: a knife, a pitchfork, a belt buckle. The muzzle of a gun, perhaps. The two women stood bathed in light, framed by a curtainless window. So vulnerable. Such easy targets, the two of them.

The moment of caution was past. Anger was back. It was a way of life these days, but this time, Tara was going to make it work for her. This was her home, her friend, and Bill Hamilton couldn't have either. This was no ghost, no figment of her imagination. It was Bill Hamilton, liar and felon, she caught sight of out there.

Tara headed out the front door, hesitating on the step. The wind was up. She pulled at a long strand of hair that blew across her eyes, and lifted her head as if she could smell him. She walked around the house, her guard up against his tricks. He could pop up anywhere or be found languishing near a tree. She could pass him in this dark and not know it until he chuckled. She would spin only to see that white bright grin of his.

"Not this time, Billy," Tara muttered, slowing

her step, keeping her eyes wide open for any sign of life on this cold, now miserable, night.

Finally she saw him. He stood quietly with his back to her, his hands in his pockets, contemplating the flow of the river at his feet. Slowly Tara moved forward, steeling herself against any sport in which he might indulge. She moved almost noiselessly until the waist-high brush kept her from going farther without commotion and greater effort. Still Bill Hamilton didn't move, and Tara breathed hard, hoping he wouldn't hear it. Bill liked fear. He fed on it. Tara took a moment before she spoke. It was too long. Bill beat her to it. His voice was so beautiful on this clear and chilly night, so different from the happy, manic cowboy who'd probably paid compliments while he shot that poor, pregnant woman. This wasn't the voice of a sanguine seducer. This voice could have brought her to tears, so lovely and low, the words heartfelt and anguished. He was unrecognizable because of them.

"It's so sad to be loved and thrown away because someone's afraid of you." He turned his head but only far enough so Tara could see his profile. His head was raised, his handsome face turned just so as if to be admired, hoping to be caught for eternity by an artist's hand. But his eyes were on a star and it seemed he was not as aware of her as she imagined. "I cry when I think of the babies thrown away. Abandoned in trash cans. Mothers who don't love them. My mother loved me. Oh, how she loved me. And look what I've become. Donna loves me. She's not afraid. You can't make her that way, Tara. She sees what I am because she wants me in a way you'll never understand. You see the wrong thing because you're afraid. You won't admit it, but you are. And the funny thing is, you're afraid of the wrong thing. Oh my, yes, the wrong, wrong thing."

He sighed as if he was saddened but Tara wasn't sure who he sorrowed for—himself for being in such a situation, her for not being able to understand the depth of him, or Donna for loving him so well that she'd lost all reason. He sighed and turned his body. His hands were still in his pockets. He talked to her as if they had lazed the day away and were now at the end of it, getting down to twilight talk. "I'll bet there are a lot of people who are afraid of you."

"There's no reason for anyone to be. Least of all you," Tara said, using her voice just to see if it still worked.

"Oh," he said, laughing bitterly, "but there is. You are a mighty fearsome person." She could have sworn his lips pursed as if he might throw her a kiss. "You are the keeper of secrets, Tara, and that is darn powerful. Maybe that's why Donna's afraid of you. You know all her secrets. Ugly little things that could show the world how really useless she is." One hand lifted and he underscored his words with an almost raised fist. "Tell your secrets and you could ruin lives, shame people. You could make it so people die." He slid his eyes her way and Tara thought for a minute the old Bill was back. "Hell, you could panic a whole city with what you know about me. It wouldn't be right for you to tell. But you could do it, couldn't you? There's nothin' really holdin' you back 'cept a promise, is there?" He looked away, almost talking to himself again as he stooped to pick up a rock and toss it in the river.

"Think about that, just one little minute. Oh,

just think about it. Don't it make your skin tingle to think what you've got in your head that nobody else knows?" He was smiling now, that famous good old boy grin. His voice dropped, he bent from the waist as if to tell her another secret. But what he said came as little surprise. "I would love to have that kind of power, Tara. I could have it. If only I had been born a different man."

"You've got the power, Bill," Tara answered in kind, her voice as bare of emotion as the branches of the winter cottonwoods. "You've got a fearful power if what you told me is true."

"Aw." Bill's body swayed as if embarrassed by the compliment. Did his boot chuck at the ground? Had she flattered him? Then his gray eyes were back on her and Tara lay her hands on the brush to steady herself. He wasn't smiling anymore. "Tara, to make someone afraid is so easy. To make them live with fear, to have enough power to make them wonder day in and day out if you're going to tell somethin'—whoee, that's mighty."

With a sad smile, he turned away from her and looked back to the river. Did he think of throwing himself in? Wouldn't that be a blessing?

"I'd like people to respect me, Tara. They should because of what I can do. But everyone doesn't know what I can do, and I'm so afraid to tell 'em. If I do, they'll expect so much. I'm not brave enough to be what they expect. Are you?"

Tara didn't move. She only stared at him, wondering how a man like him could ask all the right questions, point out all the wrong things. He chuckled and threw another rock.

"There's even something worse. To be weak when you look like you shouldn't be. Oh, damn," he sighed. "When people find out this cowboy ain't got the power, they dis him, Tara. Dis him bad." He sighed deeply. "Have you ever felt like you couldn't make somethin' happen? It's a lousy thing. Hell, I haven't been able to make life happen. Those pills made me feel like I was someone. Problem was, it wasn't the someone I should be. Do you get it? Do you know what I mean? Do you see why I need help so badly? I don't think the someone I am is a very good person to be. I'd like to be you, Tara. I'd like to be the two of you. One lady in her home, on her ranch; one the keeper of secrets, hard and tough and no one can make her tell."

Tara's heart slowed, the night around her stop-framed for an instant. Her head swam. Who was this man? How did he get into her life? Was he weak and sad and looking for the finale to the very poor play in which he'd been cast? The magic he attributed to her was nonexistent. She had no power to protect herself against the fear Bill Hamilton inspired, and there was certainly no power in knowing his secrets. She proved this every day as one by one friends turned against her.

Quietly, she drew on everything that made her what she was, calling on all the strong spirits that had, over a century, imbued her with tenacity, if not strength. She would act out the role that Bill Hamilton had assigned her. Tara Linley made her demands.

"I don't want you to leave here tonight. Talk to Donna. She'll listen to you."

Bill didn't face her, but she knew he was listening hard.

"It's time I used my power to help you then. I want numbers where I can reach your family. I want to talk to your old girlfriend. You will see a psychologist tomorrow. His name is Ben Crawford. I'll pick you up and drive you to his office in the morning. You give me these things and do these things, or I cut you loose, Bill. I'm taking risks for you. I'm not losing Donna because of you. I will tell my secrets and you will fry along with me unless you do as I say."

"Really?" Bill asked.

"Really," Tara insisted and she knew he didn't believe her. She didn't believe herself "Nine o'clock, Bill. Be ready."

Fifteen

Tara took the steps two at a time and rang the bell. The buzzer unlatched the door and she pushed through, walked into the house and down the hall.

"Ben!" she called. "You can relax. I'm all alone."

She'd swung into his office before he made the hall. They met in the doorway and Ben backed off.

"You are alone!" Ben looked around her, checking for himself.

"I am." Emboldened by the adrenaline rush of this morning's surprise, Tara skirted past as if she'd been popping in for years. "Have any hot chocolate?"

"I'm not that creative in the morning. Sorry. Coffee?"

"I'll settle." She shrugged out of her jacket and looked over her shoulder as she went to the sideboard. "Want some?"

"Already got it." The wheelchair was on automatic pilot. It whirred while he settled himself behind the desk. She slid on top of it and cupped her mug with both hands as she blew on the hot coffee.

"You keep a clean desk."

"Only when I know I'll have visitors who prefer

it to the couch," he said. He was ready for business. "So, what's the scoop? I was expecting to take a meeting with the devil this morning."

"He took off. I didn't hear a thing. Donna obviously didn't mind leaving. She didn't even say goodbye."

"And you're sitting here instead of calling out the militia?" Ben asked. "Can't even work up a good fury?"

Tara shook her head. "Guess I finally got smart."

"That's fairly amazing."

"Something happened last night. It's hard to explain." Tara took a sip of her coffee, slid off the desk, and walked to the windows. She looked past the well-manicured grass onto the street. Cars went by, people walked, everyone went about their business. She turned around and propped herself up against the sill. He was smiling at her. She laughed. "What?"

"Nothing." He shrugged, but there was more. She smiled back, liking the way the few strands of silver in his hair brightened his face. He was still grinning. She put a hand to her hip and he gave in. "Okay. You look great this morning. That's it. You just look great."

Tara chuckled. "That's nice. And this is crazy."

"I don't know, I think seeing a beautiful woman in the morning has its merits."

"I meant it's crazy that I should be so pleased that you noticed. Given the fact that Donna's taken off with a crazy man, our friendship is probably over, my client is still loose, and I am more convinced than ever after last night that he's a nut case, I should be hysterical."

"Hysteria uses a lot of energy," Ben said. "Besides, it's not your style." Ben touched his coffee cup, gave it a quarter turn, then tapped the top of his desk. "But I have to admit you have good reason to worry. Any idea where they've gone?"

"He's not a fugitive. They've probably gone back to Donna's place. She built a mansion in the middle of the desert about an hour from here."

"Must be hard to get a good maid out there."

"She pays well. Besides, now she has Bill. I doubt they ever get out of the bedroom long enough to mess anything up," Tara said.

Ben was amused. "There are some aspects of this guy's psyche that work just fine if you ask me, Tara." She gave him a withering look.

"Be serious. Last night was so weird. I found him by the river. We talked. It was spooky because he was so controlled—or maybe exacting is the word. He knows why he's angry, yet he spoke like he was sad. He knows what he wants, but understands the violence isn't the way to get it. His voice was completely different than all the other times I've spoken to him."

"That's not unusual. Some who are mentally disturbed actually seem to change their appearance depending on the depth of the psychosis."

"It was really spooky, but we also came to an understanding. I told him that I'd cut him loose if he didn't give me something to work with. The other part of the equation was keeping this appointment today. I slept well last night because I was seeing an end to this whole mess. Then he does this." She threw up her free hand, a gesture of frustration. "And I think the reason I'm not more upset is because I'm worn out trying to second-guess him. I don't know if he's thumbing his nose at me, afraid of me, afraid that if I had the information I wanted,

he'd actually be committed. Without his cooperation, I'm forced to give up."

"It would seem that way," Ben agreed. They sat
silently for a moment. Tara pushed away from the
window and paced slowly.

"The only problem is, he's still got Donna."

"Tara, he isn't holding her hostage," Ben chuckled. "Donna went with him. If he had dragged her
off by her hair, I'd be suggesting we call the police
right now."

"I know," Tara moaned. "I know that. Oh, God,
Ben sometimes I think what he has is catching and
Donna's got it. Do you know Donna actually thinks
I was attracted to that man? Can you believe it?"

Ben laughed. "I believe anything. I'm a psychologist."

"Don't make fun."

"I'm not," he said, and she believed him. "I'm
just saying there isn't anything you can do short
of running after them to change the situation, and
that's hardly productive. So it seems you made the
right decision."

"I know. But it would be easy to just pick up
the phone and tell her what I know about him.
I've already come so close. Why not go the rest of
the way?" Tara cupped her hands around her mug
and leaned her elbows on her knees. "Until last
night I thought I could wait it out. I was so sure
something would break. Now I don't think it will."
Speaking softly, Tara looked at the floor, unable to
meet Ben's eyes. "You know, when Donna leaves
my house, there's always something of herself left
behind, like a little bit of her spirit. But this time
I don't feel her. This time I feel him and it's awful.
And," she sighed, "since there is nothing I can do
about any of this short of giving Woodrow Bill's

name or telling Donna she's sleeping with a murderer, I'm going to have to move on. If I don't, I'll be the one who's nuts."

"I would have loved to meet this guy, Tara." Ben was almost wistful.

"I would have been happy about that, too."

"Meanwhile?" Ben asked.

"Meanwhile, there's one last thing I can do." Tara stood up and put her mug on the edge of the desk.

"Can I help?"

"Let me use your phone."

"What's the number?" He punched in the numbers as she gave them and held the phone toward her. She could hear it ringing.

"Gina Patton, please," Tara said when someone answered.

While she waited for her connection, Tara looked at Ben and Ben mouthed, *Dinner, tonight?* She nodded and smiled, then her party was on the line.

"Gina? Tara Linley. I need you to find someone."

Tara walked out to the courtyard to hang a ristra. A pro bono client had brought the string of dried chiles with great fanfare the day Tara told Ben he wouldn't be keeping his appointment with Bill Hamilton. That day she'd contacted Gina, one of the best private investigators in the city, and put her on the payroll. Three days ago. There had been a dinner and two lunches with him since then. Tonight would be dinner again. The time she spent with Ben almost overcame the dread she felt with the passing of silent days without contact from Donna or Bill.

But now the only thing on her mind was the ristra. She already had one hanging on the post near the far side of the wall where the bougainvillea climbed, almost obscuring it. Finally she hooked the new ristra near the front door. When she stepped back to admire it, Tara saw the car.

It wasn't hard to spot and it wasn't difficult to figure out what to do. She'd been aware of it for days now and it hadn't bothered her a bit that Woodrow, or George, had put someone on her tail. Actually, it had been rather amusing when they kept their distance, but now they were too close to home. In fact, they were trespassing.

Sticking her hands into the back pockets of her trousers, Tara pushed through the gate, her eyes trained on the olive green sedan. Joseph ambled toward her from the barn. She held up a warning hand, then pointed toward the end of the drive. He came alongside quietly.

"You need help?" he mumbled.

"No thanks. I can handle this. Go on back to Shinin'. Think you can get him out for some exercise today?" She looked over her shoulder.

The horse stood at the fence watching his mistress. Tara smiled, then looked back at Joseph. He nodded, glared at the car at the end of the road, and went back to his chores.

Tara ambled down the long dirt drive toward Rio Grande Boulevard. Her heel hit a rock and her ankle twisted. She stopped to shake it out. The person in the car hadn't spotted her. All was quiet. She went on until she was close enough to run her hand along the rear of the car and over the fender until she stopped and stood quietly watching the man in the car. He slept with his head on the open window, his mouth gaping and a cup of coffee balanced on the center console. Tara leaned down, bending from the waist. It was time to send him on his way.

"Hello? Hello?" Tara sang softly, but it was enough to startle the man.

He bolted upright and almost lost the coffee onto the gear shift. One hand went to the Styrofoam cup, the other to his face. He rubbed frantically, leaving a red blush up the left side. His eyes were heavy and his lips weren't working quite right.

"What? Yeah. What? I was just turning around. Sorry, ma'am. Was just trying to find my way. Got lost." Tongue-tied, he sounded as ridiculous as he looked. George should train his men better. Tara sighed and put her hands on the car door.

"It's all right. Don't worry about it, Detective. It is Detective, isn't it?" She was patient. She was kind. "I appreciate the position you're in, but let's agree that this isn't getting you anywhere. I can't be intimidated, and you can't find who you're looking for here. Tell Woodrow and George that he's gone."

"He might come back," the big man grumbled, almost finished, rearranging himself. He'd even found the top to his Styrofoam cup and replaced it meticulously.

"And then what are you going to do?" Tara laughed. "Arrest him for being a house guest?"

"We weren't going to arrest him," the man complained.

"Okay. Intimidate him. That's a great way to pass the day. Save yourself time and effort. Sleep at home. Drive only when you have somewhere to go.

Don't drink coffee in the car. Woodrow is not going to get anything out of me, because I have nothing to give him. And tell George I'm really disappointed in him, too. This is a terrible waste of taxpayers' money." Tara stepped back from the car. "If I ever have what they want, I'll get it to them. But right now that's a slim possibility."

"I don't think they'll like this." The detective hunkered over the steering wheel and started the car.

"Tough." Tara stood back. "Now, on your way, or I'll show you how much I know about tying up people's time with frivolous lawsuits."

He breathed heavily, and it wasn't even close to a sigh of disappointment. George would have him doing something else equally absurd by noon. But the detective knew George better than she did. "I'll probably be back. Just want you to know."

"Park on the road," Tara said.

"I've got to do my job," the man groused.

"Then wait until there's actually something to do." The suggestion was lost in the drone of the engine. She waved him off, watching until he was out of sight, knowing that Woodrow must be desperate.

Slowly she walked back to the house, imagining how her silence now gave Woodrow sleepless nights. He needed Bill Hamilton more than ever. Woodrow was no longer campaigning. He was simply defending himself against new, and ever more sensational charges that he had used his power as the district attorney to hand out favors. Fortunately Charlotte's good works didn't go unnoticed and her pretty face still smiled out from the society page as usual. Opening the front door, Tara wondered if they would ever speak again. If there was no resolution to this problem with Bill Hamilton, if he remained untouchable, culpable only in her mind, would the broken relationships ever be mended?

Tara checked the clock. It was time for work, not time to reflect on what could have been had each of them acted differently. Tara grabbed her car keys and briefcase and checked to make sure the answering machine was on just in case Donna called. She might decide it was time to make amends. She might need Tara. There was always that possibility. Living with Bill Hamilton, it was likely.

"Morning, Caroline. Any messages?"

"Johnnie Rae Riskin's mother called to thank you for making arrangements on the billing. The doctor wants to know why you haven't been back in for him to check your arm. I made an appointment for a consultation next week. Civil matter. Ben called." She waggled that particular message slip mischievously. Caroline had been having a great deal of fun since she realized Ben was not a professional acquaintance. "He wants to know if you'd like to go riding with him before dinner. He's going to start training for a marathon. Actually he said he'd wheel while you rode."

"Funny." Tara pulled a face.

"I thought so," Caroline said. "You've got a light day so I could make a doctor's appointment anytime. And I think a ride with Dr. Crawford would be just the thing."

"Thank you, Dear Abby. And no thanks, I can make my own doctor's appointment." Tara took the mail and messages from Caroline, who looked awfully disappointed. "But I'll compromise on Ben. Tell him I'll come by his place after work. I'll run, he can wheel. The way it looks, it'll take me the rest of the day to go through this stuff. I must say, I am feeling popular today."

"Oh yeah? What else besides a lot of mail and phone calls?" Caroline put a chubby fist under her chin and waited for Tara to entertain her.

"Nothing earth-shattering. Just an unexpected visitor at home." Tara grinned, thinking she'd like to sit and gossip all day. "But I can get some mileage out of it. Would you get Woodrow on the phone, please? I'd like to give him a little grief. After that, we'll give George Amos a little what-for."

"You got it." Caroline reached for the phone, disappointed it was going to be a business-as-usual day.

"Give me three minutes to stash my purse." Caroline nodded and Tara headed to the inner sanctum. Settled, she shoved aside the more mundane number ten envelopes, preferring to see what had been sent in the padded one. The intercom buzzed. She hit the button on the phone.

"Mr. Weber's office on line two. We're on hold."

"Okay." Offhandedly Tara picked up the receiver, kicked back, and held it on her shoulder while she ripped open the envelope. She left the staples hanging. Inside was no freebie from a promotional house, but a pile of fabric, soft and smooth to the touch. Slowly Tara pulled it out. Carefully she laid it on her desk. The phone had slipped from her shoulder. She caught it and held it close to her face, half missing her ear while she looked at the mess on her desk. Mesmerized, Tara unfolded it slowly, knowing she had seen it before.

"Woodrow Weber."

Woodrow's voice seemed far away and of little interest. Tara picked away at the fabric until it resembled a ruby sunburst, not the red blouse it had once been. In a revelatory flash Tara relived the moment she'd touched it before. Angry words. Donna furious and cold. Packing. Leaving. Donna leaving with the red blouse in her suitcase. Now it was here, in Tara's office. Destroyed not by accident but with passionate slashes of something sharp. A knife? Scissors? The phone popped from her shoulder and clattered to the desk. She could hear Woodrow's indignant voice as if he himself had been dropped so rudely.

"Hello! Woodrow Weber. Who is this, please?"

Frantically Tara shoved her hand into the envelope, drawing blood as the staples scraped over her skin, not caring what happened to her until she found what she was looking for. It had to be there. Subtlety wasn't Bill Hamilton's specialty. She pulled at that padded envelope until it tore, she found a scrap of paper, nothing more than that. A scrap of paper with an apocalyptic message.

"I can hear you. Who is this?" Woodrow hollered. Tara grabbed the phone and put it to her ear, the note in the other hand.

Look what I can do. Look what I have done. Look what I can do.

The message was typed until the words ran off the page. This was a typewriter, not a computer printout. Donna's typewriter? Donna! Weak with fright, she steadied herself with a hand on the pile of fabric and pushed the phone tighter against her ear as if that would keep her from reaching through it to strangle Woodrow Weber.

"Start praying, Woodrow," Tara growled. "He's

lost it. If I find a body where I'm going, it's on
your head."

Before he could utter a word of protest or horror, before he could ask a question, Tara slammed
down the phone and vaulted out of the room,
holding the mess of red silk against her breast.

"Call the sheriff, Caroline. Call them now.
Donna Ecold's house. Ten miles east of Highway
25 off 518. It's an emergency. Life and death. Tell
them it's an assault with intent to kill. Tell them
anything, just get them there."

"Oh no, is it really?" Caroline called after her,
but Tara was gone, the question ringing in her
ears as she took the fire stairs two at a time instead
of waiting for the elevator. She was too far away
to answer, but did anyway.

"I hope the hell not."

Forty-five minutes to Donna's. A record, accomplished because the roads were clear, the snowfall
had been insignificant, and there wasn't an icy
patch to be found on the blacktop. Potholes
slowed her down on the more poorly kept road
that led to Donna's isolated home, but the Jeep
took those with gumption and Tara sped onto
Donna's land like a downhill cart on a rollercoaster. Out of the car she moved fast, her coat flapping, the remnants of Donna's red blouse still
clutched in her hand.

"Donna? Donna!"

Tara took the steps fast and banged on the front
door with her fist. Nothing. She rounded the
porch. It was a big place, a monument to Donna's
success as a writer and a triple divorcee. Tara
paused, shielded her eyes, and peered into the din-

ing room through one of the long windows. Everything as it should be. She headed down the porch
and took a right. Donna's car was there. Another
with a pointed star painted on its side sat next to
it. The sheriff had arrived. But one car for a man
like Bill Hamilton?

Suddenly light-headed, Tara stopped and held
on to the side of the house. She held her stomach.
Nausea, dizziness, visions of Donna viciously at-
tacked were clear in her mind's eye. They were
almost too much to bear. It would be her fault if
Donna was dead. And for what?

Lifting her head, Tara tilted it back and took a
deep breath. In the desert silence she heard voices.
They spoke without urgency.

Tara fell against the wall, leaning on her shoulder, turning her head to it with a moan. There
was no frantic activity. No paramedics. No one to
help Donna, because Donna was beyond help.

Raising her hand, Tara buried her face in the
soft silk. She couldn't smell the scent of her
friend's perfume. She closed her eyes and couldn't
remember the look on Donna's face when she
smiled or cried. All Tara could remember was Bill
Hamilton standing by the river.

Tara pushed wearily away from the wall, and
steeled herself to look at him now. Three male
voices came from the kitchen. One of them
laughed. Confused, Tara opened the kitchen door
and looked in. Around Donna's antique table sat
two sheriff's deputies and Bill Hamilton. Cups of
coffee and smiles all around.

"Tara!" Bill was up, his arms held wide as if he
would embrace her. She backed off, glaring at him.
The cowboy was here and he was good.

"Where's Donna?" Tara was aware that one of

the deputies had stood up. The legs of his chair grated on the wooden floor but her eyes didn't leave Bill Hamilton until the deputy spoke.

"You must be Ms. Linley."

Tara whirled on him, her face flushed with anger and shock. "Where is Donna Ecold?"

Taken aback, he nodded toward the double doors that led to the living room. Tara cut a wide berth around Bill and pushed open the doors with such force they banged against the opposite wall. They swished closed behind her, and sealed the men into the kitchen and her in the living room with Donna.

Donna was bent over the typewriter, her little fingers pounding the keys as if each of them were a thing despised. She didn't stop when Tara stood trembling beside her desk. When Tara shoved the torn red blouse in front of her, Donna sat quietly, stony-faced as if waiting for Tara to tire and leave.

"What in the hell is this? What?" Tara demanded, tears of anger and relief swelling painfully behind her eyes. Her hand was shaking and her fingers were weak. She held it higher, as if for Donna to take it.

"I don't know," Donna replied. A split second later she shoved Tara's hand away. She was typing again.

"Stop. Stop it," Tara cried. She slapped Donna's hands away from the keys and shoved the machine away from Donna. Hair flying over her face, she pushed Donna's chair back, planting herself between her friend and the fairy story that held her in thrall. "Look at me, damn you. I thought you were dead." Tara's voice caught on a high note and was tempered by a sob. She pushed her hair away and turned her head to compose herself, embarrassed to find so much emotion in her and nothing returned in kind. Her voice softened to a whisper. "I thought you were dead."

"Why didn't you just call? The telephone is an amazing invention." Fake lashes swept over her cheeks, her eyes glittering angrily beneath them. Donna wore a new color of blush and it was harsh against her pale skin.

"I did call." Tara swung her head back to look at Donna, amazed that her friend would think her so stupid. "I called from the car three times. When you didn't answer, I thought the worst. If you were all right, why didn't you answer?" Tara's fist hit the desk hard. She ignored the hurt. It was nothing compared to what was in her heart as Donna sneered at her.

"Gee, I don't know," she countered sarcastically. "Maybe I was indisposed. Maybe you called when the police burst in with their guns drawn and caught Bill and me in a compromising position. Yes, I did hear the phone ring, but for some reason they didn't want me to answer it. Or maybe you called when they had him down on the floor, handcuffed, and I was screaming for them to let him go. Or"—Donna tapped her cheek with a finger and rolled her eyes ceilingward—"perhaps, you could have let it ring a little longer when they dragged him out to the car to question him. He was half dressed and it was cold and he'd done nothing wrong." Donna's eyes narrowed. There was fury in them and her voice was frigid. "I don't know, Tara, maybe you should have let it ring longer."

"I don't give a damn what they did to him," Tara countered, moving half a step toward Donna as if closer, she would be made to understand. "I was so scared that you were hurt, and it was all my fault." Donna made a sound of disgust and got up. She walked away, but Tara dogged her, taking hold of her arm and pushing the red blouse at her again. "Look at this, and tell me you wouldn't have completely freaked out if you'd seen it. He sent it." Tara gestured toward the kitchen. "He sent it as a warning. I thought it meant that he'd already hurt you, but I think it just means he could. He told me he wouldn't, but now I think that was a lie or at least it's a cry for help. Please look at it, Donna. Please."

Slowly Donna turned and looked at Tara with a lazy up and down. Finally, she took the fabric and unraveled it, holding it away from her with a great show of distaste. She eyed it dramatically, judging the amount of time Tara seemed to require and said flatly:

"It's not my blouse."

"It is your blouse," Tara cried in disbelief. "I saw it the night you left, the night I tried to tell you that this guy was bad news. I picked it up off the floor and handed it to you, remember? Donna, why are you protecting him like this?"

Tara hurried after Donna, who didn't break stride as she headed for the main staircase. Dressed in white from head to toe she looked angelic and avenging, skating over the hardwood floor in her haste. She pounded up the stairs to the second floor and threw open the door to her bedroom. Tara dashed after, studiously ignoring the tangle of sheets on the big bed. She was just headed in to the walk-in closet when Donna was coming out. The smaller woman pushed past her.

"Here. Now tell me about whatever it is you think you have there." Donna held up a red blouse.

"Three buttons, Tara. No cuffs. That's not even my size, or didn't you look at the label? That thing is polyester, Tara, not silk. Now, I don't know who did that, but it wasn't Bill and it wasn't my blouse."

Tara ran her hands over the blouse, crushing the other one in her hand. They weren't the same. Not even close. She looked toward the door, half expecting to see Bill Hamilton standing there, getting a charge out of his little joke. Tara threw down both blouses and stormed out of the bedroom. This time Donna was the one doing the chasing.

"Give me some paper," Tara demanded.

At the desk again, she ripped a sheet off the stack next to the typewriter and shoved it into the machine without waiting for Donna. She twirled the platen and the paper fed through askew. Tara typed, *Look what I can do. Look what I have done.* She ripped the sheet out of the machine and dug in the pocket of her coat.

"Look, Donna. Your typewriter. See? The dropped *e*? Now tell me you don't think your honey did this. You can't be that blind. He used this typewriter. Don't you think that could be construed as threatening?"

Donna stepped forward and took the paper. Without looking she crumpled it and dropped it on the floor.

"Tara, please," Donna said softly, so sadly it made Tara turn away. She had lost.

"Don't do this. He isn't worth it." She looked back at Donna. "I am not freaking out. I'm not having some sort of after-forty breakdown. When have you known me to be anything but responsible?"

"There's always a first time."

"This is ridiculous. That's your strategy where Bill Hamilton's concerned. Turn a blind eye. I don't know why I should be surprised. You did it when your husbands cheated on you, when your lovers beat you. You never questioned them until it was almost too late. I've stood by you through everything. I've offered my advice, my friendship, and my home when you wanted to run away. You always came back and told me I was right about those men. Well, I'm right this time, too. But you've got to admit it before the fact. After may be too late." Tara sniffed and threw back her head, blinking away frustrated tears. "I wouldn't have called the sheriff if I wasn't totally convinced that Bill had hurt you, or was planning to hurt you. I did it because I love you."

"I appreciate that, Tara," Donna said, her calm oddly unnerving in the face of such an outburst. "But you're driving me crazy and you're not going to change anything. I'm an adult, and so is Bill. Whatever is going on here is very, very strange, and I understand that. But whatever is between you two has to stay there. I don't want to know about it even if you could tell me."

"I will, if it will help—"

"Don't. Stop. I don't want to hear a word." Donna held up her hand. "Bill told me that you couldn't tell anyone about his confidence. That it was the law. If you disregard that oath and tell me something you shouldn't, it would kill you."

"I don't care anymore."

"I do," Donna said instantly. "I don't want anything to change between me and Bill. He's always been loving. I haven't seen anything that will convince me he's going to change. So if you can't accept the fact that I am happy with him, and that he is going to be a part of my life no matter what, then we can't be with each other. It's that simple."

"Ms. Ecold?" Both women whirled toward the open kitchen door, where the dark-haired deputy watched them.

"Yes?" Donna stepped forward, her voice pretty and girlish. Turn the spotlight her way and the act began.

"Since there's no problem here, we'll head back if that's all right with you." The man held his hat in hand, respectful of Donna's wealth and Bill Hamilton's winning ways.

"No, it's not all right." Tara stepped forward. "I'm Tara Linley. I'm an attorney and I think you should do some serious talking with that man in there. I want you to listen carefully to what he has to say. I want you to ask him if he wrote this." Tara held out the original note. The deputy's eyes flicked to Donna. Then he stood straight and put on his hat.

"Ma'am, with all due respect, there just doesn't seem to be any reason to hang around. The only one I see making a fuss here is you. So unless Ms. Ecold, or Mr. Hamilton, would like us to remove you from the premises we'll be saying goodbye."

The deputy cocked an eyebrow toward Donna, then turned to the doorway. Bill appeared as if on cue. His handsome face was set in a dutifully concerned expression.

"No, of course we don't want that," Donna said, holding her hand out. "Bill?"

Bill slipped past the deputies to stand beside Donna. His arm went around her shoulders. She was so small in the crook of his arm. He laid eyes on Tara and her face burned scarlet. He looked triumphant. He looked powerful, as he had wished he could be.

"Yes, you do," Tara said icily, accepting defeat. "You don't want me here, so I'll go."

"Tara, I don't understand all this." Donna turned her face into Bill's chest. He put his hand in her hair, a comforting gesture. "Why are you doing this to us?"

Tara walked close to Donna, almost touching her. "I am not doing anything that Bill didn't ask me to. Maybe he's the one who can't figure out what he wants."

The deputies passed a glance. Tara had their attention. She stepped forward once more, sanctioned by the hesitation. "You retained me as your attorney to help you, didn't you? Then let me help you."

The deputies' ears pricked. Little watchdogs waiting to see if there actually was anything interesting going on here.

"Things have changed, Tara," Bill said quietly with a small smile. "Donna and I are getting married. She's gonna need me here, with her. I got me some thinkin' to do, Tara. But I don't think you have to worry none."

"Maybe you're right. I shouldn't worry anymore at all."

Without another word Tara left Donna Ecold's home, walked across the porch, and climbed into her Jeep. Turning the key, the engine came to life. She threw the gear into reverse and, with her arm over the backseat, spun the wheel. The car bolted, overcompensated when she pushed the shift into drive, then tore down the desert road. She was anxious to get back to the city. She had one more stop to make before she went home.

***

"The polls aren't looking good, Woodrow. I don't know what else you want me to say. We knew this was going to be tight from the very beginning. But with all this controversy, I don't know anymore."

Sandy Parker sat back and tossed his pencil on top of the papers spread out over Woodrow Weber's desk. He'd done his best. Couldn't make the numbers look any better no matter how he massaged them and he couldn't change history—which was exactly what it looked like Woodrow was going to be.

"I don't understand this, Sandy. I've poured money into radio spots in the last few weeks, I've gone to every group that's asked me to speak, and I'm not gaining proportional points even in the short term. It may still be early, but after all this damage control there should have been a change for the better this week. Chris is slime for doing this to me."

"That's politics." Sandy picked up the pencil again and ran it through his fingers.

"That stinks."

"Look, Woodrow. I think it's time we back off from this strategy. We won't try to explain it anymore. You won't address it. You're going to stand up in front of people and say that you've already discussed the matter. Period. We'll look better than Chris. We'll look classier."

"We'll get killed."

"It's the only alternative strategy. Unless we can get something tight on him and give as good as we're getting, I don't see any other way."

Woodrow sighed and pushed his glasses up on

his nose. He glanced at his campaign manager, who was studiously considering the poll results. For a minute Woodrow thought of telling Sandy about Tara. There might be a percentage in committing her client. He'd like to explore the possibility anyway. He hadn't talked to Tara in over a week, so he had to assume she was going to hold out until she got what she wanted.

"Woodrow?"

Charlotte stood in the doorway. She was as good a reminder as any that compromise shouldn't be a part of the Circle K equation. He would hold tight a little longer.

"Yes, Charlotte?" He smiled.

"Would you and Sandy like something to eat? I've got cookies, cake. I could make some sandwiches." Charlotte came into the room quietly and put her arm around her husband's waist. She pulled him close and lay her head on his chest as she smiled at Sandy. Sandy envisioned her face plastered all over the city on posters. She was a blessing. He smiled back at her.

"I've gotta go, Charlotte, but thanks anyway." He looked at Woodrow. "Want me to leave these?"

"Sure, I'll go over them again later."

"I'll see you out, Sandy." Charlotte held out her hand to usher him to the door. She gave a backward glance to Woodrow and knew it had been bad. So she walked quietly to the door, beginning her goodbye as she pulled open the door.

"Tara!" Surprised, Charlotte stepped back.

"Where's Woodrow?"

Tara was in the house before Charlotte could say another word. Sandy moved to the side, knowing better than to offer his hello. Tara looked like a hornet.

"He's in his office in the back, but . . ." Tara walked past Charlotte, ignoring Sandy. Charlotte was on her heels. "Tara, he's busy right now, and I don't think we should disturb him. He's had a terrible day."

Tara whirled on Charlotte, surprising and intimidating her in her own home. For that, Tara felt a twinge of regret. She took a breath and calmed herself.

"Charlotte, I don't mean to be rude, but I didn't stop in for a chat. I'm sure Woodrow will fill you in on the details and that's his prerogative. But right now, I've got to see him."

Tara was gone, leaving Charlotte and Sandy stunned in her wake. Down the hall she threw open Woodrow's door and slammed it behind her.

"Do you want me to stay?" Sandy asked.

Charlotte shook her head, "No, thanks."

"Looks like Woodrow has his hands full, huh?"

"More than you know," Charlotte answered, then murmured her goodbyes.

In the kitchen Charlotte poured herself a cup of tea, decided that wasn't what she wanted at all, and dug in her purse for her pack of cigarettes. Even that wouldn't do it. So Charlotte sat at the kitchen table listening to raised voices. Tara's voice drowned out Woodrow's and Charlotte cringed.

Charlotte left the kitchen table when she heard the door of Woodrow's office open again. She was waiting in the living room when Tara appeared looking drawn and pale, moving slower than when she'd come in. As she passed, Tara put a hand out, but Charlotte stopped her, taking her arm and pushing it away before she could be touched.

Startled, Tara looked up and she saw a person she didn't know. There was an edge about Charlotte. Her smile was gone, replaced by a grim mouth that lacked definition without her signature pink lipstick.

"Don't ever do that again, Tara," Charlotte said, and the order was more unnerving because it was delivered without emotion. "Don't ever walk into my house and go past me as if I don't matter. Don't ever come here on the warpath looking for my husband. He deserves more respect than that, and so do I."

"I'm sorry, Charlotte," Tara apologized cautiously, deciding against the hundred other things she'd like to say. Quietly, she went out the door knowing Charlotte was watching through the leaded glass. When she was sure Tara was leaving, Charlotte went to Woodrow's office. She stood in the doorway.

"I'm sorry I didn't stop her, Woodrow," Charlotte said, happy to see he looked no worse than before Tara had come. "What did she want?"

"There was some trouble tonight. She thought her friend had been hurt. She says it's my fault."

Charlotte walked into the room and sat in the leather chair in the corner. It was the only place that wasn't covered with campaign materials. From this angle he did look tired. He sounded it too.

"Is this about the Circle K killer?" Charlotte asked.

"One and the same." Woodrow ran a hand through his hair and closed his eyes. "Jeez, my neck is tight. Do you mind?" Charlotte shook her head and smiled, doing as he asked. She kneaded the muscles that ran across his shoulders and waited until he was ready to talk again. "Charlotte, I just don't know what to do. I don't want to be responsible for anyone getting hurt. I couldn't live with myself if her friend had been killed."

"You wouldn't be responsible, Woodrow. Tara knows what she has to do, and so do you. She's the one with all the information. She's the one who should use it wisely."

"I'm not making it easy for her," Woodrow admitted.

"It shouldn't be easy. Someone has to have backbone, Woodrow. I'm proud that you're not caving in."

Woodrow sat up straighter. "Really?

"Really," she whispered and kissed him on the cheek, letting her arms wind round him. "Remember, Woodrow, you're a public servant. You have considerations that transcend the personal. Tara's never been in the position of being responsible for anyone but herself. Her scope of loyalty has always been focused on herself, her father, her friends. She's never had to work for the good of the whole. I'm not sure she could."

"You're right." He patted her hand. "I've done what I can. There isn't any more I can do at this point. It's a pity. I think I could do a lot of good if I could bring that guy in. Not just for myself, Charlotte. I know you understand that." Woodrow slid away from his wife, feeling better because of her. "Let's go upstairs."

"That's a good idea. It's been a long day," Charlotte said. They held hands as they walked up the stairs toward the bedroom. At the landing, Charlotte paused. "You know, Woodrow, I have a funny feeling things are going to get better for you real soon."

Woodrow squeezed her hand in thanks. But she knew he didn't believe her. She also knew that he should.

Tara was on his doorstep. Again. Without an invitation. Again. The place was dark, but that was to be expected. It was later than she'd imagined. She was hungry. She was tired. She was humiliated. But she wasn't worried anymore. She wouldn't be that. Donna had made her bed, let her lie in it.

Tara rang again, cupped her hands, and blew on them. The door opened. She grinned, hoping she didn't look pathetic. Ben smiled back. He obviously hadn't been expecting visitors.

"You're ruining my social life, Linley."

"Guess you're starting to feel used, huh, Crawford."

"What the heck, let's see how much I can take."

Ben whirled his wheelchair back and smiled. Tara stepped through the door gratefully.

Sixteen

"I'd give anything to get this guy into the office for a session. He is a piece of work." Ben shook his head, amazed at the story he'd just heard. "You know, I didn't think I was missing anything in my work, but Hamilton sounds like the kind of challenge that comes along once in a lifetime."

They dined in the living room. The sun porch where they'd eaten pizza was just off to the right, the kitchen was straight ahead. Tonight they feasted on chicken. No bucket. Ben had cooked. Tara was impressed. The sauce was creamy, Albuquerque chiles forsaken. There were peas, a salad, and bread. She'd run out for wine and dessert while he managed the feast in record time.

One gallon of cherry marble fudge had found its way into her basket. Ben was kind enough to rave over her choice; Tara was smart enough to know she could have left out the cherry and made him happier with more fudge. Either he'd changed over the years or, as when they were teenagers, he'd let her run roughshod over life's little decisions. Tara stood in the doorway of the kitchen and held up the ice cream.

"More?"

Ben patted his middle. "Better not. I've only got

half of me to keep in shape, but I still have to work at it full time."

Tara put away the carton, grateful to have a minute to herself. It was hard to listen to his jokes. She went back, folding herself into the chair, wineglass in her hand.

"So the bottom line is?" she asked.

She put aside the dessert bowls. Little dotted cows painted on the bottom caught her eye. They were unlike Ben, who seemed to prefer clean lines. Perhaps he hadn't chosen the cow bowls at all. Perhaps a woman had been with him, lived with him. Maybe they'd sat like this one night when she gave him this frivolous gift. Maybe he'd smiled at her the same way he smiled at Tara now. The notion made Tara feel odd. She was jealous. After all these years, she still cared. After all he'd been through, she still wanted him.

"I haven't the foggiest idea what the bottom line is." Ben laughed and she joined in, ignoring the painted cows. His laugh faded, but not the pleasure she saw in his eyes. "You look so beautiful when you do that."

"Thank you," she answered, only to find herself uncomfortable in the silence that followed. She prodded. "Where were we?"

"A dead end. I haven't got a clue what to tell you." He put his elbows on the table. One finger drew little sketches on the hard wood as he thought. "Since I haven't met Bill, I can only speculate on the outline you've sketched for me. I can't see the dimensions. In my line of work you don't discount vibes.

"For instance, I could interpret his offhandedness with the police any number of ways. He doesn't rock the boat by acting normal, he skirts arrest on a lesser charge. On the other hand, he could be pushing the system to the limit. Kind of thumbing his nose at it. I'd tend to think it's the latter since he knew there would be some consequences for sending you that shredded blouse."

"Where do I fit in? If that's what he wants to do, let him play games with the police. George would love it."

"If he wanted to do that, he'd kill someone else." Ben laid his hands flat on the table. "Then it would be between him and the cops. But that's not what he wants. You're the system. You're successful within it, you're able to work through it, understand it, and he thinks you can manipulate it. Maybe it's keeping you on edge that's fun. When you get the commitment papers, he's won. If he was playing the same game with the police, he'd eventually lose and be put in prison."

Tara set down her wineglass and pushed it away. "Ben, do you think he really wants help?"

"At first he asked for it as honestly as he could. Just because he seems up all the time doesn't mean there isn't something eating away at him. He could be tortured, he could be troubled, he could be evil." Ben shrugged as if to say *take your choice*.

"When we were by the river, I thought he was a tortured soul, but he changes so quickly. The things he says sound normal, yet the look behind his eyes isn't."

"Content and form of thought," Ben said, his bottom lip disappearing for a moment. He bit it and Tara had incredibly juvenile romantic thoughts about the way he looked. Ben's, though, were still on the problem at hand. "From what you say, there seem to be disturbances in those areas. Let's assume that his actions were imposed upon him by some external force when he killed that woman."

"Oh. The hand of God came down and helped him pull the trigger?"

"Not quite. He might have seen something that reminded him of a particularly terrible time in his life. The woman he killed is doing something, and it's that something that triggers his violence. The content of this fugacious tableau intersects with reality and *boom*." Delighted, Ben opened his hands as if to show her how realistic all this was. Tara tapped one of those hands.

"In English, please."

"Sorry. There's a delusional explosion, so to speak. When Bill complains about being nowhere and feeling nothing, that could be what he's describing. Bang, that poor lady is dead and he doesn't actually remember the other bang—the one in his head. His memory of a particular incident blacks out an actual physical response to it." Ben let her think about that for a minute, then added, "The form of thought problem seems a possibility, too. Statements that seem to lack meaningful relationships to one another when you and he are one-on-one."

Tara unwound her legs. Bending over the table, she became reflective as their heads came closer and she shared her secret thoughts. "He was so charming, and part of the charm was that he was surprising. Talking about his mother, then about country-Western songs, then about needing help."

"Did you notice any change in tone when he spoke? Like a flat, inappropriate affect in speech pattern or expression? For instance, his voice monotonous, his face sort of immobile, like he's not reacting?"

"Yes and no." Tara sat away again, smiling as she realized the futility of trying to describe Bill Hamilton. "I can't tell, Ben. Ever since I found out what he did, I think my vision of him is clouded by the danger he might present to Donna. That's exactly what I've been fighting against, that emotional involvement. It's not possible for me to be completely objective," Tara answered as honestly as she could. "And now he's out of my reach. I'm tired of him moving in and out of my life so fast. That's the one thing that really unnerves me."

"Schizophrenics do that," Ben said lazily. "They force relationships, cling to people."

"Sounds like half the people I know." Tara laughed.

"Putting aside angst-ridden middle-aged professionals we both know," Ben countered.

"I resent that," Tara insisted, flirting and enjoying it.

"Which part? The angst-ridden reference or middle age?" His hand covered hers and it felt so good to have him touch her.

Bill was right. There was power in secrets, but not in keeping them. She'd shared hers with Ben and those secrets had the power to bind them. But her grin faded. She saw only one part of him: chiseled face with the full-lashed eyes, purposefully ignorant and all-seeing at the same time. His shoulders were broad and inviting, his arms muscled. Ben's chest was so broad she could lay her head on it and want to stay there forever. But she could never forget the other part of him. Tara turned away and slid her hand from his, privately shamed by the limits of her compassion—her passion—and he knew it.

"For goodness' sake, Tara. Come on. Don't do

this. Let's at least talk about it." He reached and took her hand in both of his. "We knew it would come to this the minute we saw each other. Let's get it out of the way and move on and up or wherever you want to go."

Tara looked at their entwined hands long and hard, then used her free one to lift his to her lips. It was a gentle kiss, lasting only a moment before she lay them back on the table and rose.

"I don't want this to go anywhere, Ben." Tara moved off. She didn't know what she wanted, where she should go or what she should say. Ben came round the table. She looked down on him.

"You don't know what you want, do you? You never have where we were concerned, and it's worse with me in a wheelchair. But you're a big girl now, I'm a big boy. I've done my thinking and it took years. I was alone after the accident. I had plenty of time."

"Don't try to make me feel guilty, Ben," Tara warned, knowing she'd made herself feel worse than he ever could.

"I'm not," he insisted and he chuckled a little. "Funny your first thought should be of blame or guilt. You just hate being wrong or less than perfect." Tara crossed her arms, and studied the floor, refusing to look up. Ben backtracked. "Okay, I'm sorry. You hate being weak. Maybe that's part of your attraction to your client. He makes you feel ineffectual and you have to prove him wrong." Tara glared at him. It hurt that he should know this secret about her, and talk about it so openly.

Ben twirled his chair and in one swoop caught up the two wineglasses. With his other hand he took up the half-filled bottle of wine and gave her a smile. "Come on." His wheelchair was on automatic. It whirred past her. He stopped and looked over his shoulder. "Come on. It's now or never, Tara."

Unsure, she finally followed him into the living room. Ben pointed to a chair. Tara sat. He handed her a glass, but she shook her head so he set both aside along with the bottle.

"Don't stare at me like that." Ben grinned.

"Don't analyze me," she groused.

"Why not? I've done nothing for years except try to figure us out. Even when I began living a full life again, when I began to enjoy women again, you were always there, Tara. I missed you. I loved you. I love you still. I can't ask you to love me back, but I can ask you to let go of all the things you've buried for years. I think you want more than my help. I think you want my forgiveness for being cowardly. But it wasn't cowardly to be afraid of what happened to me. We might have grown apart anyway, even if that car hadn't left me like this."

Tara shrugged. "We might have. But I like to think that we wouldn't."

"I think you're right," Ben said. "I can tell you're still feeling something for the good half of me, and then you think about the defective part of me and it scares you. But there isn't a defective part of _me,_ Tara." Ben leaned forward and said gently, "There's only a defective part of my body. It took me a long time to understand that. I'm willing to wait until you do, too."

"I do understand."

Tara pulled her legs up beneath her and then realized how oddly subliminal that action was. Was she trying to meet him on his own level; did she truly view him in pieces? She planted her feet on the floor again. She wouldn't apologize for being whole, but there were apologies to be made.

"Once I was in Washington, I remembered the way you'd been. I convinced myself you'd be that way again. You had your mom and dad, all of our friends, a ton of people to take care of you. I convinced myself you didn't need me. I convinced myself you wouldn't miss me the way I missed you."

"Tara, I needed you so much. I missed you every single day. But I was too proud to pick up the phone and tell you I was scared." Ben shook his head. He poured half a glass of wine, then forgot to drink it. "My parents tried desperately to be strong. Our friends had other things to do. There was no one to just sit and hold my hand and let me be afraid. I would have killed to have just one hour with you."

"Ben, please."

"That was only a wish, Tara. Now I'm glad you weren't there. If you had been, you would have seen me as half a person. You would have hated me for being so needy."

"I could have done whatever you needed."

"Yes, you could have," he agreed. "The question always was, would you have felt the same way if the only thing I'd needed from you was strength? I don't think so. But I'm not half anymore. I'm whole and I don't think all that love is dead. I really don't."

"Of course it isn't," Tara said quietly, closing her eyes. She was aware of everything around her: the warmth of his home, the nubby fabric of the chair, his closeness, his curiosity, his feelings—hers. Without opening her eyes she began to speak.

"My father was a very strong man. I watched

how he dealt with his hurt and fear when he was dying. Then I understood why I am the way I am.

"He dealt with it by not acknowledging it. Three days before he died he talked about my mother and how her death had left him weak with sorrow. He told me that he was proud that he'd kept me out of harm's way by teaching me how to snap my eyes forward and put one foot in front of the other. He could die happy because he'd taught me how to control my feelings." Opening her eyes, she looked straight at Ben. "Dad thought I'd be safe if I knew how to do that. And I was safe, Ben. When I saw you again, I realized that might not have been a good thing to learn. Now I think it may be too late to change."

Tara looked at Ben without moving her head. Instead she shifted her eyes, and her lashes made phantom shapes on her cheeks.

"And now here you are. Stronger than me because you learned how to live with what you've been dealt. Stronger than me because you didn't just struggle on, you really lived your life. Stronger than me because you recognized that love has failings and you accepted mine, then turned around and welcomed me with open arms again. You want honesty, Ben? I am honestly shamed by you and your understanding, and I truly do still care."

"And what," he asked, "do you honestly want?"

"For you and me?" Tara moved her head on the back of the chair. "I don't know. I'm not that courageous. I'm coming back to you again and again, almost hoping you'll throw me out and make the decision for me."

"So far I haven't had the urge," he chuckled. "But I'm not even sure we can get to it until you figure out what you want from this thing with Bill Hamilton."

"I just want it to be over," Tara said, then qualified her statement. "I want my life back."

"Then take it back. He's stealing all the things you love. Your security. Your sense of control. Take them back, Tara."

"I can't do anything to jeopardize my license, my standing as an attorney, and I don't want my life back at the expense of justice," she insisted.

"I'm not asking you to. I'm asking you to make a decision that's based on something other than written rules. You've got to make a decision that will let your conscience rest. There are ways. There are things you can find out about Bill Hamilton. Bring pressure to bear wherever you can. On Woodrow, on George Amos, on Bill, on Donna. Do it, Tara. Don't just look straight ahead. Start playing Bill's game."

"I've never played like that before. I don't think I can do it and still keep my integrity."

"Anything's possible, Tara," Ben said and reached for her hand. He touched it with his fingertips. Those eyes of his looked right through her. "Anything at all."

"I may make it worse."

"You may make things better." He wound his fingers through hers. "Take a chance." He tugged on her hand and she pulled away. He tugged back and she was his. He reached up and touched her shoulder. "Life can be what you want it to be, Tara. All you have to do is want it badly enough."

He murmured and he whispered and he guided her down until she sat in his lap. Tara curled atop him and her head lay exactly where she had wanted it—against his broad and strong chest. He buried his lips in her silky hair and they sat together like that for a very long time.

"Can you?" Tara whispered as she climbed onto his bed. "I mean . . ."

"I know what you mean." Ben laughed in the darkness at all the things she found so curious that he had come to take for granted. He was on the bed beside her, lifting his legs, graceful in the shadows because of his strength.

"I didn't even see you leave the chair," she whispered. "I thought it was harder than that. I thought it should be—harder."

Tara lay on her side, her black hair tumbling over the pillow and the spread and over her shoulders. Ben pushed it away so that it streamed behind her. He smiled sweetly and touched the button at the high neck of her sweater. He popped the first. Tara lay her hand at his waist, feeling the muscles underneath his shirt, trying not to imagine the rest. He popped the next button and his fingers touched her throat. She shuddered, still looking him in the eye, hoping he would see she wasn't ready.

"How do you get out of that thing so easily?" Tara's voice shook; she gestured toward the chair. Ben gave it a quick glance as if he'd forgotten it was there. Head back on the pillow again, he moved closer.

"Upper body strength," he murmured, amused at her anxiety, determined not to let his own show. They should have done this in high school, but then maybe the memory would have made it more difficult for them both. He moved. He kissed her.

She kissed him back. Ben Crawford was in heaven. Tara Linley, in his arms again, at last.

"Do you . . . ?" she said against his lips.

"Adore you?" he asked. "Yes."

He kissed her again.

"Do I hurt? No."

He lay his lips against her cheek.

"Can I do what other men do? Yes."

The kiss was longer this time, his mouth open, his hands coming slowly up her sweater.

"Will you have to work harder? Absolutely." He slipped the sweater over her head, then kissed the swell of her breast. "But you've always been such a hard worker, Tara."

She sighed, she shivered, and she put her arms around him and pulled herself closer. With each breathy word, each tender touch, the questions became as unimportant as the answers. Tara rose to the challenge, but worked no harder than he. The man she loved was complete, more so than any man Tara Linley had been with.

She had touched his legs, but desire had made them as lovely as if they could have wrapped around her. Later she would remember to cry for them—she never had in all these years—but at that moment, those wonderful minutes when they kissed and touched and his hands went everywhere, and her arms and legs covered him, Tara thought only of what was and not what could have been. That was the first thought on her mind when they lay together, covers over them, naked bodies molded together, her head on his shoulder, his arm under hers.

"I've made a decision," she said lazily.

"Really?" Ben was sleepy. She could hear it in

his voice so she plucked at the lovely light hair that ran across his chest.

"Yes, really. I've decided you're right. I have to make things happen."

"Oh, Tara." Ben moved his head so that he looked away from her. He closed his eyes and pleaded, "Don't ruin it. I don't want to hear about work or Bill Hamilton or crazy people or anything. Please, Tara, let me just lie here a little while longer."

"Not on your life. You're the one that started all this nonsense," she teased, running her tongue over her lips and lowering her voice. "I just want you to know that I've decided I've done everything I can for Bill Hamilton. I haven't been running away at all. I've begged Woodrow for help. I've told Bill what needs to be done and he's refused to cooperate. I've all but broken my pledge of confidentiality with Donna and she still won't listen." Tara kissed Ben's chest and smoothed over the spot.

"So I will not breathe a word of what I know about Bill, but I won't let him rule my life. I won't beg Woodrow for help. I will be ready if Donna needs me."

"Bravo, Tara," Ben murmured. "Bravo." And he kissed her.

"And I will start living life as it should be lived." She gave him a sly look. "So whaddya say? Shall we play it again, Sam?"

"I think I remember the tune," he whispered, and they were at it again.

Bagels. Cream cheese. Butter. Jelly. Lox. Capers. Ben in bed beside her. If it could be better, Tara didn't want to know about it. Unfortunately, after

the food, and between the touching, Tara managed to convince Ben the day must begin. He convinced her to postpone it a little longer. It took
another hour and a half to get dressed, twenty
more minutes to tear herself away.

In her Jeep, heading home to change before the
office, Tara came to her senses. She had to wipe
the ridiculous grin off her face by the time she
deposed the girl who had witnessed Johnnie Rae
Riskin run into the pickup truck with all the kids
in it. So Tara put Ben in his proper niche inside
her head and her heart and edited her deposition
as she drove. She was whistling by the time she
reached the house. She ended the tune with a
flourish while she parked, and walked into the
house just in time to answer the phone.

"Hello." It sounded like she was singing. Knowing that was ridiculous, she smiled anyway.

"It's Caroline. There was a reporter here, Tara,
about one of your clients." Caroline paused. Tara
could hear her hesitate. "He wants to talk to you
about the Circle K killer."

"Wonderful," Tara muttered.

"He's coming out to the house."

"Oh, no."

Wrapped in a serape, her feet up on the wall,
Tara kept her eyes on the long road that led to her
house. In her great-grandmother's day she would
have had a rifle slung over her lap. A well-said word
or two would have sent the scoundrel packing. Unfortunately, it wasn't her great-grandmother's day
and a few choice words could make front page news.

The last thing Tara wanted, the first thing a few
other people wanted, was to make the front page.

Apprehensive as she was, now wasn't the time to sort out how this had come to be. So Tara stared blankly at the road. Finally, a small white car, much the worse for wear, came coughing and clanking up the road and stopped at the gate.

Out of the egg-shaped vehicle stepped a man in desperate need of a makeover. His black hair stood angled out of his head instead of lying upon it. His shirt sleeves ended before his wrists began. His lovely Hispanic complexion was at odds with his rather bulbous nose, eyes, and lips. He was a sight to behold, but a guy to be reckoned with.

"Tara Linley?" He handed her a card with great ceremony. Tara didn't move. He lay it atop the stucco wall. "Martin Martinez. Reporter for the *Journal*. Heard you made a call the other night to the sheriff's, and got the deputies out to see about a disturbance. Possible felony assault? Like to talk to you about that." He sighed and looked about as if this were incredibly trying for him.

"Please go, Mr. Martinez. I have no comment about that incident. It was personal."

"Not so personal if the cops were called." He looked around with a lazy eye but Tara was sure he saw a lot. She didn't like it. "You check up on every police call?"

"Nope. Just heard this was a little different. My source says you have a client that's a real doozy." He'd had a visual tour and was now back to her. "Thought that call might have something to do with that client."

"What client might that be? The doozy?" Tara asked wryly.

"Don't have a name. No charges were brought, so I don't have a public record to check on the other night."

"Mr. Martinez? Can we get to it?" If he had anything, he'd show his hand now.

"I hear you've got something going on the Circle K killing. I hear you're keeping the DA from getting this guy. Love to talk about that, Ms. Linley. Two sides to every story." She thought he might yawn. If he did, she'd laugh. But he didn't, and she knew then how serious this was.

"I have no comment." She stood and pulled the serape close. He didn't stand away; he held his notebook at the ready. "But I do have a question, Mr. Martinez. Where are you getting your information?"

"Sorry, ma'am. Privileged. Can't reveal a source, you know. I talked to someone, who had talked to someone else. Circle K killer would make a pretty good story. Lot of people had a hard time letting that one go. Just doing my job, you understand."

"Of course," Tara murmured, and picked up his card. She looked at it to have something to do, then she tossed off the serape. "I have to get to work. I'm in the book. If you want to bring your source to my office, feel free. I'll discuss anything you like as long as everything's on the table."

"No other comment, right?"

"Nope."

"Can I quote you?"

"I don't think an offer of hospitality constitutes a story, Mr. Martinez. And I might remind you, there are laws against posting fiction as fact. But you're a reporter. You know how careful you have to be."

"Yes, ma'am. My source was pretty good, but I'll double-check. Could make a story out of what I've got. You know, a retrospective. Put it in front of the public one more time. Would be great to have

something from you, though, to round it out."
The man gave another Eeyore sigh. Tara wasn't
fooled. She'd met reporters she thought were
brain-dead only to find them sharp as tacks. So
when Martinez held up his hand in what passed
as a wave, Tara took the initiative.

"On some other matter, Mr. Martinez, and only
at my office, please."

"Sure thing," he said, not put off by her rejection. "You never can tell how these tips are going
to work out, can you?" He looked at her, heavy-
lidded, then looked away and began the tortuous
ritual of leaving.

Back in his little Good & Plenty car, he coaxed
his cranky clutch into gear and drove down the
road he had come up only moments before. Tara
rested her hands on the low wall and stood looking after him. When he was gone, she tilted her
head back and howled like an animal, just once,
just loud enough and long enough to get it out
of her system. Finished, content knowing no one
had heard her lose her last shred of composure,
she calmly went into the house, got her car keys,
and headed out.

"Woodrow, I thought we were done with this
nonsense. I can't believe you're still trying to force
this issue. Does an election mean so much to you
that you would sell me out to the press just so you
can look good? You've not only put a wedge between Charlotte and me, you've brought George
in on it, and now you're whispering in a reporter's
ear that I've got the Circle K killer in my backyard."

Woodrow sat in front of Tara's desk, she behind

it. Not a harsh word passed between them because Tara knew it would do no good to scream, and Woodrow was still in shock. This wasn't what he'd anticipated when Caroline had called and asked him to stop by.

"What are you talking about? I did no such thing."

Tara was surprised, too. She hadn't expected him to look honestly dumbfounded. It threw her for a minute, but she recovered nicely.

"Woodrow, I came to you in good faith with this problem. In good faith, I assumed, you took a stand that wasn't concordant. I accept that, Woodrow. And I assumed that after we'd been to see Sepada and it was clear that neither of us had recourse, we would let the matter drop. Didn't we agree to that?"

Tara sat back and looked at him full face, her blue eyes icy. To his credit he looked back quietly, waiting to hear what was next.

"What possible good could come from planting a story and scaring the public half to death when there's no solution for our problem? I don't see how you could think that you could forward your campaign when you can't deliver on an indictment? And Woodrow, did you honestly think sending a reporter to my home would intimidate me?"

"I didn't think anything, Tara, since I didn't talk to any reporter. I didn't send anyone to your house and I resent being called here and spoken to like this."

Woodrow no longer looked surprised. He didn't look angry and Tara finally saw what kind of governor he'd make. A good one because he didn't back down and he lied like a pro.

"Resent it all you like. You've been free with information before. I don't see why you should balk at telling the press," Tara said. "I'm willing to forget this. I'm willing to go back to the original deal. A psychiatric workup and state commitment or nothing. We'll just wait.

"But if you pull anything like this again, I'll talk to the press. And I'll tell them how you refused to get a murderer off the street. You had the opportunity, and you blew it. I think it'll make a fine story. They can run it next to the Strober inquiry."

"You wouldn't dare!" That got a cool rise out of Woodrow, but it was Tara who stood.

"Yes, I would," she said calmly, gathering her papers. "I just realized, Woodrow, there's very little percentage in not being creative. This is the new Tara Linley. Be on your toes. Now, I have a deposition to take. I just wanted to make sure we were clear about everything. Don't pull any fast ones, Woodrow, 'cause I'll pull them right back, and I'll do it better. If you'll excuse me."

"I will not." Woodrow was out of his chair, meeting her halfway around the desk. "You're really arrogant, Tara. You think everything is being done to you. Did it ever occur to you that you might have done it to yourself? I'm not the only one who's been asking about this guy. You've been trying to get a psychiatrist to see your boy. Since I don't have a report, I'll assume nobody wants to touch him. Didn't you tell me you saw his old shrink? Why should I believe that you didn't spill it to him? Or maybe he knew all along and he's been talking. So get off your high horse, Tara, because there are a hundred ways a reporter could get something like this."

Tara looked at him, knowing in her gut that he was grasping at straws. But her gut was telling her something else too. Standing face-to-face, she didn't feel the vibes she'd expected. Indignation, yes. But guilt was missing.

"Look," she said, "I was ready to wait. But now I have to make a judgment call based on the facts in evidence. Those facts tell me that you have a history of sharing information, you have a use for my client, and you could manipulate the press in your favor. I have no choice but to assume the leak is coming from you or is directed by you. I'm asking you to stop now, Woodrow." Tara hugged her papers tighter and raised her chin. "I promise you, no more confrontations. Neither of us wants to be running in and out of each other's lives screaming. From here on out I take my cue from you. You send reporters sneaking around, I promise to give them a story. And you won't come out looking like Prince Charming."

Tara started to walk around him, but Woodrow stopped her.

"Tara. Please believe me. I had nothing to do with leaking this information. And remember this is my life we're talking about here. You're saying you'll tell on me if I tell on you, like this is a game. This could ruin my campaign, my standing in the community. This guy's a murderer. He deserves what he gets. I'm only trying to do what's right."

Tara softened, seeing in him a man afraid, and she was sorry for that. "And I'm trying to do the same, Woodrow. There are real lives at stake here. My client's, for one, and that's where my loyalties lie. I've promised to be his advocate. I'll do that to the letter of the law and in the spirit of it, too. I can't worry about your professional future."

She walked out the door with a nod. There was

nothing more to say. Ten minutes later, Woodrow was gone, and Tara was deposing a witness to the fateful crash involving her client Johnnie Rae Riskin. At least Johnnie Rae's case would have a conclusion. For that Tara was grateful, and she gave her full attention to the matter at hand. Even when Caroline slipped into the conference room and pushed a note onto the table beside her, it took Tara a minute to realize Caroline was waiting for an answer.

Tara unobtrusively slid her right hand toward the note, still listening to the woman being deposed. She read it, and jotted her directive. Caroline was to call Dr. Crawford and advise him that she would be unavailable for an early dinner. She would be leaving as soon as the deposition was done.

Gina Patton had found Bill Hamilton's parents.

Seventeen

"Good." Tara flipped through Johnnie Rae's file and found what she wanted. "Caroline, do me a favor and contact Johnnie Rae's employer. Ask him if we can change the time of his deposition."

"His lawyer's Phil Harmon. We already asked for an extension on this guy. Harmon likes to keep his appointments. This time he's going to be mad."

Tara snorted softly. "Phil only gets mad because changes interfere with his manicure appointments. Leave a message on my machine if you have any trouble getting him to agree. I'll call him at home tonight to see if I can straighten it out. Do you have the calendar?"

"Yep." Caroline flipped open a black, leather-bound book.

"How about a week from now? Same day. Same time."

Caroline shook her head. "No. You've got a meeting with the U.S. attorney about the casino and the Women in the Judiciary reception. The next day you're handling a pleading first thing in Judge Ferguson's court for Shirley Templeton. Remember? She's on vacation and Ferguson screwed up the calendar before she left, but you're free that afternoon."

"Okay, let's do it then." Tara put on her coat. "If you finish early, go home."

"Thanks," Caroline said, knowing she'd be lucky to leave by five. She handed over a neatly typed sheet of paper. "Here's all the information including directions. Gina didn't contact Bill Hamilton's family per your instructions, but she's confirmed that someone is living at that address."

"Okay." Tara slung her purse over her shoulder, leaving her briefcase behind. "If there's anything important, give me a call on the car phone or page me."

The elevator came quickly, but it wasn't soon enough for Tara. She was itching to get where she was going. Finally she'd have something concrete to put under Woodrow's nose. Maybe even a living, breathing human being who would add a voice to hers and convince the DA that Bill Hamilton needed the protection of the law. Maybe two.

Tara pushed open the glass door of the office building. She hoped to bring both parents back to the city with her. Outside, the afternoon was cold and bright. Tara decided to settle for either mother or father, when she realized that the insistent blaring of a horn was directed at her. A van pulled around the island in the parking lot and Tara waited. It stopped right in front of her. Automatically, the tinted window rolled down, and for an instant, Tara's heart stopped. She imagined that window was a curtain and Bill Hamilton the actor behind it. But her heart was beating again and she was smiling a second later.

"Need a ride, lady?"

Tara put her hand out and touched the dark green van.

"Nice wheels, Ben," she said, before climbing into the passenger side.

"Turn here." Tara put her hand under Ben's nose and pointed excitedly. He chuckled and pushed it out of the way. She apologized. "Sorry. Do you see any numbers?"

"I haven't been out this way for a hundred years, but I do remember that no one worried about their address numbers being legible." He squinted behind his dark glasses. The sun was brilliant. Unfortunately, even a bath of bright light couldn't make this lay of land look hospitable. They'd left the freeway twenty minutes earlier, and the highway ten minutes after that, in favor of a long stretch of road that seemed never-ending and never-changing.

"Do you even know what town we're in?" Tara's hands were folded in her lap, but she could barely contain herself. She would have gotten out and run if she thought it would do any good. Instead she lifted her sunglasses as if that would help her identify something significant in these generic surroundings.

"I know it isn't Albuquerque. There." Ben pointed with a tip of his nose, simultaneously braking with the controls at his fingertips. Another magical motion with his hands and the van went backward.

"That's wonderful," Tara said, delighted as a kid learning how to work a Christmas train. "This is the ultimate boy toy."

Ben laughed and revved the engine. Backward they went again, Ben in full control. He pointed over her shoulder when they stopped. "Can you see a house number there?"

Tara looked in the direction he indicated. "Yes—2010."

"We're close then." Ben threw the car into gear and they were off again.

"How come you don't roll?" Tara asked. No question or turn of phrase seemed wrong or awkward now. Walk, run, put your feet up, take a load off, were all words and expressions Ben had assured her would not have to be stricken from her memory bank.

"You want the official explanation?"

"We can start there," she said.

"On the base of the chair are metal brackets which support a vertically centered bolt under it, allowing a few inches for clearance. Without that I'd be bolted to every nook and cranny around." Ben looked out the window as he lectured. His voice slowed along with the van when he tried to identify a number and picked up again as he drove further.

"Underneath me is an electronically activated receiver. When I roll over it properly, the receiver is activated and automatically grabs the bolt. It's the same technology tractor-trailers use to hitch the rigs together. Only problem is, they have to take out the seat so my chair will fit. I don't even get to choose the upholstery when I get a new car." Ben chuckled, but his amusement didn't last long. They'd arrived.

Ben pulled to the side of the road. The car idled. They were silent as they scanned whatever part of nowhere they were in. If it wasn't the middle, it was darn close. Tara counted ten houses scattered around the flat and rocky land. It was impossible to tell how far the farthest was and the closest seemed uninhabited. Three unleashed, mangy dogs ran about. A horse was tethered in an area that someone had forgotten to fence in. The house was as ill cared for as the poor mare. Tara's heart broke, but out here people would just as soon shoot her as listen to her run on about animal rights. This was the place where people came to disappear. Their choice of location was an unequivocal social statement.

· If anyone was about, they were inside, alert to the arrival of strangers in a car that was far from ready for the junk heap that sprawled off to the left. To their right three trailers were planted in a neat row, oddly close considering the grand expanse of desert around them.

Dead plants in dusty bowls were strung from the metal awnings of the middle one. A lone azalea struggled for life on the trailer nearest the road and that shared the porch with a rusty bike and an ice chest. The home in the back was up on blocks, a fairly new model with splendid white siding and an awning striped yellow, green, and blue. The awning had seen better days but it still looked almost new compared to the ones on the other trailers.

"Guess we better do it. Time's awastin'," Ben muttered, eyeing their target. They rode in silence as the van bounced over the rutted dirt road and finally stopped in front of the trailer on the third terrace.

The windows were curtained, the curtains drawn. Air-conditioning units poked from two windows. Bedroom and living room, Tara guessed. She gave them as much consideration as they deserved. A metal chair, with specks of rust on the legs, and a ripped, ineffectual screen door were the only two items that were ill kept on this homestead. Ben rolled down his window, stuck his head outside, pulled it in, and grinned, happy to have accomplished what they set out to do.

"Let's get to it," he said.

Before Tara could object, before she could suggest that he stay in the van while she dealt with Mr. and Mrs. Hamilton, the rear doors flew open, the electronically activated bolt disengaged, and Ben was rolling backward, doing a wheelie halfway down the length of the van. He shot her a grin from the lift.

"Race you to the door." The lift whirred and Ben was lowered. Tara was waiting for him when he rolled around the side.

Ben took the lead, his beautifully engineered wheels moving over the uneven ground without so much as a shimmy. Instinctively Tara reached out for the handles on back of Ben's chair to help him over the lip of the porch, but he was too quick. Throwing his body weight, he balanced on the back wheels until the front cleared the few inches between porch and ground. He was on the wooden slats at the same time Tara stepped up.

"Nice moves," she said.

"You ain't seen nothin' yet," he shot back.

"Why do I have the feeling that's a prophetic statement?"

She knocked on the door. He straightened out the chair. Eyes forward, they waited, giving no indication that they were aware of what was going on inside.

Furtive steps could be heard headed their way, only to stop at the door. They could sense the person inside tiptoe to look through the dusty peephole. The footfall sounded again, this time in retreat. A curtain swayed. There was a face behind it, unidentifiable regarding sex, age, or intent. Tara slid her eyes toward Ben. He didn't acknowledge her. The curtain fluttered again. Tara could have sworn she heard someone inside thinking. In the extended silence the only sound worth listening to was the slam of a door somewhere far down the road. The desert was a wonder of acoustical engineering, something Tara was sure the person inside the trailer wasn't aware of.

Tara bided her time, letting whoever watched feel at least complacent, if not comfortable, regarding their presence. She knocked once more. This time the footsteps they heard were slower, heavier, and resigned. The door opened wider than Tara would have expected. A woman stood behind it, head and shoulders showing. She stared through the ripped screen assuredly as if it afforded some protection. She didn't speak, but watched with the look of someone for whom wariness was a way of life and the unexpected never brought good news.

"Mrs. Hamilton? Vera Hamilton?" Tara asked gently, to put the woman at ease.

The woman wasn't fooled. There wasn't even the hint of an acknowledging smile. Just a twitch so deep down in her jaw Tara wondered if she really saw it, or was simply desperate for a sign of confirmation. Ben sat quietly, comfortably beside her, impatience not in his repertoire.

"Mrs. Hamilton, I'm Tara Linley, your son's attorney."

It was a nice introduction, Tara thought, but the lady inside had a different take. She sagged like a rag doll. Her face turned into the door as if the wood were comforting. She made a noise, sort of a sigh and sort of a hiccup. Maybe she was crying. Tara didn't know.

"They got him then," she whispered. "They got him and you have to help him. Boy, oh boy. They got him."

Tara moved forward. Gently she opened the screen door frame and passed it to Ben, who held it open as Tara put a hand on the older woman's thin shoulder. It should have been frail. Instead it felt hard, all bone and muscle. It was her demeanor that was brittle.

"Mrs. Hamilton, I'm trying to help your son, but no one has him. He isn't in jail. Don't worry about that. We're going to try to keep him out," Tara reassured her softly.

Suddenly Vera Hamilton was all arms and hands and voice. She pushed at Tara, shoving her back out the door, open palms slapping against any part of Tara's body she could find. Instinctively Tara raised her hands to ward off the blows as she jumped away. But the doorway was narrow and unfamiliar and she backed into the jamb, caught between wood and a crazy woman.

"No!" Vera Hamilton shrieked. "Get out of my house. Get out now if you don't have him in jail, behind bars where he belongs. Don't tell me you brought him with you. Oh, damn, you didn't, did you?" She half hopped, trying to look through the window to the left of the door as she pushed and pummeled Tara. "Don't tell me you brought him here. I don't want him. I finally found a place to escape from him. Don't tell me you don't want him in jail. Don't—"

Vera's tirade was silenced as quickly as it had started. Ben had flipped and maneuvered his chair so rapidly that Vera jumped back in alarm. He was almost between the two women in the cramped doorway, his hand held high, Vera's arm clasped in a viselike hold. Stunned, the older woman looked at him fearfully. A man, no matter how he was incapacitated, was capable of many fearful things.

"Mrs. Hamilton," Ben said quietly, "please listen to Ms. Linley. Please."

In slow motion he lowered Vera Hamilton's hand, still holding longer than he should to make sure it would stay where he put it. She lowered her other one without being asked. In Ben's eyes there was enough power or goodness or common sense to convince the woman to move away. As she did, Tara stepped cautiously over the threshold into Vera Hamilton's world.

The place had a closed-up feeling and was uncomfortably warm despite the cold outside. The air was oppressive and stale, not with the odors of cooking, but the scent of old tobacco and perfume. Tara noted the perfume wasn't cheap and that, in itself, was curious. There was, or had been, a cat in residence, but no litter box was evident. Two sofas upholstered in a lovely spring green print, three needlepoint chairs, and a plethora of knitted afghans decorated the living room. Vera Hamilton had a penchant for green and apricot roses crocheted in 3-D. On the couch was another work in progress, the crochet hook still laced with her last stitch. In the corner was a console television and a basket full of beauty magazines. An enormous crucifix was on the north wall. Crazily, Tara thought to ask where the garlic necklace was kept, for Vera Hamilton didn't strike her as one of the faithful. Frightened, yes. Religious, no.

From where she stood Tara saw into the kitchen

and a small eating area beyond. The table was of
good wood, surrounded by four chairs painted
bright white. She doubted any had been pulled
out for a friend of late. This wasn't a home that
carried the spirit of neighborliness even if there
had been anyone to entertain. A coffee cup with
a red lipstick stain sat on a saucer, obviously left
over from the morning. Now Vera Hamilton's lips
were colorless. The whole thing was odd. Lovely
furniture pushed into a mobile home in the desert
far from what Tara considered civilization.

She walked a few steps farther into the living
room and sat down. Ben settled himself opposite
Tara. Together they waited for Vera Hamilton, who
still clung to the door. Finally, disgusted by their
tenacity and her own impotence, she closed the
door and faced the inevitable. She sat on one of
the sofas and pulled an afghan over her, holding
it close to her chest like a shield.

"Mrs. Hamilton," Tara said, "I apologize for surprising you the way we did. I should have called."
And you would have bolted. Good decision, Tara. "But
we're here on urgent business. As I said, I'm your
son's attorney. This is Dr. Ben Crawford. He's a
psychologist. Hopefully, at my request, Dr. Crawford will evaluate Bill's mental state."

"Fat chance," the woman muttered, pulling her
lips tight. Vertical lines were etched into them. Lipstick would bleed right through the little canals.
Her skin was sallow; around her eyes, deep wrinkles. A smoker's face. Yet beneath it all, there was
a remnant of beauty. Tara could see Bill there. The
high cheekbones, the clipped jaw, the confident
tip of the head. He was his mother's son, and Tara
wondered if the resemblance was only skin-deep.

"I'm sorry, I didn't hear you."

"Fat chance Bill would let you near him, much less treat him. He won't have anything to do with psychiatrists anymore," the woman grumbled.

"I'm a psychologist, Mrs. Hamilton. I can't prescribe medication and, from what I hear, Bill objects to medication, not to talking." Ben rested his elbows on the chair arms and opened his hands, a sign of hope and friendship. Vera Hamilton tensed, arms clenched across her chest.

"No," she sighed. "He doesn't object to talking. How could he? It's the thing he does best. If nothing else, Bill likes to show off what he does best." She rearranged the afghan. It was beautifully constructed but didn't seem as if it would keep a body warm. It would be a long haul with Vera unless Tara found some way to lighten her up.

"Mrs. Hamilton, perhaps it would be better if your husband was here while we talked. When do you expect him?" Tara asked, and Vera Hamilton actually smiled.

"Who told you about my husband?"

"Bill."

"Still spinning tales, is he? Everyone believes him. Even you, a lawyer and a doctor." Vera sighed and set aside the afghan in favor of a pack of cigarettes from the end table. Taking her time, she lit one, sat back, and crossed her legs. She was ready to settle in for a chat. "There is no Mr. Hamilton. In fact, it's amazing I had Bill at all considering how long his father and I were together. Must have been a virgin birth," she chuckled sadly.

Surprised, but far from stunned, Tara asked, "Has there ever been a man in the home?"

"None to speak of." She raised a shoulder, shrugging off her love life as if it were an unimportant thing. "I was married for a few years, but Bill didn't like him."

Ben sat forward.

"Did you divorce because Bill didn't like your husband?" In Vera's eyes there was venom. *Bingo.* He smiled at her. "Did you do everything Bill wanted you to do when he was small?"

"You watch out for your kid," Vera said, and took a long drag off her cigarette, her eyes never leaving Ben's. He could figure it out and she was going to let him. But it was Tara's turn to tug the leash. She pulled Vera's attention her way, anxious to peel away the layers and find out exactly who Bill Hamilton was.

"Mrs. Hamilton, why were you so relieved when you thought he was in jail? Have you been in touch with Bill? Are you aware of the crime he says he committed?"

Sliding her eyes toward Tara, she stared at the younger woman. The change in Vera was incredible. She filled out, or up, with her importance. She smiled, sucking on the cigarette and blowing out her information with the smoke.

"Which one? Burning down Mr. Taylor's shed in the back of the house when we lived in Albuquerque? Chasing after that other woman when she didn't want anything to do with him, scaring her half to death? Scaring me half to death? Killing animals and driving like a madman? Talking like a madman? Staring at you, putting his arm around you, whispering things? Which crime are you talking about? He's a criminal no matter what you're talking about, and I'd be the first one to turn the key in the lock if you could get him near a cell."

Tara's eyes flicked toward Ben, who looked back expressionless. Vera Hamilton saw it all and it pleased her to no end to have them looking so hungrily at the carrot she dangled. She narrowed her eyes and warned, "I don't want him back. I'll tell you what you need to know, but I don't want him. Do you understand? I had to pick up and move because I was afraid he'd come back."

Tara gestured toward Ben and included herself. "If you're afraid of Bill, arrangements can be made to help protect you."

"Hah!" Vera was getting cocky now. Cocky and nervous and neither Ben nor Tara missed the last inflection. Uncomfortable in the silence, Vera talked. "I'm afraid of Bill. He's got a mean streak in him. But I'm more afraid of him because he can make me do anything. I can't help that. I don't want to see him because of it. I'm tapped out. There's nothing left." She looked from Ben to Tara, received no pity, and let out a deep sigh. "Oh hell, what's the use. What do you want to know?"

"We want to know your impressions of your son, some factual details about work, education, friends. Fill us in on his mental state. Diagnosis. Times he's most vulnerable to violence. Things he dislikes. Anything."

Vera's eyes flashed and behind them, behind the gray eyes so like her son's, were memories that obviously had been wrestled with. She began slowly.

"He's a creature. That's what he is," she said quietly. "I don't think he's even human. He's handsome. Damn, he's handsome. But then you've seen that for yourself."

Vera Hamilton bowed her head as if mourning, before raising it slightly so her eyes found a midpoint between Ben's feet and his face. Maybe if he'd been a priest, there would have been solace in this confession, some peace gained by looking him in the eye.

"I loved that boy like nothing you've ever seen. Having him was the best thing I ever did. It was a good pregnancy. An easy birth. I held him in my arms and it didn't matter if he had a father or not." She sighed. "I guess that's why his father didn't stay around too long. When you're that crazy in love with your baby, there isn't a whole lot of room for a real man."

The cigarette had burned down to her fingertips. Vera stubbed it out and lit another.

"Women would come up to me in the grocery store and tell me what a heartbreaker Bill was going to be. Even then he'd smile so prettily. Those women would swoon over a little boy: five, six, seven. Just a kid, and he had power over them." Vera's head was shaking again. She took a drag and blew a perfect smoke ring. "I swear I didn't know how I got so lucky. His father wasn't any great shakes in the looks department." She looked at Ben, needing to tell someone. Then she decided Tara was the one who would understand.

"One day, when he was bigger, everything changed. I didn't love my son anymore. I was *in* love with him, and the worst part was he knew it. When Bill figured that out, he used me for target practice. The way he talked. The way he touched. I gave him everything he wanted. All my money, everything. I was so taken with him. For a while I thought I was just being a good mother. But when he was twelve, maybe thirteen, I figured out something was wrong with us. That's when I sent him to therapy."

She smoked faster, but talked slower now.

"I thought if he could learn to control himself,

then maybe I could get back to being a regular woman, get rid of all those weird feelings. It worked for a while, but then he'd come up and put his hand on my hair or look at me with those eyes just like a movie, for goodness' sake. You know where two people just fall into each other's arms, all hot and bothered. But this was my kid." She put her free hand to her breast and pounded lightly for emphasis. "My son. How could I ever have felt any of that?" Her hand went down, and when the smoke cleared, Vera Hamilton showed them a face full of pain. Tara wanted to look away. She didn't.

"Was there anyone to help you?" Tara asked.

Vera rolled her eyes, "Please. Who'd help with something like that? Who would I tell?"

Tara had no answer. The shame this woman felt plainly consumed her. Vera talked to Ben.

"We never did anything. I want you to know that. And for a long time the pills helped. Then, out of the blue, he'd be strange again, like he was trying to seduce me." Vera smiled.

"I used to be an executive secretary, you know. Fabulous job. Benefits, everything." The smile was gone as quickly as it had come. "Then Bill started hanging around work. He hung around the boss's wife, and I got jealous. Lord." Her head fell back, snapped forward almost immediately, and she reached for another cigarette. "He banged the boss's wife. I made a scene like a jealous lover. Got another job; it happened again. Let me tell you, don't believe a thing he says. Don't do anything for him except put him in jail. Don't talk to him, or he'll convince you he's something he isn't. Don't let him touch you," she spoke to Tara now, "or you'll be the same as every other woman he ever touched. You'll be lost."

Tara stared at her. She knew what his touch could do. She knew what his eyes looked like in the dark. She knew what she had felt and it chilled her that his own mother had felt the same.

"Was your husband a cowboy? Did he work on a ranch?" Tara asked softly, knowing the answer already but needing to hear it.

"Is that what he's saying his father was? That's good. That's funny." Vera stayed quiet for a minute. "That's sad." Then she pulled herself together. "No, he's not a cowboy. I don't know or care what he is, or where he is, as long as he's not in my backyard. Some things are best kept secret, and I want to keep my secrets. I'm ashamed of them. I'm ashamed I'm his mother. You tell him where I am, and I'll sue. Then I'll run. So if you want anything from me, or Bill wants anything from me, you can just forget it."

That was an invitation to leave. They stayed where they were. What an amazing man Vera's son was. His own mother was shaken with fear that he might return and Donna Ecold sat quivering, fearing he might leave her.

"Bill doesn't know we're here. I want something from you, Mrs. Hamilton," Tara said.

"You're lucky you got in here." Vera Hamilton cautioned Tara not to press. She ignored the warning.

"I've promised to represent your son, Mrs. Hamilton, and I intend to do that. Bill wants to be hospitalized. He may have committed a horrible crime, and if the district attorney can petition for hospitalization, your son would be free from self-incrimination. Instead, the district attorney wants to arrest Bill and bring him to trial."

"Remind me to vote for him," Vera muttered.

Tara ignored the aside.

"I came here because I wanted to meet you and find out more about Bill. Now that I have, I'm convinced more than ever that Bill needs psychiatric help. Unfortunately, since the DA and I can't agree on what we want, I'd like you to sign the commitment papers. Unfortunately, that won't protect Bill from prosecution should he confess this crime to a doctor. But he'll be out of the mainstream for the time being, and he won't be dangerous to anyone else."

Vera Hamilton stood up. She was a determined woman and she was determined not to listen any longer. "I don't want to talk to you about Bill, and I sure don't want to sign any papers. Maybe you've never seen Bill mad. Maybe you have, and you don't care because you have friends to watch out for you. I've got nothing except shameful memories. No mother should have felt the things I felt. Not that kind of love, and not this kind of fear. Leave me out of it. Go on now. There's nothing more I can tell you." Vera made a little shooing motion.

"Mrs. Hamilton, he's asked for help. Think what it took for him to do that," Ben said. She spoke without looking at him.

"And he'll bite the hand that gives it to him."

"Do you have any of Bill's medical records?" Ben asked.

Vera shot him a withering glance. There was pain behind it. Finally she nodded and went toward the back of the trailer, returning a minute later.

"Might as well take them. I burned his picture book."

Ben reached for the envelope and for a minute both of them were holding it, linked together. They looked at one another for a long while then Vera Hamilton let go.

"It's all I've got left."

"You sure you want me to take it?" Ben asked.

She nodded. Tara and Ben went to the door in silence. They were on the porch again when Tara remembered she had one more question.

"Mrs. Hamilton?" The door was almost closed. It didn't open again but it wasn't shut either. "The woman Bill lived with. Where can we find her?"

"You want to eat now? Before we see her?"

Ben drove slowly, the envelope Vera Hamilton had given him on his lap. Tara was once more bent over the map looking for the address Vera had given her.

"Definitely not."

"It's dark. It's getting late. You're sure?"

Tara lifted her head, noted the street, then went back to studying the infinitesimal type. "I'm sure. Listen, you're going to make a left on Zuni, then another quick left on San Pedro. Looks like about five minutes more. I want to hear from everyone we can tonight. We'll go back and look at those records, piece everything together, then I'll know what to do."

"I'm starving," Ben complained.

"Suffer," Tara said, adding a smile.

He responded in kind and they were quiet until they pulled up in front of a small blue house. Two

bikes were out front and the garage door was
open. Inside was a battered Toyota, surrounded by
tools, boxes, skates, and the other stuff life with
kids was made of. Tara got out of the van, paying
no attention to the whirrs and clunks of Ben's de-
scent.

They were halfway up the cracked and crumbling driveway when the door of the house burst
open, expelling four children of varying ages. They
screamed, hollered, hit one another for no reason
whatsoever, and were precariously close to career-
ing into Ben's chair before they suddenly scattered
and disappeared into the gathering dark. Tara
drew close to Ben. They watched the kids go, then
looked toward the house and the woman standing
in the doorway, backlit by a low-light bulb.

"Hello," Tara called as they went closer.

"Hello," came the wary reply. Mothers didn't
like strangers in the driveway when dinner dishes
waited and kids were loose. Tara and Ben were
close enough now to see the woman's round face.
Her skin was beautiful without makeup, but she
looked tired and worried.

"Can I help you?" she asked.

"We hope so." Tara went close to the door, holding out her card as she did so. "I'm Tara Linley,
an attorney here in Albuquerque. This is Ben
Crawford, a psychologist who is working with me.
We're looking for Paula Maxwell."

"Paula?" The woman looked confused. "You
mean Paulette?"

Ben and Tara exchanged a glance. Ben talked
to the woman in the doorway.

"We were told to find Paula Maxwell." Tara
looked to Ben, who nodded his agreement.

"Who told you?" The woman was suspicious now.

"Vera Hamilton. Bill Hamilton's mother." Tara hitched her purse a little higher. "We're looking for the Paula Maxwell who lived with Bill Hamilton." Even in the dark Tara saw the woman pale. Her voice wasn't quite so sweet anymore.

"Paula's dead."

That was it. The door was closing. Tara would have thrown herself through it to keep it open. Another dead woman. Oh, Donna.

"Please, wait," Ben called and the woman hesitated. He smiled gently, his hand was out to her. "We really need help. Please. That wasn't what we expected to hear."

"What do you want?"

Tara stepped in.

"I have a friend who thinks she's in love with Bill Hamilton. She's crazy about him and I'm worried about her."

The door was open, the woman stood back, dish towel slung over her shoulder. "I don't have a lot of time."

"We won't need much. I promise." Tara stepped into a neat-as-a-pin tract house.

"My mom was a wonderful lady. She had a sense of humor. Her name was Paula and she named me Paulette. Everybody got us confused and that just made Mom laugh." Paulette shook her head sadly. She was a big, attractive woman, serene and engaging. But there was nothing shy about her. She looked Ben and Tara in the eye and kept her head moving so she didn't leave either of them out.

"Anyway, she had a real sense of life. She

shopped and went to the bars. She loved to dance and shoot pool. My mom wasn't a lush or anything, you understand," Paulette said quickly. Ben and Tara shook their heads simultaneously, offering appropriate though indefinable murmurings. Paulette smiled uncomfortably, not sure they really understood.

"She met Bill in a bar one night and fell head over heels. Now, my mom was really good looking. I mean really good looking," she insisted, "but she wasn't twenty. Heck, she wasn't even forty. And here's this man who is just beautiful to look at. He was funny, paying attention to her in a way no man had before. My mama was in seventh heaven. He wanted to be with her all the time and the next thing I know they moved in together. I couldn't believe it."

Paulette looked heavenward as if hoping her mom could hear her talking about the good times. She snapped the towel and laid it on her lap, smoothing her memories out along with it.

"Was your mother a wealthy woman?" Tara asked. Paulette looked up, her eyes gentle. She shook her head emphatically.

"No, ma'am, not at all. She was comfortable, for sure. More than we are, I'll tell you. But not dumb like me. She knew enough to keep her legs shut and not have four kids." Paulette laughed and it was so sweet Tara smiled. Obviously hanging around people under the age of ten did good things for the soul.

"But she wasn't smart enough to get rid of Bill Hamilton."

Paulette looked startled. "Why should she? He was just wonderful to her. He didn't look at another woman that I could see. He didn't take her money. And when she got so sick, he was at the hospital with her all the time. And that was a long ride. We were all living pretty far out, and he would get to that hospital any way he could. Finally he let her buy him a secondhand car, but he put up a fight about that. Never could understand it. And then"—Paulette shrugged—"she died."

"In the hospital?" Ben asked. He and Tara exchanged a look and they both knew they'd been waiting for the same thing: the gory finale. "Are you sure?"

"Well, yeah. She just died. Bill was devastated." Bewildered, she looked from Ben to Tara and pushed a strand of hair in back of her ear.

"Bill had nothing to do with her death?"

Paulette blinked. "Gosh, no. He was really broken up when she died. I think he really loved her."

Hope was quashed. Tara stood. This woman couldn't be a witness to Bill Hamilton's madness. She arranged her purse, and tried to smile through her disappointment.

"We've taken up a lot of your time and we've made an awful mistake. We understood they had quite a different relationship," Tara said. "We'll be on our way. Sorry to have bothered you."

Ben moved, Tara turned, and Paulette popped up, her hand out to stop them.

"But don't you want to hear the rest?" she asked. "Don't you want to hear what happened *after* my mom died?"

Puzzled, Tara looked at Paulette. She had changed. There were fearful memories too. She just hadn't gotten to them yet. Tara sat again. Ben was settled. They'd hit pay dirt.

* * *

"I loved my mom. Actually," she said, looking a little embarrassed, "I adored her. I always wanted my life to be like hers but, well, guess I wasn't as good at looking ahead like she was. I liked the boys too much." Paulette colored and it looked lovely on her. "I had three of my kids by the time I was twenty-one, and I've always been sorry about that. For them mostly. Kids shouldn't have kids.

"Anyway, there I was feeling so down when my mom passed, and I guess it didn't strike me as odd that Bill didn't leave when it happened. I could see that he was broken up, too. So, since we were both grieving, it seemed natural for him to hang around where she'd been. I knew it would take a while for him to find a new place and get used to being without her. But then I realized it was six months after my mom died and he was still with me and the kids in the house." She tipped her head and asked Ben, "Don't you think that was weird?"

"I wouldn't say that was terribly normal." Ben punctuated his opinion with an encouraging smile. Paulette seemed grateful and went on, plucking at some unseen flaw in the sofa upholstery.

"Oh"—she rolled her eyes—"this is so embarrassing. But it was kind of scary so I might as well tell you. I said a few things to Bill, about him maybe looking for another place to live. But instead of taking the hint, he just settled in more. In fact, he got real friendly, if you know what I mean." She wiggled her brows. There was no doubt about what she meant but Paulette filled them in anyway. "He was acting the same way he acted with my mom. It was like he couldn't tell the difference between us."

Paulette rubbed away the goose bumps on her arm.

"Now I can't tell you I wasn't flattered in a way." She laughed deeply and rolled her eyes as if to say see-how-stupid-I-can-be. "But it was a really small way. I always thought he was handsome and everything, just there wasn't any chemistry between us. I didn't like him, or want him, or anything. I told him to stop but sometimes I thought it was my imagination that he was coming on to me at all. He started doing these little affectionate things. Touching my shoulder, giving it a rub. Kissing the top of my head. And when I complained, he just laughed and told me I was dreaming. Well, one day I knew it wasn't my imagination and I told him to stop."

Paulette pulled the dish towel tight in her hands and twisted it to match the expression on her face. Tara felt along with her. She felt those eyes of his, the small touches, the final, unmistakable come-on. It made her sick to think of them.

"He can be intimidating," Tara murmured and Paulette looked at her closely. The two women understood something that Ben could not, even if he spent the next ten years locked in a room with Bill Hamilton.

"Yes. That's the word," she agreed quietly.

"You want to go on?" Tara asked. Paulette nodded.

"I had a boyfriend. He's my husband now, but he was my boyfriend then, and Bill knew it all along." She caught herself, hearing the nervous undertones of her protest. Paulette took a deep breath and began again. "Mom had left him some money and he had plenty to move out on, but every morning I'd wake up and he'd still be there:

saying all those things, touching me. He was starting to scare me."

Paulette's voice shook a bit, just a quaver on the deep tones. Tara sat up straighter and noticed Ben was leaning closer. Without thinking, Tara touched Paulette's shoulder for encouragement. Paulette smiled weakly.

"One day, Bill was sitting on the couch, and I was folding clothes at the dining room table. Always a load going with so many kids. Anyway, Joey, my littlest one, was just learning to walk. So he was talking baby talk and toddling by when Bill stuck out his foot and tripped him. This little tiny boy."

Paulette's eyes were wide and disbelieving even now. She had shoved her own foot out as if Ben and Tara needed to see exactly how Bill had done it.

"Joey fell down and hit his head on the coffee table and started to cry. Bill just looked at him. That was all. I ran and got Joey and held him and patted him. I gave Bill a dirty look, but I didn't know what to say, so I didn't say anything. And I'm ashamed of that. But I was scared right then. I mean, if he could do that to a little kid and watch him cry, what would he do to me? I just hoped he would get tired of the kids and noise and me not liking him. But that day I knew he wouldn't go just because I was mad at him or because I wanted him to. That man had his own mind about things, and there was no way to plan because he never did anything the normal way."

"Was that it, then?" Ben asked. "He let the baby cry?"

"Sorry." Paulette had lost her train of thought but she was back on it now. "Joey was crying and

Bill stood up and put his fingers to his head, like this." She put her fingers on her temples, her eyes closed. "Then he put his hands down real slowly."

Paulette's eyes came open. She looked at both of them and lowered her voice as if they were around a campfire and she was charged with telling a horrible tale.

"Joey was only whimpering by that time, and Bill took two steps and he was right beside me. I held the baby closer and turned away 'cause I thought he might hurt him again. But Bill reached out and gently put his hand right on top of my head. But it wasn't a nice touch. It felt real heavy and he let it lay there for a long, long time while he looked at us. I thought I'd had it then. I was hardly breathing."

Paulette gave three short hard breaths as if she wanted to make sure she could breathe now.

"Do you need a drink of water?" Tara offered, wanting to do something to keep her own skin from crawling, knowing Paulette had to feel twice as bad as she. Tara could feel Bill Hamilton's hand as if it lay on her own head.

"No, thanks." Paulette brightened momentarily.

"Do you want us to come back? Do you want to do this another time?" Tara asked.

"Oh gosh, no. I don't think I'd ever want to tell this again. I never told my husband 'cause he'd kill Bill if he knew." She laughed a little as if pleased that she should inspire such passion. She continued, "So, he has his hand on my head. Then he just walks outside. It was strange because he didn't make any noise and he had that great smile on his face. I bet you've seen it. Handsome as can be." Tara nodded.

"He went outside and disappeared for a minute.

I watched through the door because he left it open, and then I saw him come back. He had a sledgehammer. Well, I'll tell you, my heart just stopped." She put a hand to her ample chest as if to make sure the beat went on. "He looked at me. Him out in that sunshine, me in the dark of the house. Then he smiled bigger and he picked that hammer up and whacked the dog right in the head.

"Poor thing never knew what hit him. It made this sound, a thump and crack all at the same time. Bill dropped the hammer near the dog, then he came back in and sat down. He left that dog out there rotting in the sun. He was all bloody. Bill, I mean. It was really ugly."

Paulette closed her eyes, seeing it all again in her mind. She shuddered. Tara wanted to do the same. Ben was intent on the story.

"I kept the kids inside the rest of the day so they wouldn't see the dog. By the end of the day I was near crazy myself. My boyfriend was out of town, and I had to do something.

"After I put the kids down for the night, I made coffee and told Bill I was getting married. I told him he'd have to go because it wouldn't do to have two men in the house.

"I must have put twenty measuring spoons of coffee into that machine waiting for him to answer. I thought if I kept doing something he wouldn't hurt me. And you know what he did?" Paulette's eyes widened as she looked from Tara to Ben and back again. She lowered her voice. "Nothing. He said good night, went to his room, and the next morning he was gone. That was that. I haven't seen him since. I don't want to see him. But I guess you figured that."

Paulette fell back, the couch pillow puffing out under her weight. She had survived Bill Hamilton and was proud of it. They sat in silence until the troop of kids came rushing back through the door. Paulette shooed them away but Ben and Tara were done. They thanked her and left.

"Did you hear what she said?" Ben asked when they were halfway to Tara's house.

"Every word."

"I mean the part about what she was doing when she told Bill he had to leave." Tara flipped her hair over the headrest. She was exhausted and Ben was hyped. "Paulette was making coffee." He tried to lead her train of thought with a little whirly gesture of his hand. Tara looked at him. "The Circle K clerk was making coffee. Come on, Tara. Remember I said that there was just a pinpoint of time where reality met fantasy, where anger at something in the past triggered fury in the present." Tara sat up straighter, nodding as she realized what Ben was saying. He grinned. "I think you better call Donna. It's time she started serving tea."

"You don't think he'd do it again? Not to Donna."

"Who knows?"

Tara planted her chin in her upturned palm and looked out the window. "I haven't talked to her since I left that day."

"Then leave a message." He hit the steering wheel with his open palm. "I can't wait to get to those medical records. Actually, I can't wait to meet the real Bill. Tara, I can give you a report that will send Woodrow reeling. We'll have Bill Hamilton committed in no time with what we've learned."

"So you do think he's mentally disturbed."

"From the little I know, there's no doubt."

"Then I should do whatever I can to help him."

"Yes. I think you should."

Tara fell silent. The lights of Albuquerque shone in the distance, a glittering, liquid blur as they sped toward them. Tara lay back on the seat and wished it would be a good long while before she or Ben came face-to-face with Bill Hamilton.

"I think there's wine in the refrigerator. Soft drinks too if you'd rather. You must be beat. I didn't mean to drag you all over creation," Tara called as she went ahead and turned on the lights.

"Don't worry about it. I don't get tired very often." Ben's voice was lost in the hall as Tara headed to her office to make a swift pass at the answering machine.

She punched the message button. There were two. Caroline had called with the good news that she'd managed to reschedule the deposition they'd canceled, and Donna had called. Tara smiled, so deeply relieved she thought she might cry. Tara kicked off her shoes and listened. Donna, apologetic, was frenetic in her brightness.

"This is silly, sweetie. I miss you so much. Please, let's make up. My place. Saturday night. It's an engagement party. Stop rolling your eyes. Be happy for me. All's well. I'm in New York—I'll be home Saturday afternoon. You'll be surprised. Bill's handling all the arrangements. If you're not there, we're coming to get you Sunday. Please, Tara. I need a maid of honor. I'm sorry. I know you are, too."

Kisses were thrown from the East Coast and Tara

smiled behind the hand she put to her lips. Donna was fine, safely away from Bill for a while at least. But best of all, Donna had missed her too. Bill Hamilton would be in the hospital as soon as Ben could help put him there. Life was good and Ben was calling to her now, insisting she enjoy it after a very long day. Tara walked into the kitchen to find Ben grinning ear to ear.

"Who did you get to do this?" he asked. "What a great surprise. No wonder you didn't want to stop for dinner."

Tara's mouth dropped. Paralyzed by shock, gripped by misgiving, Tara could do nothing more than stare at the butcher block. It was a veritable showcase of dining chic. The candles had been burning for some time and were stunningly misshapen, melted almost to the lips of the silver holders. Between the flickering tapers were two flutes and a bottle of champagne, sweating as it lost its chill.

He had done it.

He was there—or had been there.

Fingers to her lips, Tara moved swiftly into the kitchen, whispering as she did so, "I didn't do this, Ben. I didn't make any arrangements."

Ben tensed, vigilant as she. He scanned the kitchen, slowly doing a three-sixty, looking for anything else out of the ordinary. It was Tara who spotted the wet-edged dinner card propped against the champagne. She read it before handing it to Ben.

"Dinner's in the oven," he said softly as he started forward.

Tara held him back with an open palm. She was the one who put her hand on the oven door, opened it, and took out the cold roasting pan. Me-

chanically, she turned and held it out to Ben,
showing him an enormous hunk of newly butch-
ered bloody meat. Tara's eyes were on him. Ben's
mouth was open. She was about to speak when
suddenly she dropped the pan. It clattered on the
ground, the noise horrendous and frightening in
the quiet kitchen. The meat spilled out, blood
spattering everywhere. They both jumped as it
came to rest near the legs of the kitchen table.
Something else fell too, the thing that had
spooked Tara. Ben was the first to reach it.

"What on earth is that?" he breathed, leaning
over, adjusting his chair to get a better look.

Tara's mouth opened, but nothing happened.
She couldn't speak. She couldn't make a noise.
Her hands trembled as she touched the golden
hank of rope that had been wound around the
animal flesh. Her mouth worked, her lips moved,
she pulled her hand back as if burned.

Ben bent further, touched it, picked it up, then
wished he never had. It took a minute, but finally
it dawned on him what this thing was in his hand.
Tara's frantic eyes were on his as he held it—a
hunk of Shinin''s tail.

Eighteen

Tara leaned over and flipped off the radio.

"I can't listen anymore."

"I never knew you could hear people sweating through the radio. I think Woodrow's broken ground," Ben said, his eyes on the road. One hand held Tara's; the other was on the steering wheel as they listened to Woodrow defend himself, only to have the interviewer parry with another embarrassing question.

"It's his own fault," Tara said without sympathy. Ben gave her a glance that was as good as a whack on the behind. She shifted, but wouldn't back down. "Okay, I'm being catty but he deserves it. He's the one that started this. That reporter Martinez wrote the profile and as much as said there's a suspect. Woodrow's leak backfired, and I'm glad. He can't say that he doesn't know who or where the suspect is, so he sounds like a fool." Tara slid her hand from Ben's. "I'm not really worried about Woodrow, it's Bill. He's bound to hear about this. Then what will he do?"

"Considering what I know about him, I think he's too narcissistic to be worried about this. If anything, it might give him a sense of well-being, that he hasn't been forgotten."

"I don't think Bill Hamilton will ever be forgotten—by anyone whose life he's touched." Tara sat up straighter and put out her arm to point the way. "There's the turnoff. Ecold Drive."

"Cute," Ben mumbled. He had both hands on the wheel. "At least she could've paved it and put in a few lights."

"Donna may be eccentric, but she's not stupid when it comes to her money."

"Smart woman."

"She was," Tara murmured. "I don't want to go tonight. Every time I think about Shinin', about that man being in my house, it makes me furious."

"I know, but you've got to hang in. Remember, this isn't personal. It can't be if we're going to put him where he belongs."

"I know. I'll do my best. You are going to try to get enough evidence tonight, aren't you? Enough to give me some leverage with Woodrow."

"I'll do my best. I need time and he's the only one that can give it to me. Remember, he's been through this before with a psychiatrist. He'll know instantly what I'm up to."

"Then we have to hope that he wants to give you time. He can't go on playing sick jokes forever."

"Maybe he'll want to prove that he's better than me. Depending on what you represent to him, I could be a hindrance as much as a help."

"There is that," Tara said quietly, hoping she never had to find out what she meant to Bill Hamilton.

Ben put both hands back on the wheel and Tara flipped down the passenger mirror. It was lighted. She checked her lipstick. Hardly there, a bare color like the one on her cheeks. In this tiny bit of light she looked ghostly with her dark hair falling down. Was this who Bill saw when he looked at her? Pale with apprehension? Did he see the fear behind her eyes? She flipped the visor back up.

"So who's going to be at this shindig?" Ben asked. "Couples carrying white-wrapped, silver-bowed engagement presents?"

Tara laughed, grateful he was there to step between those memories and her mind.

"I don't think there will be a paper wedding bell in sight. You're going to be hobnobbing with the cream of Albuquerque, plus Donna's hairdresser and his significant other of the moment. Probably one or two people from New York. Sometimes I think Donna built this place far away from everything to test how much her friends love her."

"Sounds like I may have my hands full with more than Bill Hamilton. Maybe I should go back into private practice."

"Maybe you'll be happy you're not in it when you meet these folks. We'll know in a minute. There's the manor house now. Ain't it something?" They both eyed the incredible structure. Tonight the place was lit up. The party was in full swing, it seemed. Silhouettes of Donna's guests moved across the windows and Tara could see the place was packed.

"Where do they all come from?" Tara whispered.

"The woodwork." Ben laughed. "Throw a party, people come." He pulled on the emergency brake and looked at the house instead of her. "Shall we?"

Tara frowned. "If you're ready, so am I."

* * *

"Tara, over here."

Ben called from the back of the house. She found him a second later.

"I love this woman," he said and pointed toward the porch. Laid over the three steps that led to it was a large piece of wood that had been stabilized into a ramp. Tara walked toward him, leaned down, kissed him in the darkness.

"She can be very special. I never said she wasn't," Tara whispered.

"Shall we?" Tara asked, her arms still lying lightly around his neck.

"Neck in the dark?" Ben mused. "Nah, we better go in now that we're here."

Tara laughed against his lips, then lay her forehead on his, wishing she could stay this way forever. She was afraid to go in, even with Ben. Bill Hamilton might touch her again, or look at her with those metallic eyes and know that she knew everything about him. What could Ben do to save her then? Straightening, Tara stood beside Ben and knew that she had come to hate Bill Hamilton on one level and admire him on another. He posed questions she couldn't answer without thinking deeply. In the challenge of him was a challenge to herself.

Was she better than he? Was she as good as the system? More honorable than Woodrow? Yes. And she would prove all of the above. But the persistent fear was something she hadn't expected. She wasn't quite sure where that fit in at all.

"I'm so glad you're here!" Donna had Tara in a Lilliputian bearhug, her little face tipped up so that her cheek lay against her friend's. She whispered so only Tara could hear. "I was so worried you wouldn't come. But Bill said you would."

Tara held Donna away. Yellow was the color of the day, bright and young and joyous. Donna was her own little ray of sunshine. She thought she saw something in Donna's face that didn't belong. Triumph? As if she'd proved her upper hand, and Bill's. But the look was fleeting and Donna was her own self again. So Tara smiled.

"I'm really sorry. I've just been so worried about you," Tara began, but Donna talked over her.

"Stop it right now. I'm not going to fight with you again. I know you can act your way out of any paper bag. So act happy for me."

Tara held back. Everything was shaded by the anticipation of seeing Bill Hamilton. She looked over her shoulder now, wishing he would appear and grin at her so it could be over. But Donna was pulling Tara close, giving her a pep-up look when her attention was diverted and the flirt meter began running overtime.

"It's Ben, isn't it?" Donna let go of Tara and shook Ben's hand. "I've heard about you since I was a girl. It's about time you two got together. Tara's been pining long enough." She winked at Tara. "He is a dream." Back to Ben. Donna's version of tennis. She didn't even work up a sweat. "If you get tired of this horsey woman, just let me know."

"I thought this was an engagement party. I wouldn't want any trouble from the lucky guy," Ben said.

"I promise. No trouble from Bill. He's very open-minded no matter what you've heard." Her voice dropped a tone to show her displeasure but she recovered nicely, before Tara could take of-

fense. "You both need a drink. Then we'll find
Bill. And Tara," she warned, "I'm assuming the
only words out of your mouth are going to be congratulations or something of that nature. Ben, I
expect you to make sure she doesn't get out of
line."

Donna led them away before Tara could reply.
She held her arm up, cradling the champagne
glass like Lady Liberty's torch. Ben and Tara followed, Ben taking time to whisper.

"Do you get the feeling that you just lost Round
One?"

"Funny you should mention it," Tara said under
her breath as Donna ushered them into the heart
of the party.

For ten minutes Ben and Tara were the center
of attention of a group of people who thought
black was the proper color to wear to a joyous occasion. They were introduced from right to left
and heads nodded. Donna left first. Ben and Tara
made small talk, holding hands, Bill Hamilton's appearance uppermost in their mind. More than
once Tara saw Ben scan the room, heard him falter because he couldn't remember the thread of a
conversation, so intent was he on finding the man
in question.

Finally, the others melted away, leaving them
with a clear path to the bar. Polite smiles still plastered on their faces, they breathed a sigh of relief.
Ben raised Tara's hand to his lips. She smiled,
ready to tell him how she loved him, and then he
was there.

Bill Hamilton materialized, resplendent in new
jeans and black and gold boots, a shirt pressed just
so, open to show off a marvelous chest. He was
smiling. Good old boy grin. *Had she missed him?*

He swooped down on Tara. He touched her. Fingertips at her waist, body turned into hers so the tips of her breasts barely touched him. His face was close. She thought he might kiss her. Tara shuddered, paralyzed by surprise and the intensity of her reaction to him. Alarmed, she lifted her face, then with disgust, she raised her hands to push him away.

He kissed her.

On the lips, moving one step closer like a lover. His tongue darted out to cross her lips, a fluttery thing that she could have imagined, but knew she hadn't. Tears were coming, filling up hard and painful behind her eyes. She stepped back. It had taken no more than seconds for him to terrify her. No more than a blink for him to become the aggressor instead of the one in need of protection.

"Tara," he greeted her with a whisper.

She moved back two steps. He lost interest in her and turned to Ben, hoping to find another victim.

"Bill Hamilton," he said heartily.

"Ben Crawford." Ben put out his hand. "Dr. Crawford. We had an appointment a week ago. Nice to meet you."

Bill's knees cracked as he hunkered down, ignoring Ben's hand in order to put his arms on those of the wheelchair. Ben was imprisoned. Bill looked him up and down, his eyes lingering on Ben's useless legs. Bill's expression was concerned. He shook back his long hair and finally made eye contact again. His face was hard, his expression cruel, but he smiled still.

"Can't say I recall, Doc, and I am truly sorry. I'd forget my head if it wasn't screwed on, but usually I'm pretty good at details. Don't you think, Tara? It's the big picture I have trouble with."

His eyes never left Ben's; Tara never looked down at him. "Yes, you're excellent with details."

Tara stood statue-like, afraid to move, wanting only to push him aside, away from Ben. She wanted to do something heroic, something that would put Bill Hamilton in his place. But Ben seemed to need no defense.

"See, Doc, what'd I tell you. Tara and me, we're on the same wavelength. She's a good woman. You're a lucky man. Funny she'd pick a guy like you, though. I seen her out with that stallion of hers. This lady likes a good hard ride, if you know what I mean." Tara swallowed hard and closed her eyes, tensing with each contemptuous comment. Finally she stepped forward and faced him, her hand on Ben's shoulder.

"Ben, I think this might not . . ."

Ben smiled, but it was at Bill. For Tara he had only a pat on the hand. He was enjoying himself.

"It's fine," Ben said.

"Hey, little lady," Bill said, slapping the right arm of Ben's chair. "Come on now. You been around. You know how it is with man talk."

"Yeah, Tara," Ben rejoined. "This is guy stuff. Why don't you go find something else to do and leave us to it? I think Bill and I'll get along great."

Tara bridled at this ridiculous game. Posturing for a dangerous man only undercut their mission.

"I don't think so. I know Bill. He'll talk your ear off if you give him half a chance. Among other things," she added.

Bill threw back his head and laughed. "Don't you worry none about that. I wouldn't want the doc to lose an ear when he's already lost those legs of his. What else you missin', Doc?"

"Bill! Please."

Ben squeezed her hand. She stopped talking. Ben smiled pleasantly and pinched harder, a warning for her to back off. She was happy to oblige.

"I think I need a drink," she said. "Ben?"

"No, I'm fine."

"Me too." Bill laughed. She glared at him.

"I'll leave you two alone then."

"Great." Bill stood up and put his hand on the back of Ben's chair. "Take your time. Me and the doc probably have a lot to talk about." Bill pushed the chair and Tara almost went after him. She didn't want him to take Ben anywhere, not out of the house or out of sight. But she held back and was about to wander away when he called her once more.

Leaving Ben where he was, Bill came back. Tara tensed, ready to fight if he touched her again. He smiled genially, but his voice was hard.

"I saw the paper. Someone's nosin' around about the Circle K. They lookin' for me, Tara?" He touched the tip of her hair. "Did you tell, Tara? Did you tell so someone would come get me?"

Tara stared at him, her own eyes cold and equally harsh now. "You know I didn't. I gave you my word."

"You made trouble with me and Donna about it."

"You made that trouble yourself, Bill. I haven't said anything to anyone that you didn't give me permission to say. You're the one holding things up. Talk to Ben if you're serious about help. No more crap."

Bill looked around him, considering the people, the house, the food, and the waiters who passed drinks so generously.

"I don't know anymore. Maybe I was wrong to say anything. Maybe I don't need you. Maybe you're lyin' to me."

He went back to Ben. They disappeared, swallowed up by the crowd of revelers. Donna's laugh tinkled high above the rest of the noise and it sounded forced to Tara. But what did she know? Maybe that's the way real happiness sounded. Or perhaps, it was the sound of obsession, or a cry to be rescued. Who knew anymore? Certainly not Tara.

"Here you go."

A drink landed on the bar at her elbow. She reached for it and offered a quick little grimace to the bartender, hoping it would pass for a smile of thanks. She wandered through the room past knots of people and heard them talking about clothes and hair. Another group espoused opera in Albuquerque.

Tara shook her head, dismissing a waiter offering phyllo food. Donna had come and gone twice since Ben and Bill disappeared. She was thrilled to see the two men with their heads together. Now Tara was alone, wishing they could leave. But Ben wasn't done, so she stayed.

She found herself in the foyer between the living room and the huge room Donna affectionately referred to as the family room. An odd concept since family these days consisted only of Bill Hamilton. To her right was the staircase. Big and wide, it was a sweeping half-moon shape that called to her as clearly as if it could speak.

Without another thought, Tara started climbing the stairs, setting her glass on the edge of one as she went. Single-mindedly she moved on, ever more quickly until she was on the upper landing. This house was as familiar to her as her own, yet she felt disoriented, as if traps awaited everywhere.

Slowly, Tara began to wander. She poked her head into the bathroom, taking note of the imported tile Donna had been so thrilled with during the building of this mansion. She went into the pristine guest room. No one had slept there. Bill had not been relegated to the status of company. She wandered out and into the hall again. The next room was Donna's office, in its normal state of disarray. The desk was littered with correspondence. Tara's fingernail nudged a letter from Donna's editor. There was another beneath. Both asked for a book that had been promised weeks earlier. Tara felt nothing and that, in itself, was a victory. Here, in the same house with Bill Hamilton, she was learning how to control her reactions. Her assurances of objectivity seemed so arrogant now. But it was sneaking back again. Tara could indeed view the havoc Bill was wreaking on Donna's life and feel nothing but a renewed determination to remove him from it. She patted the papers. The master bedroom was next. Tara didn't hesitate. She walked into the mauve and stone colored room.

Bill's closet. Bill's clothes. Jeans, boots, shirts. She ran her hands over the shelf above. Nothing personal. No baggage. Strange for a man who would call this his home. Quietly she closed the doors. Donna's closet was no mystery. Tara knew exactly what was in there so she ignored it in favor of the chest of drawers. One, two, three drawers were opened. She riffled the clothes carefully—or so she hoped—finding only clothes.

The bedside table was next. *Town & Country* magazine, hand lotion, oil of peppermint, pens and pencils, a tape recorder. That was Donna's side of the bed. She moved to the other side, engrossed in what she was doing. The first nightstand drawer was empty; the second yielded a stack of girlie magazines. Tara riffled through them. Finally, in the last drawer, something far more telling. Catalogs and magazines for guns and ammunition, mercenary want ads. And used as a bookmark, the article by Martin Martinez that asked whether or not the Circle K killer was indeed in Albuquerque.

Tara had begun to read, refreshing her memory on the impressive subtleties of his work, when she was touched. She froze. The newsprint fluttered from her fingers. She stood tall and rigid, her eyes closed, her back to the door. Seven seconds. Huge numbers flashed in her mind as she counted the moments. She waited for a blow, the tear of a knife, a bullet ripping through her brain and stopping the show. When it didn't come, when she still lived, Tara turned slowly and opened her eyes, wanting to see what was to come. She would look him straight in the eye for Vera, for Paulette, for the woman in the Circle K, for Donna who refused to see for herself what he was.

"Bill," she whispered.

He didn't smile as she'd hoped he would. He looked not so much at her as through her, his vision trained on the hollow at her neck. Tara didn't move. She couldn't hear her breath. She waited for a cue, but there wasn't one before he reached for her. He lay his hand on her shoulder then slid it to her throat. In her peripheral vision

Tara saw his fingers move spider-like across her body until she lost sight of them as they wound around her neck. Long, strong fingers spanned the back of her neck, his powerful thumb was up front on her pulse point. Tara's blood ran hot and scared through her veins, pumping against the softness of her skin flowing into his until they were joined in life and death. Pressure from him and she died. Simple. Straightforward. Madness.

"I'm so sorry," he said finally and flatly.

Tara bolted, slipping out of his grasp, and she thanked her luck when he made no move to hold her. She flew down the stairs, unnoticed by Donna's inebriated guests. Her head snapped right and left, searching for any sign of Ben. She saw him but didn't run. Instead, she looked up, through the sweep of stairs. Bill stared down at her. Expressionless, he watched. She left, thinking only of herself and Ben and running away to leave Donna defenseless.

"We have to go," she said quietly, leaning down so that her head rested on Ben's shoulder. The man Ben was talking to went away without question or a farewell.

"You're shaking." His arms were around her, his lips burying themselves in her hair as he spoke. Were people watching them? Did they wonder what was going on? Let them. She was going to be sick.

"We have to go. He found me upstairs looking through his things. Please, Ben, we have to go now." She stood straight, her hand on Ben's back, and shook out her long hair. Ben took her hand and they went out the way they'd come.

He got into the van. Tara reached for the door handle, slipping before she could open it. She moved the heel of her shoe and bent down, curious about a glint she saw in the dirt. Plucking some bright things up, Tara held them in her palm, jingling them, rolling them back and forth in her palm. She heard the lock of the bolt that held Ben's chair in place, and pulled herself together, sliding in beside him, still looking at her treasure. She held out her hand, flipping on the overhead light. Together they looked at the shell casings.

"Target practice," Ben mused.

"I didn't see a gun in there," Tara said quietly. "Give me a report, Ben. Give me what I need to go to Woodrow."

"I need time. Vera's information, an affidavit from Paulette. I should have clinic time with him. I want it to stand up for you. I don't want him released no matter where he ends up." Ben touched her hair. "Bill Hamilton is one weird guy. He may be sicker than anyone can imagine, or as sane as you and me. I need him in my office. He's promised to come. I think he will if for no other reason than to show off."

"I can't wait, Ben. This is terrifying. He's terrifying," Tara insisted.

"Then go to Woodrow." Ben put his hands on the steering wheel, thought for a moment, then started the car. "Have him arrested for threatening you."

"But it wasn't like that," she answered softly. "Not like that at all. I'm still bound to him."

"No," Ben said. "You're obligated to him. You're bound to me and I'll help make it right. I promise."

Tara lay her head back and closed her eyes, praying she could hold him to that.

"Let's go to your place." She didn't open her eyes. He didn't answer, but she knew he would take her there.

The last place she wanted to go was home. The ghosts of the bread-baking women had fled; there were no specters of all those who had built the house brick by brick. Tara had lost the comfort of her father's phantom. All that was left were the places Bill Hamilton had been, the things he had touched: the guest house, the pump, the kitchen, the corral. He had sprayed his madness throughout, marking her place as his territory. He had driven her out of her home, claimed her best friend, put her at odds with the Webers, and made her question the sanctity of a law that bound her to silence. There was only Ben now. Without him, Bill Hamilton might have conquered her, too.

Nineteen

> . . . *a lawyer shall not knowingly use a confidence or a secret of his client to the disadvantage of his client or the advantage of himself or a third party, unless the client consents after full disclosure.*
> —*Canon 4 ABA Model Rules of Professional Conduct*

"*Do Ya Think I'm Sexy*"? Rod Stewart. Nineteen seventy-nine? She couldn't remember the year, but the tune was clear. Ben had been playing it when she awoke. They made love to it, his magical hands leaving her wanting more. They showered to it and kissed goodbye to it. The tune pounded in her head as she drove home, sharing space with all the things she and Ben didn't talk about. The party, Bill Hamilton, Donna Ecold were all off limits. For a few hours the only thing worth thinking about was what had happened between the sheets on Ben Crawford's bed.

Home again, Tara looked at her house for a long while, waiting for that feeling of tranquillity it once afforded. It was gone, eluding her like so much else these days. With a sigh, a dejected slam of the Jeep door, Tara gave up.

She stopped at the corral and gave Shinin' a pat. The horse whinnied, objecting to her offhanded attention. He danced off and back again, agitated as if he could force affection if he complained. He was worse than a child.

"Shinin', give me a break. It was a long night."

When he didn't settle down, Tara turned her back on him and walked through blustery wind to the house. Inside, the place was shadowy, bathed in winter grayness. Tara kicked off her shoes and lit a fire in the living room. She headed back down the hall, unbuttoning her shirt as she went. Her head felt heavy, her chest scratchy, and she wanted to curl up in her robe, under a blanket. Ben would call when he had confirmed Bill's appointment. She would read the material Ben had Xeroxed for her.

Tara stopped toying with the shirt buttons. Suddenly the house vibrated with the odd hum of a noise she'd never heard before. Her hand lay immobile on her breast as she listened carefully, picking and discarding adjectives that might describe the sound. Dull. Thudding. Repetitious. Then, silence.

Water heater?

She cocked her head.

Hammering? Joseph? Not today. He didn't come today.

Silence still. Tara stepped ahead, one more button coming slowly undone, the cold air pricking her almost bared chest just as the sound came at her again. A smothered noise. Electrical? No. Plumbing? Perhaps. Cautiously Tara changed her course, instinctively hugging the wall. She peeked into the kitchen.

Quiet.

She looked down the hall.

Silence.

Thud.

Back to the kitchen, her eyes flicked to every
appliance. Something was hitting against—something else. There were no branches close enough
to throw themselves against a wall. A gate wasn't
loose, slamming shut. She looked left. Her office
was in order. Tara looked toward the window. Outside was still gray, the wind was down. The trees
didn't bend as they had earlier; there were no
shutters to heave up and back.

Thump. Thump. Thump.

"*Do ya think I'm sexy?*"

The words kept time with the noise, and the
noise got louder as Tara inched farther down the
hall to the guest room. She looked in. Nothing.

Thud. Rip.

A new note was added.

Stupidly Tara went ahead. Not back to the
phone. Not out for help. This was her house. Her
home. In the guest room she solved the mystery.
Light filtered through the plantation shutters strip-
ing the opposite wall, leaving split shadows on the
bed beneath it, the man who sat there and the
knife held above his head.

His arm came down with amazingly precise
rhythm, the blade flashing through the brightest
slats of light, dulling in the shadows, disappearing
as it was buried in the mattress. Crazily, Tara's first
thought was one of relief. Bill had a repetitious
streak in him. He hadn't destroyed the entire bed.
Her mother's quilt still lay neatly folded at the foot
of it while he reduced the middle of the mattress
to an eruption of stuffing and strips of shiny blue
fabric.

"Hey there, little lady."

Tara jumped. She had concentrated so hard on

the attack, she'd ignored the attacker. Horrified, she looked up wondering why she wasn't invisible. He had seemed so intent on his task that he wasn't quite real. Obviously she'd been wrong.

Bill Hamilton was looking right at her, the knife raised and stable above his head. He was smiling. She almost smiled back until she saw how different he was. His eyes were matte, the gleam was gone. His head angled, giving his handsome face an oddly elongated appearance. He was no longer defined; his features had been remade by the light and dark of the speckled illumination. He was a man printed slightly out of register on the paper of life. He could take a sledgehammer to a dog or put a gun to a woman's head and pull the trigger or slice a mattress to shreds for no other reason than he felt like it.

Legs quaking, dry in the mouth, Tara moved a step to the right. The backs of her knees touched the small chair beside the door. She sank onto it, hands clasping the seat on either side. Mentally Tara ran through a litany of precautions. No loud noises. No sudden movement. No trying to reason with him. She should remain as still as if he were an animal, wild and unpredictable. Could she move faster than a madman? Could she outrun him, outfox him, outthink him? This was her fault. There were things she could have done, should have done. But what were they?

Suddenly her mind went blank under a wave of sensory overload. Helplessness and horror were left in its wake. The cool air on her almost bare chest, the feel of the rattan under her palms were exquisitely clear. But not her thoughts. Bill gritted his teeth. The knife came down again. She jumped and the door was shut in her head, leaving only a large, dark and blank space where the sound of his fury could echo off the walls.

Sweating, Tara turned hot and cold, then hot again, with each flash of the knife. Two fingers had forgotten to curl around the seat of the chair and were stiffened in a half-moon position, painfully still. *Thump*. Tara's skin tingled. *Rip*. She closed her eyes, imagining the knife in her. *Thud*. Her breath had startled him. He saw her again, his attention drawn to her, a more interesting prey.

Thump.

Tara's hand jarred, the chair tipped. The front right leg was slightly shorter than the other three. It hit the floor with a rappity-tap that sounded like gunfire in her head. Bill didn't look up from his work.

Thump. *Thump*. *Thump* and *rip*.

This was so wrong. The day was dreary. She wanted a nap. The fire was blazing. She had been kissed and loved and left so warmly only an hour ago. She wasn't meant to die on a day like this, in this house, in this room. She wanted to die quietly, looking out the window from her bed and feeling the cool adobe walls beneath her fingers one last time like her father. She didn't want to fight for her life. She didn't want to beg for it when it wasn't meant to be over. And with those thoughts, she started to fight the hysteria.

She listened for a change in Bill Hamilton's rhythm at the same time tears eased out from the corners of her eyes. They lay upon her cheek before bobbling slowly and gently down her face. They came one from each eye and Tara found a strange comfort in those two tears. She was alive if she could cry and shake with fear. As long as there was that, there was hope. She closed her eyes and listened. Suddenly it was silent again.

Tara steeled herself. He would come for her now. But the silence lengthened and there was no knife in her chest, no creaking of a heavy body rolling off the bed. Her executioner didn't come teasing and prancing her way, so she opened her eyes, looked past him to the window and saw that the shadows hadn't changed at all, the day hadn't darkened. It wasn't a lifetime since she'd sat in this straight-backed chair; it wasn't even hours. Bill Hamilton still sat cross-legged on the bed looking almost sad and worn out from all his work.

Cautiously Tara manipulated her body. She loosened her grip on the chair, letting the blood flow back into them. Yes! If her hands could work, her legs could too. If her legs, then her mind. Deliberately, her eyes clicked left a centimeter at a time until, finally, they focused on the bed and then on him. She was looking at Bill Hamilton and he was sitting on the bed looking right at her.

He wore jeans and heavy boots. His sweatshirt was pale blue, emblazoned with a spray of flowers, butterflies and fairies buzzing around the bouquet. Tara felt a laugh bubble deep inside her. Donna's last book cover. The sweatshirt giveaways. How absurd, to be killed by a man wearing a children's book cover. But Tara didn't laugh, because the man in the baby blue shirt held a knife that was painful to look at. It was pearl-handled, the blade curved, the edge serrated. It was a knife well worn and used hard; a knife that men used to gut their kill.

She looked away from the knife and into his eyes. The sliced light had appliquéd his face. One eye was dark, the other opaque, one cheek hol-

lowed by shadow, the other highlighted, one side
of his hair shimmered, the other was dark and flat.
Donna wouldn't recognize him if she was there.
But Tara was alone. So she opened her mouth
ever-so-slightly. She wanted to talk. But Bill lay his
head in his hands, the knife blade pointing heavenward, his eyes down. A shuddering sigh quivered
his shoulders, and then he was quiet.

Tara waited and watched. When he didn't move,
she scooted forward, raised her heels so that her
weight was on the balls of her feet, and looked
toward the door. That was when there was one
more rip. Tara froze, closed her eyes briefly, then
chanced a look his way. Bill sat quietly, considering
what he'd done. What was it he saw there? Was it
the woman at Circle K he imagined? Donna? Tara?
Any woman? She could speculate all day; she could
also wait for him to turn on her. It was now or
never.

Half crouching, Tara swung herself into the
doorway. She held out her arms, steadied herself,
lifted up, and stepped into the hall, moving
through the exceptional silence like a whisper. She
hoped her legs would hold her up. She wished she
could hear the sound of the knife once more. But
all was silent. Decisions would have to be made in
the void.

The nearest phone was in her bedroom.

The front door was only a sprint from there.

Raising a phone was quieter than opening a
door.

The telephone could bring help.

The door could bring freedom.

He wouldn't know who she was talking to.

He knew these acres almost as well as she.

Suddenly she found herself sitting on her own

bed, receiver in hand, with no idea how she got there. She was halfway home, but the numbers on the phone were jumping like fleas and it was hard to focus.

"Stop." She half sobbed, half prayed. "Stop."

There they were. Three across. Four down. She could see them all. One. Four. Five. Nine. Each number popped up, begging to be pushed. But the order had to be right. Please, please, what numbers should she push?

Her head fell back, heavy hair lay across her shoulders, her skin itched. It was damn hot. *Help.* She listened. *Thump.* Bill Hamilton was still playing. With no room for error, she dialed. Seven numbers. The ring. The click. The greeting.

"Ben. *Oh no—*"

Tara screamed the last words. Bill Hamilton was on her, his hand tangled in her hair so tight it pulled her against his broad chest. She could smell him, musky and manly. He smelled of madness. They looked like lovers, but the arm he wrapped across her chest was tight and the hand that lay against her shoulder still clutched the pearl-handled, curve-bladed knife.

Her breath caught, her neck was at an angle that would either break the bone or suffocate her should she move to escape. In the intimate recesses of her body Tara felt a swelling and breaking, a clutching of muscle that stroked her to fearful orgasm. The knife glinted just out of her view, sending a rainbow of light toward the wall opposite her.

His chest rose and he sighed. Tara's hand fell to her lap and she prayed that Bill would talk and Ben would listen. The spirits were watching. Bill spoke. He drawled. It was the only thing a tired cowboy could do. "I thought I could trust you, sugar. Told you my secrets, asked for help. Hard thing for a man to do, Tara, to ask a woman for help."

His face moved into her peripheral vision. He was assessing her, his eyes roaming over her face. Tara closed her eyes. He shifted, trying to get comfortable. His hand tightened in her hair. He held a hank to his face and breathed in.

"Damn pretty hair. Dark. Donna's not a real blonde. Guess you knew that." His chest quivered again. What was this? What did this mean? *Ben, are you listening?* "Bad girl, Tara. You told the paper about me. You're playing with me and I trusted you." His arm tightened over her chest but it seemed he held her in desperation instead of anger. "Tara, I'm so alone. Feel so damn alone. I wish I could find my mama. Damn, don't I wish that."

Suddenly the arm across her chest was flung out and his fist came down on the bed with such force it shook. His fingers twisted again in her hair and he jerked her head back so that she was looking up at him. His face was pale with fury, then he was moving, scooting back to sit cross-legged on the pillows. She was free. Tara lay there for a moment, then said:

"I didn't tell anyone anything, Bill. I promise." Bill seemed as startled as she that she'd spoken. Tara took advantage of his surprise. She sat up a little straighter. The sound of her voice hadn't driven him to a rage, hadn't made him leer at her, hadn't made him raise the knife. She was still in control. She was the parent, he the child. If only he let her talk.

"I've ruined friendships for you," Tara offered, hoping this sacrifice would be acceptable.

"You've been trying to tell Donna I'm bad for her," he shot back.

"I've been trying to warn her that she might not be safe. Would you want to hurt her, Bill? Would you?"

He shook his head. Did he care? Probably. He'd cared for Paula. Another point for her side. Encouraged, she went on. The receiver was still in her hand, slippery with sweat. She lay it on the bed beside her, half covering it with her flexed leg. She hoped Ben was no longer listening but acting. The cops would be on their way. In the meantime, she was in control. Please Lord, was she in control?

"I don't want you to hurt Donna either. And she was my friend long before you were my client. But look who I chose. Look what I did for you. I didn't tell her what you did to that woman at the Circle K." Tara thought of Paula, Paulette, and Vera and let them lie. Who knew what he might do if he found out Tara had spoken to the women in his life? "I didn't break my promise to you even though she is my best friend. I chose you!" Bill shuffled and put the knife in his other hand. He looked at her quickly, then away just as fast. He tossed the knife again. This time it clattered to the floor. She talked faster as he bent to pick it up. "And what about the DA? I told him only what you gave me permission to tell him. Nothing else. Have I tried to convince you to go in, have your fingerprints taken? No. I've protected you because that's what you asked me to do. I haven't even tried to convince you to give me permission to do that, have I? That would have made my life a hell of a lot easier, but I stuck by you."

Tara scooted farther to the side of the bed. One foot was on the floor and with this small triumph her voice rose. She sounded too excitable. That wasn't right. Not with Bill. He would hear the hysteria. She tipped her head and blew out the bad air. When she looked at him again he was off the bed, leaning against the wall, watching her as if he, an audience of one, was waiting to see how the play would pace.

"I could have used any one of your pranks against you. I could have said you were threatening me, or Donna, or both of us with that blouse thing. What about Shinin's tail? The meat? You tried to make me think you'd killed him. I could have had you arrested for breaking and entering."

"Nobody'd believe you." He rolled his head in disbelief and disgust. "I didn't hurt anyone. I didn't leave any evidence. You tried it once. You tried to make the cops believe you."

"I could make someone believe it, Bill. Those two at Donna's house were just patrol cops. I could have made the DA listen. He'd listen to anything about you, he wants you so bad. Don't ever doubt that." Tara's voice was strong now, her belief in her own competence stronger than his madness. "I could make them believe that you meant to harm me and that is a threat. I know this system. I know how to use it, for my own benefit and for yours, too. If I used it for my own, I'd be done with you now." Tara hit her words hard, hoping he understood how little power or compassion she had. "I want to make sure you get to a hospital and not a jail. You don't want any screwups. You don't want me to mess up when we're so close. But I can't do it all myself, Bill. I need you to help, and you aren't helping. You're messing

things up because I don't know where you're coming from. So how am I going to convince anyone
that you need help when you're walking around
here like you're the Marlboro Man?"

That got his attention. He swung his head back
to her and there was a twinkle in his eye. He
swung his head up and looked down his perfectly
shaped nose at her. He looked euphoric.

"What did you say?"

Ben drove fast, but not quite fast enough to attract the attention of a cop. It wasn't as if there
was a cloud of dust billowing after him. This was
speed in fits and starts. He shot forward to make
the lights, only to slam on the brake a minute before he ran the red. He could kill someone if he
did that. Tara could die if he didn't. He ran the
next light.

The fifteen minutes between Tara's home and
Ben's was whittled to seven. He hit the floor bolt
release and the wheelchair's motor at the same
time, intending to whip toward the back of the
van, but his timing was off. The lock was still engaged, the chair's motor energized with nowhere
to go. Ben remained stationary, the bolt now
locked. He rolled down the window. Nothing. No
sound at all from the house. Ben counted to ten,
letting the mechanisms reorient themselves. But
the seconds felt like hours, and he was convinced
they were the last moments of Tara's life on earth.
It took everything he had not to scream out for
her. Ben got to eight on the countdown and gave
it another try, forcing himself to release the bolt-
ing mechanism before pushing forward on the
chair. It worked.

He wiped the sweat from his brow and shivered in the cold as the door opened and he wheeled onto the lift. The ride down was interminable, long enough for Ben to think himself as insane as Bill Hamilton. He should have called the police. Bill Hamilton was full of anger in a whole body; he was Ben Crawford, full of fear in half a one.

He was on the ground and moving forward, wishing for the first time in a long while that he could walk—run—dash forward and get there just that split second sooner. But he couldn't and he had the presence of mind to understand that.

Slowly Ben pushed open the door. The fire burned steadily but low in the deserted living room. He wheeled forward on manual motion, past Tara's shoes in the hall. Desperately he tried to sense Tara's presence.

"Nice to see you, Doc." Ben's head snapped left as he stopped, frozen by a sense of fear so deep he could feel it in his toes.

Bill Hamilton stood in the doorway of Tara's bedroom. Smiling and grinning and happy to have someone else to play with. Ben's eyes flicked to the knife. A clean blade. A good sign, he hoped, for Bill had proven to be meticulous in his mischief. They locked eyes again.

"Bill." Ben nodded and his voice was calm. "Tara in there?"

"Yep. Got her all nice and comfy on the bed. You want to see?"

Bill stepped back, motioning Ben in with one hand. Ben went down the hall as far as the doorway, his heart falling to his stomach when he looked in. She was sitting on the edge of the bed, the phone still off the hook and her looking like the devil. White skin, black-smudged, red-rimmed eyes. Her jaw was tight and her blue eyes were dull. She was fine. They would all be fine.

"Hey, Tara," Ben said quietly.

"Hi, Ben," she said back, but her voice quavered. They watched one another. He hoped she knew what a good job she was doing.

"What's goin' on, guys?" Ben asked, glancing at Bill, at the ready should he need to protect himself or Tara.

Bill shook his head. "You know, I don't know anymore, Doc. When I got here, I swear I knew what I was up to. Just wanted to talk to Tara. She's my lawyer, and I wanted to talk to her, you know."

"Looks like she's listening." Ben slid his eyes to the knife, let them linger there, then looked at Bill long and hard to let him know he wasn't afraid.

"Aw, hell, Ben, you are amazing. I swear. For a guy that doesn't have much goin' for him, you're doin' A-OK! Hot damn. You are one plucky guy."

"Thanks, Bill. I appreciate the compliment. But you know what? It's getting late and I really hate driving out here for nothing. So what about it? Why don't you and I talk and figure out what it was you were trying to do here. I'll talk to Tara when we're done if you don't think she understands. But standing here with a knife isn't the way to carry on a quality conversation."

"Christ, Ben, that's the stupidest thing I ever heard. Talkin' to me like a kid. Like a shrink." Bill tossed his head around and snuffled. He pulled his arm across his nose. "Aw hell, okay. That okay with you, Tara? Ben and I have a little mano-a-mano?"

Tara shook her head, not wanting either of them alone with this man. Ben tossed off, "She's got a lot to do, too. She better get her rear in gear and figure out a way to get you what you want."

"Now you're talkin', Doc. Whatever happened to the man part of you sure didn't affect that brain of yours. Wish we'd met earlier. We'd have had some high times. Well, let's get to it."

Ben hesitated. Bill cocked a handsome brow.

"The knife, Bill?"

Bill looked at his weapon. He pushed his hair back. "Whatever." He tossed it onto the bed and walked back to the guest room. Ben followed. Tara collapsed beside the knife. She lay on her own bed for a good long while before she went to the living room to warm her cold fear in front of the fire.

Ben found her perched on the edge of the sofa, facing the fire, half an hour later. She was huddled in a corner, her legs up, her arms wrapped around a sofa pillow. Eyes on the flames, her ears pricked for any sound from the back of the house. She heard Ben's wheelchair and steeled herself. Thankfully she heard nothing more than the whirr and click of that motor. He came up beside her, lay a hand on her arm.

"We better do something, and we better do it now."

Twenty

"You've got to make some accommodations in this house." Ben stretched for the coffeepot. It was out of his reach by a mile.

"I'll get it," Tara said, the words strained and hard to get out.

"I could've got it," he assured her, "but the cabinets are definitely off limits."

"Okay." Tara opened the cabinet on command, her voice as dreamlike as her movements. Ben gave her a sidelong glance. She was pale. She was itchy, but she was functioning.

Tara closed the cabinet above the stove and walked away. Above and to the left of the sink she opened another and reached for the saucers and cups. Two saucers in hand, she dropped one, juggled it in a vain attempt to catch it and dropped the other. They clattered to the floor. She threw herself back against the counter and closed her eyes, her head shaking back and forth. Ben went over and put his hands on her hips.

"It's okay. Tara, it's okay," Ben reassured her gently. "Bill's asleep. He's not going to get up for a while. An outburst like this can exhaust someone in his state of mind. We could probably set off a bomb, and he'd sleep through it." Ben hesitated.

"But that doesn't mean we should be stupid. We have to call the police."

"Ben. No." This time she shook her head emphatically, no mere reaction but a statement, a decision. "Having him arrested would take care of things for a few days. I'd file charges. He'd be incarcerated for a few hours, Donna would bail him out. That's not going to solve the bigger problem."

"Then tell the cops what you really have. This is the Circle K killer. He has confessed to you. He has broken into your home. If this isn't threatening, I don't know what is. Give him to Woodrow with all that, and they won't set bail."

"He didn't threaten me, Ben." Tara wrenched away from his hold. "You don't understand. Nothing he said was threatening."

"And everything he *did* here was obviously threatening. There isn't going to be anybody who questions that." Ben wheeled left, watching her but she wouldn't meet his gaze.

"I'd question it, Ben, if I did what you're suggesting." Tara grabbed for the coffee, missed it, and whirled with her back to the counter. "Listen, I know what what went on here looks like, and I won't try to kid you. I was so scared I thought I would die of fright before he could do anything to me, but I'm not ready to give in yet. You've got to understand a few things. I've lost so much since Bill Hamilton came into my life. I've lost Woodrow and Charlotte. He's taken Donna from me—at least for a while. He's made my home a house of terror instead of a refuge. I don't want him to take anything more."

Tara took a deep breath, fighting to control herself as she put her thoughts in perspective. She held her hands together, considered her fingers as if they were alien things, then reached back against the counter. She couldn't look at Ben so she stared out the window over the breakfast table while she explained.

"My law practice belongs to me. Before that it belonged to my father and before that it was started by his father-in-law. This practice has a history like almost everything else in my life. It is a part of me the same way my blue eyes and black hair are a part of a special history. I'm not going to let Bill Hamilton take that from me, Ben." Her lip quivered and tears came into her voice, but she managed to catch herself. She was strong. Generations of strong women had come before her. They were all a part of her.

"I'm not going to turn him over without being damn sure that what I feel threatened by would hold up in front of the ethics committee. I'm not going to let Bill Hamilton get another attorney and sue me from here to kingdom come, ruin my reputation, and maybe take away my license to practice. And most of all, I'm not going to let him take my peace of mind. I can't let him take everything, Ben. I can't."

Tara turned away, ashamed and yet not. She poured the coffee, and this time looked out the window over the kitchen sink. What a coward she was in front of Ben. "What an ugly day," she said. Ben followed her into the living room. She put his coffee on the table and took hers to the window. She was drawn to the view, unable to look inside the house because he was still there. Tara pulled her sweater closer. She wore two and still couldn't get warm.

"I want you to know, Ben, that this isn't all self-ish. I don't believe I could be that callous. There are many other considerations. I don't want Bill Hamilton to beat me. I need to prove I can control this situation." She shrugged. "Stupid, huh?"

"No. It makes you feel safe."

Tara hung her head, living with the thought for a minute. "I'm not ashamed of it."

"You shouldn't be," Ben agreed. She looked askance at him, but his face was expressionless. Did he agree with her because he knew to argue would be fruitless?

"But you're not safe now. I believe that in my heart."

"I want to finish what I was hired to do, and what I promised." Her head was level now and she was looking at Ben. "Maybe when I passed the bar I didn't understand the full import of keeping counsel. Now I do. If a person can't come to an attorney and know that attorney is completely dedicated to his cause, utterly trustworthy, there would be no truth. People would be afraid to tell it for fear their advocate would use it against them for their own gain. Innocent and guilty alike would never feel safe. We might as well get rid of the law, because I could use all the information in my head for any purpose I choose. Who would any of us ever trust? Where would we find help? Any of us, Ben." She paused. The gleam deep in her eyes was one of pain as she tried to convince herself that what she was saying rang true. "What if it was you, or I, whose mind was sick? What if our actions couldn't be controlled? What then, Ben?"

"Tara." Ben maneuvered his chair so that he faced her square. "I agree with you philosophically. But this wasn't an ugly prank like the blouse or the meat in the oven. This was a man with a weapon. I can't tell you what his mental state is.

A sociopath would have slashed you to pieces without a second thought. If Bill Hamilton isn't one, he's damn close, Tara. He may still be fighting the right and wrong, the help versus punishment question, or he may just be having a heck of a good time making us all dance to his tune. I don't think we can afford to be anything other than cautious."

Ben pulled on his right leg, readjusting it so that it leaned closer to the left. Ben didn't, or couldn't, look at her.

"I'll write you a report. It will be full of speculation because I would need months to properly evaluate Bill. We can't wait, Tara. We have to give him to Woodrow now. You tell him that you are afraid and have been threatened and then tell him what Bill told you about the Circle K. You give Woodrow the report, and you tell him that you'll have an insanity plea anyway. Then you can tell him it would be worse if he tried to play this out in court and lost to commitment in the end." Ben looked frustrated. He didn't know the law. He only knew there had to be options. "I know one thing, Tara. This display here today was frustration pure and simple. As simple as needing a pack of cigarettes and ending up killing a woman. As simple as being frustrated by Paulette and taking a sledgehammer to a dog. How long do we wait? Until he's so frustrated with you, or Donna, that he does something we can't undo?"

Ben pulled a face. Tara sipped her coffee and didn't look at him. Ben wheeled toward her with such force she was startled. But he was agile with that thing and stopped right in front of her. He touched her. Tara froze.

"Stop it, Tara. Just stop. You're forty years old. Face up. You're not the all-seeing, all-knowing, all-perfect hope of Albuquerque, New Mexico, or even Bill Hamilton. Just do it, damn it. Get rid of this guy." His voice lowered and softened. "Please. A lot of time's been wasted already. I want a life for us, and it isn't the one we're living."

"This is the one I have now. Help me or get out of the way," she shot back.

Ben threw up his hands. "Again? Again you're doing this? First you choose your father over me, now Bill Hamilton."

"That's ridiculous. I did no such thing."

"You chose something over me when we were kids. If it wasn't your father, then what? Sanity? Freedom from hurt? I don't know. But you set yourself up for these bizarre tests of fortitude, and then you won't back down, and then you wonder why certain things in your life don't feel right."

"And you're taking your job too seriously. I'm not the one who needs analysis. And I'm not trying to be superwoman. I just want what's right for everyone. I want this all to be letter perfect so I don't lose in the end. Is that so wrong?" Tara flared, setting down her cup and standing tall.

"Forget letter perfect," Ben said. "There's a moral call to be made here. An oath does not preclude you from keeping those you care about safe. I wouldn't let my oath stop me from—"

"Hello! Knock, knock." The front door opened and Donna blew in with the cold. The fire blazed and crackled on cue, taking the tension between Tara and Ben for fuel. "Well, you two look just like you've lost your best friends."

She grinned and loosened her coat, a red fox that almost buried her. Children all over the world kept Donna Ecold in the most politically incorrect fashion. She often thanked the little peas out loud while whipping out her charge card. Now her expression was strained under a less-than-perfect makeup job. There was worry behind her eyes despite the smile on her lips.

"Sorry. Did I interrupt something important?"

"No." Tara moved away from Ben.

"Yes," Ben said simultaneously, going the opposite way.

"Oh, this is fun." Donna chuckled nervously and moved into the middle void. "I feel like I just walked in on the Two Stooges. Listen, I'll be out of here in a second, I promise. But I was wondering if you'd seen Bill? The party was super last night, but I was so exhausted I slept in. Didn't even get up until one, and then I couldn't find him anywhere. The car was still in the drive, and I waited for him to come in. When he didn't come back I called, but your line's been busy, so I thought I'd take a chance." Donna shrugged, agitated on the verge of frantic. "I thought he might be here."

In the silence, Donna became more uncomfortable. Her head flipped from Tara to Ben and back again. Tara looked away.

"What? What?" Donna fidgeted, flinging her weight from one foot to the other. "So, you didn't have a good time last night or what? Is he here?"

Ben went to her and put a hand on hers. "He's here, Donna, but he's not going to be going home with you."

"He's hurt?" Donna squealed, grabbing Ben's hand in both of hers, pleading for him to say it wasn't so. "He was fine last night. What happened?"

"He's not hurt," Tara snapped, flinging herself onto the couch and pulling her legs beneath her, wrapping herself into a tight ball of anger. "He hasn't been fine since you first picked him up in the library or wherever it was you found him."

"Excuse me?" Donna was wide-eyed. Her brows were almost nonexistent without benefit of pencil, but she raised them anyway. She started for Tara, but Ben still held her hand. Donna shot him a withering glance and shook him off. She didn't go very far before planting herself and waiting for Tara's explanation. Tara obliged.

"You heard me. Bill Hamilton is a nut, Donna, and you should just turn around, go home, and let us take care of him." In the stunned silence that followed, Ben stared at Tara. Donna's mouth fell open, and Tara glared at them both while she talked to Ben. "Well, she should. It's for her own good, and I'm not going to pretend it isn't. Ben, didn't you just say we should call Woodrow?"

"I'm sure I don't agree that you should make any decisions regarding my fiancé," Donna broke in icily. "You may be his lawyer, Tara, but I'm going to be his wife. I doubt there's anything you know about him that I don't."

"I'd take that bet in a heartbeat, Donna." Tara patted the couch. "Why don't you just sit down and let me tell you a few things. We'll compare notes."

"Tara," Ben warned.

"Don't worry. Don't worry. I'm not going to tell her the juicy stuff. I already told you I won't breach my promise." Tara waved him away. Her voice was mean, driven by fear and frustration. "But I've got enough to make her think, which is something she hasn't been doing for months."

"How dare you," Donna shrieked. "How dare

you say something like that. I've just about had it
with you, Tara. Ben, did you hear?"

"Donna." Ben came between the two women.
"Please. You've got to listen. Come with me."

Ben took her hand and urged her away from
Tara, but Donna's eyes stayed on Tara. Both were
spoiling for a fight, the ties of their friendship
tenuous. He gave Donna's little hand another tug.
Reluctantly she followed him, the heels of her
shoes making hollow little noises on the wooden
floor. The tapping stopped. Tara heard voices, but
couldn't make out the words. There seemed to be
stretches of silence. Were they looking at the sleeping Bill, Donna's eyes softening, moistening in her
love for that maniac? Or had Ben told her everything, making Donna stare in horror? Would
Donna come flying back to her best friend, just
like a page out of *Frannie's Family*, her first big
book?

Then the sounds again. Donna's heels. Ben's
wheels spinning on the hard wood. Tara imagined
remorse. She wouldn't have to say another word.
Donna had seen it all. Tara was still in control of
herself and the world around her.

Her feet were tingling. She unwound herself and
threw back her hair, wiped her eyes, and rubbed
her cheeks. She wanted to feel good when she
hugged Donna. She wanted to be lucid when
Donna hugged her back. Tara stood up, steeling
herself for the sight of Donna's devastated face.
But Donna was smiling in embarrassment.

"I don't know what to say," Donna cooed with
a furry shrug. Her fingertips went to her cheeks.
"Tara, this is inexcusable. I'm so sorry." Donna's
tiny hands clasped and unclasped, then wrung
themselves gently around one another. Her eyes

darted to Tara's, stealing a backward glance to Ben
as if she hoped he was a supporter. She giggled.
"I don't know what got into him. I guess he
doesn't hold his liquor too well, does he?"

"He wasn't drinking, Donna. Not this morning
and not last night." Tara stayed calm in the face
of such denial. She felt wooden, rooted and unable
to move even if she had known where to go.

"You weren't there long enough to know what
we had to eat, sweetie." Donna was quick, her
comment acid. She diluted it with inane conversation. "But I can't blame you. I'd want to spend
every waking minute alone with a man like Ben
too. So, I'll just wake Bill, and we'll be on our way.
He just needs some rest. I'll have a new mattress
out here tomorrow. I promise." She worked on her
coat, inordinately intense about the closure. "What
is that? A double? You really should have at least
a queen for guests, sweetie. Or singles. Two singles
are much better in case someone has a spat with
their significant other—"

"Shut up, Donna."

Tara was exhausted. All the years of listening to
her friend's chatter had finally caught up with her
and left her weary and impatient. Donna's head
shot up, her pale, unpainted lips parted, not in
anticipation of speech, but in surprise. In the next
moment, her eyes hooded, her lips closed, and her
face set. They were friends no more.

"Ben?" she said, brittlely bright. "Would you
help me wake Bill?"

Tara arranged herself grandly. This was her
home and her life and that man sleeping in a rav-
ished bed had terrified her. Donna owed her something, if only to acknowledge that she mattered.

"Don't, Ben. Don't help her do something this stupid."

"Tara, I really thought we were over this." Donna dug in, looking more formidable for her lack of props. Without makeup her age showed and with it all the pain and disappointment she had ever experienced in her sad life. "You were very kind to come to our party last night. I appreciated that. I also noticed you didn't congratulate us on our engagement. I knew then that nothing would be the same between us as long as I was with Bill. I accepted that, Tara. We're old enough to grow apart a little bit now. I also understand that you have dealings with Bill that are professional. I know he's been in trouble, he told me that. I accept that too."

"Did he tell you why he hired me?"

"No," Donna said instantly, "I didn't ask. He told me he would let me know when he felt the time was right. I do understand he may have to— pay for whatever it is he's done. I accept that too."

"Since you're so understanding, Donna, why don't you go into the bedroom, wake Bill up, and ask him to tell you specifically what it is he's come to me for. I think it's time you knew. I think you should have time to prepare yourself. Just in case he has to pay for it." Tara tried to curb her sarcasm, softening her argument so Donna might listen. "It could be dangerous for you if you don't."

Donna threw up her hands. "I'm sick of all these half-assed accusations, Tara. You sound like a bad movie. So let's just get down to it. Why don't we take care of this between you and me. You tell me what's going on, then I won't have to bother Bill and get him all upset again."

"I'm his attorney. I can't tell you without his permission."

"Then stop trying to make trouble. Stop trying to make me guess. Stop trying to scare me!" Donna dug in her pockets for her gloves. "Ben, what do you think?" Donna turned toward him. "I'll abide by what you think."

"I don't think it's a good idea for you to leave with Bill."

"You too, huh? Do you know what he did that makes Tara so crazy?" She shook her hands in front of her face and said quickly, "Oh. I forgot you're a therapist. I've been down that road. Hush, hush, hush. Fine. Keep your secrets. I saw what Bill did. I saw the knife. Okay. That was really stupid. And I know he wasn't drunk. But he does things like that—dumb things that end up breaking stuff. But it's just stuff."

"No, it's not just stuff," Tara insisted.

"People? You're telling me he hurts people. No, I won't accept that." Donna shook her head furiously. "This is an uneducated but intelligent, happy but depressed man taking out his frustrations. That's it. He feels ineffectual and out of place in this world, and I'm the only one who seems to understand that."

"And you want to marry someone like that? You want to commit yourself to the kid on the block who sets cats on fire? Donna, what he did to my mattress was a sign. Even if you did nothing your entire life but watch talk shows that glorify bad gene pools, you'd know that this is not normal behavior."

"Then I shall show him the light. I'll make sure he understands he can't do these things," Donna said, sweetly sardonic as she batted her pale lashes.

"And this is a waste of time being where we're not wanted. Just let me get him, and let me get out of here."

Turning on her heel, Donna headed toward the hall. Tara sprinted after her. Ben called out to both of them. Tara didn't stop until she grabbed Donna's arm through the soft fluff of her fur and whirled her around.

"He is sick, you idiot."

"I don't care," Donna snapped and yanked her arm, but Tara held tight so Donna stood and fought. "I hate to shatter your self-image, darling, but you are not the end-all and be-all in this world. The rest of us can think and make choices without your amazing input. Bill isn't well. He has episodes. He needs medication, and I think I can get him to take it if we're left alone. I could tell you I love him, but I don't even know if that's the truth. The real truth is I need him. N-E-E-D. A word you don't even have in your vocabulary, so don't waste your energy trying to figure it out."

"Donna, that's absurd. You've got yourself. You've got money. You've got your work," Tara objected frantically.

"I've got nothing when I don't have someone like Bill. Bill adores me. He makes me feel like I'm the only woman on this earth. So he has episodes. So do I. But I shop or lock myself in my room. He tears up mattresses. Okay. Okay. We're strange. But I need him to validate me. There hasn't been a man who looked twice at me in the last few years. Don't you think I know that? They see the clothes and they think 'babe'; they get a little closer and they say 'old broad.' Not Bill. Not him. He loves me. He needs me and I damn well need him, so let go of my arm if you don't want to help me. Get out of my life if you don't want to be a part of it."

Tara's hand dropped. Ben was moving closer, holding out his arms as if he might need to catch her when she fell. Tara threw her arms around herself, swaying as she tried to get back on track. Carefully she spoke, calming herself and hoping to calm Donna too.

"Need isn't a reason to stay with a man. Especially not a man like him."

Donna laughed, hard and sharp and without humor. "Honey, at our age it's the only thing. Need and love are one and the same, and you're the only one who hasn't figured it out. Just look at you, what kind of role model are you?" Donna skirted around and pegged Ben with her sharp eyes. "Look at this marvelous man. He's suffered so much, and you left him to do it alone. He's a good man because he's loved you all these years and helped you when you needed him. But you turned your back and didn't take him to your heart until you felt a need, Tara. Need, not love. Deny it." Donna whipped back to Tara. "Well, I'm not like that. I'm sticking by my man, and you aren't going to be my role model. So just stand here, Tara, and let me get Bill. We'll be out of here in no time, and you can forget about us. I'll make him see he needs a new lawyer, and when that happens, you won't have to talk to us at all. Just leave us alone."

Twirling away, Donna flew out of the room, returning only when she had Bill Hamilton in hand. His arm was thrown around her neck and his hand lay buried in the deep red fur of her coat. He grinned. He looked like a drunken sailor and he

was oblivious to the warning that shot from
Donna's eyes to Ben and Tara.

"Leave us alone. I'm telling you. He doesn't
need you. He needs me."

"Damn straight, babe," Bill mumbled and tried
to turn her into him. Tara turned away, knowing
she'd be sick if he kissed her. But Donna was full
of strength. She had him in tow and out the door,
this drowsy insolent man in the baby blue sweatshirt. Tara shivered in the cold wind that blew
through the open door. It slapped her in the face
and brought her to her senses.

"Ben, I can't let her do this. I can't."

"Tara, leave it be," Ben warned, his hand on
her arm as he watched Donna help Bill Hamilton
into the car. "We'll go to Woodrow tonight, okay?"

She looked at him long enough for him to know
she couldn't accept that. They were already in the
car when Tara ran out after Donna, but it was Bill
Hamilton she grabbed, Bill who was like a slap-
happy rag doll so easy to handle. The eyes that
looked at her were bright and . . . cocky? She
wanted to slap him.

"Bill, listen to me," she whispered wildly. "Are
you going to hurt anyone? Bill, answer me."

But Bill held out his hand, putting it against
Tara's shoulder, and Donna leaned over the console and slammed the passenger door shut. Tara
was outside, hollering at the closed window. She
was still holding on to the door handle screaming
when Donna hit the gas. Tara's grip slipped, but
she ran next to the accelerating car. "Bill. Give me
permission to call Woodrow. I'll get you help tonight. I promise. I promise."

By the time Tara had run as far as she could,
she was sobbing. She stood in the middle of the

long drive that welcomed people to her home and she cried in frustration and anger. And the last thing she saw was Donna hunched over the wheel, speeding away from the Linley spread with Bill Hamilton next to her. At the last moment Bill's head turned, his eyes on Tara, a smile on his lips.

Tara watched a minute longer then trudged back toward Ben, who waited sadly by the gate. Without a word she headed into the house, but he caught her hand. She knew what he wanted to hear. She couldn't say the words, so he did.

"This is wrong, Tara. I'm going to give Woodrow what he wants."

"You could lose your license. You're not a psychiatrist. You haven't dealt with people like this. Your board could question your motives given our relationship," she said, exhausted and defeated.

"My motives are moral. At some point that obligation takes precedence."

"Are you doing this for me?" Tara asked. When he was silent she said, "You could lose so much."

"I've lost before."

Tara nodded and walked back into the house, wondering if she was going to let Ben make that call, wondering if she was that much of a coward or that much of a heroine. Clinging to her oath? Her license? She turned back as Ben came in and closed the door. She wanted to discuss this with him, to ask his opinion. Instead she said:

"Donna was wrong, you know."

"About what?" Ben asked.

"Love and need aren't the same. Not for me. Not when it comes to you."

Twenty-one

They had lain side by side, fully clothed, on top of the covers after Ben made the call to Woodrow at eight. An hour later Woodrow called back. Bill Hamilton had been picked up for questioning over the strenuous objections of his girlfriend. Ben took the call. Tara felt sick. This wasn't the way it was supposed to be for her, Bill Hamilton, Donna, and definitely not Ben. The second call came at eleven. Tara dragged herself from the bed, showered, and changed. It had already been a long night that would now be interminable. Tara was in the Albuquerque police department waiting to be escorted to a very angry Woodrow Weber by midnight.

"Ms. Linley."

A uniformed deputy held the door, pivoting to get ahead of her the minute she was through. She followed him into a large room, turned left staying on his heels, then made a sharp right and started down a long hall. She heard Woodrow before she saw him. She recognized the way he walked when he was mad. Precise. As if he were keeping time to a Sousa march. The deputy stood back, having done his duty by bringing the two of them together. Tara went past him, eyes forward, heading right for Woodrow. They met at the halfway point. The hall was deathly quiet and all Tara could think of was how amazing it was that Woodrow was freshly shaved at this hour.

"It's about time. I called you an hour ago," he complained.

"It's been tough all around, Woodrow," Tara said wearily. "I know that you know exactly what went on at my house so let's not play games."

"If it was that bad, you should have called 911. If you'd done that, we wouldn't be having problems now. We could've picked up that idiot and had the whole thing wrapped up after we got his prints."

"He didn't hurt me, Woodrow, and it's my prerogative to press charges or not," Tara responded. "Can I see him?"

"No. No. I don't want you to see him until we have an understanding. The guy is denying any knowledge of the Circle K killing. We can't budge him. I want you to advise that client of yours that it's time to cooperate. Obviously you thought he was whacked out enough to finally tip us."

"Woodrow, get your facts straight." Tara snapped out of her lethargy. He was getting in her face and she felt bad enough about letting Ben take the fall she should have taken. "I didn't make that call, Ben did. And for your information, Ben was concerned about Bill Hamilton *and* me. I didn't hold the same concerns he did, and I am still bound by confidentiality. Ben is working on a report as we speak. That, and the last few hours you've spent with my client, will convince you that you must petition to commit him. Forget everything else. Let's get him help, and let's get it tonight."

Woodrow wasn't buying it. He turned, looked over his shoulder, and cocked a finger. "Follow me."

Tara dogged his steps, wishing she'd worn a blouse. The station was hot even without all the daytime bodies. She was running her finger around the high neck of her sweater when Woodrow stopped in front of a door. He opened it. He stepped back, arm outstretched as he held the knob. He looked inside, his eyes sweeping over the gentlemen who sat there.

George Amos gave Tara a nod, but didn't lift his head from the cushion of his upturned hand. The detective who had slept in her drive was there, still looking sleepy. And of course, the guest of honor: Bill Hamilton.

"Hey, Tara. Ridin' in to save the day. That's my lady." Bill grinned. He sat in a small, hard chair, leaning back so that he balanced on the back legs, one boot-shod foot firmly planted on the beige linoleum, the other crossed casually over his knee. One arm was thrown over the back of the chair; the other lay on the table in front of him. A casual man. A happy man. Not the same man Tara had seen in her home, not the shell of a man Donna had led away from it. Woodrow closed the door. They were alone in the hall again. He put his back to the wall.

"Your madman has been talking cars, Tara. Old cars, new cars, engine torque, and tire width. That man knows more about cars than I ever wanted to know. He has a quick wit. He can even make car jokes. He's crazy about cars, Tara. He's driving me crazy. But if he's insane, I'll eat my hat." Woodrow ran a hand across his brow. He was tired. It was a shame men didn't cry. Woodrow looked like he'd like to. "Tara, do it. Get him to talk about Circle K. Get him to do anything but talk about cars. Ben gave me enough to send out a car and bring Hamilton in. Now you get him to talk, Tara, or I swear I'll put a tail on him. The minute he sneezes too loud, I'll arrest him. I'll fingerprint him. I'll indict him. No chance for a hospitalization petition. This is your last chance. Get him to talk to me and I'll be objective about all this. But I swear, as I look at it now, that guy is sane. I see no reason to entertain your request for any special treatment on your client's behalf."

Tara eyed him, judged the tension factor, and said:

"I'd like to see my client alone, Woodrow."

"Fine. Fine."

He opened the door again. Tara passed in; the others came out, leaving her alone with Bill Hamilton.

She went no closer than necessary. She held his gaze, despising him yet challenged too. The dichotomy was hateful. Her hands were in her pockets and her coat hung open. She suffered Bill Hamilton's lazy looks, the happy little hey-ho shake of the head he gave her.

"You having a good time, Bill?" Tara asked quietly.

"Rather be home in bed. Had a hard day," he breathed, taking his hands and clasping them behind his head as if they were having a porch chat on a summer day.

"I know you did." She sighed and kicked out at nothing as she walked to the back of the small room. The lighting was a horror, bleaching everything a shade paler than was even remotely attractive. Yet somehow Bill Hamilton looked wonderful, full of life, delighted to be here. Tara put a hand to her eyes and rubbed, trying to banish the exhaustion. "Why don't we talk about that first, Bill.

Why don't you tell me exactly what you were trying to communicate to me today? What were you trying to accomplish at my house?"

His smile faded into an expression of distress. He let himself down, the chair landing on the floor with a thump. He crossed his arms on the table, his expression defining the word *sincere*. He'd practiced and perfected the effect. She thought to give him a hand but restrained herself.

"I am sorry about that, Tara. Damn if I know what got into me. I was just so darned mad, you know. I lost it. What can I say? I keep telling you I need help. I need somebody to just take me in hand 'til I can learn to control all this."

"So, you hitchhiked all the way from Donna's house to mine, waited for me for who knows how long, then decided to rip up a mattress." Tara lay her head against the wall and stared down at him. "That's the longest fit of madness I've ever heard of. I don't know much about insanity, but from what Dr. Crawford's told me, I would have expected manifestations to be a bit more spontaneous. A long ride and a little wait for me would take away a bit of that capriciousness, wouldn't you say?"

"I don't know about that, Tara. I don't know about any of these things. Damn but you use some dollar words!" He was smiling again. She was moving.

Tara pushed off the wall, took two steps to the table, and splayed out her hands. She leaned over, her hair falling to the scarred surface.

"Yes, you do. You know damn well what you're doing." She looked at him hard and thought she saw, for the first time, concern in those eyes of his. That sparkle couldn't quite be called fear, but she sure as heck wouldn't call it confidence either. Her voice was low and intractable. "Ben thinks you're nuts. I think you're a liar, a cheat, a con man, and a murderer, and I'm beginning to think the only thing you're really good at is hurting things. I think you walked into my life and turned it upside down because you felt like it. I think you like freaking people out. I think Woodrow's right. You're no more insane than any of us."

The accusation took form and hung heavy between them. Bill's gray eyes shaded from the color of fog to the three dimensions of steel. Every range of emotion ran through them instead of his mind, his heart, or his conscience. A shiver of recognition gripped him. He knew what she was thinking. Damn, he could read her mind.

Bill stretched out, extending his long, hard body until it seemed he simply leaned against the chair instead of sat in it. His lashes were down over his eyes, and he shifted his hands to make his head more comfortable in them. Yet he still looked at her. She knew it. She could feel it.

"Remember the first night we met, Tara? I bet you do. You had the hots for me that night. I know you did." He chuckled a little longer when she remained silent. "You were jealous of Donna. Your very best friend's new beau was just the ticket that night, huh? Whooeee, you thought I was cute."

"Those comments might make you certifiable." She'd finally found her voice and it was dry. She licked her lips. "Let's talk about those other nights. All those ridiculous things you did that made it seem like you were on the edge. Why, Bill, when the risk was so great? I could have broken the client confidence the minute I felt you'd stepped over the line.

"But I didn't step over it, did I? Even today was a call, wasn't it?" His hands came down and hung limply at his sides.

"The clerk in the convenience store?"

He pulled his lips into an exaggerated frown as if it helped him think. "Same thing. It was a call."

Tara stood up and pulled out a chair, wanting to ask him about Paulette's dog. She didn't.

"Do you know right from wrong?"

"Yes."

"Dr. Carrol thought you were dangerous. He had you on heavy medication."

"And they all worked, doin' their thing on my head. Put a damper on this old boy's fire, I'll tell you." He was teasing again, but he seemed unhappy, maybe a little angry. He didn't want to play anymore. He hooked his thumbs over his belt, defiant in his casualness. "I didn't mind seein' that shrink. It was better than being alone with my mother. Now there's a case for you," he scoffed and Tara half expected him to spit. "But the doctor wasn't bad. Just the pills. He should have talked to her. She was crazy. I was a big boy. But all that was a long time ago. Now all I know is I'll be a nut if they lock me up."

"Then why even come to me, Bill? Why put yourself in this kind of jeopardy, Bill? You had to know there was a risk. You had to know that no one could snap their fingers and get you what you wanted."

"I figured if anyone could, you could," Bill drawled. "All I'd heard from Donna was how great you were. You could get me what I wanted, or die tryin'."

"That still doesn't answer the question. Nobody was looking for you. The Circle K murder wasn't even making the papers anymore. Why wave the red flag, even to me?"

"Cops leave that kind of thing open forever." Bill's chin fell to his chest. He plucked at the button on his shirt. Looking up and right at her before he raised his head. He talked low. "It'd come one day. Thought I'd head it off at the pass." He tired of playing with his buttons. "My prints are there, on a mop." He chuckled and looked away for a minute as if embarrassed. "Tried to clean up the mess I made. Can you believe that? Got scared. Wouldn't my mama yell if she saw that mess." Tara shivered, feeling what Vera must have when she was close to him. He didn't notice her aversion. "Didn't do a very good job. Got blood all over that poor woman. Smeared it everywhere. On her face, her clothes. Got kind of sick seeing that. I dropped that old mop and needed some air. But the air was hot. So I started drivin' again. Couldn't get cool. Then I remembered that mop. Damn nice of me to clean up. Damn stupid to drop it without wiping . . ."

"Stop it. Stop it." Tara slapped the table. She was up. She was appalled. She was still his attorney.

"Okay. Sorry." He held up his hands to calm her and tried the smile. It didn't work. So he enjoyed himself instead. He told her more.

"I killed her and it was a damn hot night. The sand was in my teeth, and I wanted cigarettes. I walked in there and I swear, Tara, everything just looked so incredible. Colorful and quiet, then I saw her making that coffee and ignorin' me." It wasn't as fun as he anticipated so he threw away the telling with a wave of his hand. "Aw, there's no excuse. I killed her, and I knew that one of these days somethin' stupid was gonna happen. I'd get pulled over. I'd try to get me a credit card. I'd touch something where another guy did the deed and they'd get me. Someone's gonna put my old fingers on the ink pad and that'll be that. Better to nip it all in the bud now, huh, Tara? Better to have someone smart to do the nippin'. So I found someone smart, didn't I?"

"I don't know, Bill. I think you're just a lucky guy. You were lucky to meet Donna, and lucky she knew me. You've been lucky your whole life that no one told on you or turned on you. There were some who should have, weren't there, Bill?"

Bill laughed, surprising her. His face softened, his smile was affectionate. "Christ, you can be so sweet."

"I don't see what's so funny."

"You are. You're right I was lucky, fallin' into your lap. That was luck beyond belief." He sat up straight now and matched her posture across the table. "But I didn't just happen on Donna. I wouldn't be caught dead in a library 'less I had somethin' to do, and I had somethin' to do that day. I had a little lady to catch."

Tara breathed and hung her head. A minute later she looked up again. "Why? She's almost twice your age. What would you want with her?"

"She's cute. She's rich. Not hard to tell where a woman fits in this life."

"But you haven't taken anything from her. No clothes, no money, no cars. I know that."

"Those things aren't nothin' compared to what I got from her." His smile looked almost boyish. "I got me a slave. I got me a woman who'll stick by me no matter what, and that's worth its weight in gold. She doesn't want to know about the past, and she wouldn't believe you if you told her. She doesn't want to think about the future 'cause she might be there alone." He chuckled and ran a finger in circles on the table. "Naw, between the two of you I feel pretty safe. I think you'll get me where I want to go. Sure as the day is long, you'll get me there." He sighed and clasped his hands. "If you don't, I'll just stay out in Donna's great big ol' house and keep her happy."

"So it's all a game. All planned out with a winner and a loser," Tara said.

He put his hand down flat, then lifted it and put it through his hair.

"You can be damn wearisome, Tara. I get tired of your questions about why this and why that. I don't know what it is or why it is. Killin' that woman was just somethin' that happened. Findin' out about you was somethin' that happened. I'm on this road and I just gotta walk it. You're walking the same way. Too late to turn back now."

"I don't think so, Bill. I could walk right out of here and file a complaint about what went on at my house today. You'd be fingerprinted, Woodrow would know enough to cross-check them against that mop. You'd be booked for the Circle K killing so fast it would make your head spin."

"You won't," he said, chuckling softly. "You won't. I've never seen a human being pushed the way I've pushed you and still keep comin' back for more. You'll get me what I need. You can't say a word against me. I'm safe with you, Tara."

Tara considered how much the wall needed washing. Woodrow was waiting. She had a decision to make. Her head swung back to Bill Hamilton. He still lounged in his chair, content and as unconcerned as he could be.

"Safe? That's how I've made you feel?"

"Damn straight, sweetheart. Safe as a baby in its cradle."

"Don't bet on it, Bill."

She stood up, towering over him.

"Don't bet on it."

Woodrow didn't approach her when she stepped into the hall. Tara thought that was fair. She had a lot to think about during her short walk, and Woodrow needed to stand his ground. Ben was working on a report without documentation based on real time with Bill Hamilton. Tara had a practice and a friend to protect. Bill was wondering about her now, not quite as sure of her as he had been. He could bolt as easily as he could stay once he was released, which would be inevitable if Woodrow rebuffed Ben's report. A step away now, it was time to make some choices. Her last-ditch efforts may be nothing but smoke, but Tara would give it her best shot.

"Woodrow." She planted herself in front of him, her hands in her pockets, her head cocked just enough so she didn't look confrontational. "Let's compromise. Guarantee me he'll receive an immediate psychological evaluation. Guarantee me that Ben sits in and allow his evaluation to be taken into consideration. Find some reason to hold Bill without booking him. I'll get Ben here as soon as you can get your shrink in line. If your independent psychiatrist or psychologist or witch doctor or whatever comes back and corroborates Hamilton's precarious state of mind, you petition for hospitalization and out he goes. If there's a question in your expert's mind that Ben agrees with, I back off. You conduct your investigation and see where it gets you. No reporters. No political issues. Just do this as fast as you can and we're headed to some sort of conclusion."

"I'll see what I can do, Tara," he said without the flicker of a lash. Tara grinned. She couldn't believe it. Woodrow cooperating.

"It will solve a lot of problems," she said quietly and put out her hand. He shook it and smiled. "I'm sorry for all this, Woodrow." They said a few more words neither of them paid attention to. George Amos materialized at Woodrow's elbow as soon as Tara was gone.

"What's the deal?" he asked.

"She'll settle for a fast psych workup with her guy in on it. Don't book Hamilton, just detain him and wait for Ben Crawford. Soon as she gets a prelim on the examination from our man and Ben, she'll either step away, or I'll have to petition."

"Who you going to call this time of night?" George asked.

"Nobody. She's this close to surrender; we'll just help her along a little. Tara's left me twisting in the wind on this for weeks. Let's see how she likes it. Anyway, the guy's as sane as you and me. I want a shot at him. I want him to make a mistake." Woodrow turned to George and put his hand on the other man's shoulder. "Cut that guy loose. He's a citizen. We have no reason to hold him. Apologize to him for me."

George laughed. He chuckled. When the district attorney got with the program, he went all the way.

Tara buttoned her coat, anxious to tell Ben what had been decided. She wondered if she should call him or just wait until she got home to tell him.

She wondered about Woodrow and how he was going to keep Bill Hamilton where he was. She wondered about Donna, and if she was all right. Tara stepped off the curb, her sights on the Jeep. She wondered if she was going to sleep that night. She wondered why she'd made such an empty threat to Bill Hamilton. Then Tara Linley wondered what in the heck that little white Good & Plenty car was doing parked on a street in the middle of the night, next to the police station where Tara had just been and Bill Hamilton still was.

Slowing her step, Tara finally stopped dead in her tracks. Damn. Woodrow, double damn. He had called Martinez. Well, there'd be a story for the morning edition all right. Only it wouldn't be the one Woodrow would be expecting. She crossed the street and stood by the car.

The windows were fogged and Tara could just make out the shadow of a person in the driver's seat. She headed for the passenger door, grabbed the handle, and threw it open. Instead of flinging herself inside, Tara saw that two people fogged up those windows with their warm breath and one with a cigarette.

"Charlotte!"

"Tara!" Charlotte's initial surprise passed quickly. She seemed more perturbed at the cold air than Tara's dramatic arrival and pulled her coat closer. She touched her tam, the cigarette wedged between two fingers so she wouldn't burn the wool.

"Charlotte, what are you doing in there? With him?" Tara leaned low, trying to see the both of them more clearly.

"I'm talking to a friend, Tara. One who has always been very kind to Woodrow in his professional dealings." She smiled at him.

"But Charlotte, he wrote . . ." The light dawned before she could finish her sentence. "You're the one who tipped him about the Circle K." Breathless, Tara half laughed. "Charlotte, do you know what you've done?"

"Yes, of course I do." Charlotte tossed her cigarette past Tara and pulled herself out of the car. Martinez settled in, happy to wait until the ladies were done, straining to hear whatever he could.

"I don't believe you do." Angered at such stupidity, Tara stuffed her hands in her pockets to keep from flailing her fists. "You've compromised my position as an attorney. You've angered my client, who isn't someone you want angry. But most importantly, you put Woodrow on the hot seat, Charlotte."

"I know," she said, her voice clipped and tight. "I was stupid. I gave Martin too much leeway and not enough information. That's changed tonight. The next article will answer all those questions Woodrow couldn't until now. I believe he has a name and a face to go along with the rest of it."

"Oh Charlotte," Tara moaned. "Charlotte." Tara looked heavenward. Nothing up there but stars.

"Tara, please," Charlotte said quietly. "You have to be practical. Woodrow doesn't know anything about this. Now that you know what I'm willing to do, it will be so much easier to resolve all this."

"You're going to have to talk faster than that to convince me Woodrow didn't put you up to this," Tara hissed.

"Tara, you have never given me or Woodrow enough credit. He's more moral than you will ever know, and I am more pragmatic than you can ever imagine." Charlotte stepped into Tara's line of sight, a formidable obstacle to what Tara wanted.

"So put the credit where it's due. This is my game. Woodrow has enough to worry about."

"But why? After all these years that we've been friends, why would you do this to me?"

Charlotte laughed, obviously amused. She raised her face to the night and was rejuvenated by the cool air.

"Don't be ridiculous, Tara. There are degrees of loyalty and love same as there are degrees of hatred. My allegiance would always be to you if you were at odds with someone else. But when it came to you and Woodrow?" She shrugged. "There can't be any choice. My loyalty will always be to my husband. I was home when George called to say your man had been picked up, I called Martin, and it's as simple as that. I'm Woodrow's wife. My job is to support him and help him in every way I can. I don't really expect you to see that as clearly as I do, but that's the way it is."

Aghast, Tara stared at Charlotte Weber, a woman she didn't know anymore. Charlotte took a pack of cigarettes out of her coat pocket. Dipping her head toward the match, she was illuminated for an instant. She looked beautiful in the light, soft and pink-tinged by makeup. But her eyes were hard on Tara when she looked up.

"I admire you to no end, Tara. You've never needed anyone to help you and you've gotten along so beautifully. But now you do need help and there's no one. That's why Woodrow will win. Because he has me and George Amos and a whole lot of others rooting for him."

Tara shook her head, but it wouldn't clear. The world was upside down.

"I have Ben," Tara whispered. Charlotte eyed her.

"I hope so, for your sake, Tara." Charlotte

dropped the cigarette, wasting half of it. She moved back to the car and was half in when she said, "I really do hope you have Ben, Tara. It's awful to be alone."

The door closed. Charlotte was seated in the Good & Plenty car with Martin Martinez and Tara was left to wonder if Ben was still with her. She had left him to do her dirty work, and clung to a killer as if he were the most important person in the world. She'd thrown away her best friend for the sake of an oath. She'd allowed her home to be dishonored. It was a circle of misery that she hoped would be broken tonight. She was halfway to the Jeep when she heard:

"Ms. Linley, could you tell me why you were in the Albuquerque police station at midnight?"

Tara kept going, ignoring Martin Martinez. Even when Charlotte called after her, trying to coax her back, reminding Tara that the public wouldn't quite see things her way, she didn't turn around. She got into the Jeep and dialed Ben from the car phone.

"Woodrow is going to arrange for a psych evaluation. I told him you'd be there. Tonight. Do you mind?" Tara listened, knowing exactly what he'd say before he said it. He was thrilled. He'd run home and get his notes and the records Vera had given them. The end was near. She'd tell him about Charlotte later. Before he hung up she told him she loved him, but the phone was already dead.

Exhausted, hoping Ben would be there when she drove in, but knowing he wouldn't be, Tara headed home.

* * *

She walked to the window and looked out. Still dark. Two A.M. This was the sixth—no, seventh—time she'd gotten up from her bed on the couch to look for Ben. She'd called him once. He was still working, pulling together more information. He threw her a kiss over the wires. It was as distracted a gesture as the conversation had been. Tara could do nothing but wait. Now Ben was Bill Hamilton's hostage. At least for another few hours. She sat down on the couch, started to put her feet up under the blanket, and changed her mind. She wasn't really hungry, but she would eat to pass the time.

Tara heaved herself off the sofa, trying not to even think the name *Charlotte,* or let herself wonder what Donna was doing. She schlepped to the kitchen, stopping to run her hand along the dining room table. Spotless. Life had gone along without her. The cleaning lady still came and did her job. Joseph managed his chores and was gone before she got home most days. Carlos had left a message saying he was handling his family problems and would be back soon. Everyone was coping.

With a sigh, Tara rubbed her hands together, snuggled in the old sweater she was wearing, and pushed her hair back. She couldn't wait for a good night's sleep. She needed a vacation. Her stomach grumbled. She needed food, too, and hadn't known it.

Tara opened the refrigerator door. The little light was welcoming. She bent from the waist, pushed aside the mayonnaise, a plate of cold chicken, two cans of soda. Pickles. She opened the vegetable drawer. The lettuce was almost dead, its heart salvageable. She needed some bread. Ten minutes to make a sandwich, another ten to eat it. Cleanup would take at least five. She was almost laughing, wishing away her life in minutes spent doing mundane tasks. In the split second between standing and reaching for the chicken, Tara realized she wasn't alone.

Bill Hamilton was planted in her kitchen, the light from the refrigerator not enough to illuminate him, only give him an otherworldly glow. His hands were by his side, his shoulders squared. He was smiling. Tara's body convulsed with shock and fear, the refrigerator door between them a pitiful shield. The cold wrapped around Tara's ankles and worked its way up her legs. A great paralysis gripped her. Every joint in her body shook, arteries pumped the blood so fast through her body she could hear the rush of it. Her vocal cords constricted and Tara could do nothing but feel the terror. Bill Hamilton reached out and touched her cheek, drawing one warm finger from cheekbone to jaw, lifting up her chin when he came to it.

"Don't bet on it, Tara," he whispered, then whispered again, "Don't bet on it."

Raising his other hand, he grinned wider, and rested his arm atop the refrigerator door to show her what he had. A gun. He pointed it at her chest.

Self-preservation became the order of the moment. Weak legs became strong, instinct triumphed over reason. Tara slammed the door shut. There was a sucking noise as the seal caught. The clatter of the gun falling to the ground and Bill Hamilton's laugh following her as she sprinted out of the kitchen. In the split second it took for him to take chase, Bill seemed to be truly enjoying himself.

"Come on, Tara. Talk to me. Woodrow told me you wanted him to hold me without chargin' me.

Not nice, Tara." He was coming, so close on her heels that Tara did the only thing she could. She ducked into her office and lay against the wall trying not to breathe hard. She closed her eyes, listened, and was grateful that he still loved the sound of his own voice. "You gonna turn me in, Tara? You can't do that. Tara? Come on, babe. You gonna do me in, then I ain't got nothin' to lose by havin' a little more fun."

A door slammed against a wall. Tara jerked as if the sound were a body slamming. He was in the guest room. He'd gone right and not left. Her bedroom would be next before the office. There was time. She could make it to the door. There had to be time.

"Tara?" He was half singing now, enjoying himself immensely. She imagined him standing spreadeagled in the door like a town sheriff waiting for the piano player to notice him and head for the hills. His gray eyes would be like night vision goggles, searching and searching for any movement. He'd tire of the guest room; he knew it too well. Tara counted to herself, counted the mother-may-I-go-slow steps it would take Bill to get to the master bedroom. When he reached that room, he would have to search the bathroom too. That would be her chance. Tara counted, forcing herself to get to ten. The door of that room already stood ajar so she wouldn't hear it open. Her best guess placed him at the doorway of the master bedroom by an eight count. Worst-case scenario, she'd meet him in the hall. Ten. Nothing to do but pray and go.

She dashed. He was quick and did the same a split second later. Tara's stomach lurched. So fast, so little effort, and he was on her. The trajectory of her flight was shorter than his, but Bill Hamilton's legs and arms were long, his intent gleefully evil. That gave him the edge; he was having fun. He grabbed for her the moment their paths crossed. Lunging, he managed a handful of hair. Silky, it slipped through his fingers like water. His grunt of anger was the last thing Tara wanted to hear. She stumbled, crying out once, then dashed on, knowing her home better than he. But the doors and windows had been locked for so long now, the only sure escape would be where he had jimmied one to get in. She hoped he'd been bold and come in the front.

Tara slipped on the tiled floor but she recovered and hit the hall running. The Navajo rugs she loved were now a scourge, sliding beneath her. She fell. Her shoulder slammed into the wall. The breath went out of her but Tara threw herself forward, colliding with the door, scrabbling up to find the knob.

"Christ," she hollered, but the word came out garbled, half sob, half incantation. Everything was unfamiliar in her terror. But flight hadn't diminished her reason. Bill Hamilton should have shot her twice by now. She should be dead in the hall and she knew it. Clinging to the door, she glanced over her shoulder. The hall was empty. Her breath caught in little ticks of terror. How quiet it was. A prank? Another gaslight? Hide-and-seek when escape was so close, yet help incredibly far away, was cruel.

Sniffing. Blinking. A sob working its way up her throat only to be cut off by the need for breath, Tara forced herself to ease away from the door. Fingers shaking, she concentrated on the knob, knowing Bill Hamilton would be on her in a second. He'd throw himself out of the dark just when

she thought she'd mastered the lock. He'd slam
the door shut just when she started to open it.

Hands sweating, blouse clinging between her
breasts and under her arms, Tara flushed hot then
cold, then relief warmed her all over as she heard
the click of the lock and the door was open. No
one came to close it. She could breathe again.
Outside there was hope; there were options.

Then she heard it. A creak. Her ears pricked,
her frantic eyes widened. Had it come from behind? Ahead? Was he crawling through the walls?
Whimpering, calling Ben's name under her breath,
trying to silence herself even as she did, Tara
stepped out into the night. She turned toward the
drive, began her run for freedom, and stopped
when Bill Hamilton stepped in front of her, raised
his gun, and pulled the trigger. The sound was
deafening. It was the sound of death.

Tara's gut clutched. She stood her ground, un-
hurt, in shock. She bolted left, realized she didn't
stand a chance of getting around him, then
changed course so that she was running back toward
the river. No. No. Shinin' was spooked and dancing.
She was running toward the corral where there was
some defense. She didn't bother with the gate. Tara
hurtled over the fence with more ease than she had
since she was a kid. Behind her Bill Hamilton
laughed. Close, but not on her heels. Cocksure, he
ambled her way. Tara breathed hard and held on
to the fence, looking at him between two slats. He
was a shadow coming slowly, enjoying, perhaps sa-
voring, every minute of the chase. Shinin' was behind her, nudging her with his knee only to dance
away again. She took a chance, using the one
weapon that had held her in good stead throughout
this nightmare: her voice.

"Bill. Stay there. Stay where you are before you do something stupid."

"Aw, hell, Tara, this *is* stupid," he hollered, throwing back his head to laugh. It was a sad sound, devoid of humor. "My whole *life* has been stupid. Every minute since I was a kid *has* been stupid. Doctors and pills and my mother looking at me like she'd like to eat me up. My own mother." His head was down again and he was coming crisscross toward her as if he were stepping through a mine field. Tara didn't want him any closer. She called back.

"Your mother's out of the picture, Bill. You've got Donna. She loves you like a woman should, and now you're doing this? It won't do any good."

"This is fun, Tara," he whispered, and in the silence of the night it sounded as if he was beside her. He raised his voice again and it boomed through the cold night. "But I don't know why." He swung his gun hand, keeping time to a beat she didn't hear. "I don't know why I'm here, or with Donna, or even botherin' with you. I swear I don't. Guess it was just a stoppin' place, huh? Just another town on the Rio Grande where I could get a shave and a beer. Whoee, I'd love to have been a cowboy. Just a damn cowboy." He twirled the gun above his head like a lasso. "Come out here, Tara. Come out here, you little filly, and tell me what to do."

"I want you to put the gun down. Throw it this way, and we'll work it out," she called back, slipping into the dirt and sitting with her arms around the fence post, her eyes on the man coming closer. Suddenly he was quiet and standing still. She wished she could see his face, and immediately knew that was stupid. She'd been looking at his

face for weeks now and hadn't a clue who he was
or what he was thinking.

"I don't want to, Tara. I'm tired. Why don't you
just come right on out here and get it. That would
be better. I've paid you. You work for me. Remember, Tara?" He sang in whispers and cadences that
were ever changing. "I'm all paid up and I want
some action. Come on, little lady. Come right on
out here to me."

He took a step and another, and Tara was sure
his boots would be the last thing she saw on earth.
But behind him, in the distance, a quarter mile
down the drive, she saw lights. Two distinct lights.
Yes. She half sat up, ignoring Bill Hamilton in favor
of the slim hope of rescue. Woodrow had sent someone. Let it be someone effectual. Not a sleepy detective on stakeout. Not Woodrow on his own.
Please, not that.

"Tara?" Her head snapped back toward Bill just
as the lights winked out. She looked again They
were gone.

Please no. They couldn't have left. It couldn't
have been someone simply turning around. It
would be too cruel.

"Tara?" he called again and behind her Shinin'
reared. Tara had no choice but to pay attention.
She narrowed her eyes. Shinin' was telling her Bill
was near. Tara breathed deep and let her eyes flit
over the landscape. There. He'd gone right, heading to the gate. Bent, Tara half ran over the soft
earth of the corral, toward the horse's stall. The
pitchfork. Where had she put the pitchfork? Was
it back where it should be? Still leaning against
the wall in the guest house where Bill had last
held it. Where? What other weapons could there
be? Shinin'? Shinin' would keep him at bay for a

while. He may have gotten close enough to whack off a hunk of tail once. Shinin' wouldn't let him again. No one was coming to help. The river lay between her and the open fields on the other bank. Neighbors were too far away to scream for help. It was up to her. He was near. She could smell him.

"I'm in, babe. I'm here."

Tara threw herself into Shinin's stall, rolled awkwardly, and came up on her hands and knees. Her hair grazed the dirt. Her face was wet with tears though she couldn't remember crying. Lifting one hand, she swiped at her eyes and muttered a curse. Dirt and manure were swabbed in and immediately her eyes teared to wash it all away. Tara blinked, trying desperately to see where Bill Hamilton was through her reddened eyes. A shot rang out. Tara threw herself to the ground.

"Whooeee! Is that a noise, Tara? Is that a noise or what? Sounded like a damn atomic explosion in that Circle K when I did it. Thought for sure there'd be an army on my head, but nobody came. Hey, Tara!" She sniffled, she flinched, fighting the desire to wipe her eyes. She needed to see but her tears wouldn't come. From the sound of his voice, Bill Hamilton was midway between the gate and her. She could hear Shinin' snorting and weaving, the ground shuddered beneath her. She pulled back into the shadows. "Hey, Tara. Did I tell you I tried to clean up the mess in that store? Damn, that woman bled. Like a pig. I got a mop, ended up making a mess. Made me mad. I even mopped her. Jesus, it was a mess. Did I tell you that, Tara?"

Tara lay her face in the dirt, her hands over her ears. She didn't want to hear it again so she moved her lips, praying for the woman Bill Hamilton had painted with her own blood, praying for herself. What had she been thinking all this while? Was her practice, her reputation, a promise, anything on this earth worth this terror?

Another shot. Her arms went over her head. Her face buried itself deeper into the earth. A chip of wood flew off the wall beside her. Shinin' screamed and ran the length of the corral.

"Damn. Goddamn horse!" Bill Hamilton screamed and Tara looked up. Shinin' loomed in the center of the corral. He reared and his hoofs came down hard on the ground. He did it again, and this time she thought she heard Bill Hamilton scream. "Goddamn horse. I'm going to take out this goddamn horse, Tara."

"No!" Tara pushed off, half crouching, terrified he would make good on his promise. Shinin' reared, but this time it was away from the intruder as he tried to find his mistress. In that moment Bill Hamilton stood facing Tara Linley with nothing between them but the cold air and the gray light of a night that was leaving them.

"Tara," he murmured like a lover. He lifted his pistol, and pointed it at her. She heard the click of the hammer. She waited for it to fall. Bill Hamilton was brought to his knees at the same time Tara heard a click, a whirr, and the sound of an attack.

There were grunts and the thud of a body hitting the ground and Tara, her eyes glazed with the view of death she'd just glimpsed, realized she'd been saved. Sweet Jesus, she was saved and the man who had done such an amazing thing was the man Bill Hamilton had laughed at, the man Bill Hamilton had held in such contempt.

Ben Crawford had Bill Hamilton's face in the dirt, one arm wrenched in the air. Ben's other hand pushed against Bill's windpipe. One move and Bill Hamilton would be no more.

Tara hesitated, tried to move again. She found her feet and scrambled up. Breathing hard, she stood in front of Ben, looking from him to Bill, and back again.

"I called the cops. They told me Bill wasn't there. They told me they'd released him." Ben was out of breath too. There was fright and triumph and pride in his voice.

"You? You were the lights I saw?"

"Thought I better come quietly. Just in case you were entertaining."

"Good thought." Tara's voice shook and the words quivered.

"Tara," Ben said quietly. "This isn't easy to do in kung fu class, but it's a darn hard move to do in real life," Ben said. "Could you please call for help?"

"Yes. Yes. Oh, yes." Tara almost skipped away but came back just as quickly. She leaned down, dirty and tired, cold now beyond belief She looked Bill Hamilton in the eye.

"You were wrong, Bill. There's no power in keeping secrets. The power is in telling them." Ben tightened his hold for emphasis. Stunned, Bill grunted in pain.

Tara left, staying in the house long enough to call the police, load her shotgun, and thank her lucky stars that Ben Crawford was on her side.

Twenty-two

"Don't you want me to drive you around back, Tara?"

Caroline kept her hand on the wheel but bent low enough to peer out the passenger side as they eased up on the courthouse. Tara sat quietly beside her, briefcase in hand, eyes forward, as she unbuckled her seat belt and wished Ben were beside her. But it wouldn't do. She worried about his chair in an unruly crowd. Marvelous though he may be, there were some things he couldn't do for her.

"Nope. My head's up and there's no reason it shouldn't be. I'll defend my position until I'm blue in the face."

"You may have to if the media's going to write about you the way they did. *People* magazine wasn't exactly kind."

"Good picture, though, don't you think?" Tara laughed wryly. The belt retracted. She adjusted her jacket and looked at the magazine she had tossed at her feet. She retrieved it, took a good long look, and held it up for Caroline to see. Caroline took it and tossed it behind her.

"Yeah, great. But they made you sound like you were some money-grubbing weirdo who wouldn't turn Hamilton in so that you could keep milking him."

"There wouldn't have been enough money in the world," Tara sighed, then she laughed. "Guess we couldn't expect anything less, huh? The gentlemen of the press don't have to promise to keep anyone's secrets or even tell them when they come out."

"Well, I'm sorry anyway. I know that was hard to read."

"No harder than what's coming up. Come on. Might as well pull up a little closer, and I'll see if I can get through." Caroline stepped on the gas. The car glided to a stop. It didn't take long for the crowd to zoom in on her. They smelled blood.

Tara put her hand on the door handle, pausing to identify the various groups that were so anxious to have a go at her. NOW women walked in circles chanting slogans and raising placards denouncing Tara. She had bought into a man's world, protecting those who would kill her sisters. The media, of course, was everywhere. Three cameras that Tara could identify, one a network. She was coming up in the world. A gaggle of men and women with notepads and microphones. Spectators were everywhere, their only agenda to see a spectacle. And to the far right, the hot dog vendor. It was a big day in Albuquerque. The nation was waiting to hear what Tara had to say, to see what a morally corrupt attorney looked like, to try to find out why one woman would protect such a man when so many other women had suffered at his hand.

"I gotta do this, Caroline. Might as well do it now."

Caroline touched Tara's shoulder. "You'll do great. I'll park and come in."

"No," Tara said. "Go on home. I'm not going back to the office. I want to try and talk to Donna after the hearing. I may be a while. I'll be fine. I promise."

She opened the door and swung her long legs out. White blouse, blue blazer, gray skirt, and black heels. Power dressing. She felt right and she'd done right. No matter what they all said, no one could convince her that she hadn't.

"Ms. Linley . . ."

She heard her name called by many different voices. Her name sounded ugly. Though her eyes stayed steady, looking straight ahead as she walked up the courthouse steps, Tara was aware of the faces around her. Curious faces, angry faces. Mouths opening and closing and saying things that she couldn't quite make out. Tara pushed away a microphone without hostility. She muttered no comment like a mantra, but stopped when it was clear no one was paying attention. She was almost to the door when someone cut through the clutter, someone caught her attention. In fact, the man caught everyone's attention. The roar faded to a murmur and Tara, surprised by the sudden quiet, stopped. The man stepped forward. He didn't put out his hand. He had no microphone. He had with him children. Four beautiful children.

They didn't really need an introduction but he made it anyway.

"I'm Marge Hogan's husband. These are her children. The ones that were born." Tara remained silent. She couldn't look at the little ones so she held the man's gaze. His eyes were red-rimmed. She was sure they had looked that way since his wife's murder. "Why didn't you just turn him in? Why didn't you put an end to this?"

"Mr. Hogan, I couldn't," Tara said quietly. "I was bound by the law, by an oath I took."

"That's more important than us? Than these kids? Keeping your word to a killer is more important than letting a good woman rest? What kind of woman are you?"

Tara lowered her eyes then looked at him once more. "I'm an attorney, Mr. Hogan. This is the United States, and everyone has their rights."

"What about my wife's right to live, lady?"

Tara couldn't listen any longer. She'd never put a face to a crime the way this man forced her to do. She walked through the courthouse doors, a roar of disapproval following her. Behind her, two guards stood well within view of the crowd. She felt their opinion as she passed. Putting her briefcase on the conveyor belt, Tara walked through the metal detector. No one spoke to her, but everyone looked. She wanted the day over, but it had to begin first.

Pulling open the door, Tara walked into the courtroom where Woodrow Weber sat confidently at the prosecutor's table. Behind him was Charlotte, dressed in an exquisite blue dress. Everything was in place: her pearls, her poise, her loyalties. She offered Tara a sad, pitying smile that was all mixed up with a little chin-lift of encouragement. Across the aisle to the right, Donna looked chic in a black dress piped with gold. Tara walked past her slowly, knowing she would stop at any sign that Donna was willing to talk. Tara was through the bar and into the well. Donna hadn't even bothered to lift a finger. Behind her, there was a murmur of excitement from those counting themselves lucky to be at this impromptu hearing. She put her briefcase on the counsel table and suddenly the room was silent.

Bill Hamilton appeared, escorted into the court

by a female bailiff. God only knew what people were thinking as they gazed upon this man. Did they think Bill Hamilton handsome? Did the women sigh at his smile? Were they curious about him? Frightened of him? Tara had thought and felt all these things for so long, she no longer felt anything.

Tara let him be placed next to her, stopping the bailiff before she unlocked Bill Hamilton's shackles. After the hearing, they could do as they pleased. While he sat next to her, he would be chained.

"Come on, little lady," Bill cajoled.

She would have preferred him gagged.

Bill settled back with a chuckle when she ignored him. He was turning to flash Donna a smile when the court was called to order. Judge Timothy DeMar presiding. People stood. People sat. The judge spoke.

"In the case of The People vs. Hamilton, counsel, please make your appearance for the record."

Woodrow stood straight and ready. "Good morning, Your Honor, Woodrow Weber on behalf of the people."

He nodded to Woodrow, then swiveled toward Tara. "For the defense?"

"Tara Linley for defendant Hamilton, who is present in custody before the court." Tara's fingertips touched the table. She was tired. "Good morning, Your Honor."

" 'Morning, Ms. Linley. Now, shall we see what we have here?" The judge tucked his hands in the wide sleeves of his robe. Tara remained standing. He looked at her frankly. "This hearing has been placed on calendar at your request, Ms. Linley. We weren't set for pretrial conference 'til next month.

As I'm sure counsel is aware, this court is very busy and doesn't look favorably upon hearings being scheduled on short notice. You wreak mayhem on my clerk's schedule and she didn't become a public servant in order to work." Those in attendance chuckled politely. Judge DeMar seemed pleased. Then he got down to business. "What's so important, counsel?"

Tara swallowed, the laughter grating on her nerves. It had been a long few weeks. The end of her personal trial was in sight and it pained her that no one truly understood the import of this moment. She cleared her throat.

"Your Honor, I respectfully request to be relieved as counsel of record. I believe my client has the means necessary to retain a new lawyer."

To her right, almost, but not quite out of her view, Bill Hamilton started then caught himself. Slowly a grin spread across his face. She heard him whisper "hot damn." He may have terrorized her, but she had the last laugh. She had sucker punched him. Judge DeMar didn't miss a trick.

"Is your client aware of this request, Ms. Linley?"

"No, Your Honor. I only made the final decision early this morning."

DeMar began to take notes. "I assume there's justification for this change considering your actions may be detrimental to your client."

Tara smiled wryly, her eyes trained on the bench. She had no desire to look at Woodrow and see the triumphant look on his face. He would never know that he hadn't beaten her. She couldn't look at Bill Hamilton and have him assume that his evil had sent her running. She wouldn't try to explain that it was heartache, pure and simple, that had done her in. Those she loved had turned against her. Albuquerque no longer felt like home, her house was no longer warm and welcoming. She was so angered by all this, so hurt that there could be no heartfelt explanation. If she tried, her words would be turned around and against her. Holding her head high, she said clearly:

"Your Honor, my continued representation of this client would certainly be to his detriment. I believe a new attorney would be in his best interest at this time."

The Judge shook his head and said to Tara, "I'm sure you're aware that such a request is highly unusual, especially given the fact that your decision seems to come as a shock not only to this court, but to your client as well. I'll need a reason, Ms. Linley, and it better be a good one."

"It's the best, Your Honor. Mr. Hamilton is charged with a serious crime. He needs an attorney that can aggressively and effectively speak on his behalf. This man needs attorneys who can devote their best efforts to his defense and make sure that all of his rights are fully protected." Tara's eyes flickered to the table. It was hard for her to speak. When she raised her eyes, they were moist. It was difficult to admit she was not all she had thought herself to be. "I thought I was that counsel. I am not, Your Honor. In all seriousness and candor I make this request and ask the court to relieve me. Allow a new attorney who will be best able to do what is necessary in this case."

The man on the bench sighed and put his chin on his upturned hand. "Mr. Hamilton, do you understand what your attorney is asking?"

"Yep. Think it's darn cowardly of her. Darn cowardly, Yer Honor. I thought this little lady had more guts than that." Suddenly Bill was up, the shackles binding him from ankle to waist, and waist to wrist, rattled like the ghost of Christmas past. Tara ducked, her arms instinctively covering her face. There was a collective gasp.

DeMar called, "Bailiff."

The bailiff moved like lightning.

But no one was fast enough for Bill. He was sitting back down, grinning up at her, before anyone could reach him. Donna had reached over and touched his shoulder, calming him with all her maternal and lustful energy. Bill laughed.

"Yeah, I understand, Yer Honor," he drawled crudely.

Timothy DeMar's mouth dropped, then twisted into an angry grimace as he controlled his courtroom and his temper.

"This court finds there has been an irrevocable breakdown in the attorney-client relationship. I believe any further representation by Tara Linley of William Hamilton would not be in the defendant's best interest. I do relieve Ms. Linley as attorney of record." DeMar took a breath, calming himself. Tara almost smiled. How often had she had that delayed reaction after one of Bill's little misbehaviors? But DeMar would get over it. She might not. He was talking again, to Bill. "How long will it take you to retain new counsel?"

"Not long, I should think, Judge. I'd say there's going to be some press in this, wouldn't you? Couple of attorneys probably out there right now lookin' to take me on."

The man on the bench stared at Bill Hamilton while giving the nod to Tara.

"Thank you, Ms. Linley. You are excused. Please turn over all of your files when contacted by the

new attorney so there will be no delay. I think this
is one I'd like to see settled as expediently as possible."

"I would think so, Your Honor," Tara answered
quietly. "Thank you, Your Honor." She picked up
her briefcase and turned her back on Bill Hamilton.

Tara saw Donna Ecold's eyes trained on the
madman she needed more than she needed Tara's
friendship. Tara didn't hesitate. She walked down
the aisle and pushed through the doors. She suffered the anger that greeted her outside. And
through it all, through the din and the accusations
and the anger, she heard the sound that made
everything all right. She heard the horn and saw
the green van. Tara Linley walked right to it, jos-
tled right and left, finally managing to get in and
behind the door.

"Where to?" Ben asked.

"Anywhere, Ben," Tara said. "Anywhere but
here." He spun the wheel and the van pulled away
from the courthouse. Tara still looked out the window. Ben let her be. Finally, she found her voice.

"It will never be the same, Ben," she whispered.

"No," he answered. "But it will be good again.
I promise."

Tara turned her head and looked at Ben Crawford. She reached for his hand, closed her eyes,
and knew, without question, that he was right. Of
all of them, she and Ben would have a life worth
living again.

WHODUNIT? . . . ZEBRA DUNIT!
FOR ARMCHAIR DETECTIVES—
TWO DELIGHTFUL NEW MYSTERY SERIES

AN ANGELA BIAWABAN MYSTERY:
TARGET FOR MURDER   (4069, $3.99)
by J.F. Trainor

Anishinabe princess Angie is on parole from a correctional facility, courtesy of an embezzling charge. But when an old friend shows up on her doorstep crying bloody murder, Angie skips parole to track down the creep who killed Mary Beth's husband and stole her land. When she digs up the dirt on a big-time developer and his corrupt construction outfit, she becomes a sitting duck for a cunning killer who never misses the mark!

A CLIVELY CLOSE MYSTERY:
DEAD AS DEAD CAN BE   (4099, $3.99)
by Ann Crowleigh

Twin sisters Miranda and Clare Clively are stunned when a corpse falls from their carriage house chimney. Against the back drop of Victorian London, they must defend their family name from a damning scandal—and a thirty-year-old murder. But just as they are narrowing down their list of suspects, they get another dead body on their hands—and now Miranda and Clare wonder if they will be next . . .

A CLIVELY CLOSE MYSTERY:
WAIT FOR THE DARK   (4298, $3.99)
by Ann Crowleigh

Clare Clively is taken by surprise when she discovers a corpse while walking through the park. She and her twin sister, Miranda are immediately on the case . . . yet the closer they come to solving the crime, the closer they come to a murderous villain who has no intention of allowing the two snooping sisters to unmask the truth!

LOOK FOR THESE OTHER BOOKS IN ZEBRA'S NEW *PARTNERS IN CRIME* SERIES FEATURING APPEALING WOMEN AMATEUR-SLEUTHS:
    LAURA FLEMING MYSTERIES
    MARGARET BARLOW MYSTERIES
    AMANDA HAZARD MYSTERIES
    TEAL STEWART MYSTERIES
    DR. AMY PRESCOTT MYSTERIES
    ROBIN LIGHT MYSTERIES

Available wherever paperbacks are sold, or order direct from the Publisher. Send cover price plus 50¢ per copy for mailing and handling to Penguin USA, P.O. Box 999, c/o Dept. 17109, Bergenfield, NJ 07621. Residents of New York and Tennessee must include sales tax. DO NOT SEND CASH.

PINNACLE BOOKS HAS
SOMETHING FOR EVERYONE —

MAGICIANS, EXPLORERS, WITCHES AND CATS

THE HANDYMAN (377-3, $3.95/$4.95)
He is a magician who likes hands. He likes their comfortable shape and weight and size. He likes the portability of the hands once they are severed from the rest of the ponderous body. Detective Lanark must discover who The Handyman is before more handless bodies appear.

PASSAGE TO EDEN (538-5, $4.95/$5.95)
Set in a world of prehistoric beauty, here is the epic story of a courageous seafarer whose wanderings lead him to the ends of the old world — and to the discovery of a new world in the rugged, untamed wilderness of northwestern America.

BLACK BODY (505-9, $5.95/$6.95)
An extraordinary chronicle, this is the diary of a witch, a journal of the secrets of her race kept in return for not being burned for her "sin." It is the story of Alba, that rarest of creatures, a white witch: beautiful and able to walk in the human world undetected.

THE WHITE PUMA (532-6, $4.95/NCR)
The white puma has recognized the men who deprived him of his family. Now, like other predators before him, he has become a man-hater. This story is a fitting tribute to this magnificent animal that stands for all living creatures that have become, through man's carelessness, close to disappearing forever from the face of the earth.

Contents

ACT III: THE THREAT TO GLOBAL DEMOCRACY

PENGUIN BOOKS

UNFREE SPEECH

Joshua Wong was born in 1996. He has been named by *Time*, *Fortune*, *Prospect*, and *Forbes* as one of the world's most influential leaders. In 2018, he was nominated for the Nobel Peace Prize for his leading role in the Umbrella Revolution. He is Secretary-General of Demosistō, a pro-democracy organisation which he founded in 2016 that advocates for self-determination for Hong Kong. Joshua came onto the political scene in 2011 at the age of fourteen, when he founded Scholarism and successfully protested against the enforcement of Chinese National Education in Hong Kong. He has been arrested numerous times for his protesting and activism and has served more than one hundred days in jail. He has been the subject of two documentaries, including the Netflix original documentary, *Joshua: Teenager vs. Superpower*. This is the first time his work has been published in English.

Jason Y. Ng is a lawyer, activist, former president of PEN Hong Kong, and author of three acclaimed books charting Hong Kong's postcolonial development, *Hong Kong State of Mind*, *No City for Slow Men*, and *Umbrellas in Bloom*. He has followed Joshua's story from its beginnings in 2011 and has continued to report and advocate for his cause ever since.

UNFREE SPEECH

The Threat to Global Democracy and Why We Must Act, Now

JOSHUA WONG

with JASON Y. NG

Introduction by

AI WEIWEI

PENGUIN BOOKS

PENGUIN BOOKS
An imprint of Penguin Random House LLC
penguinrandomhouse.com

First published in a slightly different form in Great Britain by
WH Allen, an imprint of Ebury Publishing, a division of
Penguin Random House UK, 2020
This edition published in Penguin Books 2020

LIBRARY OF CONGRESS CONTROL NUMBER: 2019056792

ISBN 9780143135715 (paperback)
ISBN 9780525507413 (ebook)

Printed in the United States of America
1   3   5   7   9   10   8   6   4   2

Set in Bell MT Std

For those who have lost their freedom
fighting for Hong Kong

Introduction: A New Generation of Rebel

Joshua Wong represents a new generation of rebel. They were born into the globalised, post-internet era, raised in the late 1990s and early 2000s under a modern societal and knowledge structure that was relatively democratic and free. Their worldview is markedly different from that of the established capitalist culture fixated on profit above all else.

From the Umbrella Movement in 2014 to today's protests that have spurred on over a hundred days of resistance, we have seen the rise of a very special and brand-new rebel in Hong Kong. Joshua and his contemporaries are the vanguard of this phenomenon. They are rational and principled, clear as crystal in their objectives and as accurate as numbers. All they require and demand is a single value: freedom. They believe that through safeguarding the liberties of every citizen by demonstrating their rights in a highly visible way, we can achieve justice and democracy in any society.

This generation understands, lucidly, that freedom

is not a given condition; rather, it is something to achieve through constant effort and struggle. These young people have borne a great responsibility, and many are now suffering because of it. Some have lost their promising young lives. But these activists can and will reach their goal, because we all know that freedom without hardship is not true freedom.

True freedom finds its value in hard work and determination. This is what Joshua's generation have come to realise through their own experiences. They are confronted with an authoritarian regime – an embodiment of centralised state power and the repression of human rights that we see in China and in other countries around the world. The scale of what this regime symbolises elevates the efforts of Joshua's generation to a heroism found in myths: the underdog locked in a struggle against powerful dark forces. I am confident that the citizens of Hong Kong, and those who march for their own rights and causes elsewhere, will overcome the massive establishment and will shape the world with the most powerful message: freedom, justice, and liberty for all.

Joshua's generation advocates for two of the most precious values created by humankind over thousands of years: social fairness and justice. These are the most important cornerstones of any civilisa-tion. Throughout history, in pursuit of these principles humans have paid a great price, with too many deaths, misfortunes, betrayals and grave instances of opportunism.

Today we see that betrayal and opportunism everywhere in the so-called free world. In the West, it is ubiquitous. Joshua's generation is openly challenging all of these acts of duplicity, weakness and evasion in the name of defending humanity's core beliefs.

The young people of Hong Kong are realising a great social ideal in the spirit of sacrifice, similar to faith or religion. Together, their actions, their inherent understanding of the conflict and their awareness of the difficult realities they face are helping the whole world recognise what a real revolution is. This is what we have been waiting for, and I hope that the revolution, guided by Joshua and his generation, will be witnessed all over the world.

Ai Weiwei
18 October 2019

Prologue

In August 2017, as the baking sun bore down on the streets of Hong Kong and university students were finishing up their summer jobs or returning from family trips, I was sentenced to six months in prison for my role in the Umbrella Movement that sent shock waves through the world and changed Hong Kong's history. I was immediately taken to Pik Uk Correctional Institution, a short walk from the school I used to attend. I was 20 years old.

The Department of Justice had won their appeal to increase my sentence from 80 hours of community service to a prison term – the first time anyone in Hong Kong was sentenced to jail for the charge of unlawful assembly. In doing so, the appeal had also made me one of the city's first political prisoners.

I had planned to keep a journal while I was in prison, both to make the time go by faster and to record the many conversations and events I was privy to within the prison walls. I thought that perhaps one day I would turn those notes into a book – and here it is.

This book comprises three acts. The first chronicles my coming of age, from a 14-year-old student campaign organiser to the founder of a political party and the face of a resistance movement against the ever-reaching long arm of Communist China in Hong Kong and beyond. It is a genesis story that lays bare a tumultuous decade of grassroots activism that lifted a population of 7 million out of political apathy into a heightened sense of social justice, capturing the imagination of the international community in the process.

In the second act, readers will find stories and anecdotes from my summer behind bars, captured in letters written every evening after I returned to my prison cell, as I sat on my hard bed and put pen to paper under dim light. I wanted to share my views on the state of the political movement in Hong Kong, the direction it should take, and how it is expected to shape our future. I also wanted to capture the essence of prison life, from my dialogues with prison staff to time spent with other inmates watching the news on television and trading stories of prisoner abuse. The experience brought me ever closer to other imprisoned activists like Martin Luther King Jr and Liu Xiaobo – giants who inspired and guided me in spirit through the city's darkest hours and my own.

The book closes with an urgent call for all of us around the world to defend our democratic rights. Recent incidents, from the US National Basketball Association social media controversy to Apple's removal of a police-tracking app in Hong Kong, have shown that the erosion of freedoms that has plagued Hong Kong is spreading to the rest of the world. If multinationals, international governments and indeed ordinary citizens do not start paying attention to Hong Kong and treating our story as an early warning signal, it won't be long before everyone else feels the same invasion of civil liberties that Hong Kongers have endured and resisted every day on our streets for the past two decades.

Through *Unfree Speech* – my first book written for the international audience – I hope readers will get to know a young man in transition, both in mindset and in experience. But the book also reveals a city in transition, from a British colony to a special administrative region under Communist rule, from a concrete jungle of glass and steel to an urban battlefield of gas masks and umbrellas, from a pre-eminent financial hub to a shining bastion of freedom and defiance in the face of a global threat. These transitions have made me more committed than ever to the fight for a better Hong Kong – a cause that has defined my adolescence and continues to shape who I am.

Every day at Pik Uk Prison began with the same, exacting morning march: each inmate was expected to fall in line, march, halt, make a 90-degree turn, look up at the guards and announce their presence one after the other. Every day I heard myself shouting those same words at the top of my lungs: 'Good morning, Sir! I, Joshua Wong, prison number 4030XX, have been convicted of unlawful assembly. Thank you, SIR!'

I am Joshua Wong. My prison number was 4030XX. And this is my story.

UNFREE SPEECH

ACT I

GENESIS

'Let no man despise thy youth; but be thou an example of the believers, in word, in conversation, in charity, in spirit, in faith, in purity.'

— 1 Timothy 4:12

To the Promised Land: The Rise of the New Hong Konger

到應許之地：新香港人的崛起

I was born in 1996, the Year of the Fire Rat, nine months before Hong Kong reverted to Chinese rule.

According to the Chinese Zodiac, which runs on a 60-year cycle, the fire rat is adventurous, rebellious and garrulous. Although as a Christian I believe in neither Western nor Eastern astrology, these personality predictions are fairly spot on – especially the part about me being a compulsive talker.

'When Joshua was still a baby, even with a bottle in his mouth he would make all sorts of sounds like he was giving a speech on stage.' This is the way my mum still introduces me to new church people. I don't have the faintest memory of what I did as a baby, but her description is entirely believable and I take her word for it.

When I was seven years old I was diagnosed with dyslexia, a writing and reading disorder. My parents had noticed the signs early on when I had trouble with even basic Chinese characters. Simple words that preschoolers learned in a matter of days, like 'large' (大) and 'very' (太), looked indistinguishable to me. I would make the same mistakes in homework assignments and exams well into my teens.

But my speech was unaffected by my learning disability. By speaking confidently I was able to make up for my weaknesses. The microphone loved me and I loved it even more. As a child I would tell jokes in church groups and ask questions that even the bigger kids wouldn't dare ask. I would bombard the pastor and church elders with queries like 'If God is so full of mercy and kindness, why does He let poor people suffer in caged homes in Hong Kong?' and 'We make donations to the church every month, where does the money go?'

When my parents took me on trips to Japan and Taiwan I would grab the tour guide's megaphone and share factoids I'd found on the internet about places to see and things to do, moving from topic to topic like it was the most natural thing in the world. The audience would cheer their approval.

My motormouth and innate inquisitiveness earned me praise and chuckles wherever I went. Thanks to my small stature and chubby cheeks, what might otherwise have been considered annoying or overbearing was forgiven as 'cute', 'quirky' or 'precocious'. While there were teachers and parents who wished this little know-it-all would shut up occasionally, they were usually in the minority and I was doted on in school and at church. 'Your boy is special. He'll make a great lawyer one day!' the churchgoers would tell my father.

In the West, people may see an aspiring politician or rights activist in an outspoken child, but in Hong Kong – one of the world's most capitalistic regions – neither of these career choices would be wished upon even your worst enemy. A lucrative career in law, medicine or finance is the epitome of success in every parent's eyes. But mine aren't like that and they didn't raise me that way.

My parents are both devout Christians. My father was an IT professional before he took early retirement to focus on church affairs and community work. My mother works at a local community centre that provides family counselling. They married in 1989, just weeks after the Chinese government sent in the tanks to crush student demonstrators on Tiananmen Square. My mum and dad agreed to cancel their wedding celebrations and sent out handwritten notes to friends and relatives with a simple message: 'Our nation is in crisis, the newlyweds shall not stand on ceremony.' In a culture where an expensive wedding banquet is as much a rite of passage as the act of getting married itself, their decision was both bold and noble.

My Chinese name, Chi-fung, was inspired by the Bible. The characters 之鋒 mean 'something sharp', a reference to Psalm 45:5, which instructs, 'Send your sharp arrows through enemy hearts and make all nations fall at your feet.' My parents didn't want me to pierce anyone's heart, but they did want me to speak the truth and wield it like a sword to cut through lies and injustice.

Other than my unusual loquaciousness, I was a pretty typical child. My best friend in primary school was Joseph. He was taller than me, better looking, and got better marks. He could easily have hung out with the popular kids, but we bonded over our common tendency to prattle on and on, chatting during class despite sitting seven seats apart. In Primary Two (ages 6–7) our teacher Mr Szeto was so fed up with our non-stop talking that he petitioned the head to put us in different classes in the following year groups. But that didn't work.

Joseph and I were inseparable. We would meet up at each other's flats after school to play video games and trade manga comic books. The first movie I ever watched in a cinema was *Batman: The Dark Knight*, a Hollywood blockbuster set partially in Hong Kong – and I watched it with Joseph.

We had something else in common. My class was the first to be born after the Handover. We are the generation that entered this world during the most important political event in Hong Kong's history. On 1 July 1997, after 156 years of British rule, Hong Kong shed its colonial past and returned to Communist China. The sovereignty transfer was meant to be a cause for celebration – a reunification between mother and child and an opportunity for the local business elite to tap the still emerging mainland market – except that for most ordinary Hong Kongers it wasn't. Many of our relatives and friends had left Hong Kong years before that fateful date out of fear of Communist rule. By the time I was born nearly half a million citizens had emigrated to countries like the US, the UK, Canada, Australia and New Zealand. To them, communism was synonymous with the political turmoil that resulted from the Great Leap Forward – a failed economic campaign between 1958 and 1962 to industrialise China that caused the death of an estimated 30 million peasants from mass starvation – and the Cultural Revolution – a sociopolitical movement between 1966 and 1976 led by Chairman Mao Zedong to purge capitalistic tendencies and political rivals. Communism was the reason why they and their parents had fled to Hong Kong in the first place; the idea of being handed back to the 'thieves and murderers' – to use my grandmother's words – from whom they had escaped was terrifying and inconceivable.

But it was all hearsay as far as I was concerned. To someone who grew up knowing only Chinese rule, those accounts were nothing more than tales and urban legends. The only flag I had seen flying in public places and outside government buildings was the Five-starred Red Chinese flag. Other than the London-style double-decker buses and English-sounding street names like Hennessy, Harcourt and Connaught, I don't have any memory of colonial Hong Kong or feel any attachment to British rule. Even though many local schools like the one I attended continue to teach in English, students are taught to take pride in the many economic achieve-ments of modern China, not least the way the Chinese Communist Party had lifted hundreds of millions of people out of abject poverty. At school we learned that the Basic Law, Hong Kong's mini-constitution and a heavily negotiated document that China and Britain laboured over before the Handover, begins with the declaration that 'The Hong Kong Special Administrative Region is an inalienable part of the People's Republic of China'. China is our motherland and, like a benevolent parent, she will always have our best interests in mind under the so-called 'one country, two systems' framework.

The principle was memorialised in the Sino-British Joint Declaration, an international treaty signed by Britain and China in 1984. 'One country, two systems' was the brainchild of the then paramount leader Deng Xiaoping, who needed a solution to stem the exodus of talent and wealth from Hong Kong during the Handover talks. Deng wanted to reassure fleeing citizens that the city would be reunited with mainland China without losing its distinct economic and political systems. He famously promised the city that 'horses will still run, and dancers will still dance' under Chinese rule.

Deng's strategy worked. 'One country, two systems' helped Hong Kong transition smoothly from a Crown colony to a special administrative region. For most people, the Handover turned out to be much ado about nothing. Shortly after the clock struck midnight on 30 June 1997, 7 million Hong Kongers with their eyes glued to the television screen watched Chris Patten, the last colonial Governor, walk out of the Governor's House for the last time. As Patten boarded the Royal Yacht *Britannia*, accompanied by Prince Charles, everyone heaved a sigh of relief that, despite the dramatic pomp and circumstance, almost nothing had changed in Hong Kong. Many people thought that those who had fled the city out of fear had overreacted and underestimated China's goodwill.

My first encounter with 'one country, two systems' was more visceral than international treaties and constitutional frameworks. When I was five, my parents took me on a short holiday to Guangzhou, the capital city of Guangdong Province, of which Hong Kong is also a part. It was 2001, the same year that China joined the World Trade Organization and began its economic miracle.

Back then, Guangzhou was still a backwater compared with Hong Kong. Internet connection was patchy and many websites were blocked. Even though people in Guangzhou spoke Cantonese like we do, they behaved differently – in Hong Kong we never squat or spit in the streets; we always queue up and wait our turn to speak to sales or service people. Not so in China.

What's more, cars drove on the other side of the road and shoppers paid with tiny tattered notes called *renminbi*. Signage and menus were in simplified Chinese characters that looked familiar but not quite the same as the traditional ones we used in Hong Kong. Even Coca-Cola tasted different because the water they used had a funny aftertaste. 'I prefer the way things are in Hong Kong,' I remember telling myself.

From my parents' generation to mine, children in Hong Kong have grown up with anime from Japan. By far the most advanced economy in Asia, Japan has long been considered by Hong Kongers a trend-setting culture and exporter of all things cool. I've been a diehard fanboy of a sci-fi series called *Gundam*, Japan's answer to the Marvel and DC franchises. Many of my favourites – such as *Mobile Suit Gundam 00*, *Gundam Seed* and *Iron-Blooded Orphans* – share a common thread: they each tell the story of a young orphan who struggles to find their place in the world as they move from one foster family to the next.

The recurring theme of foster children in my Saturday morning cartoons makes me think about my own city. In many ways, Hong Kong is just like a foster child who was raised by a white family and, without his consent, returned to his Chinese biological parents. Mother and son have very little in common, from language and customs to the way they view their government. The more the child is forced to show affection and gratitude toward his long-lost mother, the more he resists. He feels lost, abandoned and alone. 'One country, two systems' may have navigated the former colony through its smooth transition to Chinese rule in 1997, but it does little to ease its deepening identity crisis. Hong

Kong is a city that isn't British and doesn't want to be Chinese, and its need to assert a distinct identity grows by the year.

This about sums up the state of mind of my generation – the first to grow up after the end of British rule, but before Chinese rule had taken hold. The ambivalence my generation feels towards our purported motherland motivates us to search for ways to fill the emotional void. We are struggling to carve our place in the world and develop an identity in our own image. More and more we look to our pop culture, language, food and unique way of life as the foundations of that self-image. Efforts to preserve quaint neighbourhoods, support local products and protect Cantonese from its replacement by Mandarin are gradually evolving into a youth crusade.

When I was ten years old, the biggest news story in Hong Kong was about massive protests to save two beloved and historically important ferry piers – the Star Ferry Pier and the Queen's Pier – from demolition. The campaigns were about more than a pushback against cold-hearted urban redevelopment and gentrification: they were about defending our fledgling identity. Those spurts of resistance and anger were only the tip of the iceberg. The rise of the new Hong Konger had only just begun.

*

But my political coming of age was put on hold when I turned twelve. As soon as I began my last year of primary, the only thing that mattered to me and my classmates was getting admitted to a decent secondary school. We have a saying in Hong Kong: 'high school is destiny'; it isn't an overstatement. The local education system is cut-throat and the school we attend has the power to determine our future: which university we get into, which course we choose, what kind of job we get when we graduate, how much money we make, who we can date and marry and, ultimately, the level of respect we will be able to command from society. That's why so-called 'helicopter parents' go to great lengths to design elaborate 'portfolios' for their children to make them more marketable to schools. Mastery of multiple musical instruments and exotic foreign languages are the rule rather than the exception.

I wasn't optimistic. Without a killer CV and with a report card hamstrung by dyslexia I knew it would be a struggle. But I wasn't going to give up. If Moses could spend 40 years wandering in the desert before Joshua finished the job and led his people to the Promised Land, what was a bit of hard work for this fire rat?

There's a common Chinese saying: 'diligence can make up for all shortcomings'. That year, I put away my video games and manga and put in over 20 hours of private tutoring every week. I worked especially hard on my weakest subjects – Chinese and English – which tended to bring down my grades. As a result of my hard work, I managed to score 0.1 points above the minimum grade point average I'd needed to get me on my primary school's 'recommended students' list. Thanks to my outspoken requests, both the head and my form teacher agreed to write reference letters touting not academic prowess per se, but rather my 'potential to excel'.

At the final round interview for secondary school, the admissions officer asked me, 'If one of your friends told you he had been bullied, what would you do, Joshua?' Without a thought, I shot back an answer as if I had been asked the same question a hundred times: 'I would take my friend to church and let God guide him. I might even do the same for the bullies. God has a plan for everyone.' The officer smiled and I smiled back. The next thing I knew, I got a letter informing me that I'd been admitted to United Christian College after someone else had forfeited his offer. The school was my first choice.

The Great Leap Forward: Scholarism and National Education

大躍進：學民思潮與國民教育

Secondary school was refreshing. Instead of being treated like children, as we had been for six years in primary school, we were now young adults, given the latitude to express our opinions in class and run our own activities after school. What's more, the school curriculum was less about rote learning and memorisation and focused more on analysis and critical thinking, which meant my dyslexia was not as big a disadvantage as it used to be.

I loved taking pictures and videos, so I went everywhere with my handheld camera, capturing moments in school, big and small. I would upload my photos to my Facebook page and meticulously organise them into albums. I also started my own blog to document school events with funny commentaries. It quickly gained traction and soon had thousands of followers, many of whom were parents eager to find out what their children were

15

up to during the week. Despite being a newcomer at United Christian College, I quickly made a name for myself as the school journalist, filmmaker and gossip columnist. But among my friends I was mostly known as a *dokuo*, the Japanese term for a young man with no girlfriend who delights in being left alone with their video games and gadgets.

Girlfriendless or not, I saw myself more like the child in Hans Christian Andersen's 'The Emperor's New Clothes' who, when none of the townsfolk would say what was on their minds, took it upon himself to point out the elephant in the room – and there were so many elephants in the local education system. One time my Chinese teacher, who had lost patience with my constant talking in class, ordered me to be quiet and stand in the corner. As I got up from my seat I looked him in the eye and said, 'This is no way to teach a child. Do you honestly think I'll become a better student by facing the wall?' My question left the teacher speechless and the rest of the class stunned.

My penchant for challenging the authorities soon took a new turn as I combined my outspokenness with the power of social media.

I had always enjoyed good food and considered my palate as sharp as my tongue. In Secondary Two (ages 13–14), after suffering a whole year of subpar canteen food at UCC, I decided to take matters into my own hands. I set up a Facebook page and online petition and invited all my classmates to voice their grievances over the school catering's bland, oily and overpriced lunch boxes. The campaign went viral and more than 10 per cent of the school signed the petition.

Because of its popularity, the unprecedented campaign, titled 'How much longer should we tolerate bad food at UCC?', immediately caught the attention of the school authorities. A few days later I was called into the principal's office with my parents. 'Joshua is a nice boy,' Principal To said to my parents, before narrowing his eyes, 'but what he did wasn't . . . well . . . ideal. He instigated other students and put us in a difficult position. Worse than that, he named our school in a public petition without our approval.' 'But with all due respect, our boy hasn't done anything wrong,' my father said, jumping to my defence, before my mother, ever the peace-maker, offered a sensible assessment with which even Principal To had to agree. 'Look, the Facebook page is already out there,' she said. 'If you make Joshua take it down, the repercussions will be much worse. I think we should just let it be.' Thanks to my parents, I walked out of the head's office unscathed; no suspension or any form of disciplinary action.

But that was the first and last time I organised a social media campaign at school. I decided to stop, not for fear of getting into trouble again, but because I realised there were bigger fish to fry. Why bother with petty issues in high school when there were far greater injustices playing out every day and right under our noses? I decided to set my sights much higher and focus on bigger, more pressing things.

A few weeks before the canteen petition, I'd had an epiphany. It happened during a regular community visit on an ordinary Saturday afternoon. My father is a devout Christian and spends much of his spare time volunteering. I used to accompany him on his visits to the elderly, to underprivileged families and children with special needs.

On this particular Saturday, we went to a senior citizens' home that we had visited a year before. A few dozen octogenarians had already taken their seats in a big circle in the day room, expecting us. I recognised the same peeling pastel walls and tattered furniture from a year ago; I saw the same faces staring back at me; the home was every bit as short-staffed, the amenities as dated and the residents as lonely and destitute as they were when my father and I left them last time we came. My eyes welled up despite myself, but deep down I was more angry than sad.

I asked my dad, 'What's the point of these visits? What's the point if nothing ever changes?' He answered with a pat on my shoulder. 'We cheered them up for a couple of hours, didn't we? Let's keep them in our prayers. That's the best we or the church can do.'

As much as I respected my father, I couldn't disagree with him more. There was much more we could do for these people, only we hadn't tried hard enough. It wasn't fair that my family could live in a middle-class neighbourhood, attend a fancy mega-church and go on overseas holidays while nearly a fifth of the local population struggled below the poverty line, with barely enough to eat and no decent home to live in.

In school we learned that Hong Kong has one of the world's highest Gini coefficients, a measure of income inequality. That's why every day we see old people picking through rubbish bins and pushing heavy carts of recycled paper up hills to sell them on for a pittance; it's such a common sight that we no longer even notice them. All this is allowed to continue because too many people think like middle-class churchgoers: let's pray and pretend we've done enough.

I was convinced that God had put me on this world for a reason: He wanted me to do more than just praise His name and study the Bible. He wanted me to take action. My father once taught me the acronym WWJD, which stands for 'What would Jesus do?' I didn't think Jesus would walk out of that senior citizens' home with a self-congratulatory pat on the shoulder. If He did I would call Him a hypocrite, just like the boy who calls out the naked emperor.

After this episode I began to feel restless. I'd realised that there is often a gulf between good intentions and actions, but I didn't know what, in practical terms, I might actually do for the people in that home, or anyone else for that matter. Crucially, this turning point in my adolescence happened not long before I met my partner-in-crime at UCC.

Justin was another *dokuo* in my class and we shared the same passions for video games, anime and getting up to mischief in school. During the summer holiday after Primary Two, two of our favourite teachers announced their plan to marry. Justin and I decided to create a sketch in their honour. He played the groom and we enlisted a bunch of other classmates to play the bride and her well-wishing relatives. I was the filmmaker who recorded the mock wedding. To up the emotional impact I even added a soundtrack. When the newlyweds finally saw the video on YouTube they were moved to tears.

Incidents like this spread through the school like wildfire and, despite causing trouble from time to time, they made us our teachers' favourites. They also made Justin and me best friends.

But Justin provided much more than companionship. He had been a politics junkie long before we met. 'This stuff is what really matters,' he would say to me matter-of-factly while swiping through news feeds about local elections and government bills on his iPhone.

Over time, some of his hot-bloodedness began to rub off on me. We would visit local bookstores together and spend hours in the politics section. We would trade books with one another, instantly doubling the number of titles at our disposal.

I spent the summer of 2009, when I was 12 years old, reading up on local politics and discussing what I learnt with Justin. 'This is insane!' I remember shouting after I had read about Hong Kong's bizarre electoral system and how it had been designed to help government stonewall the opposition. 'Our government is so messed up. Why is it that no one ever talks about this?' I exclaimed in exasperation.

Justin rolled his eyes as if to say, 'I'm glad you've finally caught up. Welcome to Hong Kong!'

Our political system is truly one of a kind. It is the product of numerous painful – some say callous – concessions made by Britain during the Handover negotiations with China that resulted in the Basic Law.

The Basic Law prescribes three branches of government – the executive, legislature and judiciary. Under the system, ordinary citizens have no say in choosing the chief executive, the highest office in Hong Kong and the head of the executive branch, a position akin to the mayor of London or New York. Instead, he or she is selected by a small committee stacked with Communist Party loyalists, business tycoons and special interest groups, most of whom take cues from central government in Beijing before they cast their votes. The result is a head of government who is unaccountable to the people and who answers only to the bosses up north who have put them in office.

Our legislature isn't any better than the executive branch. The Legislative Council, or LegCo, is a 70-member parliament divided into two 35-member chambers: geographical constituencies (GCs) and functional constituencies (FCs, drawn from the business and professional sectors). Whereas the GCs are all elected by nearly 4 million registered voters, the FCs are far from democratically elected. Nearly all of the functional lawmakers are hand-picked by a small circle of voters within their own trade or special interest groups. For instance, the real estate functional seat is selected by a few hundred industry practitioners and construction companies, just as the legal and accountancy seats are selected only by licensed lawyers and account-ants. Together, they constitute a powerful bloc of lawmakers who vote in lockstep with each other and at the bidding of the government. In other words, the FCs give the executive branch near-complete control over LegCo.

I learned all of this from my summer reading – and from many late night heart-to-hearts with Justin over video games and bubble tea. I felt angry and frustrated that such a blatantly unjust system had been allowed to fly under the radar for so long. I also came to realise that everything that's wrong with Hong Kong – from old-age poverty to skyrock-eting property prices and the wanton destruction of historic buildings to make way for pork-barrel rede-velopment projects – was attributable to a single culprit: our unaccountable government and the lop-sided electoral system that created and facilitates it.

It didn't take me long to turn my political awakening into action. The following winter, in January 2010, a number of pro-democracy lawmakers resigned from office at the same time, triggering simultaneous by-elections to fill their seats. The idea was to turn the by-elections into a referendum on electoral reform and put pressure on the government to abolish the hated functional constituencies.

Ahead of the election, I composed a long Facebook post targeted at both students and their parents – especially the parents since they were old enough to vote. I spent hours drafting summaries and bullet points, condensing into plain language the convoluted political process so that any reader could understand what the referendum was about. I made a case for why Hong Kongers needed to work together to get rid of FCs once and for all. The post received over a thousand likes, which surprised me because no one knew who I was at the time and the subject matter itself wasn't the most enticing.

In the end, the government ignored the results of the by-elections and passed a disappointing electoral reform bill with only minor tweaks to the existing system. It fell far short of abolishing the FCs. Still, for a 13-year-old it was an important lesson in political activism: you can try as hard as you want, but until you force them to pay attention, those in power won't listen to you.

The real test would come after I celebrated my 14th birthday. In October 2010, the then Chief Executive Donald Tsang issued his last policy address before the end of his second term in office. According to the address, the government would introduce a school curriculum which introduced a new and mandatory subject called 'moral and national education'. This new subject had several objectives:

1. development of moral qualities;
2. development of a positive and optimistic attitude;
3. self-recognition;
4. judging in a caring and reasonable manner;
5. recognition of identity.

Anodyne as these points sound, at the heart of the vagaries was a more sinister aim: to shape the first generation of Hong Kongers into the Chinese mould and teach us to accept and adopt Communist Party principles – without us, or our parents, even noticing. In Hong Kong, anything with the word 'national' in it arouses suspicion. The name 'national education' raises the spectre of Communist propaganda and brainwashing, the very kind that students in mainland China have been subject to – and have continued to suffer – for decades. If nothing was done about it, this new curriculum would be implemented in all primary schools in Hong Kong by 2012 and all secondary schools by 2013. A four-month public consultation would supposedly commence in 2011, but I knew that in reality, this 'consultation' would not result in any changes in the curriculum at all.

National education hit very close to home for me. It was the first government policy that deliberately targeted and directly impacted my classmates and me. I was a key stakeholder – a term we had just learned in liberal studies class at UCC. And if the people who had the most to lose didn't speak up, who else would?

Sure enough, during the four-month consultation period the pro-democracy lawmakers and even the teachers' union expressed only mild annoyance, responding to the Education Bureau with verbal disapproval and wagging fingers. 'These adults have all been out of school for two or three decades,' I said to Justin, 'why should they care about what goes on inside the classroom? But we need to care and we need to protect our education before it's too late.'

Justin's parents had a different plan for him. Mindful of his future, they were sending him abroad to finish his schooling. In a year's time he would leave Hong Kong and I would part with my best friend and my political muse.

Justin and I continued to hang out right up until he left for America, but deep down I knew that if I wanted to fight the Dark Force, I needed to recruit some new Jedis.

I zeroed in on Ivan Lam, a Secondary Four (ages 15–16) student at UCC. I'd befriended a number of like-minded students at street rallies and exchanged contact details – Ivan was one of them. Like Justin, Ivan had been politically active from a young age. The 16-year-old was also known for his artistic talent, having won many design competitions at UCC and beyond. I began to follow him to various anti-government protests and demonstrations, including the annual 1 July protest march that marks the anniversary of the Handover, and 4 June Tiananmen Square Massacre candlelight vigil, the two biggest events in Hong Kong's civil society calendar, both of which draw thousands of citizens onto the streets. Back then, not that many students would attend political gatherings so it was easy for us to spot each other, especially if we were wearing our school uniforms. The circle of friends we made at those rallies would later become the first members of our anti-national education campaign and provide the critical mass for its early events.

In May 2011, Ivan and I launched a Facebook page and named our group Scholarism, 'scholar' because we were a student group and 'ism' to signal a new way of thinking (and to give the name more gravitas).

Over the next few months we made banners, printed flyers, set up street stalls, staged small-scale sit-ins and recruited more student volunteers to do the same. Ivan was responsible for all of our campaign artwork; the use of snappy graphics and punchy sound bites was critical in spreading the word online. By May 2012, on Scholarism's one-year anniversary, our following had grown from a close-knit group of friends to 10,000 people. Among our members was Agnes Chow, who was the same age as me. Eloquent, strong-willed and linguistically gifted, she would become one of Scholarism's core members and its sole female spokesperson.

Founding Scholarism was a natural extension of what I had already been doing in the preceding year. It was the canteen petition all over again; except this time, it involved many more stakeholders and targeted an entire generation of young people. In fact, the idea of running our own youth activist group felt so natural that I didn't even discuss it with my parents before we launched it.

In the months following the creation of Scholarism, I spent nearly every day giving soapbox speeches on street corners and sitting for press interviews. I became a regular feature in the local media after one of my impromptu interviews went viral and was viewed 150,000 times within two weeks. My mum started saving newspaper clippings about me and recording the radio shows I appeared on. 'This is part of our history,' she would say. 'You are making history.'

But it wasn't all glamour and fame. For nearly 18 months I lived the life of Peter Parker. Like Spider-Man's alter ego, I went to class during the day and rushed out to fight evil after school. I would take the bus to the government headquarters in Admiralty – our equivalent of the Houses of Parliament or Capitol Hill – to meet with civil society leaders and pro-democracy lawmakers and discuss what could be done to stop the implementation of national education. While my peers sang karaoke and went to the movies, I was strategising Scholarism's next moves while coordinating mass protests with adults many years older than me. With donated funds we rented a tiny office in an industrial building and set up a campaign HQ there. I would miss important school assignments and even exams and, after a disastrous semester, fall to the bottom of the class. Fortunately, UCC was supportive of my efforts and gave me a pass. One time my maths teacher pulled me aside and said, 'I have a teenage girl who's about your age. I want to thank you for doing this for her.'

In July 2012, our anti-national education campaign intensified. Chun-ying (or C.Y.) Leung, a self-made millionaire widely rumoured to be an underground Chinese Communist Party member, took office to succeed Donald Tsang as chief executive. Soon after Leung was sworn in, a teaching manual published by a government-funded think tank was distributed to primary and secondary schools citywide. The manual praised the Chinese Communist Party as an 'advanced and selfless regime' and criticised Western democracy by arguing that 'toxic bipartisan politics' in the United States had led to the 'suffering of its people'. It confirmed all our suspicions and fears about Communist propaganda.

This bombshell publication set civil society ablaze. Within days a new alliance was formed comprising a dozen organisations, including Scholarism, the Hong Kong Federation of Students (HKFS) and Civil Human Rights Front (CHRF), the most prominent civil liberty group in the city. On 29 July I led the alliance in a massive street rally that attracted nearly 100,000 participants, most of them parents and students.

Despite the massive turnout, Leung's government, as I had expected, remained intransigent. Though Leung claimed that he was open to a dialogue with concerned groups, he reiterated that the curriculum would go ahead as planned. Heartbroken and enraged, Ivan took to the stage in Admiralty that night. Fighting back tears, he said, 'We don't need dialogue. We haven't come this far to make deals with politicians!' Within hours of his speech, another 700 student volunteers joined Scholarism.

By mid-August, more than 15 months since we began our campaign, there was a real sense of urgency within Scholarism. The new school year would be starting in a month's time and so would the new curriculum if we didn't stop it in time. 'Protests alone aren't enough,' I said to Ivan. 'We need to shift things up a gear.'

In the following weeks, Scholarism members fanned out across the city, stepping up their protests outside school entrances and launching a street petition campaign. Within a week we had collected 120,000 signatures from concerned students.

Supporters of all ages came by our street stalls to drop off pizzas, sushi, baked goods and drinks to keep us going.

With only days left before students were due to return to school, Ivan and I knew we had reached a now-or-never moment. On 31 August we called on students to head to Admiralty and occupy the front yard of the government headquarters. We baptised the open space with a new, symbolic – and catchy – name: 'Civic Square'.

On the same day, Ivan and two other Scholarism members began a hunger strike: the first of its kind by secondary school students in the city's history. The aim was to build public sympathy and attract more press coverage for our campaign. I wanted to go on hunger strike too, but Ivan said I should save my energy to do what I did best: speak to the press.

On 3 September, 72 hours after it began, our medical team ordered the three to end the strike as their blood sugar levels had become dangerously low. Ivan's lips had turned paper white and he was groggy and could barely sit up. Still, not a single government official bothered to visit them. In a PR stunt, C.Y. Leung showed up at Civic Square to shake hands with the demonstrators, without even checking on the hunger strikers.

By the end of the week, the anti-national education campaign had reached fever pitch. On Friday 7 September we called on parents and children to join us in a mass protest outside the government headquarters dressed in black, the colour of mourning. Thanks to our hunger strike and media blitz, over 120,000 black-clothed citizens descended on Admiralty after they finished work and school to show solidarity with the Scholarism demonstrators. It was the largest assembly without prior police approval in Hong Kong's history and the highest turnout ever for a rally organised by secondary school students. The crowds were so huge that protesters spilled over onto Harcourt Road, a major highway running through the city's financial district.

That night I gave the biggest speech I'd ever given. Everything I had learned from my parents, the church elders, my teachers and Justin culminated in that one moment. Even though I was exhausted from weeks of sleeping in a tent and giving interviews, I didn't want to let down all the people who believed in me and counted on me. I had to give it everything I had.

'This is the ninth straight day of our Civic Square sit-in,' I said in a hoarse voice as soon as I was handed the microphone – which I thought of as my weapon of choice, like Thor's hammer or Captain

America's vibranium shield. I was still only 15, after all. 'We've made history and shown Hong Kong and Beijing the power of the people. Tonight we have one message and one message only: C.Y. Leung, withdraw the brainwashing curriculum!'

The crowd cheered and I went from a shout to a roar: 'We've had enough of this government. Hong Kongers will prevail!'

On the following day, C.Y. Leung held a press conference announcing his decision to suspend the curriculum. We watched the announcement at the Teachers' Union conference room, which had been Scholarism's second home for the last 18 months. In front of the flickering television screen parents cried, students cheered, and activists were locked in a tight embrace.

I turned to Ivan and said, 'We've won!'

Where Are the Adults?
The Umbrella Movement

成年人在哪裡？雨傘運動

The anti-national education campaign catapulted us to political stardom. The members of Scholarism had gone from a group of young anti-government rebels to household names – and now history makers. Never before had a group of secondary school students led a political movement of such scale and with such success. Back at UCC, teachers came up to me and Ivan to shake our hands. Everyone at church gave me their congratulations. I didn't feel I deserved such praise and attention because I knew I didn't do it by myself – no one could. To every 'great job' and 'well done' I replied: 'The victory belongs to all of us. All I did was speak the truth.'

But I also understood the euphoria and excitement all around me. Political victories, like the mysterious tanhua flower that only blooms once in a blue moon, are rare for Hong Kongers. The last time a mass protest in Hong Kong had yielded tangible results was almost a decade before, in 2003, when under the disastrous leadership of the city's first Chief Executive Tung Chee-hwa the government was forced to scrap a controversial National Security Bill after half a million citizens took to the streets to demand its retraction. The hard-fought victory buoyed our spirits and strengthened our collective identity.

The axing of national education had the same effect on the city nine years later. It gave every freedom-loving citizen a shot in the arm and reminded them that they didn't need to roll over and play dead in the face of bad government policies. Real change could happen if we worked together.

But, euphoric as we felt, we knew better than to rest on our laurels. Hong Kong remained a city of freedom without democracy – citizens had the right to kick and scream but they still couldn't choose their government. As long as our political system stayed the same it was only a matter of time before another dangerous government initiative would erupt. And next time we might not be able to hold our ground. We had to set our sights on the ultimate goal of bringing universal suffrage to Hong Kong. Every time someone congratulated me on the national education win, I would respond in the same way: we might have won a battle, but the war is far from over. I wasn't being humble, it was the hard truth.

Hong Kongers are pragmatic. Few bother with political drivel like electoral reform that may or may not happen, much less benefit them in the short run. It is often said that there are two types of people in the city – those who don't care about politics and those who do but choose to do nothing about it. But where the adults have failed, young people will take up the mantle. If the national education campaign taught us one thing, it was that students have a say in adult issues. Politics is no longer an exclusive sport for grey-haired politicians and lifelong bureaucrats.

In 2012, if I had asked anyone on the streets what universal suffrage meant, very few people would have given me a straight answer. Fewer still would have told me that Beijing had promised the city the right to elect its own chief executive and the entire LegCo in a few years' time. Unbeknown to most Hong Kongers, there existed a largely forgotten political promise, an axis around which a full-scale popular uprising would soon turn.

To understand how this political promise came about, we have to go back to the early years of the Hong Kong Special Administrative Region of the People's Republic of China.

The first decade after the Handover was nothing short of catastrophic. Even though the transition to Chinese rule in 1997 had been smooth, the newly minted special administrative region began to crack under the weight of a regional debt crisis, a deadly epidemic and an incompetent government.

I was just a baby when a crippling financial crisis hit East and Southeast Asia in 1997. It took years for the region to recover and Hong Kong had barely got back on its feet when the 2002–3 SARS (a viral respiratory disease) outbreak killed nearly 300 people and decimated the local economy. I remember my parents taking me to a neighbourhood restaurant for dim sum that summer only to find the normally jam-packed dining hall completely deserted. It was like being in a post-apocalypse sci-fi movie.

And things got worse. Tung Chee-hwa's misguided housing policy led to the burst of the property bubble and the foreclosure of thousands of homes, sending the suicide rate to a record high. Then a controversial National Security Bill, which was required under the Basic Law but had never been enacted, proposed long jail terms for sedition, secession or treason and gave the government greater rights to arrest citizens and ban political organisations that are deemed a threat to national security. It was the straw that broke the camel's back – 500,000 angry citizens marched down Hennessy Road in the largest ever 1 July rally to demand government accountability and political reform.

I was too young to march at the time, but my parents were there. I asked my mum why she had gone and she replied, 'Once the bill is passed, the government can search any home they like and even seize personal property. Do you want all your video games to be taken away?'

In the years that followed, calls to democratise the territory got louder with every Handover anniversary – an annual reminder of the city's slow decline since its reversion to Chinese rule. Senior leadership in Beijing needed to quell public anger in Hong Kong before they lost their grip on the city. In 2007 China's central legislative body – the Standing Committee of the National People's Congress (NPC) – found a quick fix. They made a promise to the people of Hong Kong that they would be given the right to freely elect the chief executive by 2017, and all members of LegCo by 2020. It would mean that Hong Kongers could choose their leaders and their democratic representatives for the first time in history.

If kept, this promise would be the single biggest step towards Hong Kong's democratisation. Even though the Basic Law guarantees universal suffrage as an 'eventual goal', it is silent on when and how this goal should be fulfilled. The 2007 promise answered at least the question of 'when'.

The 'how' question, on the other hand, continued to make many in the pro-democracy camp uneasy. Still, Hong Kongers can have a short memory and an even shorter attention span. By the time the national education saga unfolded in 2012, most citizens had forgotten all about the NPC promise. Even SARS had become ancient history.

The first person to recognise both the necessity and the urgency of working out the details of electoral reform was Professor Benny Tai, a respected expert in constitutional law. I met Professor Tai during the anti-national education campaign in 2012, when he would come to our protests to show support as an academic. We didn't get to know each other too well back then but I had a strong feeling that our paths would cross again soon.

In late 2013, four years before the first prong of the 2007 promise was to be delivered, the Hong

Kong government announced the initial round of public consultations to discuss the mechanics of the 2017 election of the chief executive.* In the following spring, Professor Tai, sociology professor Chan Kin-man and Baptist minister Reverend Chu Yiu-ming threatened a civil disobedience campaign if the government refused to listen to people. They called it Occupy Central with Love and Peace (OCLP).

The so-called 'Occupy Central Trio' proposed a mass sit-in at the heart of the city's financial district if Beijing were to renege on its promise or sabotage the chief executive election by pre-screening candidates, or introducing unreasonable nomination criteria. The non-violent campaign would paralyse business activities, the very lifeblood of Hong Kong's DNA. To make their threat credible, the Occupy Central Trio even picked a venue and date: Chater Garden, 1 October. Expected turnout: 3,000.

Along with my Scholarism colleagues, I watched the unfolding events with great interest. If universal suffrage was the answer to all of society's problems, then we students wanted to be a part of

---

* On 26 March 2017, Beijing's preferred candidate Carrie Lam was elected chief executive under the current, highly restricted, electoral design.

that solution. Professor Tai and I appeared together in several high-profile media interviews to discuss how the fight for universal suffrage might play out in the coming months.

In June the Occupy Central Trio organised an unofficial eight-day citywide referendum, posing to the general public three alternative methods for carrying out the 2017 chief executive election. The most progressive of the three options was jointly proposed by us at Scholarism and the Hong Kong Federation of Students in the hope of nudging us closer to our promised universal suffrage. It was the only option that insisted on a feature called 'civil nomination', which would allow individual citizens to nominate candidates in order to circumvent any pre-screening by Beijing. I had been the first to propose civil nomination in 2013 when the public consultation began and had been its most vocal advocate ever since. In all, 800,000 citizens – one in nine Hong Kongers – participated in the poll, casting their votes at physical ballot boxes set up on university campuses or via a smartphone app.

Although civil society could talk about civil nomination and other fancy features all we wanted, ultimately it was Beijing that called the shots. On 31 August the NPC Standing Committee issued their own definitive framework for the election. It capped the number of candidates for the chief executive post at 'two to three' and required each candidate to be selected by a 1,200-member nominating committee, in much the same way as our past chief executives had been chosen. Beijing had found a way to present us with what looked like universal suffrage – without giving it to us at all.

Sitting in our rented office, I and other Scholarism members watched the announcement of this 31 August framework in disbelief and disgust. 'That's why my parents tell me never to trust the Communists,' I confided to Agnes Chow. I felt like someone had just kicked my stomach, 1,200 times.

Hours after the announcement a teary-eyed Professor Tai appeared at a hastily organised press conference. 'Today is the darkest day of Hong Kong's democratic development,' he said. 'Our dialogue with Beijing has reached the end of the road.' He told his supporters that he had no choice but to press ahead with the Occupy Central campaign on 1 October.

Professor Tai might have been heartbroken but I was downright furious. The people of Hong Kong had waited seven years for nothing. Beijing's version of electoral reform was as much a walk-back on its promise as it was an insult to our intelligence. The 31 August framework was an open taunt to Hong Kongers: too bad, so sad.

And what are you going to do about it?

I knew I wasn't the only one who did want to do something about it. Empowered and emboldened by our anti-national education campaign from two years ago, students were among the first to act on their outrage over the NPC bombshell. While the Occupy Central Trio were still busy running rehearsals and workshops in preparation for their 1 October launch, student groups like Scholarism felt we had to take matters into our own hands. Instead of waiting for the adults to act, we fired the first shot and set off a chain of events that would change the course of our history.

Two weeks after the NPC announcement, on 13 September, I led Scholarism in a mass demonstration in Admiralty outside the government headquarters. We called on participants to wear a yellow ribbon as a show of solidarity with our cause.

The following week, the Hong Kong Federation of Students, headed by Alex Chow, Lester Shum and Nathan Law, announced a five-day class boycott at all eight of Hong Kong's universities and staged massive student assemblies on various campuses. To find strength in numbers, the HKFS subsequently moved its on-campus demonstrations to Admiralty to merge with ours. Likewise, Scholarism extended the HKFS citywide class boycott to secondary schools across the city. By the end of September our joined-up campaign had been staging daily sit-ins in Admiralty and the crowds surpassed 10,000.

It all came to a head on Friday 26 September. At a meeting between Scholarism and HKFS that afternoon, Nathan raised the concern that had been on everyone's mind for some time. 'The government has grown used to our banners and slogans: we need an escalation plan.' We were sitting in a circle behind a makeshift stage set up outside Civic Square, as it was now widely known, the very place where only two years ago I had delivered the speech of my life.

For weeks, on the pretext of public safety, Civic Square had been walled off with a 10-foot fence by the police, turning it into an intimidating fortress. My eyes were trained on the fence surrounding the square when an idea came to me. 'Tonight, we will reclaim Civic Square,' I said.

By sundown, nearly 10,000 citizens had gathered outside the government headquarters, as they had every night for the past two weeks. For hours, student activists took turns going up on stage to give rousing speeches demanding immediate government action to address our call for universal suffrage. At around 10.30pm, Nathan handed me the microphone and I called on the crowd to occupy Civic Square. Hundreds of demonstrators answered my call and rushed towards the fence and began climbing over into the square. Within minutes law enforcement arrived and responded with pepper spray. As I was clambering up the fence, from out of nowhere I was pulled down by the police and arrested on the spot. My glasses fell off my face and one of my trainers slipped off as I was carried by my arms and legs through the crowd by eight officers to a police vehicle. I couldn't see, I was kicking and screaming, and I had no idea where I was. The following day, Alex and Lester were arrested and taken into custody.

It was the first time I had been arrested – I was 17 years old. I was taken to a detention cell at the nearby police headquarters where I would spend the next 46 hours cut off from the outside world. The tiny cell had no windows and no furniture other than a bench. For two whole days I subsisted on tap water, inedible food and hardly any sleep. I couldn't see clearly without my glasses and, with only one shoe on, I had to limp as I was taken by the police from one room to the next for questioning. Numerous officers asked to take my statement and video my interrogation. I didn't know what to say and so I said nothing like the suspects do in crime movies. One of the guards sneered at me, 'You could have stayed in school but you chose to be a troublemaker. How much money did the Americans give you to do this?' I felt alone, helpless and incredibly guilty – I couldn't bring myself to think how worried my parents must feel not knowing what had happened to their son.

By the time I was released on bail, it was the early morning of 29 September. After a long shower at home, I turned on the television to see what I had missed. I learned that within 24 hours of my arrest, the number of protesters in Admiralty had surged to nearly 200,000. My jaw dropped when I saw powerful images of tear gas being deployed by riot police outside the government headquarters and unarmed demonstrators using nothing but umbrellas, rain ponchos, cling film and other household objects to fend off pepper spray and tear gas. 'This isn't the Hong Kong I know,' I thought to myself, shaking my head while the same footage looped on the 24-hour news channel.

As it turned out, the tear gas crackdown on 28 September was precisely the shock needed to jolt the adults into action. That same night, Professor Tai took to the stage in Admiralty and fired the shot that he should have fired weeks ago: 'Occupy Central officially begins!' he declared. That was the start of the 79-day occupy movement that the foreign press dubbed the 'Umbrella Revolution'.

The movement didn't happen in a social vacuum. The broken promise of electoral reform and subsequent police crackdown catalysed the unrest, but they didn't cause it. It took decades of pent-up frustration over income inequality, social immobility and other injustices for public anger to finally boil over. Martin Luther King Jr famously said that freedom is never voluntarily given by the oppressor and that it must be demanded by the oppressed. The Umbrella Movement was our way of making our demands heard.

The Umbrella Movement had not only put Hong Kong on the map, it had also brought out the absolute best in us. Everywhere we looked we saw citizens of all ages and professions handing out free food, water and medical supplies to protesters. Office workers showed up during their lunch breaks with cash donations; parents and retirees took shifts to manage the provisions; students sat for civic lessons that no class could teach them. The crowds at the three main sites – Admiralty, Mongkok and Causeway Bay – were ten times bigger than those at the anti-national education campaign. The movement's symbol, the yellow umbrella, captured both the humility and humanity of the non-violent protesters.

On 1 October, China's National Day, I called on everyone to bring tents and blankets in preparation for a prolonged struggle. Shortly after, a tent city emerged on Harcourt Road as protesters began to spend the night in the world's largest outdoor sleep-over. To support a self-sustaining community, amenities like supply stations and medical centres grew up like mushrooms. I was particularly inspired by a makeshift library made out of donated marquees and furniture, where row upon row of secondary school students, still wearing their uniforms, read and did homework under the supervision of volunteer tutors. 'You think that's impressive?' Agnes said to me. 'You should see the women's toilets. There are more skincare and cosmetic products than a department store. And they are all free!' The Western press called us the world's politest protesters, but in my mind we were also its most resourceful, creative and disciplined.

Still, defying Communist China was hardly fun and games. Although law enforcement had pulled back after being widely condemned for the tear-gas crackdown, within days hired thugs began to descend on protest sites. The situation was especially tense in Mongkok, a rough-and-tumble working-class enclave on the other side of the Victoria Harbour. Reports of physical altercations and even sexual assault began to appear on online news sites and caused unease among protesters over their personal safety. 'My mum just called and begged me to go home,' Agnes said. 'The mobs are trying to scare not only the protesters but also their parents!'

I woke up one morning in my tent on Tim Mei Avenue – the camping ground for Scholarism and the HKFS – soaked to the bone. Someone had sneaked into my tent while I was sleeping and cut open a water bottle. I ruled out the possibility that the act was a practical joke as nobody was in the mood for pranks.

Actual and threatened violence was coupled with verbal intimidation. Since the class boycott in September, accusations against student activists that they were receiving support from foreign governments had been swirling on Chinese state media. Pro-Beijing politicians in Hong Kong had gone on television and radio talk shows slinging mud against Alex, Nathan and me, trumping up conspiracy theories about our supposed connections to the CIA and MI6. Even ordinary citizens weren't immune from this so-called 'white terror'. For fear of upsetting the Chinese government, many companies forbade their staff from visiting protest zones or showing support for protesters on social media.

As the movement dragged on, cracks started to show within the loose coalition of student activists, the Occupy Central Trio and veteran pro-democracy politicians. The challenge of a largely leaderless movement – the Occupy Central Trio and student activists like myself were the faces of the movement but hardly its commanders – was that it was often difficult, if not impossible, to reach consensus among multiple stakeholders. Weeks could fly by without any decision being made or action being taken. Other than one televised debate between student activists and senior government officials in mid-October that resulted in no resolutions, neither side had moved an inch. Every day, protesters alternated between pushing back the police on the frontlines on the one hand, and doing homework and feeding themselves on the other. The protest sites became a bubble isolating the campers from the outside world. As the autumn chills set in, the movement continued to drift further and further away from its original goal of electoral reform.

Unhappy with the lack of progress, splinter groups calling themselves 'localists' began to coalesce. They were particularly irritated by the 'kumbaya' atmosphere in Admiralty and viewed our coalition with as much disdain as they did the government. Their attempts to break into government buildings were foiled by moderate protesters, which only deepened the discord. Just as the movement had polarised society into so-called 'yellow ribbons' (pro-occupy) and 'blue ribbons' (pro-police and government), the movement itself had been split into moderates and radicals. This played right into the hands of C.Y. Leung and his bosses in Beijing, who had hoped that a war of attrition would lead to division and infighting, which would in turn weaken and eventually destroy the movement.

That was exactly what happened. By late November, two months after the first shot of tear gas was fired, pro-Beijing trade groups succeeded in obtaining court orders to clear the protest zones on the grounds that campers were disrupting business activities. Bailiffs and removal crews began dismantling barricades and tents, often with the help of police officers and even thugs. Meanwhile, protesters didn't put up much of a fight, in part because they didn't want to defy the court, and in part because they themselves knew that the movement had to come to an end one way or another.

Still, some of us refused to give in just yet. On 25 November, Lester Shum and I were among several activists arrested in Mongkok for violating a court injunction to stay clear of the protest zone. While being carried off by the police, I shouted, 'Why are you doing this? We are fighting for you and your children too!' It was my second arrest. After spending 30 hours in a cell, I appeared in front of a judge and was charged with contempt of court.

In the coming days, one after another the protest sites began to fall to excavators and dump trucks. On 15 December, bailiffs cleared the last camping ground in Causeway Bay, bringing to an end 79 days of student-led street occupation. Even though the movement failed to deliver the political results it set out to achieve, the sweeping political awakening and civic engagement it brought about are indisputable. It was a paradigm shift that reshaped and continues to reshape the political landscape in Hong Kong, forever altering the relationship between state and citizens, the oppressor and the oppressed. Like the anti-national education campaign in 2012, the Umbrella Movement gave Hong Kongers, especially my generation, new confidence to challenge Communist China.

For me, the biggest takeaway from the movement had nothing to do with the question of success or failure. Even the harshest critic must acknowledge that it was the first popular uprising in Hong Kong and that we had neither a precedent to rely on nor a manual to follow. We did the best we could under the circumstances.

What mattered was what we would do with this transformative experience. The movement might have ended with the dismantling of the last protest site, but its legacy and spirit would live on. It had to, because our struggle was far from over. We needed to turn our frustration into resolve and motivation, and rebuild our trust and respect for each other.

Towards the end of the Occupy Wall Street campaign in the US in 2011, Slovenian philosopher Slavoj Žižek addressed the crowd in Zuccotti Park:

> All we need is patience. The only thing I'm afraid of is that we will someday just go home and then we will meet once a year, drinking beer, and nostalgically remember what a nice time we had here. Promise yourselves that this will not be the case. We know that people often desire something but do not really want it. Don't be afraid to really want what you desire.

We could use some of that fighting spirit right about now.

From Protesters to Politicians: The Founding of Demosistō

從抗爭者到政治人物: 香港眾志的創立

I was the student activist who organised the first series of mass protests in the lead-up to the Umbrella Movement and the first to be arrested for actions relating to it. My role as a teenage revolutionary captured the imagination of the international community and became a teachable moment for young activists the world over. Whereas the national education campaign made me a household name in Hong Kong, the Umbrella Movement turned me into a global poster boy for resistance against Communist China.

In October 2014, *Time* magazine put me on the cover of its international edition next to the headline THE FACE OF PROTEST. Within the same month, I penned my first *New York Times* op-ed, titled 'Taking Back Hong Kong's Future'. By then, every media outlet from every corner of the world had descended on the protest zone on Harcourt Road seeking an interview. I was named Young Person of the Year 2014 by *The Times* and ranked tenth on the World's 50 Greatest Leaders list by *Fortune* magazine. 'If I had known *Time* would use that picture on the cover, I would have got a haircut first,' I joked to my parents.

In truth, I never asked for fame, and I certainly didn't do what I did to get famous. As much as I was humbled and often embarrassed by the overwhelming media attention, I wanted to harness it and turn it into political capital for our pro-democracy struggle. At the first post-Umbrella Movement Scholarism meeting in 2015, I said to a roomful of our activists, 'Recent events have awakened many Hong Kongers and we must transform every ounce of that new energy into ballots.' The Umbrella Movement had taught us many important lessons; one of them was that fighting on the streets alone wasn't enough. We needed to change the political system from within, and we would do that by sending young people into the legislature. We had to beat the government at their own game.

To do that, we needed a new platform that would appeal not just to students – I'd recently graduated from secondary school and was in my first year at the Open University – but also adult voters who were motivated by a different set of priorities and concerns.

In April 2016, 17 months after the last protest zone was cleared, we relaunched Scholarism as Demosistō, a youth political party. The name is a portmanteau of the Greek for 'people' and the Latin for 'I stand'.

Our launch was hardly smooth: the press conference started several hours late due to a microphone malfunction and the live streaming on YouTube was interrupted so many times that the number of viewers dropped at one point from a few hundred to below 20. Localist groups that had been critical of us poked fun at our name (they said it sounded like 'Demolition') and accused us of selling out to become greasy politicians. But as Nathan reminded me after the rocky press conference, democracy is a process. Part of it is to win over those who don't like us. Remembering this made me feel a whole lot better.

As soon as Demosistō heaved into life, we plunged ourselves into preparing for the 2016 legislative council election, which was only five months away. There was unanimous support within the party for Nathan Law to run, not only because he was old enough to do so (Agnes and I were both one year shy of the minimum nomination age of 21), but also because he possessed the perfect blend of temperament, maturity and public profile we were looking for in our candidate.

We agreed to run on a platform of 'self-determination'. Under the Basic Law, the one-country, two systems framework – and thus the city's semi-autonomy – would expire in 2047. At that point we believed that Hong Kongers should be given a say to determine their own destiny by means of a referendum, in contrast to what happened during the Handover discussions when Britain and China negotiated our future without our participation.

Self-determination is an established concept in international law and is a recognised human right in the United Nations International Covenant on Civil and Political Rights. But it was a new concept in Hong Kong, and newer still to the pro-Beijing camp, which often falsely accused Demosistō of advocating independence or a colour revolution.

Election campaigns are backbreaking work for any political party, especially one with limited resources and an unhelpful student union image to shake. Unlike well-funded pro-Beijing parties, Demosistō relies solely on crowdfunding and public donations we collect from street rallies. Despite Nathan's boy-next-door appeal, his poll numbers hovered between a measly 1 to 3 per cent, even down to the final month. 'Why are our numbers so low?' we asked each other in disbelief every morning when we checked the news.

We learned the hard way that likeability doesn't always translate into electability, especially in Nathan's Hong Kong Island constituency, which consists mostly of well-educated professionals and affluent business elites – many of whom would almost always choose stability over freedom, profit over principle.

Compared to his opponents, Nathan's youth was a handicap and his leadership role in the Umbrella Movement was an original sin that turned off the protest-fatigued middle class. 'We've put every last cent we have into this campaign. If we lose, we'll be left with nothing,' Nathan said to me on the one-month countdown to Election Day.

In a superhero movie, the situation always looks the most hopeless before the good guys bounce back to save the day. In our case, we hit that point of inflexion less than three weeks before voters headed to the ballot box, when even friendly media outlets had all but written us off. After a series of stellar televised debate performances, Nathan's poll numbers started to rise. 'Yellow ribbon' celebrities like

Cantopop singers Anthony Wong and Denise Ho – who both figured prominently during the Umbrella Movement – offered their endorsement. Our outside-the-box marketing campaign using Instagram Live and virtual reality videos, managed by our chief media officer Ivan Lam, generated massive buzz on social media. In the final month before Election Day, Demosistians were on the streets every night past midnight handing out flyers and greeting voters. We were by far the hardest working political party in all of Hong Kong. 'You guys are working even harder than you did during Umbrella and that's saying a lot!' my mum would complain to me, as she had to put up with my late nights and endless strategising with fellow Demosistians. Still, we clenched our teeth and pressed ahead. The Chinese saying that diligence can make up for all shortcomings was still keeping me going.

Shortly after midnight on 4 September, after the voting booths had closed and the ballots counted, the results were in: Nathan won over 50,000 votes and, at 23 years old, became the youngest ever elected legislator in Asia. Every Demosistian at the counting station broke down in tears of joy, even Agnes who is the hardiest among us. Five gruelling months of crashing overnight at our messy campaign room and standing for days on street corners under the punishing sun had finally paid off. Wiping away my tears, I gave Nathan a bear hug and said, 'We did it!'

As the city's only student lawmaker, Nathan entered LegCo with a clear mandate. He would focus his efforts on education reform, youth employment and housing policy. As an avid video gamer and semi-professional e-sports commentator, Nathan also wanted to position Hong Kong as a hub for international video-game competitions, although privately he acknowledged that this was more a pet project than a priority on his political agenda.

Nathan's LegCo seat was barely warm when a constitutional crisis, dubbed 'Oathgate', blew up and eventually cost him his job. At the swearing-in ceremony in October, half-a-dozen freshmen legislators, including Nathan, strayed from their oath to make a political statement. When he swore his allegiance to China, Nathan modified his tone on the last word in the sentence, essentially transforming the pledge into a question.

It had been a tradition within the pro-democracy camp to use the oath-taking ceremony as a platform of protest by displaying props, shouting slogans or adding words to the prescribed oath. But this time, in an act of mission creep to rid the legislature of unwanted newcomers, the government brought legal action to remove the six lawmakers for their antics.

Beijing gladly played along and issued an interpretation of the Basic Law that concurred with the government's position. In a decision issued in November, the NPC Standing Committee ruled that if a legislator-elect 'deliberately fails to take an oath in the correct way, he or she cannot retake it and shall be disqualified from assuming public office'.

Oathgate dragged on for months as the legal action initiated by the government moved through the court systems. In July 2017, ten months after Nathan's history-making election win, the court ruled against the six lawmakers in deference to the NPC. If ousting them wasn't bad enough, the government then had the audacity to demand that they pay back their salaries and expense reimbursements. Even my mum couldn't hold back her anger. 'I voted for Nathan last September,' she said. 'Who gives the government the right to invalidate my vote? And what kind of employer makes their employees return their pay after firing them?'

Nathan hit rock bottom. Not only had he lost his hard-earned seat, he and I were about to begin our trial for our roles in the Umbrella Movement. 'I'm out of a job and may need to file for bankruptcy if I have to cough back my salary. On top of that, you and I may have to go to prison in a few weeks. How will Demosistō survive all of this?' he said, his eyes all cried out and unseeing. Though he was inconsolable, I tried to comfort him. 'If we survived the worst of the Umbrella Movement, we will survive this too.'

Local commentators often likened the situation of post-Handover Hong Kong to a boiling frog. According to the metaphor, if a frog is put in tepid water which is then slowly brought to a boil, it won't notice the gradual change in temperature and will unknowingly be cooked to death. Beijing has been chipping away at Hong Kong's freedoms for years without us noticing. Since 1997, the Chinese Communist Party has been co-opting local business leaders in Hong Kong to buy up and exert influence over print-media outlets, bookshop chains, publishing houses and radio and television stations. This so-called 'United Front' campaign was designed by Beijing to tighten control on Hong Kong society while quietly implementing its own political agenda in the increasingly embattled semi-autonomous territory.

But that was then and this is now. Since 2014 the Chinese leadership appears no longer in the mood for subtle, creeping changes. In late 2015, for instance, five members of a local publishing house known for printing political 'tell-all' books about the Chinese Communist Party, went missing. They are believed to have been abducted and detained by mainland Chinese agents.

Incidents like the bookseller abductions and Oathgate are signs that Beijing is losing its patience and increasingly resorting to blunt suppression. It has turned the heat way up and put a lid over the pot. The frog can kick and scream all it wants but there is no escape from the boiling water. That's how it feels to be a Hong Konger these days.

And the bad news keeps coming. They say revenge is a dish best served cold: the Department of Justice waited three years after the Umbrella Movement to charge Nathan, Alex and I with unlawful assembly in relation to the storming of Civic Square on that fateful September night in 2014. On 17 August 2017, two months before my 21st birthday, the court sentenced each of us to six to eight months in jail – by far my longest stint yet – and in doing so made us some of the first prisoners of conscience in the city's history.

Political imprisonment is an inevitable step on the path to democracy – it was the case in South Korea and Taiwan and it's now also the case in Hong Kong. The three of us know that first-hand. Far from silencing us, however, jail would only strengthen our resolve.

ACT II

INCARCERATION: LETTERS FROM PIK UK

獄中日記 YP4030　8月19日(星期六)

Facsimile of letter written by Joshua from Pik Uk Prison, 19 August 2017.

Letter from Pik Uk Correctional Institution

獄中的信

Day 2 – Friday, 18 August 2017

I've been closely following the news in the daily papers and on the communal radio. I'd like to thank my supporters for their good wishes.

Prison life isn't easy. But that's exactly why I wanted to write you this letter and many more in the coming months. I want to share with you the thoughts that have been churning inside my head and to let you know that I'm thinking of all of you on the other side of these prison walls.

The last words I said before I was taken away from the courtroom were 'Hong Kong people, carry on!' That sums up how I feel about our political struggle.

In March 2013, Professor Benny Tai announced his Occupy Central campaign. His goal was to demand universal suffrage by paralysing our financial district – the most effective way to make our government listen. Professor Tai had warned us that imprisonment would be the final and inevitable step in a civil disobedience campaign.

Since Occupy Central – and the Umbrella Movement that succeeded it – ended without achieving its stated goal, Hong Kong has entered one of its most challenging chapters. Civil society has been stuck in a rut, not knowing whether or how to proceed. Protesters coming out of a failed movement are overcome with disillusionment and powerlessness. Some of them have decided to leave politics altogether, others, like myself, have ended up in prison.

The appeal sentencing of myself and my fellow Umbrella leaders Nathan Law and Alex Chow by the Court of Appeal has dealt yet another devastating blow to the morale of pro-democracy activists. So too has the conviction of the so-called 'NNT Thirteen' – 13 activists who clashed with police during a protest against a controversial government development project in the north-eastern New Territories near the Chinese border.

Even though it feels like we have hit rock bottom, we need to stay true to our cause. We must. To my friends who have decided to walk away from politics, I hope my being here and writing you this letter will convince you to reconsider. If not, our sacrifices – the loss of freedom by all 16 of us – will have been for nothing.

I want to tell you about everything that has happened to me at Pik Uk since my incarceration 36 hours ago. I'm glad to report that so far I haven't experienced any mistreatment by prison authorities. I hope it will stay this way until the day I walk out of this place. Being a new inmate, I'm required to go through a ten-day orientation. My actual prison routine won't start for a few days and I haven't got the faintest idea what's in store for me and whether I can handle it. Things do seem stricter than I expected from a juvenile prison. For instance, all inmates must learn military-style drill commands and march early every morning. It makes me wonder if Nathan and Alex are required to do the same in their adult prisons.

To my surprise, the meals aren't so bad – far better than what they fed us during our detention at the police station. That being said, I miss my mum's hand-brewed milk tea terribly, and the chicken hotpot at the street-food restaurant where my friends and I always hang out at. That's the first place I'll visit as soon as I'm out of here.

There are two things I'm going to really struggle to get used to here: the monotony and the absolute authority of those in charge. I need to make sure I don't let either of these dull my critical thinking or stop me from challenging the authorities the way I've always done. I plan to use my 'downtime' to figure out the way forward and find better ways to work with the rest of civil society to make full democracy a reality. I know I have to keep my mind occupied in prison or else prison will occupy my mind instead.

Tomorrow morning I'll speak to my welfare officer and request a subscription to the liberal *Ming Pao* and *Apple Daily* – the only two credible broadsheet newspapers left in Hong Kong – to stay informed of what's happening in the outside world. I'll also request a radio to listen to the morning and evening phone-in radio programmes. Without these things, time will crawl and life behind bars will be all the more unbearable.

That said, whatever I'm going through is nothing compared to the false imprisonment of Liu Xiaobo in mainland China or the illegal detention of the bookseller Lam Wing-kee.* These men are an

---

* Liu Xiaobo, a Chinese human rights activist and winner of the 2010 Nobel Peace Prize, was sentenced to 11 years in prison for co-authoring a manifesto calling for political pluralism in China. He died from liver cancer in 2017 while incarcerated. Lam Wing-kee was one of the five Causeway

inspiration and a reminder that I need all the inner strength I can muster to get through the next six months. As long as I continue to read and write I will be able to keep my mind free. The great Mahatma Gandhi once said: 'You can chain me, you can torture me, you can even destroy this body, but you will never imprison my mind.' Gandhi's words have now taken on much more personal meaning for me.

At the moment, my biggest worry is the state of my political party. Ever since Nathan and I co-founded Demosistō in April 2016 we've suffered a series of significant setbacks. Four weeks ago, Nathan lost his hard-won seat at the Legislative Council (LegCo) after he and five other members were disqualified on the grounds that they had failed to properly recite their oaths during the swearing-in ceremony. The so-called 'Oathgate' was a ploy by the ruling elite to remove pro-democracy lawmakers from the legislature and redraw the balance of power in local politics.

Nathan's disqualification has dealt a serious blow to Demosistō. Not only has it cost us our only seat in LegCo, but the loss of Nathan's lawmaker

---

Bay Books booksellers abducted by Chinese authorities for publishing exposés about the Communist leadership (*see page 63–4*).

salary means that our party has lost its sole source of steady income. We were given a week to pack up and vacate the LegCo Building. Nathan and his staff – all of whom are Demosistō members – became instantly unemployed.

Then, within the same week, three core party members including myself, Nathan and Ivan Lam, all went to jail. Nathan and I were each sentenced to six months over the storming of Civic Square two days before the eruption of the Umbrella Movement, and Ivan was one of the NNT Thirteen. In the meantime, Derek Lam, another core member, will go to trial this week for his role in another protest outside the Hong Kong Liaison Office – the de facto Chinese embassy in Hong Kong and the mastermind behind many controversial policies put forward by our government.

Nearly everyone at Demosistō is now out of a job and must find ways to keep the party afloat, while half of our executive committee is behind bars, or will be in the coming weeks. I sometimes joke that soon there will be enough of us in prison to have quorum for a committee meeting.

I can't think of another political party in Hong Kong that has gone through as many ups and downs as Demosistō has in the last 15 months. It must be disheartening and disorienting for party members, especially young graduates who have recently joined us. But as much as we moan about everything we've been through, I believe our trials and tribulations are precisely what we need to grow and prosper. As they say, 'only through fire is a strong sword forged'. Indeed, all the speed bumps we've gone over have only made us stronger and more prepared for even bigger challenges that lie ahead. After all, if we can get through the anti-national education campaign and the Umbrella Movement, we can survive anything.

And my message to the pro-Beijing camp? Don't celebrate too soon. Demosistō will use everything we've got to win back Nathan's seat in the upcoming by-elections. What we lack in financial resources, we more than make up for in determination. Hong Kong voters don't suffer fools gladly. They see right through your tricks and will send one of us right back into LegCo.

I will end by sharing with you my state of mind during the sentence hearing yesterday. Walking into the High Court, I was moved beyond words by the hundreds of supporters who had come out to cheer us on. Inside the courtroom, there was a gathering of like-minded friends who have stood by us at every step of the way through our legal battles. When the judges handed down our sentences, some of those friends broke into tears, others chanted slogans. People clapped their hands and stomped their feet – it got so loud that the judge pounded his gavel and ordered silence in court. I knew then that I was not, and would never be, alone on this journey.

I began my journey in 2012 when I led the campaign against the national education curriculum. It's been a tumultuous five years. I didn't shed a single tear when the judge announced my sentence, not because I was brave but because I wanted my supporters to embrace my loss of freedom as a necessary step on our collective path to democracy. To quote J.K. Rowling: 'What's coming will come and we'll meet it when it does.'

Hong Kong is at a crossroads. The ruling regime will stop at nothing to silence dissent. They have relentlessly pursued and will continue to pursue whomever they consider a threat to their grip on power. For those who dare to stand up to them, the only way forward is together. And tonight, alone in my cell, I ask you to keep your chin up and use your tears, anger and frustration as motivation to charge ahead.

Hong Kong people, carry on!

The Situation Outside Is More Dire Than the One Inside

監倉外的形勢比監倉內更嚴峻

Day 3 – Saturday, 19 August 2017

I've been assigned a two-person cell. My cellmate seems friendly enough, although we didn't have a chance to say much to each other before the lights went out last night.

Conditions in a juvenile prison cell aren't as bad as I thought. Even though summer is in full swing the air circulation is acceptable and the heat is tolerable. So far the biggest source of discomfort is perhaps the bed. In fact, calling it a bed is an overstatement. It's nothing more than a wooden plank with no mattress. But, then again, if I could spend 79 nights sleeping on a highway during the Umbrella Movement I'm sure I can get used to this too.

Prison is all about discipline and following orders. Every morning we have to get up at 6am sharp and every night the lights go out at 10pm.

Even when I was campaigning for Nathan in his 2016 bid for LegCo I didn't have to get up that early. I guess I'm not a morning person.

Twice a day, the news is broadcast on the PA system. This morning I was woken up by a story about Chris Patten, the last Governor of Hong Kong. 'At a public appearance,' the news presenter said, 'Mr Patten told reporters that he was heartened by the sacrifices made by Joshua Wong, Alex Chow and Nathan Law, and that he believed these three names will be carved into history . . .' It felt surreal to hear my name mentioned in this way in front of other inmates. The reality that I'm a convicted criminal has finally sunk in.

As far as I understand it, inmates are permitted to subscribe to their own newspapers. Other than that, there are so-called 'communal papers' that we can borrow and read for free. To my dismay (although I shouldn't be surprised), most of them are pro-Beijing mouthpieces like *Wen Wei Po*, *Ta Kung Pao* and *Sing Tao Daily*.

Luckily, I managed to borrow a copy of *Apple Daily* from another inmate. That's how I learned about the outpouring of public support for the 'Umbrella Trio' of me, Alex and Nathan and the wall-to-wall coverage of our imprisonment by the foreign press.

I hope what happened to the three of us will send a clear message to the international community: the rule of law in Hong Kong is crumbling and gradually turning into a 'rule *by* law'. Strict compliance now trumps personal liberty and peaceful calls for democracy. Our government's relentless pursuit of political activists through the criminal justice system not only violates freedom of expression, it also blurs the lines that separate the three branches of government – executive, legislative and judicial – and ultimately erodes our trust in the city's independent judiciary.

In many ways, the situation on the other side of these prison walls is far more dire than it is inside. I count on everyone who loves and cares about Hong Kong, whether they live here or abroad, to continue the fight in my absence. They say what doesn't kill us makes us stronger. Once we get through this round of political prosecution, we'll pick ourselves up and be more united than ever.

As soon as I finish my orientation I'll be assigned to an inmate work group. Until then I'll be doing simple tasks like sweeping the canteen floor, folding laundry and shining shoes. In the coming months I'll write frequently. I'll look after myself and keep my friends and family in my thoughts.

Looking for Answers in Juvenile Prison

在少年監獄尋找答案

Day 4 – Sunday, 20 August 2017

Prison life follows a strict timetable. Sunday is our 'day off', when inmates get to hang out at the canteen for the entire day between seven in the morning and seven in the evening.

'Hanging out' would be torturous if it wasn't for the TV. For most inmates, one of the highlights on Sunday is watching soap-opera reruns on TVB (Television Broadcasts Limited, the only free-to-air television network in Hong Kong) in the afternoon. Never mind that TVB is hugely unpopular because of its near-monopoly on broadcasting and its pro-Beijing, pro-government bias in everything it airs, from news reporting to programme selection. In prison, I suppose some entertainment is better than no entertainment.

I was happy to see fellow Umbrella Movement student leader Lester Shum appear live on TVB's current affairs programme *On the Record* talking about political imprisonment. There was also news coverage of another Sunday afternoon mass protest in support of the Umbrella Trio. Other than watching television, I killed time by reading my borrowed copy of yesterday's *Apple Daily* cover to cover.

Apart from the mattressless bed, the hardest thing (pun intended) to get used to here is being cut off from the outside world. It's one thing to have zero access to social media like Facebook and Twitter, but quite another to have zero conversations with friends. So I savour every opportunity to feel a sense of connection with the outside world, whether it's through the television, the radio or newspapers.

The most exciting thing that happened today was when I saw Ivan Lam mentioned on the evening news. The presenter read excerpts from a letter Ivan had written from his prison cell. Even though we were put in different prisons (Correctional Services always separates prisoners who know each other to avoid organised actions in prison), hearing Ivan's words instantly made me feel like he was here sitting next to me.

Over the last couple of days I've made a few friends at Pik Uk. Today I chatted with a fellow young prisoner of conscience, Mak Tze-hei. In March 2017, when he was 20 years old, Tze-hei was convicted of rioting for his role in the 2016 Mongkok Chinese New Year civil unrest* and sentenced to two years in prison. What I quickly realised was that even though our political views are different (he's a pro-independence firebrand and I'm not), we can still have a free and meaningful exchange of ideas. After all, we've both ended up behind bars for our political beliefs. Most importantly, we share the same love for our city.

Meeting Tze-hei reminded me of the many forgotten activists who have received neither the fame nor the public support that myself, Nathan and Alex enjoy and sometimes take for granted. Not being a household name makes it much harder for them to get funding to receive the best legal representation. We need to draw attention to the fact that there are scores of unsung heroes, from those who took part

---

* Nicknamed the 'Fish-ball Revolution' by the local press, on Chinese New Year's Eve in February 2016, hundreds of protesters, most of them localists who advocated Hong Kong independence, clashed with riot police after the government cracked down on unlicensed but popular food vendors in Mongkok (many of whom sold fish-balls). Scores of protesters were charged with rioting.

in the Mongkok unrest to those in the NNT Thirteen, who are struggling in silence.

On the subject of forgotten activists, today I also met a number of protesters who had taken part in the Umbrella Movement and the anti-national education demonstrations. I haven't yet had the chance to find out how they ended up in jail, but I recognised their faces from protests over the years.

The majority of the inmates – roughly 70 per cent by my estimate – are convicted on drug-related charges, some of them users, others dealing. Society labels them criminals and *fai ching* (literally 'useless youths' in Cantonese). Few realise that these young people are only symptoms of what has gone wrong with our education and social systems and not the cause. No one is born a criminal.

Mostly I find my fellow inmates genuine and warm. And there is much I can learn from them. In eight weeks' time, I'll turn 21 and be transferred to an adult prison in a different part of town. Until then I'll make a conscious effort to get to know them and hear their stories.

It all brings into sharp focus the hypocrisy of our governing elites. Political leaders like Chief Executive Carrie Lam and Chief Secretary Matthew Cheung are always talking about how much effort they've put into 'engaging the youth' of Hong Kong.

These are the same people who disqualified Nathan and other young lawmakers from LegCo, in doing so nullifying the votes of tens of thousands of young voters. They went on to prosecute youth protesters and throw them in prison. Not once has a single government officer sat down with the activists to try to negotiate a way out of the political impasse.

Earlier today, a young inmate told me that he had met Nathan on a lawmaker's prison visit. In Hong Kong, LegCo members and Justices of the Peace (JPs) – a title of honour bestowed by the government on community leaders – are among the privileged few who can visit any prisoner whenever they want. Before 'Oathgate' took away his seat, Nathan exercised that right and visited a number of prisons, including Pik Uk. The irony that Nathan himself is now behind bars isn't lost on any of us.

Closing Arguments at My Contempt of Court Hearing

旺角清場被捕結案陳詞

Day 8 – Thursday, 24 August 2017

This morning I left Pik Uk to attend the final hearing of my contempt of court case. It was good to have a break from the daily monotony of life in the facility and see a few familiar faces – even if it was only in the courtroom.

I was one of 20 activists charged with contempt after we violated a court injunction to stay clear of the protest zone in Mongkok during the final days of the Umbrella Movement. My lawyers advised me to plead guilty to mitigate my sentence; three to six months seems to be the consensus among them.

With good conduct, the six-month sentence I'm currently serving for storming Civic Square would be shortened by a third to four months, meaning I could be released as early as 17 December were it not for the contempt case. However, the presiding judge will probably combine the two sentences and keep me in detention for a few more months. In all likelihood I'll remain in prison until the end of spring next year. I'm mentally preparing myself for the possibility that I'll be spending both Christmas and Chinese New Year behind bars.

I'm quick to remind myself that other activists have received much harsher sentences than mine. The NNT Thirteen were originally handed community-service orders for storming a LegCo committee meeting in June 2014 before being sentenced to eight to thirteen months in prison after the Department of Justice appealed for harsher punishments. Among them were Ivan and fellow activist Raphael Wong. Raphael is vice chairman of a pro-democracy party called the League of Social Democrats (LSD). The heavy sentences they received set a dangerous precedent for future sentencing of anti-government protesters, which will in turn have a chilling effect on our freedom of assembly in Hong Kong.

I saw Raphael in the courtroom today. He was involved in the same Mongkok contempt of court case. After the hearing, we briefly discussed our appeal strategies with our lawyers should the court rule against us. Raphael was in good spirits as always, despite the triple threat he faces: the

Mongkok contempt trial, the 13-month NNT sentence and, above all, public nuisance charges for his leadership role in the Umbrella Movement.

The whole thing makes me feel a little embarrassed about the enormous media attention that Alex, Nathan and I received last week. Local newspapers plastered my picture on their front pages the day after I was sent to prison. The reality is that countless others are being tried or are about to be tried in Hong Kong for their activism work. Many of them face much harsher prison terms than we do.

On the subject of newspapers, I can't emphasise enough how hard life is without access to news of current events. I'm still trying to get my hands on yesterday's and today's issues of *Ming Pao* and *Apple Daily*, which means I'm at least two days behind on the news. This will remain a daily struggle until my prison subscription begins. I never thought I could crave reading the papers this much – the simple joy of bringing them back to my cell and devouring the local politics section and every opinion column!

I'm used to being constantly on my smartphone, thumbing rapid-fire text messages to friends, shooting off comments to the press and taking care of party matters big and small. Being phoneless is like having my limbs cut off or an itch I can't scratch. I guess I need to learn to let go and get better at delegating party responsibilities to my colleagues. Perhaps I may even learn to enjoy downtime – it seems unlikely but I'll at least try.

I was taken back to Pik Uk in a caged vehicle shortly after lunch. I was told that every inmate is required to take a urine test each time he leaves the prison premises. Until the urine test is cleared we are put in a separate ward away from other inmates. They call it the 'quarantine'.

The next time I leave Pik Uk will be for the sentencing hearing of my contempt case in September, and perhaps again in October if I file an appeal for that sentence. In the meantime, I look forward to receiving letters from loved ones and my first friends-and-family visit this Saturday. The anticipation will keep my spirits up for a few days.

Lawmaker's Visit

議員探訪

_____

Day 9 – Friday, 25 August 2017

LegCo member Shiu Ka-chun came to see me this morning.

Nicknamed 'Bottle',* Shiu is a veteran social worker. He was elected to LegCo in 2016 in the same election in which Nathan won his seat, although the two represented different constituencies. Bottle didn't participate in Oathgate and kept his seat on the council.

Bottle can drop in for a visit any time he wants because of the special privilege enjoyed by lawmakers and Justices of the Peace (_see page 83_). During the one-hour visitation, Bottle discussed his impending public nuisance trial for his leadership

_____

* His given name 'Chun' and the word for bottle sound the same in Cantonese.

role in the Umbrella Movement, debriefed me on various meetings within the pan-democratic camp and went through the pan-dem's strategy for the by-elections, in which they hoped to fill the half-dozen seats left empty after Oathgate.

Among the pan-dem lawmakers, Bottle has been the one who pays the most attention to juvenile delinquency. He's known to regularly visit youth prisons like Pik Uk. As expected, he asked me how I was coping behind bars and whether I had experienced any abuse by prison staff. I didn't have anything negative to report because in truth I've been treated fairly well. The other inmates have been friendly towards me and the guards' attitudes have been decent overall. 'If I even sensed a hint of animosity,' I joked to Bottle, 'you bet I would be recording it in my journal!' Joking aside, I know at the back of my mind that we all have Bottle to thank. If it weren't for his tireless efforts over the years to improve prison conditions and raise awareness about prisoner abuse, things could be far worse at Pik Uk.

I met Bottle six years ago, when I was a 14-year-old secondary school student and he a social worker and radio presenter. He later hosted some of my anti-national education rallies. In the documentary Netflix produced about me, *Joshua: Teenager vs*

Superpower, there is a scene in which I appear on Bottle's live radio show and he asks me whether I have a girlfriend. 'My mum told me it's too early for me to be dating,' I reply, and everyone in the studio bursts out laughing. It was a moment of levity. Neither of us would have guessed at the time that five years later we would be talking to each other on different sides of a glass partition.

After Bottle left, I had a bit of time to kill. Due to my quarantine I wasn't allowed to be with the other inmates in the canteen and so I went back to my room for an afternoon nap on that infernal mattressless bed. I can't remember the last time I took an afternoon nap. Once my urine test was cleared, I was told to join the cohort in the common areas. On my way to the main yard I was intercepted by two plainclothes staff who said they wanted me to participate in an inmate survey.

Most of the questions in the survey were pretty mundane:

What crime have you been convicted of?
Do you use drugs?
Are you affiliated with the Triads (organised crime groups)?

Then the questions get more personal:

Are you confident you can find work after your
    release?
Do you consider yourself employable?
Is your family important to you?
Do you have friends you can trust?
Are you in control of your moods and emotions?
Do you have violent tendencies?

I knew that based on the answers to these yes/no
questions I would be assigned to various rehabilitation courses and workshops. I tried not to be cynical
about the methodology because I know that no system is perfect, and I'm sure inmates do benefit from
some of the curriculum. I just can't help but wonder
if the approach is a touch too algorithmic. I also
don't see how they can expect a one-size-fits-all
survey to help them figure out how to re-educate
prisoners of all shapes and sizes. The survey is particularly irrelevant to prisoners of conscience like me
who don't believe they have done anything wrong,
much less wish to repent.

It's Been a While Since I Shook Someone's Hand

久違了的握手

Day 10 – Saturday, 26 August 2017

Time crawls in prison, but the days can also slip through your fingers without you noticing.

It's been ten days since I arrived in Pik Uk, which means my orientation is about to end. Next Monday I'll officially join the other 'graduates' in the group routine, including those dreaded morning marches. I'll also be required to master the intricate art of blanket folding. The task sounds simple but it's tricky for me. During the orientation I barely met the guards' standards even with help from my cellmate. From Monday I'll have to do it on my own and I'm not looking forward to getting an earful from the guards over how clumsy and useless I am.

Beginning next week, my day will be divided into two halves: classes in the morning and work in the afternoon. There are four types of classes depending on the inmate's level of education:

Class 1 – Secondary Five (Year 11)
Class 2 – Secondary Three (Year 9)
Class 3 – Secondary Two (Year 8)
Class 4 – Secondary One (Year 7)

I'm praying to God that the staff know I'm a second-year university student and will assign me to Class 1. Yesterday I overheard that they might put me in Class 3 for some reason and I panicked. I can't imagine how painful it would be to sit through a bunch of Year 9-level classes morning after morning!

Today, one of my lawyers, Bond Ng, came for a visit. We talked about the pending charges filed against at least four Demosistō core members – myself (contempt of court), Nathan (unlawful assembly), Ivan (unlawful assembly) and Derek (public nuisance). Our calendar is now filled with trials, bail hearings, sentencing, appeals and yet more appeals. The seemingly endless cycle of the criminal justice system keeps me up at night and occupies my mind at every meal. It's surreal that young people like us need to worry about repeatedly being sent to prison, and yet this is the reality that faces us.

Bond and I also discussed the recent typhoon I'd read about in the paper. He told me the winds were so powerful that bricks were seen flying through the air. One of the affected areas was the waterfront along South Horizons where I live with my parents. I really miss my neighbourhood and the people there.

Even though Pik Uk is a relatively civilised prison, it isn't a happy place. Throughout the day there's a lot of yelling – mostly the guards shouting commands at inmates or reprimanding them for something or other – so when Bond shook my hand on his way out, it felt strangely out of place. Since I arrived here, I have not shaken anyone's hand.

I am not treated as an equal by the prison authorities. As a prisoner, I operate in absolute sub-ordination. I must comply with every command without question and address every officer with the honorific 'Sir'. For example, if a guard stops me in my tracks because he wants to speak with me I must put whatever personal belongings I'm carrying – my toothbrush, face towel, books, etc. – on the floor before answering his questions without making dir-ect eye contact.

I read a news story a couple of days ago about Paul Shieh, a respected barrister and former chairman of the Hong Kong Bar Association, who caused an uproar after commenting on a popular radio programme about the recent legal troubles facing political activists. Shieh remarked that Professor Benny Tai and his fellow Occupy Central leaders deserved to go to prison, saying that 'they got what they asked for' when they organised a civil obedience movement. Both Bottle and Bond asked me what I thought of the controversial comment. I told them that the mindset of Shieh and all the other so-called 'social elites' in Hong Kong is what tears our society apart. Call it nepotism or plutocracy, the system always favours the upper rungs and leaves the powerless out in the cold. Just like it does here in Pik Uk.

The most coveted newspaper here is the *Oriental Daily News*. It's pro-Beijing but it has a daily centrefold that's popular among the men. Meanwhile, the only news broadcast on the communal television is from TVB, not a channel I would normally watch. I now appreciate what it's like to be exposed to biased news sources without even realising it. And if nobody realises it, the lemmings will head to the cliff without knowing that there is another way. Luckily for me, because everyone goes straight for the *Oriental Daily*, no one ever touches the shared copy of *Ming Pao*, and every morning my thoughtful cellmate Ah Sun brings it over without me even asking.

Speaking of bias, a prison supervisor approached me this afternoon for a chat over recent news events. He began by declaring himself to be an 'independent', and that he's neither a 'yellow ribbon' (a supporter of the Umbrella Movement) nor a 'blue ribbon' (a supporter of the government and the police). He asked me whether I had any regrets about entering politics and ending up behind bars, before launching into a 30-minute monologue sharing his views on my conviction and the government's appeal against my sentence. His point – if there was one – was similar to what Paul Shieh had said about Professor Tai: we all got what we asked for.

I didn't challenge him, mainly out of self-preservation, but also because I knew nothing I said would ever change his mind. So I just smiled and slowly walked away.

A Six-pronged Plan of Resistance

抵抗威權的六件事

Day 11 – Sunday, 27 August 2017 (Part 1)

Typhoon signal 8 is up. All outdoor activities have been cancelled.

My cellmate and I are cooped up in our 70-square-foot double cell, which gives me plenty of time to compose a longer journal entry. I'm dyslexic – hence the many typos and wrong use of characters – and my handwriting is hopeless. I must apologise in advance to the poor soul who is transcribing my manuscript.

A lot has happened in the past week. From what I read in the paper, last Sunday activists staged a massive street rally – the largest since the Umbrella Movement – in support of Alex, Nathan and me. The huge turnout was largely down to the fact that until recently Hong Kong never had any political prisoners. This new development has rattled a lot of people, especially parents who worry that their children may get locked up too if they participate in politics.

Also this week, Reuters published an exposé suggesting that Justice Secretary Rimsky Yuen had overruled an internal decision not to appeal the sentencing of various convicted activists, including mine. Meanwhile, the Court of Final Appeal refused to hear the appeal filed by two of the six lawmakers who were unseated by Oathgate. And Paul Shieh's callous remarks about Professor Tai receiving his just desserts topped it all off.

Hong Kong is gradually becoming an autocracy. At this critical juncture, pro-democracy activists must reassess the situation and devise a more effective plan of resistance going forward. Here are six ideas for how we can do that.

1. Point out the elephant in the courtroom

Under common law principles, judges are bound by precedents to ensure consistency and fairness. In the case of unlawful assembly, which is a crime under the Public Order Ordinance, the harshest sentence the court has handed out since the Handover is six months (given to anti-government budget protesters who occupied a street in the financial district and clashed with police). Yet the NNT Thirteen are serving sentences ranging from eight to thirteen months. Likewise, Nathan, Alex and myself received six to eight months for our roles in the storming of Civic Square.

In recent judgments, judges have stressed the need to levy heavy sentences as a 'deterrent' against an 'unhealthy trend' of civil unrest. It seems to me that judges are increasingly injecting ideology into their sentencing decisions, as they appear to be more and more willing to use the bench to express their own political views. Although judges are quick to declare political neutrality, the fact that they characterise youth activism as an 'unhealthy' development that ought to be curbed is ample evidence that some judges are anything but neutral.

Even the Public Order Ordinance itself is highly problematic. The law was hastily passed by the Provisional LegCo in Shenzhen, China, during the transitional period following the Handover. The legislative process was shoddy, opaque and involved no public consultation. Disappointingly, judges are now applying and interpreting the ordinance as if it were a robust and ironclad law just like any other. They give no regard to the ordinance's troubled genesis and lack of legitimacy.

Unlawful assembly isn't the only crime in the Public Order Ordinance that the government has used to charge protesters with. Rioting is another frequently used arrow in the ordinance's quiver, and it carries much harsher sentences. Case in point: dozens of protesters in the 2016 Mongkok Chinese New Year civil unrest were charged with rioting. Several of them, including Edward Leung, founder of Hong Kong Indigenous,* received six-year sentences.

In addition to overzealous judges and bad laws, activists have to wrestle with the Department of Justice, which has virtually limitless resources – funded by taxpayers no less – to selectively prosecute individuals long considered a thorn in the government's side. The DOJ appeals court decisions and sentences that aren't to their liking and won't stop until they get the outcome they want. By contrast, few defendants have the financial resources to battle the government in the appellate process and many cut their losses and give up.

Local business elites always rush to defend the city's declining rule of law. They hold up our independent judiciary as a 'bedrock of Hong Kong's

---

* A localist group founded in 2015. More radical than Demosistō, Hong Kong Indigenous advocate a militant approach to civil disobedience. Their political goals include full secession from mainland China.

prosperity' and turn a blind eye to the reality that the criminal justice system is increasingly used as a political tool to silence dissent. They look the other way as one activist after another is sent to prison, as judges hand out sentences that are each longer than the last.

To continue our fight for full democracy, Hong Kongers must wake up to the fact that neither our rule of law nor our independent judiciary is adequate in safeguarding our fundamental rights. The first step to tackling any problem is to admit that there is one: our government has turned the courtroom into an uneven battlefield.

2. Unite the opposition

Just because we fight for the same cause doesn't mean that we always see eye to eye. Indeed, many within the moderate pan-democratic camp have misgivings about the approach adopted by more radical groups, such as the NNT Thirteen who stormed a LegCo committee meeting and clashed violently with the police.

Likewise, localist groups are tired of mass marches and slogans. They blame the moderates for the lack of progress despite decades of non-violent campaigns. The result is constant bickering and finger pointing within the opposition, which plays into the hands of the authorities and allows them to divide and conquer.

Differences in tactics notwithstanding, we're all motivated by the same pro-democracy demands. Dozens of activists across the political spectrum have ended up in jail, and many more will do so in the coming months. We must honour them by setting aside our differences and picking up where they left off.

One of the best ways to demonstrate that we can all work together is to set up a fund and solicit donations to provide legal assistance to the accused, regardless of their ideology, and provide counselling and other support to the affected families.

3. Defend our LegCo foothold

As we continue to take our fight to the streets, we must also make ourselves heard on the legislative floor. The first step to defending our foothold in LegCo is to fill the seats left empty by the six disqualified opposition lawmakers.

At this moment, it's looking increasingly likely that localist candidates (such as those from Hong Kong Indigenous) and candidates who advocate self-determination (such as those from Demosistō) will be barred from running in the by-elections. Earlier this year, Edward Leung was denied his right to run despite having signed a pledge of allegiance to the Basic Law.

Even so, walking away is not an option. Taking a page from the pro-democracy movements in Taiwan and Singapore, we know that giving up on the legislature altogether will only make things worse, not least by allowing the government to pass bad laws with impunity. No matter how unlevel the playing field is, LegCo, like most legislatures around the world, remains an important check and balance on those in power.

As for who should be nominated to fill the six empty seats, I propose two simple selection criteria. First, the candidates must enjoy broad support from the opposition camp and adequately represent the political platforms of the respective lawmakers they are to replace. Second, they must possess the charisma to articulate our political demands and galvanise the public to support our cause.

These by-elections are more than a succession plan; they are a powerful symbol of resistance. Sending pro-democratic representatives back to the legislative chamber will deliver a powerful message to the ruling elites: every legislator they've ousted will be replaced by someone just like him or her.

They can't disqualify us all.

4. Keep faith in non-violent protests

Ever since the Umbrella Movement ended in 2014 without making any tangible political gains, civil society has struggled to cope with the perceived failure. Young people emerging from the movement were left with a deep sense of powerlessness and protest fatigue. Many began to dismiss non-violent protest as a potential means to our political ends.

Meanwhile, activists who advocate for more radical forms of resistance are being crushed under the full force of the law. What happened to the likes of Edward Leung has made young people think twice before hurling another brick at the police.

The pro-democracy movement seems to have stalled. Neither peaceful nor aggressive tactics have brought us closer to where we want to go. Whatever actions we've pursued so far have done little to make our government or Beijing budge.

But isn't that all the more reason for the non-violent camp and the localist groups to join forces? From here on in, let's make every street march a rallying cry to support those who are imprisoned or about to be imprisoned – from non-violence advocates like Professor Tai to use-any-means-necessary localists like Edward Leung. Activists of all stripes have reasons to take to the streets, if not to demand universal suffrage then to express their outrage over political imprisonment, a beast that knows no ideological boundaries.

5.   Cover for the imprisoned

Many supporters have asked me what they can do, aside from writing letters and sharing our news on social media, to help those activists who are behind bars. I always offer the same answer: donate your time.

Other than Alex, Nathan and me, the so-called NNT Thirteen are also doing time in prison. The media call us the '13 plus 3'. To show your solidarity with us, I encourage you to volunteer 16 hours of your time every month – that's one hour for each jailed activist – to do whatever community work speaks to you.

Here are some ideas of what you can do with those 16 hours: hand out political flyers on the streets; man a street stall on a Sunday march; share your views at a community forum; and tell your friends and family to register to vote. You can even join an election campaign for a pro-democracy candidate.

The success of any political movement relies on grassroots efforts at neighbourhood level. Those efforts begin with you. Once I'm out of prison and back on the streets I hope to see you hard at work and making a difference, behind a megaphone or at the front of a crowd.

6. Be prepared to step up

In the late 1970s, the pro-democracy movement in Taiwan took a bloody, tragic turn. Brutal crackdowns on protesters by the autocratic regime culminated in the so-called 'Formosa Incident'; martial law was declared, protest leaders were arrested, tortured and executed, and many more were tried and given heavy sentences.

Hong Kong has been spared the kind of bloodshed witnessed in Taiwan and neighbouring countries – at least for now. But the price we must pay for demanding political change is expected to rise. Before the 16 of us were sent to prison, we all operated on the assumption that an unlawful assembly conviction would result in no more than a community-service sentence. See how quickly that assumption was disproved.

In Taiwan, after the Formosa Incident a large number of activists were locked up and barred from politics. In response, their spouses, friends and even defence lawyers were called upon to run for election in their place.

Activists in Hong Kong are expected to suffer similar fates in the foreseeable future. Before long, you too may be asked to step up to take their place. When that day comes, I hope you are ready.

Fall In, the Chief Officer Is Here

高層殺到，立正站好

Day 11 – Sunday, 27 August 2017 (Part 2)

Like every other day since I arrived, a handful of inmates and I spent most of today sweeping the 2,000-square-foot canteen. We clean after every breakfast, lunch and dinner.

Most 20-somethings in Hong Kong live with their parents and many middle-class households have a live-in maid. My family is no exception. I've never cleaned this much in my life and I keep telling myself that it's good for my character.

Twice a day, a senior correctional officer visits the facility to ensure that everything is in tip-top shape. All inmates have to stand in a straight line with our chests out, make a fist with both hands, and stare, not straight ahead, but 45 degrees upwards. This last requirement makes no sense to me. I've always assumed that one should make eye contact when addressing a superior, but apparently I've had it all wrong. 'When you look up, you look like you're full of hope,' one of the guards explained.

While we're in position, the senior officer will yell, 'This is an inspection. Any request or complaint?' Of course no one ever says anything except to reply, 'Good morning, Sir!' After that, the officer will say 'Good morning' back, and we'll express our gratitude by answering, 'Thank you, Sir!'

People outside prison, such as my friends and classmates, always call me by my full Chinese name: Wong Chi-fung. It's common in Hong Kong to address friends and acquaintances by their full names and it's not considered overly formal. Here in prison, however, as a friendly gesture of familiarity, staff and inmates alike have shortened my name to 'Fung Jai' (Little Fung), 'Fung Gor' (Brother Fung) or 'Ah Fung' (Fungie).

Everyone at Pik Uk knows who I am. Inmates like to chat with me and discuss prisoners' rights. They all think I can use my 'star power' to make life easier for them. After finishing our chores tonight, a few of us gathered around to complain about some of the ways in which prisons are run in Hong Kong.

One of the biggest gripes is how restrictive 'the list' is. The Correctional Services allow visiting friends and family to bring inmates supplies from the outside, but only if items are on an approved list. This includes basic things like pens, notebooks, razors and face towels. Absent from the list are some basic personal hygiene items like talcum powder and body lotion.

The teenager sitting across from me at the canteen had a more specific request. He complained that Pik Uk doesn't allow 'photo albums' (photo books of nude or semi-nude women), even though other juvenile facilities do. 'We need to fight for equality among prisons!' he joked. 'But, on a more serious note,' he continued, 'I was roughed up pretty badly in the police car after my arrest. Do you think you can push for cameras to be installed in police vehicles?'

Teenager vs Society

少年倉裡的 Teenager

Day 14 – Wednesday, 30 August 2017

I received another large batch of letters today. Some came from Demosistians, some from supporters in Hong Kong and abroad. Other than visits from my parents and friends, the arrival of the mail is the most exciting part of my day.

One letter was from a Hong Konger living in Canada. It brought back memories of a recent trip I took to Toronto with veteran activist Martin Lee, the so-called 'Father of Democracy' and founding chairman of the United Democrats of Hong Kong and the Democratic Party, and Mak Yin-ting, the former chairwoman of the Hong Kong Journalists Association. It feels like a lifetime since I was free to travel around the world and tell our story to parliaments and university students. Those days couldn't be more different from my life here in prison.

I've spent every day of the last two weeks with the same group of inmates. There are about 36 of us – roughly the size of a class at a local secondary school. At the beginning I was pretty guarded around them, partly because some are heavily tattooed street-gang types (the kind your parents would tell you to stay away from), and partly because most of them are here for drug trafficking, robbery, assault or other serious crimes. But once I got to know them, they all seemed genuine and easy to get along with. I realise it was wrong of me to judge them based on their appearance and history.

They all seem to have one thing in common – they like to brag about their pasts. They engage in endless one-upmanship based on the number of runners they used to control in their gangs, the size of their turf, how fiercely they defended and expanded it, things like that. Sometimes the war stories get so OTT and implausible I just roll my eyes and tune them out.

But I do try to understand how they ended up in gangs in the first place. They often share common backgrounds: not getting along with their families, quitting school after Secondary Three (Year 9), and hanging out with 'the wrong crowd'. Listening to them has been eye-opening and humbling. It's completely changed my impression of youth offenders, who are so often portrayed in the mainstream media as vicious and dangerous. In reality they're kids just like me. They spend their days like any average teen, flipping through magazines and burying their noses in books. Many of them are loyal fans of Roy Kwong, a prominent activist, lawmaker and bestselling romance novelist nicknamed 'Kwong God'. When the inmates found out that Nathan and I work closely with Roy, they all wanted to know the secret of how he comes up with such gut-wrenching love stories. I think those questions are best answered by 'the God' himself.

As much as I like Roy and respect his work, I prefer Japanese manga and video games. They are my guilty pleasures. Inmates were surprised when I asked them to lend me *One-Punch Man*, a popular Japanese comic book. I also told them about my obsession with *Gundam*, a timeless Japanese anime series and the country's answer to *Star Trek*. Then it was my turn to brag – I told them I had just bought the new PS4 game console and it was waiting at home to be played.

Sometimes our conversations turn more serious and they'll whine about the local education system. One guy said, 'Kids who do well in school don't end up here. And kids who end up here won't ever do well in school. Nobody ever chooses to be in the second group. The two groups never mix and we may as well live on two different planets.'

His words really made me think. The local education system is notoriously competitive and obsessed with good grades. Lots of kids get pushed out and left behind and once they fall out of the system, no one bothers to try to bring them back. They become one more statistic for the government and scare stories for the media, who write sensationalist headlines like 'Teens arrested in major drug bust' and 'Gang youth rounded up at underground gambling pit'. When we read the headlines in the newspapers, most of us shake our heads and turn to the next page. We don't expect to hear about these kids ever again. But where have they gone and where can they go?

Just last year, Netflix released *Teenager vs Superpower*. But in the mean streets of Hong Kong, a 'Teenager vs Society' story plays out every day and no one bats an eyelid.

My First March

落場步操

Day 15 – Thursday, 31 August 2017

Today I had my first dreaded morning march. I'm a scrawny, nerdy Hong Kong schoolboy. I spend nearly all my spare time playing video games and watching Japanese anime. I don't go out much and I've never been athletic or particularly coordinated. I'll be lucky to get through the march without embarrassing or hurting myself.

All things considered though, I think I did alright this morning. Other than the few times I turned left when I was supposed to turn right, I held my own just fine. Perhaps years later when I look back on my Pik Uk days I will miss the marches. But for now, my strategy is to lay low in the second row where mistakes are less obvious to the drill sergeant. (In fact, inmates always rush to the main yard at march time to try to call dibs on the second row.)

It was a good start to a jam-packed day. I had several visitors lined up. Lawmakers Charles Mok and Alvin Yeung stopped by before the Legal Aid rep showed up with more paperwork for me to review and sign. After that came my parents, then Lester Shum and lawmaker Eddie Chu.

Before we finished, Eddie looked me in the eye and said, 'Chi-fung, don't think of yourself as being in prison. Think outside these walls.' I knew exactly what he meant. Eddie wanted to remind me that I'm a prisoner of conscience and even though I'm on the other side of the thick glass pane, there are plenty of ways I can make a difference in the outside world.

Eddie's words lifted my spirit and motivated me to think beyond Pik Uk. After all, we live in the age of social media and instant information dissemination. Whatever message I want to deliver to the public, I can say it to my visitors and have them share it on Facebook and Twitter on my behalf.

Speaking of Facebook, I received a letter from Demosistō that contained more than the usual ramblings about party affairs. It had screenshots of Facebook posts that had been shared on my wall from friends and colleagues. It was surreal to go through social media on printed paper instead of a smartphone. But it hit the spot and eased my Facebook withdrawal symptoms, however temporarily.

On an unrelated note, there's no shortage of propaganda in youth prison. Every classroom, computer room and common area is plastered with posters featuring slogans like 'Knowledge can change your destiny' and 'Reform for a better tomorrow'. Every prison poster bears the same butterfly motif. I asked one of the guards what it symbolised. Beaming with pride he told me that butterflies represent transformation. He explained that youth offenders are like caterpillars that will morph into beautiful butterflies by the end of their sentences – but only if they are willing to be rehabilitated. If they follow the programme of the Correctional Services they will spread their wings and take flight once they reintegrate into society.

I wonder how many inmates register the metaphor.

Letters from the Heart

有信有心

_____

Day 16 – Friday, 1 September 2017

I received 40 letters today – a new record for me. The senders came from all walks of life, including university students and professors, a *Wall Street Journal* reporter, a Hong Kong expatriate living in Australia and a young mother who gave birth to her son in 2014 at the height of the mass protests. She calls him her 'umbrella baby'.

I really enjoy reading the personal anecdotes my supporters share with me. One mother wrote that she had asked her son to draw me a picture of the Transformers to cheer me up, only to discover in embarrassment that she had mixed up *Transformers* and *Gundam*, the anime I like. A father talked about taking his family of five to a street rally for the first time, and how jam-packed the metro station was on that day. A self-professed 'politically apathetic middle-class citizen' confessed how he used to think TVB News was the reigning authority in news reporting until the Umbrella Movement inspired him to be more critical and take mainstream local media with a pinch of salt. A Facebook follower urged me to hang on to my imaginary 'crest of courage' (an amulet from the *Digimon* anime) and a particularly thoughtful supporter printed a copy of my mother's open letter to Chief Executive Carrie Lam, which was published on the online news portal *HK01* and urged Lam to start listening to young people, instead of trying to silence them by using the criminal justice system.

These letters are evidence of the Umbrella Movement's greatest achievement: political awakening. Even though the phrase has been overused to the point that it has lost much of its meaning, no one can deny or question the fact that the movement has jolted a generation of Hong Kong citizens out of their existential coma and political apathy. Had it not been for those 79 days of mass protests in 2014, no one would have bothered to pick up a pen and craft a letter to a 20-year-old behind bars. The outpouring of support shown to me and other jailed activists is proof that a seed has been planted in the mind of every freedom-loving Hong Konger, ready to sprout when the conditions are ripe.

These letters also answer a recurrent question many have asked me: after all that Hong Kongers went through in 2014, and given how helpless and hopeless everyone has felt since, how do I, a leading activist, plan to energise the public to fight alongside me?

My answer is this: the only way to galvanise society is to make real sacrifices and put our money where our mouth is. Bearing the cross of imprisonment as the '13 plus 3' activists have done is the best way to prove our commitment to Hong Kong and demonstrate that we are more than mere slogans and rhetoric. The heartfelt letters that keep coming are proof that our efforts haven't gone unnoticed.

Counting the Days

數數日子

_____

Day 18 – Sunday, 3 September 2017 (Part 1)

There are no classes or chores on Sundays. It's the only day of the week that inmates are allowed to wear open-toed sandals. These rubber sandals have come to symbolise idleness for me.

This morning we were given a couple of hours of free time to do our own thing in the canteen. In the afternoon, we were given yet more hours to fill in the classroom. Most inmates chose to watch television, which is pretty much the only form of entertainment in youth prison. Some half-heartedly picked up a newspaper or a book to read.

During a very slow conversation, one inmate told me that if my release date happens to fall on a Sunday or public holiday they'll release me a day early. That little prison titbit prompted me to immediately check the dog tag I have to wear around my neck where my release date is marked. My projected release date – 17 December, assuming good behaviour – is indeed on a Sunday! The idea that I'd just 'saved' one day sent me all the way to cloud nine. But I'd barely wiped the smile off my face when I realised it might be too good to be true. The other contempt of court charge I'm facing will likely delay my release date by weeks, if not months.

My contempt hearing is still scheduled for mid-September. Assuming I plead guilty (which my lawyer has recommended), I'll likely get a three-month sentence, which, assuming I get a third off for good behaviour means a net jail time of two months. That makes 16 February my actual release date. I checked again and found, to my delight, that 16 February is Chinese New Year, a statutory holiday. So it looks like I'll benefit from the one-day discount after all.

But even with that, the idea of not being able to spend Chinese New Year's Eve – akin to Thanksgiving or Christmas elsewhere in the world – with my family has once again tempered my excitement.

Checking the calendar, 16 February is 166 days away. That's less than 24 weeks – 6 more in the youth prison and 18 in the adult ward. It makes me feel a bit better to measure time in weeks and break it up into two chunks: before and after my 21st birthday.

I had no visitors today, which made the day feel even longer. My only solace was reading a letter Alex wrote from prison that appeared in the *Apple Daily*, as well as the delivery of the post at 4pm.

In Alex's article he echoed the same sentiment that other jailed activists feel, or are at least supposed to feel: that those in power can imprison our bodies, but they can't imprison our minds. I must admit that Alex's mantra is more easily said than done. The first things I think about when I wake up are my parents and my friends.

Equally torturous is seeing advertisements for all the food I can't eat on the TV and in newspapers. Sometimes prison food is so bland that I can only finish half of it and go to bed hungry. What would I give to have a sip of coffee or a coke? Or a bite of sushi, a steak or wonton noodles.

An Open Letter to the International Community

寫給國際社會的信

Day 18 – Sunday, 3 September 2017 (Part 2)

To friends abroad who care about Hong Kong:

It's been a month since I arrived in Pik Uk. Even though I'm behind bars, I can still feel the outpouring of support from the international community, in particular from human rights organisations around the world and lawmakers in the United Kingdom, the United States and Germany. All of you have expressed concern and outrage over the imprisonment of the '13 plus 3'. We are eternally indebted to you.

Three years ago, I joined hundreds of thousands of brave citizens in the largest political movement in Hong Kong's history with the simple and honourable goal to bring true democracy to our city. We asked to exercise our constitutional right to elect our own leader through a fair and open election.

Not only did the Hong Kong government – appointed by Beijing and under its direction – ignore our demands, it also arrested and charged many of us with illegal assembly. Including me. After a lengthy trial and taking into account our unselfish motivations and generally accepted principles of civil disobedience, the lower court sentenced us to community service.

Then things took an ominous turn. An investigative report by Reuters revealed that our Secretary of Justice Rimsky Yuen, an appointee of our unelected Chief Executive Carrie Lam, overruled the community-service order recommended by his prosecution committee and made a politically motivated decision to appeal my sentence. The appeal was heard by a High Court judge who had been photographed at events hosted by pro-Beijing organisations. Ultimately, the judge increased my sentence to six months in prison on the grounds that the court needed to put a stop to the 'troubling trend' of political activism.

Until recently, the charge of unlawful assembly was used only to prosecute members of local gangs. Now, I believe the real 'troubling trend' is that a counter-organised crime tool is being deployed to silence dissenters and snuff out the pro-democracy movement in Hong Kong. Until recently, participants in civil disobedience efforts had always been handed community-service orders. The prison sentences received by the '13 plus 3' represent yet another 'troubling trend' that has significantly increased the price of political activism in Hong Kong.

Tomorrow, Professor Benny Tai, Professor Chan Kin-man and Reverend Chu Yiu-ming will likely go to prison for their roles in Occupy Central, the civil disobedience campaign that led to the Umbrella Movement. Their imprisonment is yet more evidence that freedom of assembly and other fundamental rights in Hong Kong are being eroded at a quickening pace.

In the past, the term 'political prisoner' conjured up frightening images of dissidents in mainland China being rounded up and thrown into jail. It's hard to imagine that the term now also applies to Hong Kong, one of the world's freest economies. As Beijing's long arm reaches into every corner of Hong Kong and threatens our freedoms and way of life, the number of prisoners of conscience is only going to increase. The international community can no longer stand on the sidelines and pretend that it is business as usual in Hong Kong. Something needs to be done.

Unfortunately, few foreign governments are willing to take on the world's second largest economy and hold its actions to account. For instance, I was disheartened by the latest 'Six-Monthly Report on Hong Kong' published by the British Secretary of State for Foreign and Commonwealth Affairs Boris Johnson.* Despite the political persecution of activists like myself, the Foreign Secretary concluded that the 'one country, two systems' framework was 'working well'. As a signatory to the Sino-British Joint Declaration on Hong Kong, Britain has both a moral and a legal obligation to defend its former subjects and speak up on their behalf.

I hasten to add that there are many individuals and organisations in the West that have steadfastly supported the pro-democracy movement in Hong Kong. With his remark that our names will be 'carved into history', Chris Patten has been a great source of encouragement to me, Nathan and Alex. A *New York Times* editor has even suggested that the three of us be nominated for the Nobel Peace Prize.† Their words humble us. What should be carved into history is the Umbrella Movement that awakened a generation of Hong Kong's youth. The ones who deserve a Nobel are every Hong Konger

---

* Appointed Prime Minister of the United Kingdom in 2019.
† In February 2018, Joshua Wong, Nathan Law and Alex Chow were nominated for the Nobel Peace Prize. At 21 years old, Joshua was the youngest of the three. They were Hong Kong's first ever nominees for the prize.

who stood bravely in the face of an intransigent regime backed by an authoritarian superpower.

Compared to the 1.4 billion people in mainland China — that's nearly one in five people on this planet — the population of 7 million in Hong Kong is infinitesimal. But what we lack in numbers, we make up for in determination and grit. Every day we are guided by our thirst for freedom and a sense of duty to bring democracy to our children and grandchildren. So long as we follow that path, we will always be on the right side of history.

The island of Hong Kong may be small, but the resolve of its people is anything but.

This Time Last Year I Was Counting Votes at LegCo

一年前還在立法會點票站

Day 19 – Monday, 4 September 2017

Today's mail delivery broke another personal record, not by the number of letters but by its sheer weight. From my lawyer I received a 291-page printout of my entire Facebook page and Demosistō's group page since my sentencing two weeks ago.

I never thought I would enjoy this 'hardcopy Facebook' – almost a contradiction in terms – but I do. It makes me feel connected with the outside world again. I've thought about requesting regular Facebook printouts but decided against it. For one thing, the task is time-consuming (Demosistians are already time-poor and short of hands) and for another, printing reams and reams of Facebook posts would kill far too many trees. I'll just have to wait for the occasional surprise, like today's.

Every letter coming in and going out of prison will be opened and reviewed by the guards, on the grounds that Correctional Services need to check for hidden objects. They also screen for unauthorised messages, like plans to subvert the authorities or conspiracy among inmates.

Unless, that is, the letter is to or from a person who holds a public office, such as a legislator. If this is the case, the envelope will remain unopened and unread by anyone other than the addressee. Delivery is also expedited so it takes two days instead of a full week to get to the hands of the recipient. The sender doesn't even need to put a postage stamp on the envelope.

This creates a bit of a loophole and one that I'm happy to exploit. It saves me stamp money and gives me peace of mind when discussing sensitive matters. The guards grumble each time I request a so-called 'sealed delivery'. Whether they like it or not, I'm determined to send one at least twice a week.

All sealed deliveries go through the Reception Office. To avoid inmates smuggling drugs or other illegal substances we're required to take a urine test after each sealed delivery pick-up or drop-off. The Reception Office is a glorified locker room where simple paperwork is processed and prison officers sit around and gossip. While waiting in the office to take a drug test one time, my eyes were drawn to the calendar pinned on the wall. Exactly a year ago, on 4 September 2016, Nathan made history by becoming the youngest elected lawmaker in Asia, having won 50,818 votes in the Hong Kong Island constituency. All of us were in the ballot room at the LegCo Building cheering and crying tears of joy, a throng of local and foreign reporters waiting impatiently outside. None of us would have guessed that months after the historic win, Nathan would lose his seat and both of us would be behind bars.

I wonder if Nathan, too, has noticed the anniversary, and I wonder what's going through his mind tonight.

Bland and Blander

重複單調乏味的食物

___

Day 20 – Tuesday, 5 September 2017

From the day I started keeping a journal, I've expected friends and family to take great interest in what kind of food I've been eating in prison. And so I've made it a point to jot down what I ate every day at breakfast, lunch and dinner.

Day	Breakfast	Lunch	Dinner	Night snack
Mon	pork cucumbers	sweet porridge buttered bread	chicken wing vegetables	raisin roll milk
Tue	beef vegetables	savoury porridge jam and bread	fish, egg vegetables	raisin roll milk
Wed	chicken wing cucumbers	sweet porridge buttered bread	fish vegetables	raisin roll milk
Thurs	pork vegetables	savoury porridge jam and bread	chicken wing vegetables	raisin roll milk
Fri	beef cucumbers	sweet porridge buttered bread	fish, egg vegetables	raisin roll milk

Day	Breakfast	Lunch	Dinner	Night snack
Sat	chicken wing vegetables	savoury porridge jam and bread	fish vegetables	raisin roll milk
Sun	beef balls cucumbers milk tea	tofu skin porridge buttered roll	fish, egg vegetables	raisin roll milk

I stopped recording my diet after about two weeks, when I realised the menu repeats itself week after week and never changes.

An 'Ill-mannered' Speech

「不懂大體」的一番話

Day 22 – Thursday, 7 September 2017

The headline of every newspaper today relates to the government's proposed national anthem law.

Yesterday, Beijing published a draft bill to criminalise the commercial use or parodies of the Chinese national anthem, 'The March of the Volunteers'. Anyone caught 'intentionally insulting' the anthem could face up to three years in prison.

The bill is another encroachment on our freedom of expression. Like the national education curriculum that Scholarism thwarted in 2012, it's the latest attempt by the government to legislate patriotism. It didn't work in 2012 and it won't work today.

Sadly, LegCo is dominated by Beijing loyalists (especially after Oathgate's recent purge of pro-democracy lawmakers) and the government has more than enough votes to pass the bill as soon as the public consultation period ends.

Several newspapers reported a student's speech that has turned heads and earned widespread praise. At the opening ceremony of her secondary school, Tiffany Tong, the school's 17-year-old student union president, weighed in on the national anthem debate when she addressed the student body:

> The way young people choose to express their grievances about their government, such as turning their backs to the national flag, is often considered ill-mannered and disrespectful.
>
> Yes, we know that manners are important – we're taught that every day in school – but we also know the importance of our principles and beliefs.
>
> In the eyes of many adults we're rude, disobedient and unpragmatic. But we are doing what young people are supposed to do: challenge conventional wisdom and refuse to compromise. Along the way we are bound to make mistakes and stumble, but we'll emerge from our mistakes and stumbles as stronger and better people.

Tiffany's words are prodigious. They perfectly sum up the collective sentiment of the next generation in

Hong Kong. Facing ever-growing social injustices and political bullying by Communist China, young people refuse to give in and trade their ideals for what's easy and pragmatic. Instead of hunkering down and living a 'well-mannered' life, the way adults do, they are choosing to risk it all by speaking up and pushing back.

I was enormously encouraged by what I read. When we disbanded Scholarism to make way for Demosistō, some members worried that we might lose an important platform to inspire the next generation of teenage activists. Tiffany is proof that we need not worry.

The Flexible Politician

靈活的政治家

Day 24 – Saturday, 9 September 2017

A trio of Demosistians came to see me today. The main subject of conversation was the upcoming LegCo by-elections. As the nomination deadline approaches, there's some urgency for us to agree on which one of us should run. The answer depends on who we're running against.

Our main opponent is Judy Chan from the pro-establishment New People's Party (NPP). Chan was educated in Australia and worked in the US before returning to Hong Kong to enter politics. In a recent interview, Chan said her husband was against her decision to run for LegCo, not only because he was concerned about the stress an election campaign could bring, but also because she would be obliged to give up her American citizenship and in doing so, potentially make it harder for her daughter to attend a US university in the future.

The NPP is a party of business elites. Its members come from the upper crust of Hong Kong society, who cosy up to the Communist Party with their patriotic rhetoric while holding onto the foreign passports that are their potential escape route. They own luxury property abroad and send their children to universities in the West to shield them from the local education system. It makes it all the more ironic that Beijing accuses leaders of the Umbrella Movement and pro-democracy activists of acting under the influence of 'foreign powers'. Their own so-called loyalists have more foreign ties than any of us.

During a district by-election in 2014, Chan lambasted the outgoing district councilman – a pro-democracy politician – for abandoning his local constituencies to run for LegCo. She told voters she would focus on district affairs and that she had no ambition to become a lawmaker. She ended up winning the election.

Two years later, after Oathgate created an opening for her, Chan has no qualms about going back on her word and throwing her hat into the ring. I wonder what her constituencies make of that?

My Chinese-made Radio

國產收音機

Day 25 – Sunday, 10 September 2017

Two weeks ago I spent some of my hard-earned money on an FM radio.

My order arrived today. I've been looking forward to an RTHK* phone-in current affairs programme called *Open Line, Open View* and I was really excited to open the box. I was expecting the same Sony model that other inmates have purchased recently using the provision order form. But it turned out to be a Chinese knock-off. (Later on I found out that Sony have recently stopped manufacturing radios.) A Chinese brand would be fine if it worked, but when I turn on the unit in my cell I hear nothing but static. I get some reception if I stretch my arm through the iron bars of my door

---

* Radio Television Hong Kong public broadcaster.

and place the unit as far out as possible, but that's no way to listen to the radio.

So I put away my useless radio and opened my mail. One of the letters was from Senia Ng, a young barrister whose father was a cofounder of the Democratic Party, Hong Kong's oldest political party. She enclosed over 50 pages of articles relating to the National Anthem Bill, writings by Alex from prison and even a few sudoku and jumble puzzles.

On the subject of games, earlier today I played ping-pong with some inmates in the common room. We play a few times a week. I'm terrible at sports and never enjoyed them at school, but I managed to hold my own with the table-tennis paddle. I've never exercised as much in my life. My mum must be so proud!

How Much Did They Pay You?

其實你有無錢收?

Day 27 – Tuesday, 12 September 2017

Reading makes the day go by faster. My parents try to bring me new books every time they visit and friends send me reading lists.

I've just finished reading *The Protester* by mainland dissident writer Xu Zhiyuan and the three-volume *One Hundred Years of Pursuit: The Story of Taiwan's Democratic Movement* by Cui-lian Chen, Wu Nai-teh and Hu Hui-ling. I'm looking forward to reading *How Do We Change Our Society?* by sociologist Eiji Oguma, a book given to me as a present by two young Japanese professors via Agnes, who visited Tokyo earlier this year.

Most inmates read whatever is available in the library – tabloid magazines, romance novels and comic books. I try not to walk around with my serious, dense non-fiction on display. I'd enjoy leafing through cooking magazines if they didn't make me crave proper food even more. Japanese *One-Punch Man* manga comes in handy as a guilty pleasure that also helps me blend in with others.

For the past five years I've been moving in circles with politicians and activists. We sometimes live in a bubble, saying and doing things that make us look out of touch with the general population. I'm making a conscious effort to connect with my fellow inmates. Listening to them vent about what they've been through has broadened my horizons and brought me back down to earth.

More than one inmate has asked me, 'How much do they pay you to do your political stuff?' At first I thought they just wanted to provoke me with accusations that I take money from foreign governments. But I've slowly realised the questions are genuine. Most people don't understand why any sane person would risk prison to do what I do if it wasn't for money. So now I just smile and say, 'I wish I did get paid!' But no one ever believes me. I've thought about saying that I'm just like someone who volunteers their time to help others without expecting anything in return. What I really want to tell them, but don't for fear of sounding self-righteous, is that my sole purpose for entering politics is to make a difference. I do it so that I can one day tell my children and grandchildren that I've given something for the city they love. That would be worth all the money in the world.

Boredom Busters

解悶工廠

Day 28 – Wednesday, 13 September 2017

FronTiers is a group of social workers, lawyers and reporters who came together to support activists in need. Together with lawmaker Eddie Chu, the group started a letter-writing campaign called 'Boredom Busters', collecting letters and reading materials to help the '13 plus 3' fight the most formidable enemy in prison: time.

I got my first FronTiers package today – a 30-page document with newspaper clippings and printouts of online articles. Even though I make a habit of reading the *Apple Daily* every morning, some of the best political analysis and reports are only available through independent online news outlets that cover small but significant news events often overlooked by the broadsheets.

Reading a stack of computer printouts may not be everyone's idea of having a good time, but there I was, flipping the crisp pages in the canteen and feeling the warmth of every Boredom Busters' volunteer who had taken the time to make my prison sentence go by just that little bit faster.

I saw in the news clippings that my sentence appeal is now public knowledge. Some of the articles mentioned that I would be out on bail by early October. What they didn't mention was the likelihood of that happening. So far my lawyers have been trying to manage my expectations. They estimate that my chance of being granted bail by October is less than 50–50. For now, I'll continue to be what politicians call 'cautiously optimistic'.

Do You See Those Skyscrapers?

你看那到些高樓嗎?

Day 30 – Friday, 15 September 2017

I received another hefty mail delivery today. I noticed that most of the letters were dated more than a week ago and it made me wonder why my mail is taking longer and longer to reach me. I don't think I'll ever find out the reason why.

Two things I read in the morning kept churning around in my head all day.

The first is an article by *Initium* reporter Vivian Tam. I've known Vivian since my anti-national education campaign in 2012. Five years on, her pen is as sharp as ever. In her article for the digital media outlet, 'Safeguarding the truth and protecting our history', she charts the evolution of Hong Kong's pro-democracy movement and compares the Umbrella Movement to similar transformative events in Asia such as the 228 Massacre in Taiwan* and the Gwangju Uprising in South Korea.† Both were bloody popular uprisings that eventually led to the democratisation of the entire countries.

Despite the geographical proximity of Taiwan and South Korea, and that they are two of the most popular travel destinations for Hong Kongers, most of us know very little about their histories and how they came to be the modern democracies they are today. I admit I'm not as well versed in their histories as I should be and I've made a note to ask my family to send me a few books about them.

The other thought-provoking article was from a new columnist who goes by the pen name Ha Mook Mook. In her article 'Forgive me for leaving Hong Kong', she remembers the first night of the

---

* An anti-government uprising in 1947 that was violently suppressed by Taiwan's National Revolutionary Army on behalf of the ruling government. Thousands of citizens were killed and many more injured and imprisoned. The event marked the beginning of the White Terror, a 38-year period of martial law during which tens of thousands of Taiwanese were imprisoned, disappeared or died.

†A popular uprising in South Korea that took place in May 1980 in response to the violent suppression of local students who were demonstrating against martial law. Over 600 people, mostly students, were killed.

Umbrella Movement, and describes her conflicted emotions when she saw entire highways occupied by pro-democracy protesters:

> I know Hong Kong isn't perfect. It has its fair share of social injustices and urban maladies. Sometimes just getting through the day can be tough. But no matter how often I get lost in the dizzying streets and the soaring sky-scrapers, I never cease to be amazed by the beauty of this place.
>
> Everywhere I look tonight, I see courage, imagination and hope – things that I've never seen in the two decades that I've lived here. Hong Kong, you are beautiful!
>
> I won't lie to you – I'm worried that your beauty may not last. I need to hurry and cap-ture these images on film, before the colourful wall is washed out, the tents are taken down, the traffic returns and the people disappear. Before strangers no longer say hello to each other on the streets.
>
> On an anonymous stretch of the highway, a man says to me, 'Can you see the skyscrap-ers over there? That's not the real Hong Kong. Now can you see the crowds down here? That's the real Hong Kong.'

Inmate Abuse

囚犯被打

Day 32 – Sunday, 17 September 2017

Not much happens on Sundays. We spend much of our day off sitting around and chatting, or 'blowing water' as we say in Cantonese. We don't usually have a specific topic, although I've tried to steer the conversation to inmate abuse so that I can pass on any useful information to Bottle. I made a promise to him and I want to honour it. It's a sensitive subject and it didn't take long for the prison guards to catch on – they snoop around and listen in on our discussions – but, whatever the authorities think, I've taken on this issue and I'm not about to drop it for fear of reprisal.

Despite the outright denial by the Correctional Services' Rehabilitation Unit, the division in charge of prisoners' welfare, and the defensive attitude of pretty much every person of authority that Bottle has spoken to, prison violence is so prevalent in Hong Kong that it can be called an epidemic. Bottle also told me that out of the thousands of complaints filed over the past decade, only a handful of cases have been accepted and validated by the Complaints Investigation Unit. It's hardly surprising considering that the head of the unit is appointed by none other than the Commissioner of Correctional Services. There's little, if any, accountability in the system.

It's one thing to look at this issue of inmate abuse in the abstract, quite another to hear first-hand accounts of physical – and sometimes sexual – violence from victims sitting right in front of me. Many of the stories are harrowing. Some have been groped in the groin, others force-fed water mixed with cigarette ash, while some have been made to beat their own hands with wooden clubs until their fingers are broken.

I know that many inmates still believe politics has nothing to do with them and that they have nothing to do with it. That's why they struggle to understand why anyone would enter into politics if not for financial gains. Each time the topic comes up, I tell them that politics is all around them and that it affects every aspect of their lives, from the cigarette tax they pay to the minimum wage they will one day take home and the monthly rent that absorbs almost all of their parents' income. They needn't even look beyond the prison walls to see its effects. Politics is why so many inmates are abused and so few officers are held to account. 'Do you still think politics has nothing to do with you?' I ask.

Hair Politics – Part 1

髮政一

___

Day 33 – Monday, 18 September 2017

Other than prison abuse, head shaving is another institutional injustice that drives me insane.

At Pik Uk all male juvenile inmates are subject to a mandatory biweekly head shave, without exception. Our hair must be kept shorter than the arbitrary maximum length of 6 millimetres. Twice a month, 40 or so of us are turned into Buddhist monks against our will.

It reminds me of a constitutional challenge lodged by lawmaker Leung Kwok-hung three years ago. Nicknamed 'Long Hair' for his trademark shoulder-length locks, Leung was one of the six who lost their LegCo seats in Oathgate. Just before the Umbrella Movement erupted, he was jailed for forcibly entering a political event. Alleging gender discrimination, Leung took the government to court for cutting his hair in prison while female inmates are allowed to keep theirs long. The Court of First Instance, the lower court of the High Court, below the Court of Appeal, ruled in Leung's favour, but the case is currently pending an appeal.*

I understand that prisoners shouldn't expect to enjoy the same rights as ordinary citizens, and I appreciate that keeping inmates' hair short serves a practical purpose, such as eradicating hair lice. Nevertheless, there's no reason why Pik Uk needs to impose such a strict requirement when other facilities don't. I fail to see any security or health threat posed by male inmates sporting, say, a standard schoolboy haircut.

What upsets me even more is what happened when I suggested to prison management that the matter be brought to the attention of the Justice of the Peace in charge of prison affairs on his next visit. They responded with anger and threats; Sergeant Wong, who is responsible for my ward, warned, 'If you try to talk even one inmate into taking this issue any further I can charge you with incitement to disrupt prison order.'

---

* In January 2019 the Court of Appeal refused to hear Leung's appeal on the grounds that his case 'does not involve questions of great general or public importance'.

Sargeant Wong's response left me dumbfounded and angry. It revealed the authorities' utter disregard for prisoners' welfare. Expressing my concerns about head-shaving to a Justice of the Peace is well within my rights and precisely the kind of concern that is the purpose of his visits. What's more, if this is the level of intimidation levelled at someone like me, a public figure protected to some extent by the glare of the media, then I can't imagine what a regular inmate with no political connections would suffer. No wonder so many inmates choose to keep their mouths shut, irrespective of the injustices.

On a happier note, I received two-dozen letters today, many of them from friends and colleagues overseas. I was especially delighted to hear from Anna Cheung, founder of the New Yorkers Supporting Hong Kong group (NY4HK), who has worked tirelessly for years to help pro-democracy politicians such as Martin Lee and Anson Chan, who created the Hong Kong 2020 group to monitor progress towards constitutional reform by 2020, meet influential politicians in the West. Since the Umbrella Movement Anna has been instrumental in Demosistō's efforts to lobby support from the international community.

I also heard from Jobie Yip, a Hong Kong student at the London School of Economics, who I befriended after giving a talk at Oxford University in 2015. Jobie was one of the overseas students who protested outside the Chinese embassy in London during the Umbrella Movement and the first person to join Demosistō after Nathan's disqualification from LegCo earlier this year. It was a bold decision, considering that Oathgate has effectively barred anyone in the self-determination camp from future elections. If she has any political ambition her affiliation with Demosistō is pretty much a political career-ending move.

Committed overseas Hong Kongers such as Anna and Jobie are critical partners in our fight for democracy. Even though they are far away geographically, their hearts are with us and their solidarity has been one of the major engines behind the push to raise international awareness about the political situation in Hong Kong. What's more, they are a testament to the indelible impact of the Umbrella Movement, which is felt not only in Hong Kong but everywhere else in the world where Hong Kong people can be seen and heard.

Messages from friends are a morale booster, but mail from total strangers often packs the greatest emotional punch. I received a letter from a 14-year-old girl today, who wrote in beautiful handwriting about the way recent political events have made her feel. I don't often receive letters from secondary school students (pen and paper seem anachronistic in the age of WhatsApp and Telegram) and she clearly took a lot of effort and time to craft hers. It's always a treat to hear from people who are the same age I was when I first started my journey in political activism.

Another heartfelt letter came from a young mother, whose last paragraph moved me to tears:

> My baby girl was barely a year old when my husband and I brought her with us to one of your anti-national education demonstrations. We spent the entire evening in Admiralty, hoping that she would soak up the energy at the protest site and grow up to be as brave and stubbornly principled as you.
>
> That was five years ago and she is almost six now. To our surprise, she still remembers that night in Admiralty like it was last week. Each time we drive through the area, she'll point at the section of the highway where we sat for hours. She calls you 'Brother Admiralty' whenever she sees you in the news.
>
> Last week I asked her whether she wanted to do something to support 'Brother

Admiralty', who has been thrown into jail for doing what he believes to be just. I suggested that she draw you some pictures, since she loves to draw. And so here you are, three drawings from the little sister you've never met.

Hair Politics – Part 2

髮政二

___

Day 34 – Tuesday, 19 September 2017

I read in the paper today that the 26-year-old activist Sulu Sou became the youngest lawmaker in Macau in Sunday's general election.

Macau is a former Portuguese colony that, like Hong Kong, reverted to Chinese rule and became a special administrative region before the turn of the millennium. Best known for its mega-casinos, Macau too has been fighting for a free vote and battling the dual evils of corporatocracy and political cronyism. With a population of less than 700,000 (one-tenth of Hong Kong's), the city lacks the critical mass of experienced politicians for a meaningful pro-democracy movement to take hold.

But in 2014, the same year that Taiwan had its

Sunflower Revolution* and Hong Kong witnessed the Umbrella Movement, Macanese citizens exercised their civic power and said 'enough is enough' to political injustices. In May that year, 20,000 protesters took to the streets to oppose a government proposal to enrich the ruling elites with generous retirement packages. The government eventually withdrew the controversial plan and the incident was considered the biggest victory for civil society in Macau's post-handover history. Riding on the surge in political awareness, Sulu managed to make a name for himself and gain mainstream acceptance.

His election win this week is hugely encouraging for all of us, but I also feel a twinge of sadness. Sulu's success story reminds me of Nathan's dramatic political rise and fall – and of the way the youngest lawmaker of Hong Kong won and lost his LegCo seat within just eight months.

Meanwhile, there have been some developments on the head-shaving front. Pik Uk authorities granted me an audience with senior management

---

* The occupation of the Taiwanese legislature by a coalition of students protesting against a proposed bilateral agreement with China (the Cross-Strait Service Trade Agreement, or CSSTA).

this morning. At the meeting, representatives tried to justify the practice by citing hygiene and health concerns, such as excessive perspiration during the summer months.

When I pressed them about the 6-millimetre limit, they conceded that there are no hard and fast rules in the written guidelines and that the length was agreed among officials simply out of 'operational efficiency'. They said they would reach out to other juvenile facilities to establish what best practice would be.

I responded to the representatives blankly. 'The fact that you need to check with other prisons means that Pik Uk doesn't have a specific length requirement beyond the general principle of keeping our hair short. In other words, the 6-millimetre maximum is a made-up rule that I believe you should stop imposing on us.' The men looked at each other and declared the meeting over.

Losing My Cellmate

失去囚友

Day 35 – Wednesday, 20 September 2017

Every three months or so there's an inmate reshuffle
at Pik Uk and cellmates are reassigned. The idea
is that newcomers can be paired with more experienced inmates who will show them the ropes, while
any cliques or potentially dangerous alliances can be
broken up.

In this round of cell moves, not only did I
lose the cellmate I've grown to like over the past
five weeks – I wasn't assigned a new cellmate at all.
Prison management probably sees me as too much
of a troublemaker to be paired with a new cellmate
without infecting his mind. Either that or they think
I won't be much of a mentor when it comes to prison
duties.

At first I thought it would be a treat to have
all 70 square feet to myself, after all, in Hong Kong

you'd have to pay an arm and a leg to get that kind of space. But after spending the first night alone, I've realised how isolated I feel without someone to talk to at night. In the coming weeks, I'll have to get used to coming back to an empty cell after dinner – it's the eternal question of privacy vs companionship.

I remember meeting Ah Sun for the first time, 35 days ago. We didn't have much in common and neither of us was too eager to engage with the other. I was raised a Christian in a middle-class family and went to a Direct Subsidy Scheme school (private schools subsidised by the government that are considered better quality than government-run public schools). Ah Sun, like most other inmates, comes from a broken home, dropped out of secondary school and joined a local gang. When he sat down to talk in our cell I couldn't understand half of his gang speak; I would hide in a corner reading a newspaper.

But over time I picked up more and more jargon and began to understand Ah Sun better. I learned to stop dropping English words into my Cantonese to sound less elitist and pompous. Now we sit around and talk as if we were in the same gang.

Most importantly, I really got to know Ah Sun, and I'm proud to call him my friend.

Interrogation by the Security Unit

保安組問話

Day 38 – Saturday, 23 September 2017

I found out today that several inmates I often eat with have been interrogated by prison authorities. After we finished today's physical check-up, about 12 of them were escorted away by the security unit. They were taken to a room, asked to divulge the details of our conversations and warned that mixing with me might get them sent to solitary confinement.

The security unit must have gone through the canteen's CCTV recordings to identify the people they wanted to question. In truth, we rarely discuss prison affairs openly – most of the time we chat about random things like video games, exam strategies and career options. But management is paranoid that my head-shaving campaign might get out of hand and lead to an all-out prison rebellion if it's not contained. The incident echoes the unpleasant conversation I had with Sergeant Wong a few days ago when he threatened me with incitement charges if I were to involve other inmates in my prison activism. It also brings home the reality of living under 24-hour surveillance, watched over by Big Brother at all times and in all places.

Knowing that the visitation area is also closely monitored, I haven't mentioned anything to my visitors about the threats and the interrogation. Instead we talk about recent news events and campaign strategies for the by-elections.

Alone in my empty cell, I reflected on what happened at Pik Uk this past week. I realised that my vocal advocacy for prisoners' rights may have put others inmates in jeopardy. Thinking more broadly, perhaps every political movement I've either led or participated in over the past five years has had the same impact on my loved ones. I've always operated on the assumption that I'm prepared to pay whatever price it takes to fight for my beliefs, but have I once paused to think about my family and consider the tremendous pressure that my actions, no matter how noble in my own mind, have created? Have I once sought their consent, or have I simply taken their understanding for granted?

Watching *Hong Kong Connection*

看的《鏗鏘集》

Day 40 – Monday, 25 September 2017

Hong Kong Connection, one of the longest running current affairs shows in Hong Kong, airs every Monday night at 6pm.

This week's episode was all about activists in prison. I was excited to see several Demosistians being interviewed, including Derek Lam, Isaac Cheng and Jobie Yip. They were filmed opening letters from supporters addressed to Nathan and me. Seeing them chatting and working away on the small screen made me miss them even more.

Most of the scenes were shot in our new office, which is markedly smaller than the workspace we used to have before Nathan lost his seat. After Oathgate, we were evicted from the LegCo Building and had to scramble to find an affordable office space.

Towards the end of the 30-minute episode, Derek said:

> It's been six years since Chi-fung and I entered politics – we've gone from Secondary Four to our third year at university. We became activists because we wanted to make Hong Kong a better place. But has it worked?

Derek's words sum up the question that most activists are too afraid to ask: are we making a difference?* Is society changing for the better? Pushing Derek's question further: even assuming we have made a difference, is it worth it and at what personal cost?

It's perhaps easier for young people like myself and Derek to throw ourselves deep into activism without another thought – we still live with our parents and don't have much financial burden or

---

* In fact, many of Joshua's fellow Hong Kongers demonstrated against the imposition of the Extradition Bill that led to the summer protests in 2019, when 2 million people – over a quarter of Hong Kong's population – peacefully marched against the law. As a result of the demonstrations, and with the world watching, Carrie Lam was forced to back down, declaring the bill 'dead' on 9 July 2019 and announcing its full withdrawal on 4 September 2019.

family responsibility. What do we have to lose other than our freedom?

By contrast, people like Professor Tai have a different set of considerations. Before Occupy Central he was living a stable, middle-class life, teaching at a leading university and making a comfortable living. Now Professor Tai not only faces a long prison sentence, but also stands to lose his position at the University of Hong Kong and be forced to sell his home to pay for mounting legal bills. Why would any rational person make that kind of sacrifice?

There aren't many people in this world for whom I have unreserved admiration. Professor Benny Tai is one of them.

What Civic Square Means to Me

公民廣場對我的意義

Day 41 – Tuesday, 26 September 2017

As I was getting ready to turn in last night, out of the corner of my eye I spotted a black shape darting away from the foot of my bed. Before I could even react the thing had vanished. To my relief, the giant rat – I assume that's what it was – never appeared again and I was able to have a good night's sleep.

Today is 26 September, exactly 17 days before my 21st birthday. In other words, I only have 16 days left in Pik Uk before my transfer to an adult facility. I wouldn't go so far as to say that time goes by quickly, but having a transfer to break up my six-month sentence (four months assuming good behaviour) does make it feel a bit more tolerable.

I have a number of things to take care of before my transfer. First, I have reams and reams of court documents to rifle through and organise concerning my appeal. I have no desire to bring all the paper-work with me, since lugging bagfuls of legal documents into the new facility will draw unnecessary attention and raise privacy concerns. I need to spend a bit of time processing them before passing everything back to my parents for safekeeping.

Then there are over 200 letters from supporters that I've read but haven't done anything with. During my parents' visit today my mum said I should keep the letters and try to reply to them all, however briefly. She said that's what Nathan has been doing. It's not bad advice, especially since a few public holidays, including National Day and Mid-Autumn Festival, are coming up, which will give me plenty of free time.

Ever since my sentencing, my parents have been running around for me, working with my lawyers on the appeal, requesting a deferral at my university and taking care of all kinds of paperwork and errands. When a young person goes to prison he brings the entire family with him. I don't know where to begin to express my gratitude for everything my parents have done for me.

It looks like I may have to trouble them for one more thing: there's a possibility that Pik Uk may hold an open day and invite all parents to visit the facilities and meet the staff. It turns out that juvenile prisons regularly organise outreach events to 'bring families together'. Guests will be given a prison tour and asked to sit through long speeches by representatives from the rehabilitation and counselling units.

The open day culminates in a symbolically significant event: a tea ceremony for inmates to prepare and serve tea to their parents. This rather contrived ritual is followed by a 20-minute heart-to-heart between the inmate and his family under the watchful eyes of the guards.

These scenes are frequently depicted in local TV dramas: a child in prison uniform breaks down in front of weeping parents, repents his wayward past, and promises he'll make them proud once he's released. The prison staff will look on with great pride at another reformed soul thanks to their care and guidance.

While that sort of re-education model may work for some inmates, I don't believe it applies to political prisoners who will always believe in their cause. No amount of rehabilitation can make us repent. Even so, I am looking forward to it – if nothing else, it'll be a wonderful opportunity to spend some time with my parents without having a thick window pane between us.

What Civic Square Means to Me

Today is the third anniversary of my Civic Square siege, the event that set in motion the Umbrella Movement and a turning point in my life. This time exactly three years ago, on 26 September 2014, I scaled a metal fence near the government headquarters and called on other protesters to follow me. I was tackled by a dozen police officers and taken into custody. That was my first arrest, which ultimately resulted in my first criminal conviction and prison sentence.

The very name of the place – Civic Square – was coined during my anti-national education campaign in 2012. Before that, the nondescript circular public space was known unimaginatively as the front yard of the Government Headquarters East Wing. It had been sealed off with a metal fence and on the night of my arrest I attempted to reclaim it. So much history has been written in that square since then, and it will always have a special place in my heart.

Operation Black Bauhinia

黑紫荊行動

Day 42 – Wednesday, 27 September 2017

My heart skipped a beat at dinner when I heard the words 'Operation Black Bauhinia' on the news. Don't tell me the Department of Justice is pressing charges for that protest too! I thought.

The Golden Bauhinia was a gift from the Communist Party when Hong Kong was handed back to China in 1997. Every 1 July, also known as Handover Day, the government holds a flag-raising ceremony in the square to commemorate the 'reunification' of Hong Kong with the motherland.

At around 6am on 26 June 2017, roughly seven weeks before my sentencing, myself, Agnes and a number of other activists climbed the 6-metre-high monument and draped a giant black cloth over the Golden Bauhinia. We'd planned the operation ahead of President Xi Jinping's high-profile visit for the

20th anniversary of the Handover to show our opposition to Beijing's increasing intervention in Hong Kong's affairs.

If the DOJ decided to charge us for trespassing or public nuisance, it would be the third criminal case I'd be facing after the unlawful assembly charge for storming Civic Square and the contempt of court for breaching the Mongkok injunction. It would add to my prison term and throw my whole timetable out the window.

It turned out to be a false alarm. The news report had mentioned Black Bauhinia because some of the protesters arrested for the operation had refused bail and were released by police unconditionally. But we're not out of the woods just yet. The DOJ 'reserves the right' to file charges against us in the future, just as they did with Alex, Nathan and me, as well as the Occupy Central Trio, years after the movement ended.

What the DOJ does is entirely beyond our control – the Justice Secretary alone has the power and resources to take criminal actions against us. The authorities are always in the driver's seat, whereas activists can only react to their whims. Whatever the future holds for me, I have to stay focused and remain positive.

Books have helped me do both. I just finished reading *20th Century Chinese History*, published by

Oxford University Press, which dissects contemporary China from both macro (history-based) and micro (event-based) perspectives. It analyses recent political uprisings, including the 1989 Tiananmen Square protests, through the lens of a totalitarian regime, not justifying China's actions but trying to understand its motives and mindset. If I wasn't in jail I wouldn't have the time or patience to labour through a dense academic book like this. Having the opportunity to read is one of the silver linings that give me some solace.

So is getting to know a broad range of people behind bars, like this Vietnamese inmate I met in the main yard today. He's roughly my age and was arrested earlier this year for drug trafficking and illegal entry into Hong Kong. He opened up to me about his upbringing in Vietnam and the events that led him down this path. Until meeting him and other inmates convicted of similar charges, illegal drugs was something I would only hear about through the government's aggressive 'Stand Firm! Knock Drugs Out' campaign. Being here has given context and nuance to what most people consider a black and white issue.

To: Mr Joshua Wong

寄給: 黃之鋒

Day 43 – Thursday, 28 September 2017

I received an unusual letter this morning. It caught my attention because it was addressed to 'Mr Joshua Wong' instead of my prison number. It must have taken a few extra days to get delivered because most prison staff don't even know my Christian name.

The letter came from the United States Senate Committee on Foreign Relations. It was a joint letter from five Democratic and Republican senators expressing solidarity with Alex, Nathan and me and condemning the Hong Kong government for prosecuting non-violent protesters. Both the US Senate seal at the top of the page and the wet ink signatures at the bottom made the piece of paper feel weighty in my hands.

Despite the unprecedented outpouring of support received by the Umbrella Movement around the world, universal suffrage for Hong Kong remains dead in the water. In the years since the uprising Beijing has dug its heels in and taken the topic off the political table. Every time I hear words of encouragement from politicians and scholars overseas, like today's letter, it adds to the conflicting emotions inside me. I feel like we've let everybody down.

But as Alex put it succinctly in a recent letter:

> If the path to democracy was free of obstacles, then Hong Kong would have arrived at the finish line a generation ago and I wouldn't be writing to you from prison. It's precisely because the path is full of obstacles that we've taken up the mantle to continue the unfinished journey.

I know I can always count on good old Alex to get me out of a mental rut.

Joshua and Caleb

約書與亞迦勒

Day 44 – Friday, 29 September 2017

Today went by quickly. I spent the morning in the computer room learning Adobe Illustrator and the afternoon with visitors. By the time I returned to the main yard for group exercises it was almost dinner.

My lawyers had important news today. A date has finally been set for the sentencing hearing for my Mongkok contempt of court case – the second week of October. I took my lawyers' advice to enter a guilty plea for violating a court injunction and now it's up to the judge to decide how and where I will spend the next few months. If luck is on my side I'll either be given a suspended sentence or allowed to serve both my current and the contempt sentences simultaneously. I try not to think too hard about it; I know false hopes can be crushing.

Among the letters I received today was one from Raphael Wong, a friend and one of the NNT Thirteen currently serving time in prison. In it he wrote:

> Remember that night in 2014? You, me, and all those kids from Scholarism and the Federation of Students – we all wanted to find a way to energise the protesters in Admiralty. In the end we decided to storm Civic Square, but you were arrested and I wasn't. And yet here we are. Both ended up behind bars just the same. I think it's destiny.
>
> If you are Joshua, then I must be Caleb. Together we can take the pro-democracy movement forward and lead Hong Kong to the Promised Land!

Raphael and I are both Christians. He knows that my parents named me after Joshua, the prophet who led the Israelites to the promised land of Canaan after Moses' death. My parents weren't thinking about political leadership when they picked the name, but they did want me to be an upstanding citizen who does the right thing and inspires others to do the same. Ever since my parents told me the story of Joshua I've tried my best not to let them down.

According to the Book of Numbers in the Old Testament, Caleb and Joshua worked side by side to explore new land for possible settlement. They famously carried a huge cluster of grapes from Canaan to persuade the Israelites that it was the promised land that they had been searching for over 40 years.

Raphael is being humble by referring to himself as Caleb. He has made significant personal sacrifices for Hong Kong. Other than the nine-month sentence he's currently serving, he faces two other criminal charges: one for inciting others to participate in the Umbrella Movement and the other for breaching a court injunction to stay clear of the Mongkok protest site – the same contempt of court charge as mine.

In the past, pro-democracy political parties have had their differences. Even though we fight for the same cause, interpersonal conflicts and ideological disagreements often get in the way. From time to time Raphael and I argue over strategy and direction. But with so many of us locked up in prison it's time we set aside our differences and work with – and not against – each other.

Prison as Experiential Art

模擬監倉

Day 46 – Sunday, 1 October 2017

I took my mum's advice and spent my day off replying to the hundreds of letters from supporters. I knew I wouldn't be able to finish them all before my transfer, but I had to start somewhere. The other inmates kept themselves busy watching *Kung Fu Hustle*, probably the last good Stephen Chow film before he started churning out 'co-produced' films with mainland Chinese studios.

I hadn't realised that today was National Day until I heard the tired old celebratory speeches and national anthem blasting out from the TV. On the news I saw protesters surrounding the Golden Bauhinia, some holding up placards saying 'Free political prisoners'. I also saw footage of a solidarity march down Hennessy Road and the camera zoomed in on the Demosistō contingent. I saw Demosistian

Tiffany Yuen carrying a banner and shouting 'Step down, Rimsky Yuen!' If it weren't for the Justice Secretary's decision to appeal our original sentences (against the recommendation of his staff, I might add), Alex, Nathan and I would have been out there marching on the streets with the rest of the crowd.

The footage made me want to look for more coverage of Demosistō in the newspapers and I was happy to find two articles in today's *Apple Daily*. The first outlined the latest findings of an ongoing research project we've undertaken in partnership with a group called Liber Research Community, a non-profit organisation that undertakes independent research into Hong Kong's social development. 'Decoding Hong Kong's History' involves dozens of volunteers and university students poring over declassified archival materials here and in the UK documenting the discussions over the future of Hong Kong during the Sino-British handover negotiations in the 1980s.

One of the documents shows that Maria Tam, a barrister-politician who became an ardent Beijing loyalist and a political pariah, had once asked the British government to publish periodic reports to monitor the state of Hong Kong under Chinese rule – an act that in today's Hong Kong would have been considered highly unpatriotic and even subversive.

The fact that our research project continues to uncover shocking revelations and attract media coverage makes me really proud.

The second article was about a street demonstration staged by Demosistians yesterday in an effort to boost the turnout at today's solidarity march. A photograph showed two of our members (I couldn't make out their faces) dressed in prison uniform and squatting inside a papier mâché jail cell. It was a simple yet powerful way to let the public visualise what it's like for young people to be locked up like hardened criminals, and to realise that political imprisonment is no longer an abstract idea that they can brush aside.

Mooncake Season

月餅季節

―――――

Day 48 – Tuesday, 3 October 2017

Mid-Autumn Festival is a big deal in Hong Kong. It's the cultural equivalent of Thanksgiving in America, a night for families to get together for a big feast followed by a mooncake or two.

To make up for being separated from our loved ones on this special occasion – which is tomorrow, prison prepared treats for us. In addition to grilled fish and a hard-boiled egg for dinner tonight we each received a chicken leg the size of a credit card. Of course it was nothing like the kind of fat, juicy chicken leg you'd get from a street-food stall, but here in prison the surprise treat went a long way to make the day feel more festive.

Then we were told that each of us would be collecting our own mooncake tomorrow night. It was a nice touch, although I find the idea of giving out mooncakes in prison somewhat strange. Every Chinese person grows up with the story that mooncakes were used by the revolutionaries to overthrow Mongolian rule at the end of the Yuan dynasty. On a Mid-Autumn Festival some 700 years ago, rebels put secret messages in baked pastries to evade the authorities and wage a successful uprising against the Mongols. I wonder whether the irony of handing out these subversive treats is lost on prison management.

Earlier today, two new inmates arrived at Pik Uk, which means I'll no longer be the only newcomer doing all the sweeping up in the common areas. It means I'll also get help carrying the heavy milk bottles I have to lug up the stairs from the kitchen to the cells on the fourth floor. Mind you, when I say 'milk', I don't mean the fresh kind people get from the supermarket refrigerator. Here we prepare milk by mixing an inordinate amount of water with a stingy portion of milk powder. It's essentially white-coloured water. Unsurprisingly, the inmates aren't lapping it up.

Sentencing on My 21st Birthday

二十一歲生日的判刑

Day 49 – Wednesday, 4 October 2017

I found out from the news today that the sentencing for my contempt of court case has been set for 13 October, which happens to be my 21st birthday. It's not a bad thing given that it means I'll be able to see a few familiar faces – family, Demosistians, lawyers and other activists.

For logistical reasons, prison management has delayed my transfer to Stanley adult prison by a day. That means on 14 October, the day after I attain legal adulthood, I'll say goodbye to the juvenile inmates here and be bussed out of Pik Uk carrying a small bag of personal belongings and a huge bag of junk food, which I plan to purchase in order to use up my October salary.

I spent much of today going through the 200-page Facebook printout Senia Ng sent to me. I read

Tiffany's heartfelt post describing how she has been coping with Nathan's imprisonment (the two Demo-sistians have been dating for years), as well as her efforts to push back the Education Bureau's attempt to whitewash sensitive subject matters like the Tiananmen Square Protests from secondary school syllabuses.

There was also a post about Derek's trip to London alongside three pan-democracy lawmakers – Eddie Chu, Ray Chan and Ted Hui – to meet with representatives from Britain's Foreign and Commonwealth Office. It was the first visit of its kind in recent memory and an important step in forging closer relations with foreign governments to draw the world's attention to the situation in Hong Kong.

I was also excited to read about the new line-up of presenters on the popular *Demosistō Student Union* programme, a weekly show on radio D100. In the past, Nathan, Derek and I – being the party's most senior members – would always go on the show. Now that the three of us are either in prison or about to be, it opens up opportunities for more junior members to get some airtime and hone their public speaking skills. In terms of inspiring the next generation of leadership, it's a good thing.

Last Few Days with Inmates

與囚友的最後幾天

Day 50 – Thursday, 5 October 2017

Autumn is upon us. The temperature has dropped by a few degrees and we've all put on our blue T-shirts instead of going topless as we have been the last few weeks. In Hong Kong, everyone prefers chilly weather to the sweltering summer heat.

Yesterday was the Mid-Autumn Festival, which makes today a public holiday (the idea is to give people a day to rest after a night of festivities). At Pik Uk, public holidays operate like Sundays – we get to sit around in the canteen all morning and the classroom all afternoon. To get some fresh air and move around a bit, I decided to go for a jog in the main yard.

We've been getting special treats at mealtimes for three days in a row. We were surprised with Chinese pears, spring rolls and hotdogs at dinner yesterday and this morning we each got a gift pack full of snacks like Cheezels, dried squid and soda crackers. Inside was a note from the Christian Prison Pastoral Association with a short story about Christ's crucifixion, several scriptures from the New Testament and a response slip. Inmates are encouraged to fill out the slip to request a pastoral visit or some religious literature, and to tick the box to 'surrender to Jesus Christ and make Him my Saviour'. I wonder how many inmates read the note and how many simply binned it with the packaging.

For weeks now we've been glued to a TVB crime drama called *Line Walker 2*. TV star Moses Chan plays Mr Black, a fearsome organised crime kingpin. In today's episode (in prison we're one episode behind the live broadcast), Mr Black was shot three times by an assassin at point-blank range. Either he was wearing a bulletproof vest and will survive the gunshots, or TVB is willing to kill off the series' leading man, which is highly unlikely. I suppose we'll find out tomorrow.

Inmates were fired up by the climactic scene when Mr Black threw himself in front of his gang brothers and took three bullets from the assassin. During the ad break everyone talked over each other to brag about their own heroic near-death experiences, trading stories of outrunning the police and using encrypted messages to close deals.

What they left out – and I only found out from one-on-one conversations later on – was that most of them ended up in prison because they were thrown under the bus by their leaders. Those at the bottom of the gang pecking order often end up being the fall guys who 'take one for the team'. No matter how much TV shows and movies in Hong Kong glamorise the Triads, there's no shortage of cowardice and hypocrisy within the gang hierarchy.

I also learned that most inmates decided to join gangs for financial reasons – they needed to put food on the table, especially the ones who were estranged from their parents. It's entirely different from the government's narrative that young people choose to become gang members because they want to look cool or because they've flunked out of school and need to find something to do.

Something else I was surprised to find out is that I'm the only person in the entire juvenile prison who has a Christian name. While most people in Hong Kong go by their English names and like to mix English vocabulary into their everyday conversations, this is not the case in prison. In fact, there are inmates who don't even know the alphabet. This morning when I mentioned that I missed having milk tea at the 'weekend', the response I got was 'Chi-fung, no more English words, okay? Speak Cantonese please!'

Last Letter from Pik Uk

獄中札記

Day 53 – Sunday, 8 October 2017

To my supporters:

In a few days I'll turn 21 and be transferred to an adult prison to serve my remaining sentence.

I've now spent 50 days at Pik Uk. Every day I march, I clean, I go to class, I eat and I go to sleep; it's an endless loop that keeps repeating itself. Prisoners are expected to follow strict orders in an environment designed to erase independent thinking and free will. Every decision here is made for us by an unshakable authority. That's the hardest thing about being in jail.

The Bible teaches us that 'suffering produces perseverance; perseverance, character; and character, hope' (Romans 5:3–4). To make the best of a bad situation I've befriended dozens of inmates at Pik Uk. They've given me a deeper understanding of the social issues facing people my age. I've also tried my best to fight against institutional injustices, from physical abuse to mandatory head shaving. Even though I've been threatened with reprisal for speaking up, I remain undeterred and committed to ensuring fairness and dignity for all.

From the anti-national education campaign to the Umbrella Movement, from Scholarism to Demosistō, from the first demonstration I led in 2012 to my imprisonment in 2017, the past six years have been nothing short of a rollercoaster ride. I believe there's a silver lining to my imprisonment. The last seven weeks have given me a chance to take a step back and reflect on my journey of activism, to take stock of mistakes made and lessons learned, to read more books to better myself, and to thank the people who have walked with me along the way.

Many commentators, especially those from the international press, attribute the Umbrella Movement and the political awakening it engendered to the efforts of a few student activists like myself, Nathan and Alex. But nothing is further from the truth. The true heroes who deserve the credit are the amazing people of Hong Kong who for decades have stood by each other and fought for democracy despite the odds.

But we need their help once again. We need every Hong Kong citizen to direct his or her energy, perseverance and commitment to non-violence towards building a more robust civil society. By the time the next political uprising is upon us (in whatever form it may take), we'll be best positioned to make the most of the opportunity and use it to get us closer to our goal.

Over the last 50 days I've received over 770 letters from supporters around the world. Some of them were from self-proclaimed 'blue ribbons' who opposed the Umbrella Movement. Their words of encouragement, despite their political leanings, are ample proof that if we continue to demonstrate to the public that our motives are pure and unselfish, even those who disagree with us may come around.

From a semi-autonomy to a semi-autocracy, Hong Kong has entered a new era of political oppression. To lose faith now is to let our opponents have the last word. But if we each do our part, together our efforts will amount to a force to be reckoned with. The arc of history will bend towards us if we persist long enough.

Joshua Wong
Pik Uk Prison

Presence of God

主的同在

Day 57 – Thursday, 12 October 2017

Today is my last day as a legal minor.

On the eve of a milestone, I was thrilled to receive a birthday card signed by some 30 pastors and ministry leaders from my church. I was particularly inspired by Reverend Yiu's words:

> *The presence of God transcends prison walls*
> *May His grace free you wherever you are*

I've been going to the same church since I was three. The building itself is one of those heritage structures that seats a thousand and the congregation comprises mainly middle-class families from the neighbourhood. It's your average house of worship in Hong Kong.

With some notable exceptions, like Reverend Chu (one of the Occupy Central Trio), religious leaders tend to stay out of politics. Pastors often steer clear of sensitive topics on the grounds that they need to accommodate congregants of all political stripes. During my anti-national education campaign five years ago, I felt resistance and even disapproval from church seniors, which was disappointing considering the way I've always treated them as my second family.

I should point out that not everyone in my church shares this attitude and some are openly supportive of my activism. I also understand why others are sceptical, since religion and politics never used to mix and they simply don't know what to do with a vociferous youth who makes a career out of questioning authority. Besides, how could a pastor offer any meaningful guidance if he doesn't have a firm grip on the underlying political issues?

The civil awakening brought about by the Umbrella Movement is widespread and irreversible. My worry is that if churches in Hong Kong don't evolve with our shifting political landscape they run the risk of alienating their congregants. This problem will only grow as society becomes more polarised and churchgoers demand that their religious leaders take a stand. At some point, even the most loyal members will vote with their feet and find an alternative where their political views and grievances are listened to.

I heard through the grapevine that my transfer date has been set for Monday, 16 October. As requested, I'll be moved to a non-smoking ward in Stanley Prison. One of the biggest advantages of being at an adult prison is that I'll no longer be required to do those Godforsaken morning marches. In fact, I had my last march this morning and even after all this time I still couldn't get it right. I have trouble remembering even basic drill commands in English, which come out funny through the mouths of our Cantonese-speaking sergeants. Who knew that 'lap-wai-lap' is actually 'left-right-left', that 'tsing step' is 'change step' and 'fee see' is 'freeze'? My English pronunciation isn't perfect but even I can tell that the sergeants are butchering the language. Diction aside, I'll never understand why 'change step' means stomping on the ground with my right foot – the phrase bears absolutely no connection to the action.

But prisons are all about keeping up appearances. Morning marches are shown off to bigwig visitors as the ultimate embodiment of discipline and order. Whenever there's a Justice of the Peace or senior correctional officer on the premises we have to line up like schoolchildren and shout out our responses in unison.

One time a VIP arrived for a prison tour and I spotted a mysterious bird's nest on the hallway outside one of the classrooms. When asked why, the prison guard said, 'We planted the nest there to show our esteemed visitor that Pik Uk inmates are very much in touch with Mother Nature.'

ON 16 OCTOBER 2017, JOSHUA WAS TRANSFERRED TO STANLEY PRISON, A MAXIMUM SECURITY ADULT FACILITY.

Blue vs Yellow

藍絲黃絲

Day 66 - Saturday, 21 October 2017

Saturday is a work day at an adult prison. For me, that means more toilets to clean.

I've decided to skip both breakfast and lunch every day until my release. I want to save my appetite for the real food outside. Real food with friends and family.

A few cellmates told me today that the mood has changed around here since my arrival. They said that the staff are more on guard and on edge. Rules that are usually not enforced are suddenly taken much more seriously.

For instance, because of the diversity of inmates, Caucasians are given Western-style meals, South Asians get naan bread and curry, and so on. Non-ethnic Chinese often trade food for purposes of variety and as a social bonding activity. Even though prison guidelines prohibit food sharing (perhaps to prevent inmates from using it as a currency to barter for other things), the guards usually look the other way. After all, what's the harm of a few guys sharing a bite together? But all that has stopped since I got here and the guards are patrolling the canteen nearly every day to make sure it doesn't happen.

Inmate diversity goes beyond ethnicity; there's a huge variety of political views too. The younger prisoners tend to be 'yellow ribbons' supportive of the pro-democracy movement. Several of them have opened up to me about their involvement in the Umbrella Movement and subsequent protests. But there are plenty of hardcore 'blue ribbons' too. Yesterday someone from the Security Unit pulled me aside and told me that some older guys in the workshop had heckled me and yelled 'traitor' when I walked past. I didn't hear them, but I'm hardly surprised.

I received letters from a few university classmates today. We started in the same year and now they're about to graduate. By summer next year they'll be starting their first jobs and getting their first pay slips. Some of them will become architects, others will go into finance or IT. They'll be climbing the corporate ladder and moving ahead in life.

By contrast, I've just deferred my studies for another six months, which puts my earliest possible graduation date at May 2020. And then what? Politics is all I want to do and to be honest all I can do. No company or government department will ever dare come near this thorn in Beijing's side. That's the cold reality of being an activist in Hong Kong.

Path to Full Democracy

香港的民主路

Day 67 – Sunday, 22 October 2017

Since September Catalonia's independence referendum has been in the news nearly every day. The movement reached a fever pitch this week and the 24-hour news channel showed the same footage of massive street protests in Barcelona throughout the day. The more I learn about the Catalan people's demands, the more I feel we have in common.

I'm not talking about Hong Kong independence – I've never advocated for that in the past and I'm not going to now. What I'm referring to is the similarity between Catalonia's efforts to assert its cultural and political identity and Hong Kong's own struggle to do the same in the shadow of Communist China. Many issues we face in Hong Kong, from ever-increasing intervention by the central government to the marginalisation of our mother tongue and the persecution of political activists, will sound as familiar to a Catalan as a Hong Konger.

There's no shortage of popular support within Catalonia for its resistance against Madrid. Turnouts at street protests are always substantial, despite the threat of violence and arrest. What the movement lacks, however, is support from the international community. In the absence of key allies such as overseas governments and the European Union, it's hard to imagine that the Catalan movement will prevail in the near future.

The same lesson applies to our pro-democracy struggle. Pitted against the world's most powerful autocracy, Hong Kong must look globally and secure international support regardless of our demands, be it universal suffrage or some form of self-determination. That's why I've made international interaction and networking a top priority for Demosistō. I hope other pan-democracy political parties will see it too and work with us to find allies overseas.

On a lighter note, a cellmate recorded last Sunday's movie on TVB Pearl and the entire cell cheered when we learned that it was *Avengers: Age of Ultron*. Even though I'd already watched it in the theatre, being a superhero fanboy who's watched every single Marvel and DC movie (some more than once) I was as thrilled as everyone else. Seeing the Marvel logo at the start of the film alone was enough to give me goosebumps. I've already made a mental note to watch the latest *Thor* movie as soon as I'm out of here.

Last Day

最後一天

————

Day 68 – Monday, 23 October 2017

My last day in prison came and went like any other. I spent the day reading the news, scrubbing toilets and watching a bit of TV with my cellmates. It's fitting that I finished Malala's memoir just before my release. Holding the paperback in my hands, I couldn't help but feel both fortunate and humbled to be able to follow my beliefs and live out my dreams – however far-fetched they first appeared – and make a mark in history.

By the time I'm released I'll have spent 69 days behind bars. While these 69 days are a mere footnote in our decades-long struggle for democracy, they represent an important milestone in my seven-year journey in political activism. Prison has taken away my freedom, but it has given me many things too: time to reflect, space to grow and memories that will last a lifetime. What's more, I'll come out of prison stronger and more committed to our cause than ever.

In many countries around the world, the fight for freedom and democracy puts safety and even lives at risk. As my Pakistani cellmate rightly pointed out, the cost of activism in other places is much higher than what we face in Hong Kong.* Yet that can change quickly, as we've witnessed with the conviction of the '13 plus 3'. It's all the more reason for us to make as much progress and generate as much momentum while we still can, before the cost of resistance becomes prohibitively high. We have no excuse not to and we owe it to future generations to at least try.

This will be my last journal entry, at least for now. I'll be back within these walls soon enough. Our struggle is far from over.

---

* The situation in Hong Kong has deteriorated rapidly since Joshua's imprisonment in 2017. *See Act III, Chapter 1, The Extradition Bill Crisis.*

ACT III

THE THREAT TO GLOBAL DEMOCRACY

'Injustice anywhere is a threat to justice everywhere.'
— Martin Luther King Jr

The Extradition Bill Crisis: A Global Trend in Citizen-based Democracy

逃犯條例危機: 公民民主的全球趨勢

A lot has happened in Hong Kong since my first incarceration.

If I were to liken our epic struggle for freedom and democracy to the original *Star Wars* trilogy, then the two years since my imprisonment in 2017 would be a drawn-out version of the middle instalment: *The Empire Strikes Back*. While the Resistance was still regrouping and recovering from the last political uprising, the Imperial Fleet led by the new chief executive Carrie Lam had begun an all-out counter-attack on civil society.

In January 2018, three months after I walked out of Stanley Prison, the election authorities barred Demosistian spokeswoman Agnes Chow from running in the by-election to fill Nathan's vacated LegCo seat. The ban was issued on the grounds that Demosistō's self-determination stance was seditious and not in line with the Basic Law.

The announcement came after Agnes had already renounced her British citizenship in order to run for office, which meant the sacrifice she had made against her parents' wishes was for nothing. When I offered her my apologies she said, without a hint of regret, 'I'm a big girl. I knew what I was getting myself into; besides, don't make a habit of apologising for things the government has done to us.'

And the bad news kept coming. In April, after months of gruelling court trials, nine prominent activists involved in the Umbrella Movement were convicted on public nuisance and incitement charges. While some of them received suspended or community-service sentences, Professors Benny Tai and Chan Kin-man of the Occupy Central Trio were each sentenced to 16 months in prison, while 'Bottle' Shiu Ka-chun and Raphael Wong each received 8-month sentences.

Then, in July, the Department of Security took the unprecedented move to ban a political party, the Hong Kong National Party, for its pro-independence stance. Less than a week later, the government deported Victor Mallet of the *Financial Times* for hosting the founder of the banned party for a talk at the Foreign Correspondents' Club. It was the first expulsion of a foreign correspondent on political grounds in the city's history.

By shutting the opposition out of the legislature and locking its people up when they took to the streets, the Hong Kong government was forcing its opponents to pursue more radical options. No one else but our political leaders, who act at the behest of the Chinese Communist Party, is responsible for pushing citizens towards more violent forms of resistance, destabilising the city in the process. As activists, our challenge is to strike the delicate balance between principles and results, means and ends. What else can we do when our right to political participation is denied to us and non-violent protests are repeatedly ignored? How much violence, if any, can be tolerated to further our cause without alienating Hong Kong society and the international community?

We didn't have to wait long before we had to confront these questions head on. In June 2019, on the heels of the 30th anniversary of the Tiananmen Square Massacre and nearly five years after the Umbrella Movement brought Hong Kongers out onto the streets, the city was once again mired in political unrest. A controversial fugitive transfer arrangement with China tabled by the government set off a fresh round of large-scale protests. What followed was something that nobody – not the pro-democracy camp, not Carrie Lam's administration, and certainly not the Communist leadership in Beijing – could have imagined.

At the heart of the firestorm was a government proposal that would allow the extradition of criminal suspects to stand trial on the mainland. Many feared that anyone in Hong Kong, from the local business-man to the foreigner working in, or simply passing through, the city, could be arrested and delivered to the authorities across the border where a fair trial and due process are not guaranteed. The disparity between their judicial systems and legal safeguards is the reason why most modern democracies, such as the United States, the United Kingdom, Germany and Japan, have refused to enter into extradition treaties with China. In fact, this very issue was brought up during the Handover negotiations; a mutual fugitive transfer arrangement between Hong Kong and China was specifically excluded from our extradition ordinances because of concerns over potential political persecution and human rights abuses.

As soon as the Extradition Bill was announced, civil society was up in arms over the proposal's potentially chilling effect on free expression in Hong Kong; China is known to punish critics by fabricating criminal charges such as tax evasion and drug trafficking against them. The bill came within weeks of the high-profile arrest by Canadian authorities of Meng Wanzhou, CFO of Chinese tech giant Huawei. The timing had the city's expat community worried about retaliatory actions by Beijing via the extradition channel. 'If this dangerous bill gets passed,' a Chinese-American friend said to me, 'the Communists can get their hands on anyone they don't like. They can do it openly and legally without resorting to kidnapping like they did to the booksellers!'

Distrust of Beijing aside, what Hong Kongers found even more infuriating was Carrie Lam's stubborn determination to press ahead with the bill in the face of public outcry. Her intransigence had everyone asking: why is she so fixated on an arrangement that nobody wants, when society is already divided as it is and there are other, much more pressing, issues like housing and old-age poverty? Is this Beijing's idea or her own pet project designed to impress her bosses? Regardless of the answers, the self-inflicted crisis confirmed Lam's image as a tone-deaf career bureaucrat and underscored the problems of an unelected government.

When mass protests began to flare up in June, it felt as if it was the Umbrella Movement all over again, except this time protesters were angrier and more combative than their predecessors. Young people's voices went from loud to deafening as they refused to be brushed aside in the way they had been in 2014. Street demonstrations escalated quickly after two back-to-back million-person marches failed to move the political needle – both the Hong Kong and Chinese governments refused to scrap the Extradition Bill despite the record-breaking turnouts. Peaceful rallies soon gave way to full-scale urban guerrilla warfare.

A more militant breed of protester emerged, dressed in black and wearing yellow hard hats and half-face respirator masks, and the movement grew in size and organisation. Faceless and leaderless, it self-mobilised using crowdsourcing apps and began clashing with police and vandalising properties of businesses perceived to be pro-establishment. Some dug up bricks from the pavement and hurled them at the police, while others threw Molotov cocktails and set subway exits on fire. A piece of anti-government graffiti offered a poignant explanation, if not a justification, for the use of more aggressive tactics: 'It was YOU who taught us that peaceful protest doesn't work!'

In response, the police unleashed an unprecedented use of force on protesters, hitting them with rubber bullets, stun grenades, bean-bag rounds, water cannons and even live ammunition. To make matters worse, hired thugs jumped into the fray to beat up demonstrators and passers-by alike, while police officers stood idly by or escorted the assailants away. All this pushed anti-police sentiment to an all-time high. If Carrie Lam resembled Darth Vader, then the Hong Kong Police Force would be the armour-clad, blaster-brandishing stormtroopers terrorising villagers across the galaxy.

I will never forget the night in July when protesters confronted a phalanx of riot police in Sheung Wan, a stone's throw from the city's financial heart. Shortly after midnight, law enforcement began an operation to clear the area by firing a rapid succession of tear-gas rounds into the crowds, turning the quiet residential enclave into a smoke-filled battlefield. Nathan and I were on the frontline hoping to reason with the officer in command, but to no avail. We had trouble breathing and started coughing uncontrollably, our paper-thin surgical masks useless against the engulfing smoke. We tried to outrun the volleys of tear gas but there was just too much of it all around us. 'This is it – I'm going to suffocate and die,' I thought to myself, before Nathan found a way out and pulled me to safety.

In September, three months after non-stop violent clashes turned Hong Kong into an urban war zone, Carrie Lam finally relented and announced the full withdrawal of the Extradition Bill. But her concession was dismissed by protesters as 'too little, too late' and did nothing to quell public anger. By then, the anti-extradition campaign had already evolved into a broader movement for accountability and democracy; the battle cry on the streets had changed from 'No extradition to China' and 'Kill the bill' to 'Liberate Hong Kong; revolution of our times!' and 'Five demands, not one less.' Among the five demands were the creation of an independent commission to investigate police misconduct, amnesty for arrested protesters and universal suffrage.

In many ways this new round of popular uprising is part of a larger global trend of citizen-driven democracy. From the Czech Republic and Russia to Iran, Kazakhstan and Ethiopia, ordinary citizens are using what little freedom of expression they have at their disposal to voice their frustrations over corruption, failed economic policies and regression in civil liberties. Halfway around the world in Venezuela, for instance, President Nicolás Maduro's move towards a one-man rule by filling both the legislature and the courts with political allies and the subsequent collapse of the Venezuelan economy brought massive crowds to the streets demanding his resignation. Most recently in Chile, violent demonstrations against a subway fare increase morphed into a full-blown popular uprising demanding social equality. Similarly, in Lebanon protesters occupied major thoroughfares in the capital city of Beirut to oppose a series of proposed taxes and other austerity measures.

Meanwhile, some resistance movements are so powerful, and their concerns so universal, that they transcend geographical boundaries and galvanise citizens the world over. Extinction Rebellion, or XR, for instance, began in the UK in May 2018 to demand immediate government action to address climate change and treat it like the existential crisis it is. In the 18 months since its start the movement has spread to over 60 cities on 5 continents and inspired legions of 'XR Youth' to join the fight, thanks in large part to powerful voices like the Swedish teenage activist Greta Thunberg. Many of these grassroots movements, from XR to the post-Parkland gun-law campaign in the United States, are increasingly led by millennials and Generation Zers, as they are often the ones most impacted by older generations' inaction and acquiescence.

Whether it is the developed or the developing world, bottom-up resistance made possible by social networks and crowdsourcing tools is slowly but steadily coalescing into a formidable 'fifth estate' holding the ruling class to account. When the three branches of government – executive, legislative and judicial – are no longer effective in safeguarding democratic values, and the fourth estate of the free press is being targeted and silenced with growing intensity, a fifth power emerges to provide the necessary checks and balances on those in power.

Hong Kong is a case in point. The executive branch, including the head of government, is handpicked by Beijing to do its bidding. The legislature, already stacked with pro-establishment loyalists, has been rendered even more powerless with the wanton disqualification of opposition lawmakers. The independent judiciary, once the pride of Hong Kong and a bedrock for its economic prosperity, is being undermined by frequent overrulings by the National People's Congress, China's central legislative body. In the meantime, pro-Beijing businesses are exerting pressure on media outlets by pulling advertising or gobbling them up altogether, as was the case in the acquisition of the *South China Morning Post* by Chinese e-commerce giant Alibaba with the explicit goal to present China in a positive light. Where the other four powers have failed, a citizen-driven fifth estate comes in to fill the void. This global pattern of a mass protest movement acting as a counterweight to the state is best captured in a line from the dystopian film *V for Vendetta*: 'People should not be afraid of their governments. Governments should be afraid of their people.'

As Hong Kong plunged deeper and deeper into chaos, I became more convinced than ever that we could not fight this battle alone. Our embattled city needed a global influencer to rally overseas support and lobby foreign governments to put pressure on both our own government and Beijing. I was ready to step into that role. In September I travelled to Washington DC to testify in front of the US Congressional-Executive Commission on China (CECC). I was accompanied by Denise Ho, Canto-pop star turned human rights activist, and Demosistian Jeffrey Ngo.

Jeffrey is a Washington-based PhD student at Georgetown University and Demosistō's de facto foreign liaison. Jeffrey has written nearly all of my speeches on my foreign trips – his English is much stronger than mine – and the two of us have collaborated on numerous op-eds in international publications such as the *Guardian*, the *Wall Street Journal* and *Time*.

The focus of the CECC hearing, titled 'Hong Kong's Summer of Discontent and US Policy Responses', was twofold: first, to address the spiralling social unrest sparked by the Extradition Bill; and second, to rally support for the passing of the

Hong Kong Human Rights and Democracy Act of 2019. Once passed, the act will enable the US government to, among other things, sanction high-ranking government officers like Carrie Lam and Secretary for Security John Lee, as well as members of the Hong Kong Police Force responsible for violent crackdowns on protesters. The US government may deny entry to sanctioned individuals and freeze their onshore assets. A second bill called the PRO-TECT Hong Kong Act was also introduced. This bill aims to stop American exports of crowd control weapons to Hong Kong.

During the hearing I worked hard to explain the gravity of the situation in Hong Kong. 'The recent political crisis has turned a global city into a police state,' I said. 'I would describe the situation as a collapse of "one country, two systems". Now is the time to seek bipartisan support for the democratisation of Hong Kong. It isn't a matter of left or right, but a matter of right or wrong.'

It was heartening to be granted an audience by political heavyweights like Senator Marco Rubio and CECC Chairman and House Representative Jim McGovern. It was equally encouraging to speak in a room full of overseas Hong Kongers. The massive turnout was in stark contrast with a similar congressional hearing I attended five years ago during the Umbrella Movement, where Jeffrey was pretty much the only person from Hong Kong in the audience. We've come a long way in generating support and attention from Hong Kongers living abroad.

I ended my testimony with a solemn plea: 'Now is the time for the US Congress to pass the Hong Kong Human Rights and Democracy Act. I also hope that the US government will prioritise human rights issues when it reviews its policy on China.'

After the hearing, Denise, Jeffrey and I were ushered to another chamber, where House Speaker Nancy Pelosi and Foreign Affairs Committee Chairman Eliot Engel awaited us for a press conference under a giant portrait of George Washington. After we addressed the press, Speaker Pelosi gave me a hug and said, 'You are an inspiration to young people everywhere. Thank you for your courage and resolve.' This was the same fearless congresswoman who protested on Tiananmen Square in 1991 with a banner bearing the words 'To those who die for democracy in China', and who went on to become the most powerful woman in American politics. I am grateful that we have her and other powerful figures in the international community rooting for Hong Kong and fighting our corner.

As the three of us left the Capitol Building we were heckled by a throng of angry mainland Chinese demonstrators who were being held back behind a police line. They yelled 'Traitors!' and 'Running dogs!' while waving Chinese flags and punching in the air. I looked the loudest ones in the eye and said, in Mandarin, 'Take a deep breath of this air of freedom in America. You don't get much of it back home.'

Square Peg in a Round Hole: The Countdown to 2047

方枘圓鑿: 倒數 2047

In the early summer of 2016, for a single minute every night the facade of the tallest building in Hong Kong, the International Commerce Centre (ICC), transformed into a giant digital timer. Second by second, the clock counted down to 1 July 2047, the expiration date of the 'one country, two systems' framework that guarantees Hong Kong's semi-autonomy. The light installation was the handiwork of two young local artists who wanted to express their anxiety over the looming deadline and Beijing's tightening grip on the city. Once the building's management realised the subversive message, the ICC cancelled the light show and distanced itself from the artwork. But the artists had already achieved their goal: images of the so-called 'countdown machine' had been plastered across social media and in newspapers the world over.

There is the colonial-era cliché that Hong Kong is a borrowed place on borrowed time. Like all clichés, this one contains a measure of truth. Before the Handover, nervous citizens counted down to the end of British rule. As soon as the clock struck midnight on 30 June 1997, a 50-year timer began to tick. To its 7.5 million inhabitants, Hong Kong is one big rental unit and we are its tenants. Nothing ever belongs to us completely or permanently.

But we don't need to wait until 2047 to know that something isn't quite right. Two decades into the sovereignty transfer, the real impact of Chinese rule, however innocuous it first appeared, has finally registered. Citizens are coming to the realisation that 'one country, two systems' is more a myth than a promise. Popular uprisings in recent years, from the Umbrella Movement to the still-unfolding Extradition Bill crisis, have underscored the inherent contradictions within the framework: how can anyone trust a totalitarian state to run or even tolerate a free society?

'Hong Kongers have been taken in by the Chinese Communist Party,' I often say to foreigners who ask me what I think of 'one country, two systems'. 'The CCP doesn't understand liberal values, let alone embrace them. It's as paradoxical as the United States running a communist territory on its soil.'

Any way you cut it, a democratic Hong Kong under Chinese rule is as out of place as a square peg in a round hole.

China and Hong Kong haven't always been at odds with each other. It's hard to imagine that there was actually a time, not too long ago, when mother and child were on good terms. After the British colony transitioned into a special administrative region without a hitch, citizens began to see their destiny intertwined with that of their mainland brothers and sisters. They believed that if China prospered, so would Hong Kong, and vice versa. Cross-border economic integration wasn't only an inevitability, it was also an opportunity. Many who had fled Hong Kong before 1997 decided to return; some even moved to the mainland in search of better wages and advancement prospects.

After the SARS outbreak in 2003, the central government relaxed travel restrictions for mainlanders to visit Hong Kong in an effort to revive our slumped economy with tourism dollars. Grateful citizens who had been traumatised by a deadly disease welcomed them with open arms. After a catastrophic 8.0-magnitude earthquake levelled parts of Sichuan Province in 2008, Hong Kongers returned the favour and paid it forward. They opened their hearts and wallets, donating hundreds of millions in aid and provisions. The first Sunday after the disaster, my church congregation observed a moment of silence to honour earthquake victims and set up donation boxes all around the premises.

A semblance of patriotism among citizens started to emerge. It continued to grow and peaked during the 2008 Beijing Olympics, China's coming-out party to the world. Hong Kongers flocked to the capital to root for their 'home team', waving the Five-starred Red Flag and chanting 'Add oil, China!' meaning 'Go for it!' I was 11 years old at the time and one of my classmates who had gone to the games gave me a keychain with a Fuwa, the official mascot. He showed me pictures of him posing in front of the iconic Water Cube aquatics centre; the entire family was wearing matching 'I Heart China' T-shirts.

But the flash of China pride didn't last. The massive, unrestrained influx of cross-border visitors started to snarl traffic and the city gradually devolved into a giant duty-free shop for mainlanders. Retail rents skyrocketed and beloved local restaurants and family shops gave way to faceless skincare chains and pharmacies to attract the red dollar. Worse, Hong Kong became a haven for well-heeled Chinese businessmen and high-ranking officials to hide their fortunes from the authorities, bidding up property prices in the process. In the ten-year period before the Umbrella Movement, residential property prices more than doubled and Hong Kong was the world's most expensive city in which to buy a home year after year.

Our everyday grievances told only half the story. Since President Xi Jinping took power in 2012, Beijing's grip on Hong Kong society has gone from tight to choking. From the 31 August framework that dashed our hopes for universal suffrage to the booksellers' abductions, Oathgate and political imprisonment, Hong Kongers can feel the political ground simultaneously shifting and shrinking beneath their feet. Successive political showdowns bear out the notion that Hong Kong has not and will never shed its colony status. We've simply been handed from one imperialist master to another.

The growing sense of unbelonging towards the motherland contributed to a collective identity crisis. Survey after survey has shown that citizens, especially the youth, are distancing themselves from the 'Chinese' label and increasingly identifying themselves as 'Hong Kongers', 'Hong Kong people', or any other appellation that doesn't contain the 'C word'. This 'anything but Chinese' sentiment swelled as a new identity was being forged. This new self-image is best captured in the protest anthem from the recent Extradition Bill crisis, titled 'Glory to Hong Kong':

> *When the dawn comes*
> *we shall liberate Hong Kong*
> *Brother and sisters walk arm in arm*
> *in the revolution of our times*
> *Our quest for freedom and democracy will not falter*
> *May glory be to Hong Kong*

The love-and-hate relationship between mother and child is a two-way street. As much as Hong Kongers view Communist China with distrust and disdain, Communist China, too, is re-evaluating its approach to running Hong Kong. China's accession to the World Trade Organization – and the breakneck economic growth that followed – means Hong Kong is not nearly as financially and strategically important to Beijing as it once was. In fact, China has made a concerted effort since the Handover to groom Shanghai and Shenzhen as viable replacements to the wayward child. More and more multinationals are bypassing Hong Kong and setting up regional headquarters on the mainland, despite the many perils of doing business in China, from intellectual property theft to the lack of rule of law.

To the Communist leadership, Hong Kong is no longer the proverbial goose that lays the golden egg. What was once a gateway to China is now perceived by Beijing as a burgeoning base of subversion. Both the Umbrella Movement and the Extradition Bill crisis are viewed as open challenges to Chinese rule. If left unchecked, freewheeling dissent may spread to the mainland and threaten the very stability of the Communist regime. By Beijing's calculations, the special administrative region is more trouble than it's worth, and the only way to rein in what the leadership regards as a bunch of Westernised cry-babies is to keep them in a state of perpetual adolescence, never allowing them to achieve political maturity.

This mutual distrust and disdain are the backdrop against which Hong Kong heads toward 2047. The prognosis for the remaining 20 or so years is grim, as repression begets defiance and defiance begets more repression. This gloomy outlook is not lost on us. Already a second exodus is underway as Hong Kongers flee the city en masse like their parents did in the 1980s and 90s. In the past two years since I was in prison, many relatives and family friends have uprooted their lives and moved overseas. These days, local bookstores are filled with titles like *Hong Kongers' Guide to Opening a Café in*

Taiwan and *Emigration to Europe for Dummies.* The same conversations my parents' generation used to have in their twenties and thirties are once again heard around the dinner table and at the office drinks machine: 'How does the Australian point system work? Will my score go up if I purchase a property?' or 'You should leave now while your kids are still small, they'll assimilate better and learn to speak English without an accent.'

Nearly halfway through its 50-year countdown, Hong Kong is at an existential crossroads. The assumption that half a century is plenty of time for Communist China to democratise or at least meet us halfway in terms of political reform has been spectacularly disproved. Come 2047, the city will either stay put – if Beijing thinks it serves its interests to renew the 'one country, two systems' policy – or, more likely, fully integrate with the rest of China in a 'one country, one system' scenario. Based on the current trajectory, the popular lament that 'Hong Kong will become just another mainland city' seems inescapable. The other two options – that Hong Kongers will achieve total independence or outlive the Communist regime as Eastern Europe did with the Soviet Union – both appear implausible given China's seemingly unstoppable rise to economic and political dominance.

But no matter how grim the future looks, I refuse to give in to the growing sense that there is nothing we can do and that Hong Kong is finished. As the clock ticks down to 2047, I am more convinced than ever that our quest for freedom and democracy will prevail in the end. My optimism is rooted not only in my conviction that democracy is an inevitable global movement, one that even the most formidable regime cannot reverse, but also in my unshakable faith in the people of Hong Kong. We are united by our courage, tenacity, resilience, ingenuity, resourcefulness and sense of purpose, summed up in a single phrase long used to describe the core essence of Hong Kongers: the 'Lion Rock spirit'. It is the collective belief that we can overcome any adversity if we try hard enough, a belief inspired by the namesake mountain that has been watching over our land since time immemorial.

So don't count us out just yet. Throughout our history, every sceptic that's prophesied the end of Hong Kong – during the Japanese occupation in World War II, at the reassumption of power by China at the turn of the millennium, when a deadly epidemic swept through the city in 2003 and a full-scale popular uprising rocked its foundations in 2014 – has been proven wrong. No matter the obstacles, the city will achieve political maturity and reach its full potential as a beacon of resilience and defiance around the world. I am sure of it.

I will be exactly 50 years old in 2047. I want to be able to tell my children that their father once fought a good fight to safeguard their homeland. I will tell them that their father didn't make the same mistake their grandparents' generation did at the Handover, when they let other parties decide their own future.

One World, Two Empires: A New Cold War

兩雄相爭：新冷戰思為

On 1 October 2019, the Chinese Communist Party commemorated the 70th anniversary of the founding of the People's Republic of China. The day-long celebration culminated in a massive military parade on Tiananmen Square, the largest of its kind in the party's history. As fighter jets zoomed overhead in perfect fly-past formations, a convoy of nuclear-capable missiles and other never before seen weapon systems rumbled down Chang'an Avenue under the watchful eye of President Xi Jinping. During his speech, Xi declared to thunderous applause, 'The Chinese people have risen! No force can stop China and its people from forging ahead!'

For decades, since Deng Xiaoping's 'reform and openness' initiative began in 1978 – the economic version of Gorbachev's Glasnost and Perestroika that sought to reform the Soviet Union in the early 1980s – and the Tiananmen Square Massacre that nearly derailed it, the free world has operated on the assumption that economic prosperity will bring about political reform in Communist China. As quality of life improves, it is argued, the Chinese people will become more educated and connected with the rest of the world. They will demand more freedoms and accountability from those in power, forcing the latter to modernise and democratise the country's political system. The formula has worked elsewhere in Asia, for example in South Korea and Taiwan, and so why not China? Time and money, too, will run their course in the 'Middle Kingdom'.

Deng's successors, Jiang Zemin and Hu Jintao, stuck to the formula to a large extent. They were aggressive on economic growth and relatively moderate on nationalist fervour and ideological control. It was on this basis that China was admitted to the World Trade Organization in 2003 and cemented its status as 'The Factory of the World'. The 2008 Beijing Olympics was China's way of telling the world that it was every bit the benevolent economic powerhouse that it claimed to be, and that its 'peaceful rise' was not only good for its people, it was also good for the world.

Then, in 2012, everything changed when Xi Jinping beat out his political rivals in the once-a-decade leadership change and ascended to the role of Paramount Leader. The son of a prominent revolutionary who had fought side-by-side with Mao during the Chinese Civil War, Xi is a wolf in panda's clothing, whose gentle, understated public persona belies ambition and ruthlessness. Since assuming the throne he has sought to secure a place next to Mao in the pantheon of powerful Communist leaders. In 2017, Xi manoeuvred to have his political theory enshrined into the Chinese constitution alongside the teachings of Mao and Deng. A few months later, he engineered a constitutional amendment to remove presidential term limits, effectively crowning himself Emperor for Life.

Domestically, Xi has successfully consolidated power by purging political rivals using a nationwide anti-corruption campaign and crushing dissent on the pretext of social harmony. The Chinese government has deployed face recognition, online surveillance and other cutting-edge technology to monitor its citizens and manipulate public opinion. Hundreds of human rights lawyers have been arrested and charged with inciting subversion. Catholic congregations are routinely harassed and pushed underground as their churches are raided and demolished, while Tibetans have been stripped of their freedom of speech, religion and movement. In Xinjiang Province, as many as 3 million Uighur

Muslims have been imprisoned or sent to re-education camps.

Internationally, China has been flexing its military muscle by building artificial islands as naval and air bases in the South China Sea, unnerving neighbours like Malaysia, Indonesia and the Philippines. The country has grown markedly more assertive in territorial disputes with Japan, India and Vietnam. The Chinese government has also been accused of launching coordinated cyberattacks on government networks and research agencies in the US, Canada, Australia and India.

This show of hard power is matched by a full-scale sharp-power offensive. China has been wielding its growing financial and cultural influence to entice, coerce, manipulate and bully other countries into acquiescence and cooperation. It has set up hundreds of Confucius Institutes around the world to spread propaganda under the guise of language teaching and cultural exchange. Under the auspices of its ambitious Belt and Road Initiative (BRI), China has been aggressively pitching its infrastructure-based economic model to countries from Myanmar and Sri Lanka to Kazakhstan and Cyprus. Multi-billion dollar construction contracts awarded to Chinese companies are often fraught with corruption and financed with crushing debt that serves to increase China's political leverage over the foreign government.

The combination of carrot and stick in regional diplomacy has allowed China to export far more than manufactured goods and infrastructure know-how. Increasingly, Xi is seeking to spread his own brand of one-party rule in Asia and beyond, just as the Soviet Union sought to spread communism in the Cold War era. Chinese companies have been marketing and selling citizen surveillance systems, euphemistically known as 'smart city' technology, to autocracies in the Middle East and Latin America. Beijing's economic assistance to and open endorsement of North Korea and Myanmar are a key reason why these brutal regimes continue to operate with impunity despite international condemnation and isolation.

China's unprecedented economic clout and political stature have made many governments, especially its neighbours in Asia, its allies and enablers. One example hit particularly close to home. In October 2016, while I was on my way to give a talk on youth activism at Chulalongkorn University in Bangkok, I was detained by Thai authorities at the airport without being given any reason. During my confinement in a dark cell, one of the officials told me in broken English, 'This is Thailand, not Hong

Kong. Thailand is just like China!' He was referring to the lack of human rights protection in both countries. Those were by far the scariest hours in my life, not only because of the language barrier, but also because I was on foreign soil without access to a lawyer. Worse, the incident happened on the heels of the Causeway Bay bookseller abductions. One of the abductees had vanished while on holiday in Pattaya, a beach resort in Thailand. Even though I was released after 12 hours and sent back to Hong Kong on the same day, the episode was a wake-up call to me that Beijing's long arm has reached far beyond its soil and that many foreign governments have been cowed into doing its bidding. Today, my mobility in the region continues to be highly restricted; I can count all the places in Asia I consider it safe for me to travel to on one hand: Japan, South Korea and Taiwan.

By now, any pretence that China is on a peaceful rise to superpower status has been shattered once and for all. The world's second most powerful nation is contributing to a troubling global trend where autocratic regimes are encroaching on democratic rights both domestically and internationally. We have seen Russia, another authoritarian superpower, clamp down on anti-government activists at home and annex Crimea from neighbouring Ukraine.

Similarly, Narendra Modi's government in India has attempted to silence the opposition at home and invaded semi-autonomous Kashmir, just as the Turkish military regime has imprisoned journalists and displaced millions of Kurds in northern Syria.

Their motivation is singular: self-perpetuation. To consolidate and maintain power domestically these regimes have shown no compunction about crushing dissenters, crippling civil society and removing other obstacles that stand in their way. Outside their borders they flex their military muscles to make a show of strength abroad and, more crucially, to impress and intimidate their home audiences. These twin offensives are critical because autocratic regimes are often embroiled in factional infighting centrally while battling popular insurgencies regionally. However invincible and invulnerable they appear to the outside world, the two-front strategy is the only way for them to retain power and prolong its existence. China's simultaneous territorial expansion abroad and brutal crackdown on minorities and human rights activists at home are a case in point.

But that's not all. President Xi's continent-spanning Belt and Road Initiative suggests an even greater ambition: to challenge America's dominance in world trade and global diplomacy. In many ways, the 'one country, two systems' formula for Hong Kong is also how the Communist leadership views its relationship with the rest of the world. In his grand vision of a new global order, Xi is advancing a 'one world, two empires' framework in which the United States and its allies defend their liberal, rights-based ideology, while China and other one-party states demand non-interference from the free world and quietly pursue an oppressive and expansionary agenda. BRI is a thinly veiled attempt to create a strategic blockade to counter the US-led alliance system with Japan, South Korea, the Philippines, Taiwan and Australia that has been the bulwark of East Asian security since World War II.

A new cold war is brewing between China and the rest of the democratic world, and Hong Kong is holding the line in one of its first battles. Nothing captures that tension more vividly than the surreal 'split-screen' moments on 1 October 2019 when live coverage of the 70th anniversary celebrations in Beijing was shown side by side with scenes of anti-government demonstrators braving tear gas and throwing eggs at Xi's portraits on the streets of Hong Kong. The contrast between the two narratives not only symbolises the David-versus-Goliath struggle of Hong Kongers against a regime that is infinitely more powerful, it also sends a clear message to the world that China's tightening grip on Hong Kong is part of a much broader threat to global democracy.

In May 2019, five months before the National Day celebrations, I went to prison for the second time. I spent seven weeks at Lai Chi Kok Correctional Institution for violating a court injunction during the Umbrella Movement. I tried to comfort my parents by downplaying the situation, telling them that I had picked up enough prison speak at Pik Uk to blend in with the inmates. I joked that my biggest regret was having to miss the opening night of *Avengers: Endgame*, the sequel to *Avengers: Infinity War* which I'd watched and re-watched several times.

Before heading to prison, a foreign reporter asked me for a soundbite about my second incarceration and China's crackdown on pro-democracy activists in general. I thought about my discussion with my parents and said, 'This isn't our end game. Our fight against the CCP is an infinity war.'

The infinity war that has ravaged Hong Kong for years, I am afraid, may be coming soon to a political theatre near you.

Canary in the Coal Mine:
A Global Manifesto for Democracy

礦坑裏的金絲雀: 全球民主宣言

At the CECC hearing on Capitol Hill in September 2019 I issued a dire warning to the United States congressional committee: 'What's happening in Hong Kong matters to the world. The people of Hong Kong are standing at the forefront to confront China's authoritarian rule. If Hong Kong falls, the next may be the free world.'

Hong Kong is my birthplace and my beloved home. There is far more to this magical place than meets the eye. Beyond the soaring skyscrapers and glistening shopping malls, the semi-autonomous territory is the only place on Chinese soil where citizens dare stand up to those in power – because our very existence depends on it. For better or worse, the tidal waves of resistance in recent years have transformed the financial centre into a political stronghold. Notwithstanding Beijing's effort to keep the city in a state of perpetual adolescence, the latter has outgrown itself and its master. Hong Kongers, too, have evolved from detached economic beings to noble freedom fighters. Ever since the Handover we have been waging a lonely and improbable battle against an autocratic superpower with what little resources we have: our voice, our dignity and our conviction.

From Turkey and Ukraine to India, Myanmar and the Philippines, citizens are pushing back oppressive regimes in defence of their diminishing rights. But nowhere else in the world is the struggle between free will and authoritarianism more clearly demonstrated than here. In the new trans-Pacific cold war, Hong Kong is the first line of defence to stop or at least slow down the dangerous rise of a totalitarian superpower. Like the canary in the coal mine or the early warning system on a tsunami-prone coastline, we are sending out a distress signal to the rest of the world so that countermeasures can be taken before it is too late. As much as Hong Kong needs the international community, the international community needs Hong Kong. Because today's Hong Kong is the rest of the world's tomorrow.

The best way to illustrate this point is to understand the 'white terror' that has plagued Hong Kong since it reverted to Chinese rule. The term refers to the systematic attack on free expression and other democratic values, not through hard military might but by more subtle forms of fear and intimidation. For years, local businesses in Hong Kong have been pressured into keeping quiet on sensitive political subjects or openly siding with the Chinese government to avoid angering Beijing or alienating the lucrative mainland market. Media outlets in Hong Kong are known to self-censor for fear of losing advertising revenue. A-list celebrities have appeared in video confessionals to apologise for 'hurting the feelings' of the Chinese people after inadvertently wading into political debates. The feelings of the Chinese people are so easily and frequently hurt that a new phrase has been coined – we call it 'brittle heart syndrome'.

At the height of the anti-Extradition Bill protests, Cathay Pacific – Hong Kong's flagship airline that relies heavily on the Chinese market – fired two-dozen pilots and flight attendants who were sympathetic to the protesters. The airline's CEO issued a letter to all 33,000 staff warning them that they could be dismissed for making pro-protest social media posts and encouraging them to report 'unacceptable behaviour' among staff. The incident happened while I was in Washington DC, which prompted me to make a remark to House Speaker Nancy Pelosi after our press conference. 'This is a prime example of the white terror I mentioned in my testimony this morning,' I said. 'Let's hope what happened to Cathay Pacific will never happen to American companies.'

Less than a month after I said those fateful words, the National Basketball Association controversy exploded and set off one of the biggest PR crises in the history of professional sports. In October 2019, Daryl Morey, general manager of the Houston Rockets, posted a tweet in support of the Hong Kong protests. Morey's comment triggered a massive backlash in China resulting in cancelled events, pulled advertisements and a boycott by mainland basketball fans. When NBA Commissioner Adam Silver told reporters that Beijing had put pressure on the franchise to fire Morey, China's state broadcaster China Central Television (CCTV) warned Silver of 'retribution sooner or later' and 'dramatic financial consequences'.

Within the same month, US games publisher Blizzard Entertainment found itself in a similar diplomatic quagmire. Fearing backlash in China, Blizzard suspended e-sports gamer Ng Wai Chung for openly supporting the Hong Kong protesters and stripped him of his prize money (which was subsequently restored following international outcry). Then Apple bowed to pressure from Beijing and removed from its app store HKmap.live, a crowd-sourcing app that protesters had used to track police movements to evade arrest. In response to Apple's decision I wrote an open letter to CEO Tim Cook urging him to honour his commitment to free speech in the face of Chinese oppression. I did so not because I expected a response or change of heart from Apple, but because I wanted to send an urgent message to the international community. If even Apple – the world's leading tech giant and one that has in the past fought tooth and nail against the US authorities in defence of user privacy – finds itself bowing to authoritarian pressure, then how can we expect any other company or person to stand up to China in the future?

Even though these high-profile fallouts, all happening within a short space of time, have sent shockwaves around the world, they are 'old news' to us. The people of Hong Kong have grown so accustomed to this type of Orwellian state intimidation that it no longer shocks us. Sadly, what has been happening in Hong Kong for years is now happening to the rest of the world. Citizens everywhere are finally waking up to the reality that Communist China is increasingly throwing its weight around and mobilising its people to coerce foreign companies to comply with its worldview. That makes

China, simultaneously the most powerful autocratic regime and the largest consumer market on the planet, the single biggest threat to global democracy. The *New York Times* columnist Farhad Manjoo called the country 'a growing and existential threat to human freedom across the world'.

Our struggle has become your struggle, whether you like it or not. It is for this precise reason that the free world cannot stand idly by while the situation in Hong Kong continues to deteriorate. If Hong Kong fails, so goes the world's first line of defence. And if governments and multinationals continue to bend to the arc of China's gravity, it won't be long before citizens everywhere feel the same sting we have felt every day for the past two decades. In supporting Hong Kong in its resistance against the Communist regime, the international community is contributing to a broader fight against the spread of tyranny that, like climate change and terrorism, threatens the way of life and liberty everywhere. That's why to stand with Hong Kong is to stand with freedom. And that's why you must act now, before it's too late.

A perfect storm is brewing in the East. Xi's China is coming under increasing strain from the economic drag of an escalating trade war with the US on the one hand, and regional unrests in Xinjiang,

Tibet and Hong Kong on the other. Meanwhile, with a dangerous combination of rising unemployment and inflation, social discontent on the mainland is bubbling to the surface, the latter exacerbated by an epidemic of African swine fever that has driven up the price of pork, an important staple. Facing destabilising challenges on all sides, Xi is betting on strengthening his position by fomenting nationalism in China and stepping up his crackdown on dissent. He is hoping to navigate himself out of these turbulent times with a heavier hand and swifter measures, which in turn makes my call to stand with Hong Kong more urgent and critical than ever. The withdrawal of the Extradition Bill by the Hong Kong government is symbolically significant in that it is the first ever compromise made by Xi since he took power in 2012. Our hard-fought win suggests that the Mao-like strongman is not invincible and that there is light at the end of the tunnel if only we work together. Think about it: if a bunch of leaderless young people wearing basic protective gear can wring a concession from the world's most powerful autocratic regime with one of the world's biggest military forces, then imagine what we can achieve if all of us act together.

That is why I am asking for your help.

If my journey of activism has shown one thing, it is that even one person can make a difference no matter the odds. Whatever your age, wherever you are, you can be a part of something far greater than yourself. If you would like to help reverse the regression of democratic rights in Hong Kong and around the world, follow the ten-point action plan I set out below:

1. **Open a Twitter account** and follow hashtags such as #StandWithHongKong, #HongKong Protests and #FreedomHK. Translate tweets you find particularly relevant or inspiring into your own language so they can reach more people.

2. **Follow Hong Kong's news events** on independent news outlets like *Hong Kong Free Press* (www.hongkongfp.com) and, if you can read Chinese, *Stand News* (www.thestandnews.com).

3. **Participate in overseas Hong Kong protests** in your city. Create your own Lennon Walls (street murals of handwritten pro-democracy messages on sticky notes) or come up with an ice-bucket challenge-type viral campaign to promote awareness about the situation in Hong Kong and the threat to democratic rights posed by China and other autocratic regimes.

4. **Watch the Hong Kong film** *Ten Years* **(2015),** the Ukrainian documentary *Winter on Fire: Ukraine's Fight for Freedom* (2015), and the Korean drama *1987: When the Day Comes* (2017). These movies will inspire you – as they have inspired me – to join the global fight against tyranny and social injustices.

5. **Travel to Hong Kong** to get a first-hand look at the situation and speak to young Hong Kongers about their beliefs and experiences in the streets. Experience the city in all its glamour and trauma.

6. **Write to your government officials** and legislators urging them to impose sanctions on Hong Kong government officials and the Hong Kong Police Force. Write a letter to the United Nations Security Council urging them to put pressure on China to guarantee freedom and democracy in Hong Kong. You can download templates from www.demosisto.hk.

7. **Sign online petitions in support** of Hong Kong and anywhere else in the world where citizens' free expression or other fundamental rights are under threat.

8. **Support businesses and media outlets** that stand up to white terror from China or other autocratic regimes. Similarly, avoid companies that sacrifice free expression for short-term profit by yielding to oppressive governments. You can get a list of businesses we encourage you to support and those to avoid on www .demosisto.hk.

9. **Make a donation** to the Washington DC-based Hong Kong Democracy Council (www.hkdc.us /donate), which has worked tirelessly over the years to lobby the US government to support the democratisation of Hong Kong.

10. **Tell five of your friends** about what you have learned from this book and share Hong Kong's story with them. Explain to them why standing with Hong Kong is standing with freedom and democracy.

One of the questions I am frequently asked when addressing student audiences overseas is how ordinary citizens can act on the erosion of democratic values in their own countries. As much as they sympathise with the situation in Hong Kong, they are equally if not more concerned about their declining freedoms at home. With the rise of far-right political parties in the West and a similar surge in populism elsewhere in the world, even advanced economies are not spared the same 'boiling frog' scenario facing Hong Kong. Below are five things you can do to counter this global threat:

1. **Follow news events** and identify warning signs where you live, such as increased political polarisation, citizen surveillance, paid advertisements by special interest groups and the use of police force on non-violent protests.

2. **Speak up about these warning signs** by sharing your thoughts on social media, talking to your local representatives and joining a civil society group that speaks to your concerns. Remember the slogan 'when you see something, say something'. Take a small step by attending one civil society event and see whether it makes you feel more empowered and energised. If not, try a different one.

3. **Learn to spot misinformation** in social media posts and news feeds. Visit fact-checking sites and discuss news events with friends, which I believe is the best way to develop media literacy

and hone your skills in telling apart real and fake news.

4. **Volunteer in the election campaign** of a political candidate to whom you relate. Few things will give you a better grasp of the democratic process than understanding the electoral system and immersing yourself in a campaign from start to finish.

5. **Organise your own small-scale rally** on issues that concern you – or in response to the warning signs you have identified in step 1. Work with like-minded friends to create simple banners and placards. Remember: every successful campaign starts with one voice, one flyer and one speech. Believe in the power of the individual.

There is a popular refrain in the restless streets of Hong Kong: 'This is our problem and we will solve it ourselves.' It is a show of courage, faith and self-reliance. But what if our problem is also yours? What if our problem is so vast that the only way to solve it is together?

Everything that I've done since I was 14 – Scholarism, Demosistō, national education, the Umbrella

Movement, from the principal's office to the prison cell, speaking at Civic Square and testifying on Capitol Hill – has led me to this point: Hong Kong's most desperate, but also its finest, moment. With your help and the help of the international community, Hong Kong will prevail and so will democracy across the globe, because this canary may be the best hope the world has to counter China's growing hegemony.

We are all in this together.

Epilogue

結語

———

In October 2019, two weeks after my testimony on Capitol Hill, the US House of Representatives passed the Hong Kong Human Rights and Democracy Act. A month later, the US Senate passed the Act before President Donald Trump signed it into law. Senator Marco Rubio, who had proposed the legislation, said on the Senate floor, 'The United States [has] sent a clear message to Hong Kongers fighting for their long-cherished freedoms: we hear you, we continue to stand with you, and we will not stand idly by as Beijing undermines your autonomy.'

In the meantime, US Senator Josh Hawley drafted the Hong Kong Be Water Act, calling for sanctions to combat the suppression of free expression by the Hong Kong and Chinese governments. The bill was proposed two days after local election authorities barred me from running in the District

Council on the grounds that Demosistō's self-determination platform is in breach of the Basic Law – the same reason they had banned Agnes from the LegCo election in 2018.

While sanctions against Hong Kong officials are a welcome development, they have done little to ease the tensions on our streets. As I am writing this, the city is still witnessing sporadic bursts of violence. In November 2019, for instance, riot police raided the Chinese University of Hong Kong and fired more than 1,500 rounds of tear gas and over 1,300 rubber bullets at demonstrators on a single day of confrontation. A week later, law enforcement besieged the Polytechnic University, trapping over a thousand protesters on campus for over 48 hours before most of them surrendered to the police.

Prolonged unrest has paralysed the city's traffic and public transport systems. Many restaurants, shops, banks and other businesses have been forced to shut. Tourism has plummeted and major international sporting and cultural events have been cancelled or postponed.

These incidents have created dramatic consequences for our city. Combined with the impact of an ongoing US–China trade war, Hong Kong officially slipped into recession late last year after the economy shrank for a second quarter in a row. While the government is quick to point fingers at the protesters, most of the blame falls on the Hong Kong Police who have been responding to demonstrations with disproportionate force and, in some cases, acts of retaliatory brutality.

The anti-Extradition Bill protests show no sign of abating. The movement has evolved into a rolling crisis that keeps Hong Kong society on a simmer. A stunning, landslide victory for the pro-democracy camp in the November 2019 District Council elections (which I was banned from running in) was widely seen as a referendum on the protest movement and led to a temporary 'ceasefire' between protesters and police.

But this truce is fragile. All it takes is another misstep by the government or riot police to trigger a resurgence in violence in a seemingly endless cycle of clashes, crackdowns and arrests. Nobody knows when, how and if the unrest will come to an end.

What we do know is the longer it goes on, the higher the price both sides will have to pay. Nearly 6,000 protesters, a substantial portion of whom are below the age of 18, have been arrested and charged with serious crimes such as rioting, arson and assault on police officers. There have been unconfirmed reports of fatalities being dressed up by the police as suicides. They say the night is darkest before dawn. In our case, the night is still young and our journey will get darker and more perilous before it gets better.

In the meantime, I continue to travel around the world to tell the story of Hong Kong and rally international support for our struggle. In-between my trips I set aside time for prison visits as there are a few dozen activists still behind bars and they need all the support we can give them. Considering how many young people have been arrested and charged in the still unravelling political unrest, hundreds more are expected to lose their freedom in the coming months.

Political imprisonment is an inevitable step on the path to democracy; it was the case in South Korea and Taiwan and it has been so in Hong Kong. Far from silencing us, prison will only strengthen our resolve. We have unfinished business and we won't stop until our demand for the most fundamental of all rights – a free vote and an accountable government – is met. From here on out, we'll stop asking nicely and start shouting so the rest of the world can hear us.

3 December 2019

Acknowledgements

It's by God's grace that the path of political activism has taken me this far and made me the person I am today. And so first and foremost I want to thank God for watching over me, my family, and the city I fight for.

None of what I do would have been possible – or had any meaning – if it weren't for my parents: my father who named me after the great prophet Joshua, raised me to be an honest man and taught me to be every bit as stubborn and persistent as he; my mother whose patience and care have helped me not only overcome my dyslexia but also become more compassionate and empathetic toward even those I have every reason not to be. It's said that when you become an activist, you bring your whole family with you. In the past ten years, I've put my parents through trying times, given them many sleepless nights, denied them precious family time and done pitifully little to make up for the sacrifices they've made. I'd like to give mum and dad my deepest apologies and sincerest thanks.

Then there's my other family: the young men and women of Demosistō. I'd like to thank my partner-in-crime, Ivan Lam, who has stuck with me through the rollercoaster ride from the early Scholarism days to every trial and tribulation that Demosistō has seen. Ivan never asks for any recognition but I want to give credit where credit's long overdue: he's hands-down the most trusted member in our team. I'm equally grateful to have Nathan Law fighting alongside me. Nathan's LegCo win remains the most beautiful battle I've fought in my political career. Thanks also go to Agnes Chow who has persevered through the ups and downs of Scholarism and Demosistō and under the often unforgiving glare of the media; Jeffrey Ngo whose efforts in international networking have taken Demosistō – and Hong Kong – to the world stage; Chris Kwok, friend and colleague since the anti-national education campaign; Lili Wong who listens to and comforts me always; Tobias Leung who works hard and plays hard; Arnold Chung who keeps me on my toes by challenging my views; Isaac Cheng, our youngest spokesperson; Tiffany Yuen, who taught me how to carry myself in public; Ian Chan who works tirelessly behind the scenes; Angus Wong and Kelvin Lam, both of whom have devoted themselves to district affairs; and Au Nok Hin, my mentor in community outreach. All of them have guided and tolerated me over the years and made my journey in activism less lonely and more colourful.

Thanks to lifelong friends and mentors Jacky Yu, Kerrie Wong and Justin Yim who have supported and inspired me since those halcyon days at UCC; Dorothy Wong who looks after her 'kids' in Demosistō, got us through some of the worst public relations crises, and is nothing short of a fairy god-mother to all of us; S.K. who helped me 'reintegrate' into civil society after my prison release and is the sister I never had; Tiffany C. who taught me an important lesson in life and will always have a place in my heart; and Fanny Y., Oscar L. and K.C., for being trusted friends and confidantes who dispense daily encouragement and counsel. Special thanks go to S.H. who visited me and looked after my affairs while I was behind bars, stood by me through my darkest and loneliest days, and has given me a reason to smile even in the most hopeless of situations.

I'd like to express my gratitude toward every local and foreign reporter who covers the pro-democracy movement in Hong Kong. Their professionalism, fearlessness and relentless pursuit of the truth are truly inspirational. Special thanks to journalists

Vivian Tam and Gwyneth Ho, both of whom have interviewed, profiled and guided me since day one. I also want to thank my legal team, in particular Jonathan Man, Donna Yau, Bond Ng, Jeffrey Tam and Lawrence Lok, who helped me through every grueling trial and court hearing and demonstrated by example the critical role played by human rights lawyers in a political movement.

My warmest thanks go to Martin Lee, the Father of Democracy in Hong Kong, who taught me everything I know in international lobbying and continues to coach me and educate me to this day; Anna Cheung, who supports us in New York and Washington D.C.; the indefatigable Eddie Chu, pro-democracy lawmaker who has given Demosistō his unconditional support; and filmmaker Matthew Torne, producer Andrew Duncan and director Joe Piscatella for believing in me and telling my story on film.

In regard to the book, I want to thank my co-author Jason Y. Ng who has supported me and my cause since our first interview at the Foreign Correspondents' Club years ago. He has brought this challenging project to fruition by lending his craft as a skilled nonfiction writer and coaxing long-forgotten dialogues and memories that I never thought would be relevant or noteworthy and that turned out to be the glue that holds the narrative together and the sparkle that brings my story to life. Jason's writing is matched by his culinary finesse. It's always a pleasure spending late nights at his place exchanging political views over his delicious home-cooked food.

I'd also like to thank my literary agent, Penguin Random House editor Hana Teraie-Wood and publisher Drummond Moir, all of whom are respected professionals in their fields who have guided me through the process and have been a genuine pleasure to work with. I'm indebted to the support that Penguin Random House has thrown behind this project despite the political climate and potential pressure they may face. This book, my first written for the international audience, would not have been possible without their interest and faith in Hong Kong.

Last but not least, I want to thank the courageous people of Hong Kong, as well as the generous support of people around the world for me and for my city.

Joshua Wong

I've devoted my career to writing about Hong Kong – my birthplace, my sole source of inspiration and in my mind the most splendid, captivating, fickle, paradoxical and frustrating place on the planet. Telling its stories is a life's work but also a tremendous privilege. Likewise, when I was approached to co-write Joshua's memoir, I felt both duty-bound to do justice to the man's meteoric rise from a teenage activist to an international human rights icon and honoured to be entrusted with that colossal responsibility. I'd like to thank Joshua for his confidence and faith in me and, above all, everything that he has done for our city. Hong Kong is lucky to have a fighter like him.

I'd like to thank all those who have helped me in my research, especially Joshua's family and his friends and colleagues at Demosistō. I'm also grateful to my partner Jack Chang for putting up with me during these reclusive months of writing; my agent for her patience and guidance; editor Hana Teraie-Wood and publisher Drummond Moir who are as insightful as they are delightful to work with; and Penguin Random House for standing behind this project, which requires courage and fortitude.

As this book goes to print, Hong Kong continues to be embroiled in a political crisis that's unprecedented in both scale and intensity. I'd like to thank every brave young woman and man out on the streets who are fighting for the future of our city with what little they have and everything they have.

Jason Y. Ng

Timeline of Key Events

1842	China cedes Hong Kong Island to Britain
1 October 1949	Mao Zedong founds the People's Republic of China
1958-1962	The Great Leap Forward in China
1966-1976	The Cultural Revolution in China
19 December 1984	Signing of the Joint Declaration by Britain and China over the return of Hong Kong
4 June 1989	Tiananmen Square Massacre in Beijing, China
1 July 1997	Handover of Hong Kong from Britain to China; Tung Chee-hwa becomes first chief executive of Hong Kong
1997-1998	Asian Financial Crisis

11 December 2001	China joins World Trade Organization
2003	SARS outbreak in Hong Kong
25 June 2005	Donald Tsang becomes second chief executive of Hong Kong
2011	China becomes the world's second largest economy
29 May 2011	Joshua Wong founds student activist group Scholarism
1 July 2012	C.Y. Leung becomes third chief executive of Hong Kong
8 October 2012	C.Y. Leung announces the withdrawal of the national education curriculum after Scholarism leads hundreds of thousands in a mass sit-in
15 November 2012	Xi Jinping becomes president and paramount leader of the People's Republic of China
31 August 2014	China's National People's Congress Standing Committee issues '31 August framework' restricting the free election of Hong Kong's chief executive
26 September 2014	Storming of Civic Square by members of Scholarism over restrictive electoral reform

28 September 2014	Tear gas crackdown by riot police on peaceful pro-democracy protesters; start of Umbrella Movement
15 December 2014	Umbrella Movement ends
8 February 2016	Mongkok Chinese New Year civil unrest
10 April 2016	Joshua Wong and Nathan Law co-found political party Demosistō
21 July 2016	Conviction of Joshua Wong, Nathan Law and Alex Chow for unlawful assembly and incitement over storming of Civic Square in 2014
4 September 2016	Nathan Law becomes youngest ever lawmaker in Hong Kong
1 July 2017	Carrie Lam becomes fourth chief executive of Hong Kong
14 July 2017	Nathan Law loses his LegCo seat for straying from prescribed oath during swearing-in ceremony (Oathgate)
17 August 2017	Incarceration of Joshua Wong, Nathan Law and Alex

	Chow for unlawful assembly and incitement
13 October 2017	Conviction of Joshua Wong, Lester Shum and several other protesters of contempt of court
9 April 2019	Conviction of Occupy Central Trio and several other activists for their roles in Umbrella Movement
16 May 2019	Second incarceration of Joshua Wong for contempt of court
9 June 2019	Start of anti-Extradition Bill political crisis
16 June 2019	2 million Hong Kong citizens take to the streets demanding complete withdrawal of the Extradition Bill
5 September 2019	Carrie Lam announces withdrawal of the Extradition Bill
24 November 2019	District Council elections see landslide victory for pro-democracy camps
28 November 2019	US enacts Hong Kong Human Rights and Democracy Act